Apparent Wind

James N. Ellsworth

Printed by CreateSpace for

Words Worth Writing Services

Thanks Alastair for all your help & support. James (handwritten inscription)

Acknowledgements:

I wish to thank my wife Barbara and my daughter Jennifer for their support and perseverance with me through the idea and completion of this novel. In addition, I must thank my focus group for their time and forthright feedback in reading the manuscript. They are Barbara, Jenn Wilson, who was also my efficient and effective copy and content editor, Alastair Urquhart, Robert Ross, Elizabeth Gordon, and Janet Doyle. Lastly, thanks to Stephen Norton who shared his knowledge on indie publishing.

DEDICATION

**To Barbara and Jenn,
for all their encouragement and support**

Apparent Wind

Apparent wind at your face is caused more by your own motion than any actual or true breeze, like the 'wind' one feels when riding a bicycle on a calm day. It is a perception of reality rather than reality itself.

The forward motion of the sailboat plus a cross-wind will also give an effect known as apparent wind. It will cause a boat to take a different course somewhere between the two directions. Sailors must have their wits about them to calculate the effects of an apparent wind distinct from true winds.

There are many apparent winds in our lives.

CHAPTERS:

PART THREE: A Life Lived For Others

PART ONE: FORGIVE THEM FOR THEY KNOW NOT WHAT THEY DO

CHAPTER 1.

ONLY AN OCEAN AWAY

If he knew then what he knew now, would it have made much difference? He thought not. It wouldn't matter really because he couldn't make different choices then or now. That's counterfactual history anyway and a waste of time. It was hard enough to deal with what actually happened, let alone what might have happened. You have to set the course the wind gives you, not wish for one from another direction. Anyway, that was then. David thought back to that time that held so much promise...

London, Ontario, 1971

It was December and David walked the slushy street exiting the university campus. He was tired but euphoric. It had been a long day of testing but he was confident. He said to himself, "I think I've got that position in the bag."

He could feel the damp seeping through the soles of his light brown Dack's dress shoes, a concession he had purchased so he could look the serious part in the job interviews. He had asked his father's advice but he should have asked his Uncle Peter. There would have been less teasing and no judgment.

His father had said, "What? Your hush-puppies not good enough for the real world?" David admitted his new shoes were a sop to conventionality but now he didn't care; they had done the trick as part of his package. His mood was buoyant in the Friday late-afternoon, the harbinger of the weekend. He had a lightness in his step, enjoying the oblique sun and the cool mid-December air sparring to dominate the end of the day. The breeze felt refreshing on his open neck, and on his sensitive face, the ginger beard only recently shaved for the interviews. Feeling casually professional with his light brown corduroy sports jacket unbuttoned, dark brown woolen trousers instead of his usual jeans, an orange and blue-striped tie loosened, and navy blue scarf dangling, he caught a reflection of himself in a window. He approved of what he saw, tall, lean, even athletic, remarking on his light brown hair stylishly over his ears, and reddish sideburns an appropriate and modest length. Yes, he believed he looked very much like a diplomat-in-the-making.

David allowed himself a smile of triumph, maybe with a hint of narcissism; and he pumped his fist surreptitiously by his hip, letting out a sigh of relief. His future was looking less opaque.

It had been a long and arduous process. He recalled seeing the notice in the Student Union Building announcing that on Saturday, October 21, 1971, an entrance exam to apply to Canada's External Affairs would be held. That was when it all started.

It was his last year before graduating with a Master's Degree in History and he thought diplomacy would be as good as any career. Paid travel and digs in the service of the country; walking the hallowed halls of revered mandarins, the likes of Lester Pearson; applying his education to something meaningful. Dabble in foreign policy, work with immigrants and refugees; why not? Nothing better to do and he was steeped in international affairs anyway with his studies. How difficult could it be?

He remembered sitting in the upper level seats of the tiered classroom in the Indian summer heat of that weekend afternoon, missing a Mustangs' football game. Instead he was concentrating on answering true and false questions about current events and general political knowledge, followed by a timed item where he had to write a précis of a report to brief an intended government minister. He must have scored well that day because he made the short list. Round two today; a full day of further tests on writing ability and role playing scenarios, such as helping Canadian tourists who had lost passports while travelling in under-developed locales. He felt he had aced these hurdles too. And at the end of the day, the External recruiters told him he qualified for the penultimate step of security checks. Surely the hardest parts were over.

Now David felt like celebrating; perhaps he would buy a new book, Mordecai Richler's recent *St. Urbain's Horseman* maybe. Or go see that new James Bond movie, *Diamonds Are Forever*. He thought of calling Lindsay to join him in celebration but that would be a bad move and he dismissed the idea as quickly as it entered his head, even if he could couch it in Christmas good cheer for old time's sake. Who else would still be around campus that he could call?

"Oh well, I'll figure out something because this day definitely needs to be commemorated," he promised himself, stroking his slight chin dimple with a thumb.

Ottawa, 1972

Early in the following New Year, mid-February actually, David's father, Sergeant Desmond Dilman was at his desk in Ottawa. Still tanned after an assignment in Havana for his superiors in the RCMP Security Services, he sat with his reading glasses on, shirtsleeves rolled up and suit jacket draped on the back of his chair. Deep into his recollections and notes for his report, he was startled when the phone jangled.

"Dilman here, yes Fred, how are you doing? Yes, it's been a while. Yep, it was a good Christmas. No, David didn't make it. A skiing trip with his university buddies. Yes, I just got back and I'm working on that report now. No, I can't say, it's on a 'need to know' basis only. You should know that. No leaks from me, Fred, you know how it is. You still managing those External Affairs recruitment teams? Yeah, sure, I have some time tomorrow. Coffee sounds great. See you at ten then."

Des was in his mid-fifties, salt and pepper hair beginning to thin and carrying an extra ten pounds on his six foot frame. Self-conscious of his appearance, he bought clothes that hid his weight well. Since today was an office day, he was wearing a white shirt with a comfortable neck size, a charcoal grey suit with complementary slimming alterations, and a Liberal-favoured red tie in case any of the minions for the Minister of External Affairs, Mitchell Sharp, or for Prime Minister Pierre Trudeau, showed up unannounced to utter 'fuddle duddle, I want a news item for my constituents'. Des was looking very professional but it didn't stop him from thinking otherwise about his employers and the caller.

His mind's voice said, "What does that asshole Fred McNeil want? Haven't seen or heard from him in over a year. Probably wants a dinner at our house. He always had a hard on for Meg. I'd love to get inside his small brain and take away the leverage he thinks he's got on me. He never invites me for coffee. Oh well, priorities. First I gotta finish this report for the boss, and then try to weasel my way into his inner circle of 'secret' agents. Focus now, Des; you'll find out tomorrow what Fred Finger-Up-His-Ass wants."

The following day, a Friday, Des drove to the External Affairs offices in the East Block. The diplomats were eagerly awaiting their new building to be finished on Sussex Drive next year, but until then they toiled in cramped and over-heated conditions. Des found Fred's office stuffy, but smiled as he sat across from him.

"Hey Fred. Long time, no see. Have you been to see any Canadiens' games this year?"

"As a matter of fact, my kids got me tickets to a game before Christmas. Canadiens and Leafs. You should've seen that new kid, Guy Lafleur. Boy, can he fly! I figure him in the running for the Calder Cup this year."

"We'll see, we'll see; lots of good rookies this year. So what's up, Fred?"

"A couple of things, Des. Just thought a face to face would be better than the phone. More secure, so to speak," he laughed nervously at his joke. Des could tell that Fred had some information he was itching to spill.

Fred continued, "Thought you might like to hear it from a friend."

"Well Fred, now that you've got my full attention."

"Oh right," he laughed and sputtered some coffee that he had been sipping onto his desk.

Wiping it with his hand, Fred said, "I guess congratulations are in order, Des. Looks like another Dilman will be working for Canada soon."

Des, as was his practice, kept a straight face, keeping his cards close, and wondered, "What's he chortling about now?"

Instead he said, "Well, strictly speaking I don't work for the government. Remember my legend. You can't blow my cover, Fred, not even in your office." These diplomats could be so thick.

Des continued, "If you're referring to David, I suppose we do have a lot to be grateful for, although I'm sure you know more than I do," and smiled like a Cheshire cat.

"Yes, that kid of yours scored really well on all his entrance tests for External, one of the highest among the 5,000 or so applicants. Looks like after the security checks this month, we'll be able to offer him a position."

"Oh yes?" Des dissembled. "Meg and I have been encouraging him, but of course we didn't know the results."

Des's mind whirled. A part of his security service files meant he could follow university student radicals, and he used that file occasionally to keep an eye on his son's comings and goings. "How the hell did I miss this one?" he thought.

Fred said, "Of course, if he has a preference for one of the branches, you know, political, economic or immigration, you should let me know. I'd see what I could do."

"Sure, I will Fred, thanks. He usually calls his Mom on Sundays so I'll mention it to him. And the other thing?" Des figured Fred used the good news about David to get some other favour. Might as well get it from him now.

"Beg your pardon?"

Des cocked his head a bit, "You said a couple of things."

Fred remembered and said through a nervous laugh, "Oh right. Wanted to ask you and the little lady over for dinner sometime this month. Can you spare a Friday or Saturday? Valentine's is over but we'll look romantic for the girls anyway. Got your agenda with you?"

"Come on Fred," Des kidded. "You know I can't decide anything social without consulting Meg."

There was some more hockey talk and a promise to line up a dinner date. The coffee finished, they shook hands and got on with their respective days.

At home after dinner, unwinding in the living room with a glass of wine, Des got out his journal while Meg watched some insipid television show she liked, a hospital series called *Marcus Welby, M.D.* He wrote in his journal about his meeting with Fred, occasionally tapping his tooth with his pen.

Friday, February 18, 1972

While having coffee with that fop McNeil, I learned that David had taken the External Affairs exams and had done really well. Fred said that David had also passed the second interviews and they were about to do security checks before offering him a job. How did I miss that? I poker-faced my way through our gabbing but I'm going to have to throw a monkey wrench into that somehow. No goddamed way am I going to let the so-called public service get another Dilman.

Blocking out the television noise, he began to think, more proactive now. How could he throw a spanner into the works? Because come hell or high water, Des vowed, he would not allow the Canadian government, or any government for that matter, to get another Dilman to work for it. Damn David for his non-communication and trying to sneak this by him. He finished his entry for that day and resolved on a plan of action.

He waited a few days to call Fred, and by mid-week, he was sitting in McNeil's office again.

"Boy that was an ugly loss to the Rangers last night, a 7-3 drubbing. Did you see it?" Des began with some small talk, but quickly got to the crux.

"You know, Fred, it's important that we never talk work in front of Meg. She thinks I sell locks and security systems so, to be safe, you know." His voice trailed off but the message was clear. No shop talk on social occasions; he had to remind Fred each time, to be explicit with the bumbler.

"Also what I'm about to reveal to you is just between you and me. Meg doesn't know anything about this, so it's between you and me, got it?" he said tapping the side of his nose. Fred leaned in over his desk, nudging his coffee mug and spilling a bit of it onto some paper.

Inwardly Des thought, "What a buffoon!" But with no judgment on his face, he continued. "I don't think you should offer David a position with External."

"Jesus, Des, why not? The kid is brilliant."

"Thanks Fred, we think so too. But I've learned that he's tarnished." Des feigned some discomfort, squirming a bit in his seat and pausing to sip from his mug.

"What do you mean?"

"Well, the work I do on my side of the river, security stuff, well, I've learned something about David that wouldn't look good when you get into your clearance stages. In fact it would make him a risk."

"C'mon, Des, you're not making any sense here."

"I'm just trying to save you and External and the government some time and effort and money. Fred, don't even bother starting the security checks on David."

"I don't understand." Fred crunched his eyebrows and furrowed his forehead in a question.

"Damn it, Fred, do I have to spell it out? Are you trying to humiliate me here?"

"No, Des, I really don't get it."

Des looked around the office furtively as if ascertaining that they were truly alone. He leaned in and whispered something confidentially across the desk.

"Holy shit, Des, I had no idea," Fred commiserated. He patted Des's arm in sympathy. "Thanks for this information; I'll let the recruiting team know right away. What a shame."

"Of course we were all proud of his results, but I did some soul-searching over the weekend and came to the conclusion that I was duty bound to tell you." Des got up to leave.

"Remember Fred, mum's the word," and tapped the side of his nose twice again. "I think I'm going to need lots of your best scotch on Saturday night to ease my suffering," and he managed a grin.

Des sat in the parking lot for a while, not liking what he had just done. Fully aware of what innuendo can do, Des remembered back to 1935 when he himself was tainted with that limp-wristed, winking nuance that can destroy a reputation. It was that damn Frank Zaneth, the undercover cop who insinuated that Des was a homosexual and used it to blackmail him.

Des weighed the realization of what he had done. It was simply a means to an end, he tried to rationalize. He would use whatever he had to do to keep David out of the clutches of the government. One Dilman was enough. But if he could justify it, then why did he feel like a Judas, betraying with a kiss?

That night Des jotted in his journal.

Wednesday, February 23, 1972

Arranged to see Fred again. Over coffee, I said, in a conspiratorial, man-to-man voice, that I could save the department some money and aggravation in security checks. I confessed that after a lot of thought, I decided I wasn't the only father to be embarrassed by his son. So I wanted to come clean and let them know David was a risk...I hate it but it had to be done.

By April, David still hadn't heard anything from External. Finally he decided to call. When he was told that he was no longer on the list, he was baffled. How could that be? He knew a former classmate, Terry Whelan, who had been a successful candidate a year ago, and was now a Foreign Service Officer. He decided to call him.

After preliminaries, David asked, "Say, Terry, I've been going though the Foreign Service exams. Yes, I've been jumping through their hoops and doing quite well. Thanks, well you got me thinking of trying the exam in the first place actually. But suddenly with the security checks, I got dropped. Do you have any ideas why? Or can you advise me on how I can find out?"

"Dammit, Dave, that's too bad. Typically the security check flags a womanizer or someone with a criminal record or having some nefarious political background."

"That's what I thought too. I don't fit any of those descriptions. Do you think some of that stuff like attending radical meetings at school would affect my chances?"

"Maybe. I can ask but I'm low man around here. Your Member of Parliament might be able to uncover what happened."

"Ok, thanks and good luck with your first posting, man."

David hung up. This was a puzzle. He took Terry's advice and made an appointment with his local M.P.

Judd Buchanan shook David's hand warmly. He wore thick framed glasses, a dark three piece suit and was all business. Buchanan's demeanor oozed hard work and life insurance sales which was his background. After some brief pleasantries and praise for Western's sports teams, he asked what he could do for David.

David explained his dilemma and Buchanan said he would see what he could find out. He could usually cut through bureaucracy, he said confidently. A week later Buchanan's office called. It wasn't the M.P. himself but one of his aides. He said that apparently David had failed the security checks and no specifics were offered, except to say that he should pursue other lines of employment. David felt deflated and still confused. Then on the weekend, just as he was leaving to go for a run, the phone rang, a call from Terry.

"Dave, I managed to meet someone in recruiting and I think I found out what happened."

But first, David filled Terry in on his answer from Buchanan's office as a preamble and Terry said, "I'm afraid that's what I found out too. But there's more."

There was a pause and David asked Terry to spill it out.

"Well someone in your background bad-mouthed you; so the department concluded you would be too great a risk in the diplomatic corps."

It was David's turn to go quiet and pause.

"That's ludicrous, Terry."

"I know, but you're black-balled, I'm afraid. If one of your relatives was playing a practical joke, it's a bad one. Did you piss off an aunt or an uncle or some cousin?"

"Mmm, no I'm pretty sure I haven't. Thanks for finding this out though."

Actually David did have one idea about who might have done this, but it still seemed inconceivable. He and his father had been estranged for several years, barely speaking to one another. But would his father really stoop this low to conquer? David needed to blow off some steam and thought a run would help. His career plans were in a shambles and all because his father, at least he suspected his father, had planted some rumour or hare-brained inference. It just didn't make sense!

David called home on Sunday. His Mom answered as usual and he dutifully asked how she had spent her week. She answered the usual; Euchre Club with the ladies at church, her television programs and hoping to see him so they could go to a movie or two. She seemed a bit surprised when he asked to speak to his father, a rarity.

"Hi Dad. Oh you know. Lots of essays and exams. Listen Dad, did anyone from External Affairs contact you recently and ask any questions about me? Yes, I had applied to them; oh you know, thinking of doing something with my life, like you always nag me about. No eh? Well I was just wondering because something happened; someone said something that influenced the way my application turned out. Yes, Dad, I know, you don't have much influence with anyone; you're just a locks and home security salesman. No, I'm not blaming you; I was just wondering. No, not before the summer now; too much school work anyway. Yep, bye, and tell Mom I miss her."

On a hunch he decided to call his Uncle Peter, not really his uncle by blood, but he might as well be. He was David's godfather and had been a family friend for as long as David could remember. Peter was a lawyer in Ottawa and David thought he might shed some light on the situation.

"Hi Uncle Peter. You must be looking forward to golf season. Has it been a rough winter?"

"Davey, you didn't call me to talk sports and weather. As delighted as I am to hear from you, what's the reason for the call?"

David apprised him of what had transpired. Peter had not been contacted by anyone about David's character, External or otherwise, and had no explanation as to what might have stopped David's progress.

"No, David, there isn't much you or I can do. You would have to know who slandered you and the onus would be on you to disprove the claim. Canada's defamation laws are capricious, I'm afraid. It's unfortunate and a cruel joke. You have no idea who maligned you?"

After talking possible summertime plans, they hung up. David had a thesis to complete and exams to study for; but after May, he didn't know what he'd do about his future.

"Oh hell," he thought. He had worked hard at trying to find new meaning in his life and start a career. He felt the loss of opportunity deeply.

Des had worked in Canada's security services since 1935 but had axes to grind against his employer. Sometimes he daydreamed that he was like Prometheus, chained to the rock of servitude; but that somehow, someway, eventually, he would bring down the Titans that had tricked him. Then he'd smile ruefully. When the fantasy faded, he had no plan for revenge. He usually just returned to the job at hand. Even if that included spying on his son.

Yes it was deceitful, but the boy was always in danger of screwing up. Like the time he was flirting with the Commies. It was always a game for David; something to play at or with.

Des was driving home from the office and he was thinking about David. The roads were wet and the tires made a sibilant white noise in the thawing March slush. The radio volume was on low to uninteresting drivel and Des was letting his mind wander. Specifically, he remembered two occasions where David made a hash of things at roughly this same time of year.

Just last year, his informers reported that David attended a recruiting meeting on campus for the Young Communist League. "The fool," he thought, "that could be a career limiting move." And wasn't it only a few years ago that a tap on David's phone revealed that he got a girlfriend in trouble, Lindsay Something. Strictly speaking Des never intended to use the eavesdropping information as evidence so it wasn't exactly illegal, he rationalized. Besides, if David had come to him for advice or money he would have helped out gladly, but David managed to run that gauntlet himself. It had been a long time since his son had come to him for help.

Des smiled as an observation began to form. Was there a timing pattern to his son's goofs -a kind of early spring fever that drove him to act as mad as a March hare?

As he approached their house on Glebe Avenue, Des wondered, "How much longer would a father's role be necessary; when would David be beyond mollycoddling?"

He thought, as he pulled into the driveway, "Parenting is a curse that lasts forever."

him

Little did he realize how that sentiment would haunt both he and his son!

Chapter 2:

GENERATION GAP

Ottawa, December 1975

Three years later and if anyone looked closely at the lives of the Dilmans, of Des, David and Meg, as Peter had opportunity to do, the acronym 'snafu' would come to mind. To outsiders the Dilmans presented themselves with a modicum of normalcy but all was not as it seemed.

Des chafed a lot with his clandestine case files, especially the one assigned in 1965 which required him to track university radicals. He found it was getting tiresome having to keep up with the steady stream of 'with it' jargon that peppered the meetings and reports he received from his cadre of informants on Canada's campuses. He wasn't even sure how reliable the reportage was. So many of the recruits were in it for the monthly stipend rather than any deep-rooted belief that they were shoring up the Establishment from incursions by the hippie, Yippie and dippie long-haired freaks. Most of his 'spooks' didn't fit in either with the myriad leftish organizations and it was difficult to glean the real from imagined threats they saw from the periphery.

Des had his hands full keeping up. The acronyms were driving him crazy. It was more than the Old Left and the New Left; there was the Canadian Union of Students or CUS, and the Company of Young Canadians or CYC; ersatz peaceniks in the guise of the Student Union for Peace Action or SUPA, and piss artists with sit-ins and placard protests in the Students for Democratic Universities or SDU.

And David was a part of all that, cavorting with street theatre and radical or revolutionary politics. Most of it wasn't serious, such as the Chicago Seven clowns of the Youth International Party, aka Yippies, or the self-run Rochdale College in Toronto with its free dance, free love and free drug distribution, although it did cost a measly $25 to buy a Bachelor of Arts degree.

But some of it was deadly serious. Just ask the parents of the four students killed on the campus of Kent State while protesting the Vietnam War. Or comfort the mothers of the three students who self-immolated in Czechoslovakia to protest the Soviet invasion there. Des still shuddered to hear Mayor Richard Daley give the order to "shoot to kill" demonstrators at the Democratic Convention, facetiously dubbed Czechago by a Yippie. Yes, they had been troubling times; he and Meg had both worried a lot about their son then.

And the anxiety continued. David was out of university now, graduating in 1972, but working in Hungary somewhere for a rather dubious organization planning and promoting youth conferences or festivals or some such thing. Meg seemed to fret about David constantly.

However David was back in town for Christmas this year and his mother was entirely in her element, coddling and fussing. The house was festively decorated. Green and red candles at dinner, green and red place mats and napkins, white lights on the artificial tree, and always red and white wine available for toasts. Her spirits were so high that she even encouraged a plan from David to go out for a night of drinks and chat with Peter and his father, just the 'boys'.

"David and I have had our own time; now you guys go have some fun," she proclaimed, and started to clean up after dinner.

David had suggested the Prescott Hotel and Peter offered to drive them there, a mere two kilometers from the Dilman home. Des, riding shotgun, was unusually quiet on the ride over, as if he was reluctant to enter the local bar, as if it was something distasteful. David ordered a round of beer before Peter and Des could take their coats off.

"Aren't you the big shot with the big bucks?" Des growled at his son.

David rubbed his hands against the cold. "No, Dad. I just want to show you that I'm earning my way."

Peter intervened. "Are they paying you well then Davey? You're an event planner over there, aren't you? Your Mom and Dad were kind of vague."

"We're vague because he doesn't tell us much, Peter."

"Well you don't ask much either, Dad. What do you want to know Uncle Peter?"

"Who do you work for, what do you do?"

"It's called the World Federation for Democratic Youth. It's run out of Budapest and is a non-governmental group trying to connect youth organizations from around the world in festivals. It started out along with the International Union of Students promoting peace and anti-fascism after the war in 1945. I heard about it during my last years at university."

"Do you like what you're doing?"

"Ya, it's alright. I'd prefer being in the diplomatic corps but this is okay. It's good. There are over 140 countries involved. Remember I attended a festival in 1968 in Sofia. Two years ago, we got about 25,000 for the East Berlin festival and we're hoping that the next one in Havana in 1978 will be even bigger."

Des had finished his beer and decided to have another with scotch. "A Jameson too," he called out and showed his empty glass to the server. Then he asked David, "Do you know where your funding comes from? Do you ever wonder why the festivals are always in Communist countries?"

David and Peter were still nursing their beverages. "I presume it's from all the member countries, Dad. After all the WFDY is recognized by the United Nations. It's one of the few organizations where youth from South Africa can meet others from Palestine, and students from the East and West can get together."

"I asked around and some say it's a front for the Soviets and their propaganda," Des responded grumpily.

Des almost added that it was just like David to be flirting with Communists; after all, he almost joined the Young Communist League. Luckily he caught himself from blurting; that would have been a huge misstep. David mustn't know that he was aware of his campus activities. Instead he asked David, "You know you always worried your mother when you'd tell stories of your radical shenanigans."

Peter was curious and asked, "Can you tell me why you never joined the Communist Party of Canada, or even the Waffle group of the NDP, Davey?"

22

Perhaps because his uncle seemed genuinely interested in David's thoughts, whereas Des would have been judgmental, David didn't mind explaining. Des appreciated Peter's deft touch with the boy.

"Sure, Uncle Peter. It's not too deep really. Those guys were way too intense and wanted to see everything in the straightjacket of Marxist theory. I think I went to a couple of meetings because I was looking for a renewed commitment but it felt a little like joining a religion. I'm afraid it wasn't for me."

Des responded, "Peter lived under the Communists, their prison camps anyway. It certainly was no church picnic."

"Is that right, Uncle Peter? You guys were in the war together too, weren't you? You never talk about it though. That was one of the reasons I suggested tonight; a chance to get to know each of you a little better."

Peter and Des glanced at one another but neither took up the gauntlet of recounting war stories.

"That's ancient history David and, well, its ancient history," Peter demurred.

David looked at the two of them and said. "Okay, I guess that's your code for 'let's change the subject'.

And Peter did just that. He asked how long would David be around before returning and wondered about the possibility of going skiing.

"I have until the end of December, so yes, that would be great." David ordered another beer but Peter declined.

"How about Boxing Day? I don't have much on my desk right now." Peter watched Des finish his scotch and beer and wondered why he seemed to be drinking hard and fast.

Des knew he shouldn't be ordering another but there was something about being at the 'P' that stirred up memories and put him in a foul mood.

"Want to join us Dad?"

23

"You know I don't ski. You'll have to carry your own gear."

Peter looked around the tavern. Some guys were playing darts, no women allowed, and a hockey game was on, muted sound. It wasn't exactly misogynist but it was a man's lair.

"Say Des, didn't you and Meg used to come here to the Prescott a lot? Meg said you got engaged here or something."

"Ya, we used to come here when we were courting. But as you say, Peter, it's ancient history. Haven't been here for donkeys' ages."

David snorted in his beer. "Courted? Jeez Dad you use words like you're from a different century. Speaking of history, you two. Wasn't that great news that Spain's Franco died last month?"

Des seemed to bristle. "What right have you got to celebrate the Generalissimo's passing?"

"Well, Dad, every time a fascist pushes up daisies, there are more flowers to put into those oppressive rifle barrels."

Peter smiled at the quip but Des didn't.

"You don't realize how much your mother worries about you. She could just imagine you doing something stupid like putting a flower in a soldier's gun."

"Ah Dad, lighten up. Concern for my safety gives Mom something to pray for."

Des lit up a cigarette, and offered one to Peter who declined. He didn't offer David one but left the packet on the table.

Des blew the smoke towards the ceiling.

"You don't know nothing about fighting Fascists." Peter noticed that grammar was always the first casualty when Des was getting drunk. They had laughed about the tell before but Des wasn't laughing now.

"What Franco did in Spain was terrible, wiping out towns, leaving thousands of orphans. You never fought for anything; how can you

24

know what war is like? You should let the survivors who suffered and fought Fascism be the ones to dance on his grave. Or did you want to joke about what they went through too?"

"That's bullshit, Dad. I didn't have to be in the trenches to know what it was like in World War I or to commemorate Remembrance Day."

Des knew he was getting inebriated and that his judgment was suspect, not unlike a bat in a belfry, but he couldn't seem to help himself this time. He wanted to tread more carefully; he had his legend to maintain after all. But being at the Prescott and David acting like a big man on campus was getting under his skin tonight.

"Dad, c'mon, chill man."

"I suppose you fashion yourself after Abbie Hoffman or one of those yappie guys, always joking. I bet you like it when he says stuff like, 'Free speech means the right to shout 'theatre' in a crowded fire'. They're just punks playing."

Peter tried to soften the discussion. "There's nothing wrong with a sense of humour, Des. You always play with words."

Des smiled at Peter. "You're right; it breaks the tension and helps with perspective. Isn't that what you always explain to me?"

Peter changed the subject. "So David, are you seeing anyone special these days?"

"Yes, she's a colleague. We met at the World Festival in Sofia in 1968 and wrote to each other afterwards. Now we're working together. She's special but nothing serious really."

The ceasefire was short-lived. Des started to needle his son again.

"Isn't that the problem with your generation? You don't take anything serious."

"Dad, we're just trying to have a friendly get together here. I tried to be serious about Franco but you went off the deep end. Let's just bury him and the hatchet, alright? Mellow out."

"That's just the problem. You're flippant. You don't respect or appreciate what others did before you to earn freedom of speech or preserve democracy. Your lot has what we earned; you never paid for anything."

"Oh here we go. You hold up what you did as if you created Paradise. But you stopped your revolution; Hoffman says that revolution is a perpetual process embedded in the human spirit."

Des raised his voice. "That's bullshit, Davey. You can't go undercutting everything at once all the time. Like calling the courts 'fascist pigs'. We need laws."

David responded in kind, "You want bullshit, I'll give you some. Sacred cows make the tastiest hamburgers, Dad. Your institutions are just propping up injustices and they need to come down."

"Jesus H. Christ, David, in our day, we picked up guns and fought for our beliefs against Fascism. The Mac-Paps gave their lives; you just talk pap."

"Maybe you're so much a part of the Establishment now that you stopped believing in your ideals. Maybe you've become a bourgeois fascist yourself."

"You've got a lot of nerve saying that. You're so wet behind the ears, with your mincing marches and pabulum placards. Why don't you get real?"

David scraped his chair back, stood up and pointed at his father in a low voice, almost growling. "I always figured you despised me, now I know it. WELL I DESPISE YOU. Why don't you just fuck off."

Peter motioned them to calm down. Des got up quickly, knocking over his chair. He threw a twenty on the table and said to Peter, "I'll walk home. Merry Christmas, Peter."

To David, he said nothing. Sadly they would never have a chance for closeness again in Des's lifetime.

It was only one week until Christmas but Des was not feeling
26

particularly cheerful on his walk home. He pulled his collar up and thrust his hands into his navy-blue wool overcoat. He coughed a couple of times in the damp cold air, his chest tight, but he couldn't tell if it was the smoker's cough or the pain of desolation he was feeling at that moment.

"How did I fuck it up again with David? Both of us are despicable but I should know better. I'm the professional and I've been trained to stay in control in situations. How can I show such self-control in all the other facets of my life except this one of parenting? Well almost all." He snickered out loud and let his memories roll randomly on the walk home.

He thought, "Professional eh? I was trained by the best but it's not easy to keep it up day and night, on assignment and at home. Gotta be more diligent, Des. Yep that's me, diligent Dilman. Better than dilettante David. I wonder if it's my work that stops me from being close to anyone. Keeping my real intentions away from my colleagues must be taking a toll. I'll have to keep my wits about me around those bastard agents in Montreal over the next few days." Then he smiled at a recollection. He remembered a young Montreal woman in Cuba.

"Oh I can get intimate; I've had a few women in various places. But that was being intimate, not close. Meg and me were close, and intimate, for a while but that burnt out; no heat there anymore. Peter and me are close like brothers; there's hardly anything we don't share. I wonder if intimacy ruins closeness; it lets in other emotions like anger and jealousy. Maybe parents can't be close with their kids either because there's all that 'have to do' stuff that is a parent's responsibility. I was lucky in my life to have a few guys treat me like a son, a lot better than my own father did. Davey's lucky to have Peter; we both are. Funny, when thinking about close and intimacy, I didn't even use the word love."

He let out a sigh and could see his breath in the haze cast by the street lamp. He was home already. Letting himself in, he grunted to Meg that he was back and climbed the stairs to his room.

David and Peter drove home a while later, having had a further discussion after Des had left the Prescott.

"That was a bummer, Uncle Peter. Is he like that with you?"

"Not really. But he accepts me as I am. I don't think he feels that way about you yet. It's much easier to be an uncle than it is to be a father, I guess."

"How come you never married and had kids? You'd be good at it. You've always been great with me."

"Actually I was married once and had a boy. But that was long ago. You've always been like a son to me. I guess being an uncle is like being a grandfather too, all of the fun and never having to be the disciplinarian."

"Will you tell me about your marriage and your boy?"

"Your Dad knows. I might tell you someday, but not now. Want me to take your skis and get them tuned?"

"I might have to re-think that ski day with you, Uncle Peter. It will be pretty frosty at home, I don't doubt. Maybe it would be better if I go visit some friends in London before flying back to Hungary."

"Oh that would disappoint your Mom, and me. And deep down, your Dad too. Boxing Day is only a week away; you could visit your friends after that if it's still bad at home. Anyway think about it. The offer still stands."

Now David waved good-bye and entered the house quietly. But his mother was still up.

"How was your night, sweetie?" Meg was nursing a cup of tea with lemon before bed and offered to make one for David. He declined. After the beer, he would surely be up during the night anyway.

"I had fun with Uncle Peter but Dad was a bit grumpy."

"Not to worry; he's going to be away for a few days before Christmas and will get over it. He usually does after those trips. Say, how do you feel about lunch out tomorrow? I have a bit of Christmas shopping to do and maybe we could see a matinee. *One Flew Over The Cuckoo's Nest* is showing and I've heard good things about it."

"That would be lovely Mom. I have some last minute things to get too."

In his inner voice, David thought that he might learn something from the cinema about living with crazy people.

"Okay," she said. "It'll just be you and me. It's fun when you're home, Davey. Good night, dear."

Des went to sleep quickly but woke up about 2 a.m., dry mouthed, over-heated and in need of a glass of water. He stumbled downstairs to the darkened kitchen and while sipping some cold water, he flashed back to the wrecked evening with his son. He had a shiver realizing that he was in danger of having no son and no wife to speak of in real terms. What do the students say nowadays, in a 'meaningful way'? More to the point, what could he do about it? Shit, trying to keep your buddies alive in a war seemed easier than keeping a family together. He always made sure Meg and David were well cared for, food, shelter, and clothing. It seemed he was good at providing the basics but he fell short on the other needs. He just didn't get it. It's not that he didn't try. But like Midas, when he tried love, it always turned into something else, something leaden.

He didn't seem to have as much control over his mood swings lately. It was like things built up; he got angry, and before he knew it he was sliding into some dark place. It was wearing him down and repercussions were beginning to be noticed. Like tonight. And he hated himself when he'd close himself off completely from his son and wife. Never with Peter though. He could always talk to Peter.

He was trying to fix the situation at work but it seemed to be a lot harder to fix home. Maybe something would come to him while he was on his little road trip, a couple of days in Montreal 'to see a friend about a dog'. Actually he was impatient with a contact there and had to make an inquiry about an inquiry. In the meantime maybe he could come up with another salvaging scheme for his relationship with David. "Who knows?" he thought. "Maybe this cup of coffee will help my head."

David, on the other hand, had trouble getting to sleep and when he did it was fitful. Learning that his father was going to be away for a couple of days was like a reprieve. The atmosphere in the house would be poisonous with him there. The episode tonight made him toss and turn. He wondered how culpable he was for the evening's exchange. Normally he wouldn't have given a fig but something nagged at him. His one liners and repartee already had caused a rift between himself and his girlfriend Lydia and they had parted frostily for the Christmas holiday. She too had said that he wasn't taking life seriously. Could it be that his style got under his father's skin also? Whose fault was that? Did they both have personality flaws that bore some responsibility? Whoa, that was too deep. No way!

Lydia had said he had a subconscious ploy to keep people off balance and at arm's length. Sociology 101 tripe, he had responded. But did he really have anyone he felt close to? He could say he loved his mother but it was practically habitual. He couldn't remember the last time he said he loved his father. And lately he was wondering if he was causing Lydia to fall out of love with him. Love, closeness, wrong turns, nothing working out they way he planned. He punched his pillow and said, "C'mon Sleep."

Peter sat up nursing a scotch in the comfort of his condo. He wasn't particularly tired. Tonight at the 'P' depressed him. He was witness to his adopted family self-destructing and he wasn't sure what he could do to prevent it. Meg increasingly was in her own world, whether it was the church, her interest in popular culture, or her general angst about David.

And David, to his credit, did try to broach the gap between him and his father from time to time, but the alloys used in their relationship too often corroded whatever gold there might be. And he had to agree somewhat with Des's assessment made at lunch the other day.

Des had asked one of those open-ended questions he was so good at. "Peter, you're the art expert. I saw a can of soup presented as a work of art the other day. What is that about?"

"It's called pop art."

"You mean like Pepsi or something?"

Peter laughed, "Well actually there is one artist who believes that the hidden meaning behind a whole row of Coca Cola bottles is that no matter how rich or poor, everyone from the president to the hobo can drink the same drink. He uses mundane objects or celebrities in repetitive representations."

"What's that about the soup can guy?"

"That would be Andy Warhol. The National Gallery has a few of his works. Like the Brillo boxes. We can go some time if you want."

"Not especially. Do you like his work?"

"Not particularly, nor do I like his philosophy. In fact, it was Warhol who said he was deeply superficial. It's almost like he's having us on. Why do you ask?"

"Mmm, deeply superficial. That's rich. Sounds like our David, don't you think?"

"How do you mean, Des?"

"How he flits from one idea to another; never seems to stay the course or go much below the surface."

"Well he's still young and trying to find his feet maybe; trying things out."

"Peter, when we were his age... he's going to be 28...hell we had fought in a war and had started careers by then. I was already ten years into mine by 28. We had found our feet and put shoes on them for chrissakes."

Peter responded, "Different times, Des;" but he had to admit that perhaps Des had a point.

What was that expression they used to use when he lived in Scotland? At sixes and sevens, was it? Well the Dilmans certainly seemed to be at sixes and sevens, caught in confused and whirling waters. Yes, he worried about his adopted family.

Chapter 3.

WHERE ANGELS FEAR TO TREAD

It was the wee hours and Des still didn't feel like going back to bed. He sipped a cup of instant coffee, not his favourite but it would do. The den was dimly lit. He lay his head back against the sofa and closed his eyes. David had infuriated him last evening, wanting to home in on the celebration of Franco's death. Des remembered those early days when he was co-opted into participating in that tyrant's episode of Fascism. Why did he feel Spain was his battle and didn't want to share it? His tired mind wandered. It was as if it were April, 1937 and he was reliving his assignment...

Frank Zaneth was his tormentor turned mentor then. Two years earlier in Regina, Frank, the undercover cop with the pseudonym Harry Blask, had effectively tricked and hazed him into his new career as a Security Officer. Earlier, Zaneth had infiltrated the On To Ottawa Trekker's strike office where he, Des, volunteered too and one afternoon Zaneth/Blask had found Des with his pants down... Nuff said.

It was innocent enough but Zaneth twisted it and used it to catch Des up in a web, enough to co-opt Des into joining the Force. In Des's first major assignment, going to Spain during its Civil War, Zaneth made reference to the trouser incident.

Des remembered as if it were yesterday. He was travelling under a false passport made out to Barry Desmond and his cover or legend was as a reporter. Zaneth had figured, since Des was new at this undercover espionage, having a name that would seem legitimate for him to respond to 'Des', if anyone might recognize him, was prudent.

"No need to be caught with your pants down again, is there?" Zaneth had said.

Des and several other volunteers were on a ship sailing plying the waters to Europe to join up with Spain's Republicans. During the deep Depression, often there was space on luxury liners and they were sampling a first class trip on third class tickets. Des chatted up some of the men under his guise and most were willing to talk to a 'reporter'.

There were a few that Des vaguely recognized from the Trek and he mostly avoided them. But one guy older than Des by about fifteen years and sitting on a deck chair waved at him and called him over. The man, with a quizzical look and bushy red eyebrows squinted in the sun. It was James 'Red' Walsh and he thought he recognized Des.

In his gravelly voice he said, "Hey, weren't you one of Doc's boys? Sorry I forgot your name."

"Hi Red, Barry Desmond, but folks called me Des. The last time I saw you, you were being clubbed by some dick on Regina's Market Square stage."

"Ya, he clobbered me good. But I got away and hid in a garbage can, of all things. Those Mounties were firin' real bullets so I got outta there quick and headed West. The goons blackballed me but I managed to fake my way into a stevedore job on the coast. Pretty good one too, paid 50 cents a day, better than the relief and panhandling I was doin' on Hastings Street in Vancouver. So, here we are about to face real bullets again. What about you?"

"Oh you know, like lots of guys, when the Trek was over, I wandered East. I got lucky too and landed a researcher's job for a Toronto paper. Easier to hide in a bigger city, eh. Now I'm on assignment to Spain."

"Well, keep your head down, comrade."

Des moved on. There was one happy-go-lucky guy, Taffy Stockdale, a six-foot, barrel-chested, infectiously amicable Texan. They hit it off and spent lots of time getting to know each other over the seven-day crossing, drinking coffee, grabbing a bite, and enjoying each other's company. Des wavered between his task of getting familiar with other Canadians and wanting to get to know this American more. He remembered his self-pledge against his employer, his anti-RCMP mantra of 'you have me but you don't own me', and decided getting to know Taffy suited him just fine.

On the night before reaching Rotterdam, they stood after dinner at the aft deck railing, the reddish-orange dots of their cigarettes counterposed against the myriad stars. The propellers stirred a luminescent wake behind them and the two fell into conversation.

"What are you leaving behind in the States, Taffy?

The Texan blew out his smoke, his eyes twinkly and his smile an attractive white in the dark.

He drawled, "Nuthin' really."

"What? No family, no girlfriend, no job? Everybody's leaving someone or something behind."

"Nope, I'm just wantin' to give some good fortune back."

"Really, how so?"

"Well, Barry, I figure I've been lucky all my life and this civil war is just another bit of a good opportunity that's dropped my way."

"C'mon Taffy, you're just talkin' off the cob. I'm serious," countered Des.

"No really. I've had a lot of good things happen to me and now I just want to give some back."

"You'll have to explain that one for me," Des responded.

"Ya, sure. Well, I was born in 1914 so I didn't have to fight in that capitalist blood bath in the trenches. How's that for good luck?"

"Fine by me if you don't want to talk." Des started to go.

"Ok, you want the real goods, do you? Really, I do feel lucky. My parents were dirt-poor farmers but believed in education. They scraped enough outta the soil to get me through high school. Then in 1932 I saw an advertisement for a college on a farm in Arkansas where you could work for room and board while learning. I applied and damn if I didn't get accepted. It was called the Commonwealth College. Wonderful what folks can do when they think about the greater good first instead of themselves, ain't it? Since my Pops was a worker and I was a worker, I decided to study workers, you know, labour history. Liked it so much I joined the Communist Party and got a job organizing. I think someone is pretty lucky to get a job they love doing, don't you?"

"So did the Party tell you to join the Republicans in Spain?"

"Shit no. I guess I just don't like seeing anyone bullied. Sure, the Soviet Union is the only country backing the Republicans, them and us are the only ones forming militias to help. We are it, Barry-o, just us against the bullies. The Popular Front was elected so it seems an easy choice over a generalissimo, don't you think?"

"Hmm, makes sense but I'm not exactly joining, am I? I'm just gathering information and writing. But ya, I agree. You gotta try to stop the big bosses and their power. Sometimes it ain't so black and white though is it? And it ain't always easy."

"Nah but who said it would be easy? Are you talkin' some high filutin' existential philosophy now? Or maybe it's more mundane. Are you just tryin' to tell me you took on this job because you got a girl in trouble?"

"No, no, I don't have any girlfriend. No, it's more that some things force your hand and you can't always do what you want."

"Don't know nuthin' 'bout that, Barry. Whenever I've wanted something, I've either been lucky to get it or folks have sacrificed to help me get it. You help others whenever you get the chance and other folks'll help you back. These Spaniards were just workin' and votin' and mindin' their own business; seem like good American values, hell, good human values to me. So we oughta help 'em. I don't need the Party to tell me that; it's just good sense."

"Do you really think the Popular Front, you know the Republicans, the volunteers and the Soviets can stop what Hitler, Mussolini, and Franco are throwing at them?"

"Won't know unless we try. Hey, I've got an idea. Why don't you put down your pen and pick up a rifle too."

"Ho, you are a good farmer. Planting seeds all the time, eh?"

"Can't see a crop unless you plant some seeds, my Pops always said."

35

Des flicked his cigarette butt. It glowed briefly before it arced into the frothy abyss. Taffy did the same and they shook hands.

"Good luck to you Barry. Let's say so long, not good bye."

They disembarked the S.S. Volendam at Rotterdam and took the train to Paris. Taffy and Red Walsh and most of the other volunteers were travelling with duffle bags and cardboard suitcases. Some had been to Europe before but most hadn't and were in awe when they pulled into the Gare du Nord, with its iron and stone, its glass and sculptures. French contacts met them and managed their transit, many making their way to Marseilles before taking a coastal freighter to Spain. But Des left their company; he had to be about his own official business in Paris.

The Canadian Embassy in Paris was on prime real estate; the Avenue Montaigne, not far from the Seine, which formed a triangle with Avenue Georges V and the Champs- Élysées. Des entered the foyer of the elegant white building and was ushered into an office. There he was greeted formally by Philippe Roy, the minister plenipotentiary. He seemed constricted, jowls and belly stuffed into a morning suit. He was almost 70, and he conveyed his message succinctly, holding his fingertips like a steeple.

His information, he said, stated that Canadian passports were being used by Communist supporters to gain easy access throughout Europe. It seemed that when volunteers for Spain were recruited in Canada, they were asked to give up their birth certificates for the passport process; and conveniently the documents often were not handed back. Also when leaving France, they had to hand over their passports for 'safekeeping' before travelling to Spain. The contraband Canadian documents were being used by Soviet and other Communist *persona non grata* to enter various countries. The Canadian government and Monsieur Zaneth, in particular, needed names of the volunteers to stymie the use of legitimate Canadian birth certificates and passports in the wrong hands.

After his work on the Volendam voyage, Des was able to provide a number of names right away that the Embassy could track. Roy was impressed; and relayed the next part of Des's assignment, via Zaneth's instructions. Des's mission was about to become more sombre.

He was told to carry on to Spain and send back to the embassy the names of Canadians who had died in the Spanish conflict so that their names couldn't be used for false identification or show up on bogus passports for Communists. With his job thus defined, Des crossed the Pyrenees and went to Barcelona. There he met his pre-arranged contact, a free-lance photographer who would courier coded messages and names back to Paris.

Margareta Gross was an attractive woman in her mid-thirties, born in Poland and separated from her husband. She had her own studio, Foto-elis, and had been working on her own in Barcelona for a few years. Her sculpted face reminded Des of a shield that she could hide behind. She had thick, light-brown, shoulder-length hair; piercing dark eyes and a strong chin, indicating a confident and independent bearing. Recently she had done a gallery showing called *Novo Barcelona*, a stark presentation that included stills of soup kitchens, slum children, schoolchildren at their chalkboard, and a doctor bandaging a child's eyes. She had a preference for distant and overhead shots, not unlike her demeanor. And Des found her very alluring.

After meeting her at her studio, they went to a bar to talk. She ordered a crème de cassis for herself and a glass of red wine for Des. She took out a cigarette, and Des was quick to light it for her. She blew smoke out the side of her mouth and said sarcastically, "You're awfully young; do you know what you're in for?"

Des answered as suavely as he could, stretching the truth. "I may look young, but I've got more experience than you think. You grow up fast as a journalist; I've been around."

"Is that so? Well I dare say I've gone a little further around the block than you. So you're going to give me names from time to time, no?"

She paused, waiting for an answer and then added, "You know, there is something you can do for me in return for my postal service," she said, squinting at him through the smoke.

Des sipped some wine and lit his own cigarette. He leaned back in his chair; her face was giving nothing away. He could feel a stirring in his groin as he imagined what the something was he could do for her.

"What might that be?"

She laughed a throaty, sultry bit of mirth.

Des smiled. "It was that obvious, was it?"

"No, well yes. I didn't mean that kind of help, not yet anyway. No, I want to get away from Europe; it's mad here. I want to get far away somehow. You will be with many people from far away, yes, these crazy volunteers, some from Australia even. As you go searching for names, maybe you can introduce me to someone who can help me?"

"Ya, sure I can keep an eye open for you, Margareta. If that's what you're cooking. How is it you're my contact anyway?"

"It's not easy earning a living during a civil war. I can be trusted for some little jobs, so I said okay. The extra money helps but you might be able to help me more."

"Hey, maybe you'd like to tour with me, you know while I travel with the Canadians; maybe you could get some good pictures?"

She looked at him squarely. "You know, Barry, you have a nice face; I would like to photograph you."

Des insisted on paying and they left. She slipped her arm through Des's and the golden hairs on his tanned arm seemed to bristle with electricity at her touch. She was a dish alright he thought but he couldn't afford to go dizzy over a dame. Not so soon anyway.

Her living quarters were above her studio, small and cluttered with a faint nostril-pinching odor of photo developing fluids. She led him to her bedroom and started to undress.

"I thought you wanted to photograph my face," he smirked.

"Barry, I do, but let's see what else you've got first," she said looking over her bare shoulder at him...

Des opened his eyes when the furnace went on. It roused him and he noticed he was also aroused. Damn memory was too real, he thought.

In more ways than one, Des lost his virginity in Spain. Maybe that was why he cherished the experience. He wasn't ready to share it with anyone yet. He fell in love, got his first piece of writing published, and successfully completed his first espionage assignment. Those were his trophies in an otherwise unaccomplished life, he mused. Along the way he had betrayed a lot of people and values though. He had blown the whistle on his employers, the RCMP; denounced his wife on flimsy evidence; and been a lousy father to his son.

Could the dubious good he had done in his life make up for the explicit bad? He wondered. Then it struck him like an epiphany. Maybe he could work a strategy to entrap David for his own good. He had his secrets in boxed journals. Maybe somehow he could entice David to get to know him through his writing. Then David would see that he meant well. Yes, that might work. He could devise some carrot to lure David to want to accept. He'd let the idea percolate some more and use Peter as a sounding board of course. He'd have to flesh his plan out but it felt right to him.

Now he felt like going back to bed. As he quietly trudged back upstairs though, he thought of David and the wicked turns he had done to him over the last twenty years, leaving him for long periods, spying on him, and the worst one, destroying his chance with External Affairs. He knew that when he lay in his bed there would be no rest really. Instead his confidence waned, like a dream does when one wakes up. Was this a realistic strategy or was he merely being a fool rushing in?

CHAPTER 4:

SOMEONE HAS TO DIE...

Nine Years Later, Ottawa,
Friday, November 16, 1984

Des woke up realizing that time was running out. Like Socrates' hemlock, the cancer was on the move. He had always beaten the odds but grimaced at the thought that death would not be one of them. He lay still on his bed in the dark mid-November morning, the house quiet except for the click of the furnace kicking on and whirring to keep the cold at bay. His waking mind said, "Yes, I figure today's the time to put the plan into place."

He remembered their longtime family doctor, Dr. Clift, and his analysis from the early summer. "It's spreading, Des. Lung cancer can be like that. The lump on your neck means it is affecting your lymph nodes and the aching legs indicate it may be attacking your bones. Sorry but I'm afraid there will be more pain in your legs and hands, and probably sooner rather than later. I can arrange treatment but it will be a stopgap at best.

"Nah, just some pain killers, Doc."

And sooner was now. He lay in the early morning murkiness. His back and legs hurt as he rolled on his side, and forced himself to swing his legs into the chilly air from under the warm, boiled wool military blanket he preferred. Using his right arm to push himself to a sitting position, he peeked out the side of the curtain and saw bony tree limbs and the street light illuminating them like an x-ray. While hunched on the edge of the bed, he groped for his reading glasses on top of his book at the bedside.

"Better get things moving," Des thought and he opened his bedside table drawer, taking out a black-covered journal. Slowly rising, sliding into slippers and fumbling with an old cardigan on the bedroom door knob, he clutched his brown, horn-rimmed reading glasses and journal in his right hand while he ran his other hand along the walls for guidance and support. Moving quietly past his wife's room, he slowly descended the stairs to the kitchen. It was only then that he turned on a light and plugged in the kettle, filled the night before with enough water for two cups.

Then he went to open the front door where he reached for the newspaper and felt the cool blast of air. He looked at the headline without reading it. The kettle's whistle stopped his fixated stare. He must act while he still could. Pouring boiled water over freshly ground coffee, letting it drip into his mug, he sniffed the aroma and decided it wasn't too early to call Peter. It was a number he always remembered, although he was relying more and more on his worn address book to remind him of details. Another casualty of age for sure, but Peter's number was etched.

"Hello Pete, I know it's early but I need to set an appointment to amend the will; yeah, this morning. Let's do this. He will bite or he won't. No, it's the only way. Besides, I can feel it in my bones." At this last line he chuckled, allowing his black humour to enter the conversation. "Right then, see you at 8:30."

Des sipped his coffee, one and a half spoons of sugar and a drop of table cream. Every day should start with a treat because the day rarely gave you many more. He popped his meds, scanned the sports page, and rubbed his stubbly face. The Grey Cup was being held in Edmonton on Sunday, Hamilton against Winnipeg. He'd like to watch it even though his Ottawa Roughriders finished out of the playoffs; in fact they were last this CFL season. One thing for sure, he would never cheer for the Saskatchewan version of Roughriders. Never those Regina bastards, that was for sure! He flipped the page to hockey. And how were *Les Canadiens*? They had lost only three games so far and would play the Devils this weekend; but Guy Lafleur was still not scoring or playing much.

"Maybe I could advise him about retirement," he mused. His own three and a half years of retirement had been much like his life, just another phase one adjusted to. He did like his sports though, the microcosmic struggles helped him forget his own and the world's problems, at least for a while. Seated at the kitchen table, slurping a bit of coffee, he wrote in his journal for about twenty minutes, signed with a flourish; then scraped back the chair and got up.

Next he moved down the hall to the front foyer and the closet under the stairs. The door, with the top slanted to fit under the stairs, was always locked. Taking the longest key of two attached to a leather cord around his neck, he unlocked the door and switched on the light. He had to bend over to enter and was met with a co-mingled aroma of cedar and the dregs of empty wine bottles stored there.

Along the facing wall was a wine rack with a few dozen bottles, and to the right, tucked tight against the acute angle where the floor met the stairs, were six boxes, three wide and stacked in two rows. They were made of cedar, about 11 inches high and wide and 15 inches long, each with a hinged top and locked at one end. Also there were routed hand slots on the ends so that the boxes could be pulled more easily and then lifted. Each box weighed less than 10 pounds. He tugged at one.

The words *The '80s, Property of Desmond Dilman* were stenciled in black on the lid. He fit the smaller key into the lock and half opened the lid, revealing the spines of a few journals and some collectibles: newspaper clippings, postcards and other memorabilia.

He put his journal into this box and, like a finale, it seemed to satisfy him because he nodded, closed the lid, locked the box, then pushed it back. Reversing on his knees and using the wine rack for support, he shut off the light, backed out of the closet taking care not to bump his head, and relocked the door.

It was 7:30 a.m., time to go back up the stairs to his room to dress. Clouds were skidding above the trees but he saw they were peach-tinged, promising an eventful day. He tried to stay focused on what he had to do today. He would be 67 next month and the face that he was shaving was not the one of his memories. Then he had dark wavy hair; a full, confident smile with blue eyes that twinkled; handsome in a craggy way. It was a face that said he was likeable or at least tried to be; a guy that welcomed opportunities. But that was then. Now that face sagged. His creviced jowls met an incipient wattle below a receded chin. He pulled his cheeks up to shave a smoother surface." If only one could smooth out a past like that", he thought.

When Des descended again, he was neatly attired in white shirt and a red and blue striped tie, pressed grey trousers and a blue blazer, black loafers polished; not badly trimmed for his age although now fifteen pounds overweight. He wasn't as erect as he once was, but he thought he still presented his six foot frame well in spite of graying hair, sallow skin and other signs of age and pain. By this time, Meg, his wife, was in the kitchen with her cup of tea and the paper. She called out good morning but Des was abrupt. "No time now, off to an appointment." He slammed the door and took the stairs gingerly to the waiting cab that went down Glebe Avenue toward Bank Street.

Meg cradled her cheek in her hand, skimming the ads and sipping from her china teacup. "Now where's he off to?" she wondered. "That man is so full of secrets," she muttered. She got up to check the calendar for events but nothing indicated an appointment. Des had lived a separate life for so long his actions really didn't surprise her, but she did feel neglected once again. Resentment rose. She walked to the back of the house, from the kitchen through a den to the screened add-a-room. The plastic storm windows snapped in the wind and didn't keep out the chill. By the door to the back yard, there was a deacon's bench used for storing odds and ends. She opened the lid and found a bottle of vodka under some mittens. "Well I have my secrets too," she said. "Damn, he makes me need something to fortify my tea."

She returned to the kitchen and added a shot, squeezed a bit of lemon into her sugary tea, re-hid the bottle and tried to resume her reading. But now she was distracted. Meg and Des had been married 37 years but not happily. She always seemed to disappoint him somehow. It wasn't her looks because she still had a figure and lots of people said she was attractive. Even for her age, the tactless ones might add. He never talked to her, only at her, as far as she could remember. He just didn't involve her and it bothered her.

Well she had her own life to lead anyway. Maybe she would go shopping along Sparks Street; maybe she would meet a friend for lunch; or maybe she would call her son. It had been a few days since socializing after all. "At any rate, it's time to put my face on." The vodka was making her feel hopeful.

Peter put the bedside phone down and rubbed his eyes. Yes it was early but he might as well get showered and start what was likely to be a long day. He didn't resent Des's early call. They had been friends a long time, since the war. But this latest plan that they had talked about over the last few months seemed desperate. He thought, "Why didn't he just talk to David?"

Peter shook his head however; he owed Des a great deal and now Des was calling in some of his chips. Loyalty was like that. Des had been his only friend and had given him an escape to slake despair after the war.

It was Des who had sponsored Peter to come to Canada as a Polish immigrant. Tall at 6'2", lean, and fit, Peter took care of himself. Second chances could have that effect. Semi-retired from his law practice and turning 70, Peter still moved with purpose and verve for life. He was also compassionate, aware that most everyone needed a least another chance. And he had hoped that Des would try a more direct route with his son rather than this intricate one. But Des was not forgiving, even at this stage. Peter disapproved inwardly of Des's request but did not judge openly.

"Of course I will set it up and execute the will as you wish. I just think it's a bit like ruling from the grave," he had told his lifelong friend during the summer. He still thought that way.

Had it only been four months ago, in early August, when Des had asked Peter to meet him for lunch at the Lord Elgin? They arrived together both dressed in casual sports jackets, pressed trousers, polished shoes. To the restaurant diners who observed, Des was a trifle paunchier and a bit more rumpled with thinning grey hair combed to cover as much as he could while in fact, Peter who was older, looked younger, haler and very distinguished with a full head of striking white hair. Sitting by the window and quickly ordering, they were easy with one another and moved through pleasantries, like Peter's upcoming golf trip, football games, and Mulroney's chances at beating John Turner in the fall. Peter asked after Meg but Des waved at the air like shooing a fly. So Peter said, "What's on your mind, Des?" Clinking tableware muffled their sudden tête-à-tête. They were revisiting 'the plan'.

"No, every time I try to talk to him, it ends up in an argument. Talking won't work with David and me. He hates me."

"He doesn't hate you; he just misunderstands your intentions," responded Peter.

"Aagghh, you're the favourite Uncle Peter; you always take his side."

"No, I don't; I just go a little softer on him, that's all."

"Well you of all people know how the past can be a burden. I still think that if he goes on hating me, it will eat him up. I think this is the only way for him to get to know me. Ironic don't you think; getting to know me when I 'm not around."

"You're talking crazy, Des. You've got lots of time still. Use it wisely. Talk to him while you still can."

"I've tried Pete. We always end up NOT talking. This is the only scheme I hope will work."

"He'll have many questions, you know, and you won't be there to answer or explain."

"No, he'll have the journals and money. And you. It's my legacy to him so that he can let go of some of his anger and hatred."

Des stopped and quickly glanced around the room before continuing.

"And if he can't, at least he'll get some travelling out of it. But you know Pete; my worse fear is that he will be like me. He's more like me than he thinks; always trying to be one up, always thinking he's better than he's got a right to be. It will eat him up inside, just like this goddam cancer."

Peter bit his lower lip and then said, "Okay, okay, lower your voice. What if I called him and tried to arrange a visit between you, even act as mediator?"

"No, Pete. It has to be this way. You tried that, remember, and David and I both ended up yelling at you. I don't want that again. Let the bugger figure it out himself for chrissakes, if he's up to it."

"Well it still seems like posthumous meddling to me. But I'm just your lawyer. I hope you enjoy watching, wherever you might be," he said with a tight grin.

"You're more than my lawyer. You are probably, no you ARE the only person who knows most of my secrets. I didn't expect to be as bad as my own father as a parent but, shit, I was." Des looked away for a bit and then continued.

"It's just that I had a chance to raise a boy and messed it up. You, well you lost your chance. But you've been a brother to me and an uncle to David. So I'm just providing the means and hoping you can get him to grasp the brass ring. If anyone can, you will. As for ruling from the grave, you'd know about that; didn't Anna do that to you?"

Peter glared at Des for a minute and growled slowly, "*Głupi kłamca!* *(gwupi kwamza)* Damn liar! No, Anna didn't do that to me and you of all people should know that. Don't go too far, Des. I will do this because we're friends but." He didn't continue in case he said something he'd regret but his icy blue eyes held Des's unfathomable brown eyes and Des finally blinked.

"You're right, Pete. Sorry, I presumed too much. But I need you to impress on David that it's for his sake, just like Anna wanted you to carry on for the best."

It seemed a good time to end their luncheon. To carry on with small talk would be banal. Peter picked up the tab and they shook hands. "Don't thank me Des, I'll get the money back as executor expenses soon enough." Each chuckled sardonically, tension gone, and went separate ways; Peter back to his office on Laurier West and Des to walk thoughtfully along the Rideau Canal.

He took the paths through Confederation Park and walked along the canal, late summer sun casting shadows to his left. He let his mind wander...

Wasn't it about this time of year when my Dad told me I wasn't going back to school? "Eight years is enough, it's time for you to get a job and start helpin' out around here." God, the ole man was gruff...

I was about fourteen or fifteen, wasn't I? Yep, I took that farm job out in Whitby. Room and board, $10 a week with Sunday off. Christ that was hard work. Hands got pretty calloused. First time away from home and really missed my mom and sisters. Set out on my day off hitchhiking back to Toronto. I walked and thumbed and by noon I had only got to Pickering. Shit, I remember being hot and dusty and I had to turn back. Knew I couldn't get to Toronto and back in time and didn't wanna get fired. Yeah, a few tears feeling sorry for myself. Was I lonely or just feeling all alone? Boy I was bone weary, hungry with just another week of work to look forward to when I trudged up the lane to the farmhouse. Then a letter from the ole man telling me to mail half my earnings. Shit. When did I stop that job, November, 1928 I think, laid off more like. The ole man was pretty pissed off, whacked me with his cane, like it was my fault. Then I got that delivery boy job at the local grocery. I bought that bike and the big oversized carrier that I put on it...

The loud hum of the traffic from the Queensway overhead shook him from his reverie. It was like waking from a dream and he caught his bearings. Turning up Patterson Creek pathway, the sun in his face forced him to squint. But it also allowed him to go back to his daydream...

That job paid okay and I got good tips. But that rainy afternoon, the street was so slippery. I skidded on the streetcar rails and when I tried to regain balance the damn front tire lodged, stuck right in the tracks...

...Over I went, my bike twisting and me sprawling. Shit, the groceries were strewn all over the street with a trolley bearing down on me. Ha, that crumbled the bike up pretty good. I left the bike and groceries all over the street and just walked home. The ole man tried whacking me with the cane that time too but I caught it and pulled it from his hands. Ha, I showed him I was getting too big for that. Or maybe he showed me; yep that was when he kicked me out. But not before he said I was a bastard, wasn't really his son; he only married Mom out of sympathy because she was raped and got knocked up. So his taking care of me was over, it was time I got out. Boy he sure showed me...

"Jeez ", he thought, "What took me down that memory lane? Is that how my life is gonna flash before my eyes?" Des had probably walked about five kilometers, three miles by his reckoning, before he reached home on Glebe Ave., between Lyons and Bank. It was a modest home purchased with modest earnings in 1948, a two-story brick and stucco with covered veranda. It cost just under $10,000 and he was earning about $2,000 a year then. He was proud of that purchase, setting up Meg for the times he would be away and renovating one of the 3 bedrooms for little David, born that same year. Now he was tired and sweaty. He needed a shower and would treat himself with a glass of Amarone from the closet cache, patting the spare closet key hanging on his chest. It had been a full day, but it dawned on him, that like most days, and except for Peter, he had faced it alone.

Since that summertime luncheon, Peter had been and returned from a late October golf holiday in Florida and still sported a tan, looking especially distinguished in November. He got to his office early on Laurier Ave. West, a third- floor inauspicious space. Taking the stairs and too early to greet anyone, he unlocked doors to his waiting room and his office beyond. He was trying to cut down on his workload but still felt work gave him purpose. And he still liked helping people with their legal problems even if it was sometimes mundane. Coming in for Des was no hardship. There were no appointments until 11 a.m., so Des and he could get started in private. His secretary would attend to the legal copying and morning coffee after her arrival at 9:30.

Des took the elevator up and sat somewhat heavily into the leather chair opposite Peter's uncluttered desk. Both men were all business, wanting to get the deed done. Peter sat with his hands folded on the desk, leaning forward a bit and looking natty in a navy suit, blue button down shirt with a sky-blue silk tie. His framed credentials were on the wall behind him, B.Sc. from Krakow's Jagiellonian University, 1936; LL.B from the University of Edinburgh, 1949; LL.B from The Law Society of Upper Canada, Osgoode Hall, 1954; and his Certificate of Canadian Citizenship, 1955. Des had underpinned Peter's life, getting him to Canada and supporting him in a law career; now Peter was helping Des fashion an amended will that would change lives after Des died.

Peter started. "How are you bearing up? How's Meg?" Des blew some air of dismissal and Peter got the hint. "Alright Des, so we're amending the will. Why don't you explain your grand plan again?"

"It's still about Meg and David first; I'm not giving it all to cat charities, if that's what you think. You can stop the furrowed brow routine."

"Okay, I'm relaxed, just one condition. You have done enough for me in your life and I don't need anything. Remember you sponsored me when I came here and helped me when I was a student-at-law in Toronto. So I won't agree to anything for me in the will apart from my executor duties. Agreed? Alright, so you're revoking all former wills and codicils you've made. And now I am the executor, not Meg. So outline your wishes for me again."

"It's mainly about David. I want a conditional trust set up. And I need you to hold these keys." Des placed the two keys on the leather thong on Peter's desk.

"Before we talk about David, what about Meg?" Peter asked while eyeing the offering.

Des waved a hand and impatiently said, "Meg will be fine. She has the house, a survivor portion of my pension, and maybe an insurance policy unless I give it to David. But you know and I know she's a lush. She will just blow through the money when she's drunk. So I want to set up an annuity, maybe $10,000 a year that you or a designate can monitor. She can go for a cruise or travel to Europe, a holiday that she always wanted but I never had the time for; but she has to account for it. Otherwise she will just piss it away on booze or scam artists."

Peter was writing quickly in his notepad, no interruptions.

"But David is a trickier business. I gather from Meg that he's at loose ends, no full-time job. How's that for a university-educated 36 year old. So I'm thinking the lure of money and travel might do the trick, if he has the right persuading." He paused and waited for Peter to look up.

"Pete, you're the brother I never had; hell, the family I never had. You and I have helped each other in the toughest of times. You let me be a friend and you're the only person I have been able to talk to about most things. But not all things; my job wouldn't let me."

Peter's brow was furrowing again and he cocked his head slightly with curiosity and concentration.

"I've been keeping diaries for most of my working life, writing what I've been through as a kind of self-witness." Des chuckled. "It's as close to being a writer that I'm gonna get."

Peter sighed and smiled. "Yes, I remember that chat about what we would like to do once the war was over."

"So that key there will open up the closet under the stairs and the other smaller one will open up almost five decades worth of journals and clippings about my life that I have jotted down and ferreted away. That's what I want David to have. That and $70,000 to draw on in trust and with your advisement to complete as much of the journey that you can persuade him to. Each box will take him to different places and can shed light on parts of my life's story: from Regina to Spain, to Italy and Cuba, maybe even Poland with you."

Peter raised his eyebrows. Des hushed him. "There is still a bit about me you don't know, and I'm not proud about it all, but the time for secrecy is over. Call it an explanatory confessional to David if you want. Hopefully he will forgive me but at least I want him to understand me. With those journals, you helping him, and the money to travel, who knows, maybe he will be able to show me and himself a little compassion."

"I knew there was always a reason for you being reticent and wary. I put it down to your job mainly and never judged you. Are there some things I should have been more judgmental about, that I should know about?"

Des swallowed, "No, we've covered most of what you need to know about me over the last 50 years. You have always been an uncle to David and good supporter to Meg. Now I need you to be something more for David, his advisor, his mentor, a Merlin to his Arthur, if that isn't too hokey."

Peter spoke. "Des, I can set up the annuity for Meg and the trust for David, no problem. But, Merlin? I don't know magic."

"Don't sell yourself short. And one other thing. The wine under the closet. Each time David comes back to confer with you before going on his next installment, you and he should drink a bottle. Each one is vintage and wonderful, trust me."

Just then, Peter's secretary came into the outer office. "Good morning, gentlemen. Here is the coffee you wanted Mr. Nowak. Two Americanos, both black, just like you ordered."

"Thanks Nancy. When Mr. Dilman leaves, we will have some work to do on his will."

Peter looked sideways at Des. "A toast to a taste we learned in the trenches. And to our relationship." They sipped quietly, each remembering that they acquired the taste for this java style from the Yanks in the war, Americano black.

"Like that line in *West Side Story*, from womb to tomb, from our new beginnings to the end, eh? It's been good Pete."

Des struggled out of his chair. "Why don't you come for dinner on Sunday? Meg would love to see you too; but not a word about the will. And then I can come back to sign the copies next week some time." Peter and Des shook hands across the desk but Peter was quick to come around and walk Des to the elevator where they hugged and said good-bye.

"Just so long," Des corrected him.

Friday, December 14, 1984

A month later, Des was resting in bed, propped up on his pillows and a bit mellow after two glasses of Mouton Cadet Rouge with dinner. Meg had fallen asleep watching *Jeopardy!* with new host, Alex Trebek. Des's *Les Canadiens* lost last night to the Canuckleheads of Vancouver but had points in nine of their last 13 games. All their worlds would unfold as it would, but he had decided that he didn't want to see another Christmas, definitely not a New Year. He had said as much to Peter at lunch two days ago. The tingling in his legs was getting worse, his back was constantly aching, and now he had noticed a lump in his armpit. It was time.

He looked around his rather Spartan room: at his black framed print of Van Gogh's *Potato Eaters*, the dark and grimed peasant family forced to hang upstairs because Meg protested so much about having it in the dining room downstairs; at his beloved but modest three-shelf book case, where he espied his prized signed copies among a small collection of special volumes; his open clothes closet with his best blazer, white shirt and grey trousers that he had hung as an ensemble; and his bureau with a picture of David's graduation on it. He noticed that his bedside table needed dusting and smiled with the thought that he would soon be returning to that state himself. Feeling tired, Des put his current book down, a birthday present from Peter, Barbara Tuchman's new history, *The March of Folly*, which was given to him at lunch on December 3rd. Instead, he picked up another book from his bedside and lay it by his side. Then he closed his eyes and began to remember when it all started...

"It was that damn Depression wasn't it? I was 17 that spring in 1935, out of work and ridin' the rails out West. I got to Calgary and that's where I met Hugh Garner, just up from California and on his way to New York. It was in a hobo jungle, there were so many back then...

...I remember Garner telling me it was okay to be a hobo, but not a tramp or a bum. We're all wandering he said but tramps dream and bums drink; only hoboes wander and work. He was collecting material to be a writer he said. I was tempted to go with him then but I'd heard about work in Banff and headed there instead.

The government was setting up a national park run by the Army and using us working stiffs as cheap labour. Clearing logs and building roads with shovels, picks and wheel barrows, ha, some relief work. Got us transients out of the city and gave us $5 a month for 8 hours a day, food and shelter, tents actually until we cut enough logs for buildings.

Submit or starve, the papers said, but really I didn't mind it; played hockey in winter and took that literature and writing course from the Frontier College guys. I was getting good at reading and developing a book list. Then the agitators started in on us, calling us slaves and wanting us to strike and go on to Ottawa to protest. Trek or Treat I think I said to one of them and there were guffaws in the bunkhouse. But I went with them anyway, hopping the CPR in June with the rest of the boys until we got to Regina a week later. Yeah, that's when it started. And tonight is when it will end...

Des opened his eyes and reached for another glasses case beside him on the bed; it was cracked old leather and stamped with the British Government Issue broad arrow. He had won it in a poker game during the war off a Special Operations Executive bloke, a British agent, who had said he didn't need them; looked intelligent already and too cowardly to use them as designed. These had tortoise shell rims on the top and metal on the bottom of the glasses, the arms thin and malleable. Now it would all depend on Peter to do what he thought best.

Des put the earpiece in his mouth as if he were thinking and bit down hard, just like the SOE guy had said. He quickly put the glasses in his hand onto the case and held them there by his side while his breathing became very rapid and his heart raced. He twitched some, a fleeting remembering of what cyanide would do, and suddenly, death.

CHAPTER 5.

...SO THAT OTHERS MAY VALUE LIFE
MORE... (Virginia Woolf)

Ottawa, Saturday, December 15, 1984

It was about 9:30 in the morning, bright, windy and cold with some snow covering the ground. A pretty day. Meg had heard the boy shovel the walk earlier. It seemed strange though. She had to get the paper herself and there was no coffee cup on the counter. It wasn't like Des to sleep in. She had read what she wanted to in the paper; Christmas sales mainly, and there was that new movie playing, *The Terminator* by Canadian director, James Cameron. Des wouldn't go with her but maybe Peter would or even Davey if he came for Christmas.

"Oh well, surely he won't be upset if I wake him now," she reasoned as she went upstairs. She gently opened his door and looked in toward the bed. "Des? Des?" she asked gently. He seemed to be reading but his face looked contorted. Something wasn't right and she put her hand to her mouth to muffle a shocked whimper.

This wasn't for her to deal with she thought and did an about turn, her legs a bit shaky. She went to her own room, sat on the bed and picked up the phone to call Peter.

"Hello, Peter? " She started quickly and Peter could sense Meg's growing hysteria. "Something's wrong with Des. I need you to come and see!"

Peter was efficient and calming. "Go make a cup of tea, Meg. Don't touch anything in the room. In fact, don't even go into the room until I get there. "

"Thanks, Peter. And please hurry."

When Peter arrived, he noticed that Meg was sipping tea at the kitchen table. He kissed her on the cheek but motioned her to stay while he went up to Des's room. It looked like Des, but he knew instinctively that he was gone, leaving a body slightly slumped over, mouth and eyes open, Orwell's *1984* beside him. "You old goat...a wry jokester to the end."

Then he also noticed the vintage glasses case on the bed and the reading glasses clutched in Des's left hand.

"Hmm, that's odd." He ~~espied~~ *noted* that Des's regular reading glasses were on the bedside table on top of another familiar book, the recent birthday gift Peter had given him, *The March of Folly*. He pried the tortoise shell glasses from his hand and recognized the WWII British issue case. Holding the glasses up to the light he noticed they were not prescription at all and that one of the earpieces was crushed with teeth marks. And then he realized. Thinking quickly, he returned the glasses back to the army case and put them both into his inside jacket pocket.

"Now you've got me keeping secrets too, you bugger." He arranged Des into a laying down position, patted his hands and kissed him on the head. He picked up the birthday book and flipped open the inside the cover, Des had written:

It's back in your hands now, Pete, my best friend and brother-in-arms. Don't let it all be for folly. And I will be watching. I loved you, Des

Peter hugged the book and took it with him back downstairs to the kitchen.

"He's dead Meg; are you able to call the doctor, Clift isn't it?" She was dressed in a black dress already and her highlighted hair in place, her face made up. She was ready for visitors but not totally ready to function. Meg slowly focused on Peter and slurred a bit. "Geez, Peter. I don't remember ifff I put any tea in my teacup. Could you be a dear, please?"

Peter reached for the teapot but noticed that her cup was filled with clear liquid. "I mean, could you make the call please and alsho to David. I sheem to be too fortified," she half-smiled a bit coyly and gave that Lady Diana wide-eyed sideways glance that she had been practicing. Was she trying to flirt or to look vulnerable?

"No more, Meg. I'll need you to help get things done, funeral things, Des's clothes, and people to notify."

Dr. Alan Clift came and expressed condolences. He explained how

Des refused any treatment for his lung cancer so he wasn't surprised; if they needed any more from him, just ask; and left. It was all news to Meg though. She knew nothing of Des's disease. Her eyes widened but she said nothing.

David rubbed his thumb over the weekend stubble on his dimpled chin and picked up the ringing phone. His voice was flat with a hint of irritation until he realized who it was. "Hi, Uncle Pete, how's it going? What can I do for you on this lovely Saturday morning?"

Hamilton may be in the same province but the weather today was a world away from Ottawa. David looked out his window; the day was sunny, 5 Celsius, and a bit of wind, perfect for a last sail.

"I have some bad news, Davey. Your father died early this morning. It was the lung cancer that got him in the end." There was silence on the line. "David?"

"I'm here. You know, I didn't even know he had cancer." David was six feet in height with his Mom's blue eyes and light brown hair, which he kept longish and a bit unkempt over his ears. His dad was always after him to get a haircut, another bone of contention. What did his dad say? "You're getting older but not maturing."

"How are you and Mom taking it?" David asked, noting that he didn't really like the father he was supposed to love.

"Yes, sure, I'll take the train tomorrow. School term is pretty much over anyway. Well, that's just like Dad to put a downer on Christmas. No I'll talk to her later when I have my ETA sorted out. See you tomorrow and thanks, Uncle Pete."

David always had planned to get one last sail in before having the boat hauled out for the winter and Peter's news didn't change that. It was late in the season but he banked on some late balminess and today was the day. It had been gustier yesterday but he was teaching and could only covet a sail while looking at the wind from the classroom window. But today was warm enough with a 10 km south-west breeze, bringing up Gulf air, thanks Zephyrus.

David never liked to have good times interrupted or ended, and today was no different. Besides he couldn't do anything for his dad now anyway, and his mom was in good hands with Uncle Peter. So he picked up his duffle bag filled with sailing gear, a flask of coffee, a sandwich and left for the boat.

It was an older wooden sloop, 36 ft., dependable, and forgiving to the helmsman. It needed new sails and the deck needed work, leaks coming in on the forward berth and even the galley windows sometimes, but it could wait for the spring. He bought the *Barracuda* a few years ago after taking some sailing lessons. He liked getting far from the madding crowd and the perspective from the water that the seafaring few could get. Uncle Peter had said it was a good venture because sailing was David's own initiative, a mark of individualism; his dad thought he was foolish to spend the money when he was only a substitute teacher; and his mother thought it was dangerous and worrisome. There they were in a nutshell, David thought.

David raised the mainsail but left the mainsheet loose. Holding onto the mainstay he walked the Barracuda back from the dock and deftly hopped on board as it cleared. He could have started the engine but preferred to practice without mechanical reliance. The breeze slowly filled the mainsail and the sloop began to glide slowly toward the open bay. He could hear the water purl along the hull and he felt peaceful with the elements. Once out in the clear, he brought the boat into irons and raised the jib. Then heading on a broad reach, he lazily followed the Burlington shore on a north-easterly run. Straight ahead were the mooring cans of Lasalle and off to his right the slag heaps and burning torches of the steel plants. He ran this course a little longer, sliding by the expansive yards of the big shore-line estates. He tacked onto a close reach parallel to the skyway but a bit too late so that the wind made him drift toward the rocky embankment along the shore and he had to tack again away from the exit channel. What he had wanted to do was exit via the Skyway Bridge and enter Lake Ontario but with the altered course and Uncle Peter's call, he knew he wouldn't now. He had to make arrangements; duty interfered with pleasure.

"Damn it, Dad," he yelled at the gulls and cormorants.

He flicked at the stubble in the cleft of his chin and the tic helped him to calm down. "At least I'll have a picnic before I go in," he decided. He hove to and relaxed against the coaming of the cockpit, sipping coffee, enjoying his lunch and letting the sun warm him like a hug. He closed his eyes and a forgotten lakeside scene with his father came to mind. Des was trying to teach a young David to fish...

I must have been about five. He was trying to get me to bait my own line. There was a can of worms and they were squiggling and wet. When I grabbed one and started to stick it onto the hook, it recoiled and wiggled on my finger. I remember shuddering and throwing my fishing line down and it fell off the dock and into the water. Dad was disgusted. "What the hell", he said, and I said I would tell Mom that he swore. I think I began to whimper. There was a pail near me on the dock with some fish in it. They were thrashing about and Dad picked up one by the tail and whacked it on the dock to make it senseless, I guess, or it was better than hitting me. It scared the shit out of me and I remember screaming. Dad kicked the pail of fish off the pier, grabbed my arm and off we went; end of fishing.

David came out of his reverie and set sails for a return to the sailing club. He had enjoyed the outing enough but now felt a bit doleful, like the acrid smell of burning leaves at the end of a childhood's sunny autumn day. He made arrangements to have the boat hauled out next week and walked back to his apartment. Kicking the leaves along the sidewalk, the wafting aroma reminded him of dried marjoram and the pasta sauce (his mother's recipe) he would reheat for his dinner. He emptied his kit, checked the train schedule, and called his mother to say he would be arriving tomorrow, Sunday, about 2 p.m. and could Uncle Peter pick him up. He ate his spaghetti Bolognese and began packing his suitcase.

David stopped and gazed at the opposite wall, remembering...

I was playing hockey, a defenseman in the bantam division. Dad had given me a book about the legendary Hab, Doug Harvey, and I had practiced trying to copy his blocked shot move. In the game this guy was coming in on me and I thought he was going to shoot, so I slid to the ice, throwing my legs to the side to block, like Harvey I thought. But he was only deking and as he was going around me, well, I got a penalty for tripping. Dad was not impressed.

"What kind of bonehead play was that? You better play better than that if you expect me to get up at the crack of dawn to drive you to the arena." I don't think he

ever took me again.

David blinked, gave his head a shake and decided to watch some television. Whatever Elwy Yost was showing on TVO's *Saturday Night At The Movies*, or the hockey game, see how Mario Lemieux was besting the Leafs. Anything to keep the memories at bay.

Peter and Meg had spent the day discussing funeral arrangements.

"I'll make sure something goes in the obituary sections on Monday, including the *Globe and Mail*. There may be some people outside of Ottawa who might like to know."

Meg said, "I don't think he had many friends, at least it didn't seem so. You were his only friend, Peter."

"So you can't think of any work mates or old school chums? What about family?

"He did have some sisters still living but he wasn't close you know."

"Well if you could give me their names, I'll call them."

"It's here in the address book somewhere; there was Barb in Barrie I know, and Elsa in Stoney Creek."

"What about your side, Meg?"

"Oh there are a few friends, but I can call them, Peter."

"Now you know he wanted to be cremated, Meg?"

"Oh I didn't know, Peter. I don't like burning."

"Meg, he definitely did not want a church service or traditional funeral. Didn't he talk to you about it?"

Meg smiled ruefully. "He didn't talk to me about anything important. I didn't even know he was sick!"

"Really? Well, I definitely know how he felt about churches. How do you want to handle that?"

"Whatever you think is best, Peter."

"Actually I think cremation and then a memorial in a couple of weeks. We could hold that at your church, the Blessed Sacrament isn't it? If you feel that would be a compromise, or I could rent a room. With your friends and family and me and David and Des's sisters, it looks like no more than fifteen people or so, even if a few work mates show. Probably a small meeting room at one of the downtown hotels would be tasteful. What do you think?

"Yes, that would be nice, Peter, thank you. I'm getting tired now and need to nap. is there anything else?" Dr. Clift had left her some pills to help.

"Just his clothes to be cremated in and I can deliver those to the funeral home. And I'm taking this book I gave him, if you don't mind. I'll see you tomorrow when we go to collect David. Bye." He gave her a comforting hug and went.

Peter worked on the obituary announcement. It wasn't easy. As close as he was to Des, they didn't talk death-announcement details. Peter knew workmates were with the RCMP Special Branch but that name changed at least three times over his career. And Des was away a lot but never mentioned the cases directly. He remembered Des saying he served in Spain and of course they met in Italy. But apart from that...he liked his hockey; he liked to read, was generous to a few and curmudgeonly to most; estranged from his wife and son; beloved by his 'brother'. A gasp of grief bubbled up. Peter stifled it and sipped his single malt Scotch, the peaty Laphroiag, their favourite. "To you, Des; we'll get through this, just like Monte Cassino, you know we will."

He continued writing:

Desmond Charles Dilman, 67, died in Ottawa, Ont. after a brief battle with cancer. Born in Toronto, Ont., Dec. 3, 1917; died peacefully at home in the early hours of Dec. 15, 1984. Survived by his wife of 37 years, Margaret, née Tanner of Ottawa; his son David; two sisters, Barb Fellows (Barrie, Ont.) and Elsa Frazer (Stoney Creek, Ont.); and missed dearly by his friend Peter Nowak. Des worked for the RCMP until his retirement three and a half years ago. There will be a memorial gathering at the Chateau Laurier's Burgundy Room on Saturday Dec. 29, 1984 in the evening, 7 until 9 p.m. Donations in lieu of flowers can be made to the Canadian Cancer Society.

The next afternoon, Peter met David at the train station alone. Meg had begged off because of a headache she was trying to get rid of so she could be more sociable with her son and visitors. They hugged and Peter put David's single suitcase in the trunk as they set off back to Glebe.

"Good trip, David?"

"Good enough, lots of time to read. I am getting into *Hitchhiker's Guide To The Galaxy*, so it was fine.

"I am more of a non-fiction person but sometimes the truth isn't easy, I must say."

"Mmm, that sounds heavy, Uncle Pete. Is something going on that I need to know about?"

"Not really, but I hope you will be able to stay over Christmas to help your mom and me weather things."

"Yep, I'm good. Got some Christmas shopping to do and I don't mind taking Mom off your hands from time to time. Is there something I can do to help with funeral arrangements?"

"There won't be a funeral, Davey. Your dad never went in for that. But I am organizing a memorial for him on Saturday evening, Dec. 29th."

"God, that pretty much takes care of the Christmas holiday then. Dad was never the most thoughtful and he never had a knack for timing either, come to think of it."

"Oh he had his moments Davey, maybe you just didn't see them. You can help me with his books and things. Maybe there are some items you want. I thought, since I'm the executor, that we could read the will on Monday, Dec. 31st, start off the New Year with fresh business."

"Out with the old, in with the new, so to speak. I'm fine with that and then I'll have to get back to Hamilton and pick up any teaching calls."

"You know, your sense of humour is a bit like your dad's, kind of unexpected, is it left field or right field? I still get that one mixed up."

David seemed to bristle ever so slightly but Peter sensed it.

"You don't like it if I see some of your dad in you, do you?"

"Not really because I don't want to be like him. But I'll try to keep a lid on it for your sake and Mom's. You know, more reverent than irreverent."

"No need for me and your Mom enjoys your humour, if it's not too black. She'll be happy to see you too. She loves it when you're around. We all do; even your dad did."

"Really, he never showed it."

"Yes, he could be a tough nut but every nut has some protein you know. And in death we can be kind, yes?"

"Sure, and it is Christmas, the spirit of giving and peace. You're right, Uncle Pete."

Peter didn't want to press any further and they drove quietly taking in the Christmas lights until they arrived.

Meg was happy to see them both. She cupped David's face in an embrace and wouldn't hear of Peter leaving right away. Her headache was gone and it would be good to sit and have a drink together, she said. Actually she had already started. David and Peter poured a healthy dram of Glenfiddich from a full bottle that must have been a gift to Des, but they noticed the vodka bottle on the counter was getting low.

"You know dear, do you find it hard keeping up with all the new sayings when you're in the classroom?"

"Like what, Mom?"

"Oh like yuppie and dink and those acronyms. Are they like our snafu?" She giggled.

"Nah, it's not so hard. Yuppie stands for young, urban, and

62

professional.

"And dink, that sounds vulgar," Meg said.

Peter chimed in, "dual income, no kids, isn't it? I think I read that in the paper."

And David replied, "Guess that makes me a pig then."

To their puzzled looks David said, "One income, no kids: OINK", and they both chuckled at David's joke.

"Speaking of classrooms," Peter said changing the subject, "Are you enjoying teaching?"

"Yes, well enough, I guess. Four years now and still no permanent position though. I really enjoyed the long-term leave I did last year; History and English and one Geography class. Lots of preps but I enjoyed spending a longer time with the same kids."

"Why do you think it's so hard to break in, dear?" asked his mother. "I keep reading that they need teachers."

"Well there is talk about more teachers for special needs in elementary schools and more funding for Catholic schools but those won't affect me, Mom. I'm high school and not Roman Catholic. And there is also that little experiment I foisted on the staff during my long-term job."

"You could be Catholic again if you went to church, dear."

Peter looked up, "What did you do this time, Davey?"

David poured himself some more scotch, Peter declined. "Well you know how they have bells signaling the change of classes, at god-awful weird times, like 76 minutes. I was into a great discussion with a class and the bell went so they all got up while a student was making a really good point. I made them sit and listen until the end but they were late for their next class. So I mentioned this in the lunch room; found out there were some other frustrated teachers, and we organized a bloc for the staff meeting. We won a vote to have a one-month experiment where there would be no bells."

Peter guffawed, "And how did that turn out?"

"Really well, I thought. The kids felt they had some control and some teachers did too. The traffic jams in the halls rarely happened and classes started more or less on time. But the traditionalists in Math and Science couldn't stand the randomness and it was ended after a month. Man, the principal was not impressed with me though. Kids were; but not the man. It kind of upstaged him in the staff meeting, democracy and all that."

"Well of course he wouldn't be pleased, dear, " Meg said. "You can't rock the boat like that and expect any favours."

Peter shook his head and chuckled. Then he looked at Meg and David. "Do you two want to talk about Des at all, and what happens next?"

"Yes, if we must. What do you propose? Peter has been so helpful with arrangements, Davey."

"Well the funeral home has asked if you want to have a visitation at all, Meg. And the cremation is arranged for the first of the week. You could have a visitation but we do have the commemorative service in two weeks."

"I think I am fine with just a requiem mass next week, Tuesday. Get it out of the way. I can arrange that and the church announcement if you and Davey are okay dealing with his things. And then we can see everyone at the commemoration. There's no need to make Christmas a totally sad affair, after all."

Peter went wide-eyed for a second, but David and Meg were both staring at the table and didn't notice.

"Davey, do you have any friends you would like to attend the mass or memorial?"

"No, I'm good, Uncle Pete."

With a sigh, Peter got up to leave. "Goodnight then and I'll see you tomorrow; is mid-morning fine with you Davey, to go through your dad's belongings?"

Peter tried to engage David about dealing with his father's death the next day. Peter had been gathering Des's clothes to go to St. Vincent de Paul while David was going through the small collection of books. David noticed the inscribed copies of Ernest Hemingway's *Farewell To Arms*, (*To Des, may you learn to fight and write in España, all the best, Papa);* Hugh Garner's *Cabbagetown* (*To Des, it's hard to escape our history; it's just one damn thing after another, all the best, Hugh);* and Graham Greene's *Our Man In Havana* (*To Des, remember a romantic's expectations will always be dashed by reality, GG*).

"Jesus, Uncle Peter, did Dad actually know these authors?"

"Some of them, why?"

"Was he some kind of book writer groupie?"

"No, I don't believe so. He loved to read and met some authors on his conferences and travels, I guess."

"These guys wrote inscriptions like they KNEW Dad, drank with him, swapped stories. Geez, I never knew."

"Well there is more to a book than its cover. That's something your Dad, and even you, might say." Peter felt he had delivered a clever line. "Do you want to keep the books, Davey, something from your Dad?"

"No," he said almost too quickly. Then he paused and reconsidered. "Well maybe, Uncle Pete. These are interesting, maybe even valuable. Could you hang on to them for me, just in case?"

"Yes, of course, I'm sure your mother wouldn't mind. Is there anything else you might like, ties, any of his jewelry?"

"No!"

Peter was holding a signet ring, gold with an engraved **D** on it. "Have you seen this?"

"Yes, he wore it on his pinkie sometimes. Said it was instead of a wedding ring. Why?"

"Do you want it?" David shook his head. Peter looked at it again and said, "I think I'll ask Meg if I can keep it, if you don't mind."

"No, go for it."

"Davey, what did your dad mean to you?"

Peter had been holding in his feelings because he thought that Meg and David were somehow trivializing Des's death.

"Not a lot, Uncle Pete. You have to admit that he wasn't around much after I turned ten, and when he was here, we tended to fight. I guess I always felt like I disappointed him, but not as much as he disappointed me. It was like MAD-Mutually Assured Dislike. He provided for Mom and me, end of story."

"No, he loved you, trust me. He was frustrated that he couldn't be a good father, but he loved you."

"Well if love means butting heads so much that it gave me a huge headache and made me want to be free of him, then thanks Dad."

"But you saw the books; don't you think there's more to him than you know?"

"Maybe, but like the **D** on his ring, Dad was more into Des than us."

"Are you certain the **D** was for Des?" But Peter decided to drop it.

The next week until Christmas Eve was a busy week of balancing shopping, visiting, entertaining, and what David called, 'Des events', and pretty much in that order. Meg and David did some Christmas shopping together and often lunched. Then David begged off to go for a run while Meg visited with her church ladies. Instead of going out, David rented a VCR and a movie video for Meg and him. Once he got *Terms of Endearment*, which he called 'tears of endearment'. Peter declined the movie invitations, staying away rather than showing his annoyance with them. He was dealing with his own grief and was upset that Meg and David showed little feeling about losing Des. He did go over one evening but when David and Meg wanted to play a new game, *Trivial Pursuit*, he left before it was completed.

On Christmas Day evening, Meg called Peter. "We missed you today. Merry Christmas, Peter."

"I know, I meant to call but I was a bit morose today, Meg. How sweet of you to call me."

"Well, we won't have you in the dumps tomorrow. David wonders if you want to go skiing, a boys' day out while I cook a dinner for your return? Please say yes."

After a brief pause, "Yes, that would be great. I'll pick him up at 10 and we can put in a half day at Edelweiss. It's brutally cold and they've been making snow."

Peter had taught David how to ski when he was a boy and this outing was renewed fun. Also, Peter did notice that David used the event to broach the subject of the commemoration in a few days. "Uncle Peter, I was wondering if the memorial is going to be like a mix and mingle or if there are going to be speeches?

"Probably a bit of both, why?"

"Are you going to say anything about Dad?"

"I thought I'd be emcee only and give the opportunity to whoever wants to say something. We'll see."

"It would mean a lot to me, and Mom, if you could say a few words. It's obvious you saw more of Dad, and more in Dad, than we did."

By the end of the month, the cold snap was over and there was a dusting of snow on Dec. 29th. The chairs and tables were set around the Burgundy Room randomly; there was a bar, hors d'oeuvres, and some fragrant stargazer lilies. There was also a lectern beside a single table with a plain stainless steel urn atop, Des's ashes. Mingling was induced with wine and Peter moved around graciously, introducing people, inviting them to sit in clusters to chat or move about. Meg was dressed in a simple black A-line dress and was elegant with grey pearls, while David was wearing blue jeans and a tieless denim shirt with a navy corduroy sports jacket. It was a disparate and small gathering of eleven people. Meg chatted with her church friends; there were a couple of lawyer colleagues paying their sympathies on Peter's behalf; and three other total strangers. Peter handed an envelope to Meg and David and went to chat with the three unknown men, one of whom was showing a photograph around.

The envelope contained a card from the aunts who had sent their regrets. The flowers and a donation were their recompense. David read the note to his mom:

We were surprised to get the call and read in the paper about Des's passing. Neither of us had heard from him in such a long time, not since David was a wee boy. Des used to send us the odd letter or a postcard and even a birthday wish sometimes, although it was often on the wrong day. No matter, it was always the thought that counted. Des had largely been out of our lives since he was a teen and kicked out of the house, but not out of our thoughts. Our condolences to you both. And David, please call your aunties when you are in Hamilton. (Peter told us you lived close by.) We would love to have you for a meal and get to know you. Your father was always very proud of you and included news of you when he wrote or occasionally helped us out.

Our thoughts and our love,

Aunt Barb and Aunt Elsa

David was perplexed. He didn't remember any aunts. When he asked his mother why she never mentioned aunts, she just shrugged. "Out of sight, out of mind, I guess. You noticed they have thoughts but no prayers." David became thoughtful himself while his mother went back to conversing with the three church ladies and organizing a euchre party. There certainly were hidden sides to his father, and slight fissures were entering David's evaluation of his dad. Then, Peter was at the lectern.

"Welcome everyone, it's not a pleasant time to be out, remembering someone who has died, but we rarely have choices in the matter. On behalf of Margaret, and David, and of course Des, I thank you. Before I say anything else, I would like to offer the podium to anyone who might want to pay their respects."

One of the strangers stepped forward. He was a tall, slim man, erect in a dark blue, be-medaled uniform. His voice was authoritative.

"Good evening, I'm Commissioner Robert Simmonds of the RCMP. I didn't know Des personally very well. I did meet him briefly when I was posted to Burnaby in the mid-'60s. But a commander of mine at the time asked me at his own retirement to do something if I ever had the chance. That man was former Superintendent Frank Zaneth, who recruited me and was my mentor. He had one regret, however, in his long and illustrious career, mainly in undercover work. He told me that if I could ever honour Des Dilman, to do it. Frank never gave me all the details but I trusted him. He said Des deserved recognition for serving Canada and the Force so diligently. Des did his job ethically and professionally for almost fifty years. It almost seems fitting then, that an era is over with his passing. As you may or may not know, the branch that Des and Frank served in, the Security Service, was just disbanded and replaced by the civilian Canadian Security Intelligence Service or CSIS, as deemed by the McDonald Commission. I feel doubly privileged to honour two men then, if posthumously, by fulfilling a pledge to Frank and by giving the Commissioner's Commendation for Outstanding Service to Des Dilman."

With that, he smartly marched over to Meg and David, presented the medal, and snapped a salute. Meg dabbed at her eyes, proudly showed it to her attending friends, and said to David, "He didn't forget us at Christmas after all, what a dear." The others clapped. He said to David. "Son, if you ever want to join the Force, you let me know."

Then a lean, grizzled and arthritic man went to the lectern and cleared his throat.

"Well this is a strange event. I'm Robert Savage, but folks call me Doc. I just happened to be in Ottawa as part of a preparation delegation, meeting with newly elected Prime Minister Mulroney. Apparently he wants to celebrate the 50th anniversary in the spring of the "On To Ottawa Trek". You see, I was one of the eight Trek leaders chosen to meet with Prime Minister Bennett way back in June of nineteen and thirty-five. I just happened to see Des's obit in the paper and thought I would pay my respects. I remembered Des as a young man workin' hard in the strikers' office in Regina. He wanted to help out where he could, researchin', writin' some pamphlets, and was just a nice guy. We were both young but I was a little older; so like a brother, I took him under my wing. In the riot, my wing wasn't good enough and he got picked up by the police. Some of the boys say they saw him in Spain with the Mac-Paps, but I never saw him after that time in Regina. I just felt I had to come by. I'm sorry for your loss ma'am and I'm glad to hear he done well in his life."

Again there was some clapping and the third man, who somehow looked vaguely familiar to David, went to greet Meg and David personally. He was dressed a bit preppy, and shorter than David. Lean, white shirt and an orange tie with grey bubbles, light blue jeans and a black jacket. He had a full head of close-cropped brown hair, a strong chin, thin lips and American accent. His words were clipped.

"I was just on my way from Germany to Cuba and saw the memorial notice in the in-flight paper. My name is Philip Agee. I hope I'm not intruding, but I've known Des for fifteen years or so. We go back to some conferences we were covering in Cuba. I liked Des and counted him as a friend; he helped me through some tough times. I had a bit of a layover in Montreal just now and decided to come pay my respects."

Then he began to chuckle and shake his head.

"I've got a feeling Des would be having a good laugh himself at the apple of discord that has been thrown into this group tonight. That was so like him. Mountie medals and Communist strikers. Your dad could juggle with the best of them. He was a good man; the kind who would watch your back. I'm sorry for your loss." With that he shook hands with Meg and David, then with Peter and Doc and was gone.

Peter stood at the lectern, erect, dignified, dark grey three-piece suit and burgundy tie. "The time has moved on quickly, ladies and gentlemen, such is life," Peter began. "First, thank you to those who came to share some memories of Des. He was definitely a complex man. He cherished those he cared for; was impatient with those he cared less for. He gave sparingly of his friendship but when he did, he gave it fully. He wasn't perfect; who among us is. But, as we have seen tonight, Des had several sides to him. Distant but loved brother to two sisters; husband and father; true friend; and honoured Canadian. When Des was in your corner, you could trust that you'd be supported. And tonight we gathered for mutual support in this time of sorrow. "

Peter looked over at the urn and said, "*Szczęśliwej podróży*. Have a good journey, Des. Thank you for coming and good night, everyone."

David hadn't trusted himself to speak that night, more concern about being appropriate than about being emotional. Truth be told, David was reeling a bit with the revelations of the evening. Sisters who cared for Dad, a medal for service, people who relished his Dad's support.

David and Peter were having a night cap and he said to Peter afterwards, "I thought Dad was a salesman, peddling locks and safes. He always said he was a travelling salesman, off dealing in security, selling safety. I had no idea he was with the RCMP and an undercover cop. Did you?"

"Yes, but you never asked me. It seemed you'd had your mind made up about your Dad and were a bit close-minded about him, yes?"

"Well, I suppose, but I'd like to think I can reconsider when there are new facts presented."

David smiled, clinking his scotch glass to Peter's. "Good arrangement tonight. It was very appropriate. We both thank you for what you did and said."

"You're welcome. Remember the next 'Des event' is the reading of the will on Monday." And to himself rather than David, Peter said, "I hope you've opened your mind a chink by then."

CHAPTER 6.

TO DARE IS TO LOSE ONE'S FOOTING MOMENTARILY (SØREN KIERKEGAARD)

Ottawa, Monday, Dec. 31, 1984

Today was the day to read the will and David had been wrestling with recalibrating emotions and perspectives all week. Yesterday, Sunday, he had gone for a long steady distance run (LSD in runners' parlance) for ninety minutes or so, bundled against the cold and letting his mind and feet go where they would. He had run along Glebe making his way to the paths beside Dow's Lake, then Colonel By Drive, through Carleton University to Hog's Back and looped around, approximately twelve kilometers.

It was plenty of time and distance to ruminate on events. For instance, whenever they were together, Uncle Peter had kept presenting subtle little points about Dad being more than he, David, was aware of. Certainly the memorial was a revelation. And then those book inscriptions. "I mean those were famous people." He even said that out loud while running. Those writers seemed to be urging his father on to deeper understandings and maybe David should be heeding those encouragements too.

He realized his dad didn't suffer fools gladly and he knew that he didn't either. Is that what Uncle Peter meant when he said he and his dad were more alike than David was willing to credit? Suddenly David felt some self-doubt creep into his thoughts.

"Did Dad get gruff with me because I wasn't acting smart enough?" This didn't sit well because David was proud of his own intelligence. And then another Graham Greene line that David liked came to mind.

"The world is not black and white. More like black and grey." David had read that recently in a *London Observer* article one ugly February day last year in the Hamilton Library. Now he wondered if he had been looking at his dad in terms too stark and unfair.

"And what was with my grad picture on Dad's bureau? It had to be fifteen years old. Why didn't he have something newer?" And then he realized that he hadn't been around for photo ops, not even his father's retirement.

Once his thoughts trumped his running and he almost stopped. "And Philip Agee, shit, he was the CIA whistleblower about ten years ago; he had death threats against him and then he disappeared. What in god's name was Dad doing with him?"

David mulled over these recent discrepancies in his long-held judgment of his father, like a little pebble that kept chafing in a running shoe. This was not the absentee lord who quashed David's idealism at every turn, who was critical of David and rarely supportive. "Hell, he was even happy that I had failed the External Affairs exam back in, when was it, 1972? A few years after graduating when I didn't know what I'd do. Yet these memorial people, the three magi who spoke, all gave testimony to Dad being supportive; it didn't gel." That was his Sunday run.

But today was a new day, the last day of the old year. The morning was sunny, -10 C°, windy, and white with twenty centimeters of accumulated snow. Peter, Meg and David were sitting in Peter's law office, being cordial but expectant. Meg was in a grey skirt, white blouse, and black sweater; David in a black turtleneck and blue jeans. Peter also was dressed casually in grey corduroy trousers and black sports jacket. Their clothes showed vestiges of mourning, but Peter wondered if all of them were letting go of Des sooner rather than later. Except for the urn on the desk.

As if to prove Peter's concern, David started to share some news about his future. He recounted that just before he and his mother took the cab to Peter's office, the phone rang. The caller, a Hamilton high school principal had actually offered David a long term assignment, teaching History until March Break. Meg had clapped her hands and said, "My prayers are answered." David gave her a filial hug, smiled, and said thanks.

David was saying to Peter and Meg, "I had actually been thinking about Commissioner Simmonds' offer with the RCMP. I always wanted a job where I could travel and use my education, but that kind of went up in smoke after External Affairs turned me down. I never thought of the Mounties though, or maybe CSIS. And now the teaching job."

"That's great." said Peter; "Have you committed to anything yet?"

"No, the term starts next Monday though; I said I'd let him know tomorrow. Maybe my future is brightening."

Nancy brought in some coffee and Peter cleared his throat, "Shall we begin?"

Peter opened a folder on his desk and peered at Meg and David over his reading glasses. "You may not know this but Des and I discussed his will at great length since the summer and amended it in November. Everything is in order; this is his most recent and legal last will and testament.

First of all, he appointed me to be the Executor and Trustee of this will. Without question, you two will receive all of Des's assets, apart from the paying out of the capital any enforceable debts, funeral expenses, and all expenses associated with the administration of his estate and will.

The transfer of the residue of his estate is to be divided between the two of you but with some serious limitations.

First of all, Meg, you will receive the house on Glebe which is fully paid for. You will also receive the spousal portion of Des's pension, which I believe is sixty per cent, to manage as you please. I can help you with the paper work on all of that. Des also wanted you to have a travelling fund to make up for all the trips you two didn't do. So we are to set up an annuity that will allow you to do that. It isn't a great deal of money but enough. The catch is that you have to plan and account for any trips with the trustee of the annuity. For the time being that will be me. He was very clear that there be a monetary limit but I did talk him into using the following term, 'I authorize my Trustee to be generous in the exercise of his discretionary power in this regard but not to exceed the yearly limit.'

Secondly, David, your father made you the beneficiary of a small life insurance that he had for $10,000. Originally it was to go to you, Meg, but he changed it. And then he has arranged an optional plan, a challenge so to speak, that you may or may not accept, Davey. If not, the monies will stay in the estate and go to his survivors in the long term; you or your mother or if you both predecease, then to his surviving sisters. The plan is as follows, and I am paraphrasing his words:

Your father expressed a huge regret that his relationship with you was at best estranged. He had concerns that your life was going nowhere, his words, remember. He thought you were too idealistic, too devil-may-care, too arrogant, and too unwilling to commit to anything or anyone beyond yourself. As a father he had wanted the best for you, but he always said, "like Midas, I turned the boy's gold into lead." But your father's career, and ultimately his life, was a secret one. He couldn't tell you or Meg, or me for that matter, the half of it.

His hope in the end was that if you knew what his circumstances were, you might come to understand why he did what he did during your upbringing. He was not looking for forgiveness or compassion; he wanted you to know of his secret life and to learn that a life of disdain and no commitment is a dead end: a cul-de-sac of unhappiness. He watched too many people go from idealism to cynicism and hopelessness. He almost took that route himself and he was worried that you would too.

You may not know this but your father always wanted to be a writer. He kept journals for most of his adult life. He is inviting you into his life by bequeathing these journals to you on some conditions. I'll read them to you so there is no misunderstanding:

'Your life has lacked direction, partly because of attenuated commitment and goals. Therefore you have to decide to take the challenge within 24 hours of being informed or the opportunity will be lost forever.

The journals will lead you to various places in the world. I am speaking of Barcelona, Havana, Ortona, Krakow, as well as Canadian destinations. You must take some of me on each your travels and scatter ashes in each place. Each location meant something special to me. Each may come to mean something to you too.

There is an envelope at the back of the journal in the last box, if you agree to take up the challenge. The last shall be first, so to speak.

Peter has been instructed to set up a substantial trust fund to finance any and all expenses and to set up the economies needed for each step. Once you take the keys from Peter you must complete the investigation. It is a trust between you and me; don't break it. If you renege or quit your quest, Peter has been instructed to sue you for any monies used to be paid back to the estate.'

Peter placed his reading glasses on the will and looked up. "Do either of you have any questions?"

David's first response was resentful. He glanced toward the urn and blustered, "How dare he call me shiftless. I'll be damned if I'll take that from him." Peter held up his hand.

"Davey, your father really wanted me to persuade you to take this challenge. He felt you were at a place in your life where you would have time and no money to do this. Really he was offering it as an opportunity. As Søren Kierkegaard wrote 'To dare is to lose one's footing momentarily; not to dare is to lose oneself."

Then Peter did a rare thing, he raised his voice. "Dammit Davey, he didn't say you were shiftless. Don't be so defensive. He is reaching out a hand to you; please take it."

Then in a softer tone he added, "I will be here to help, even to give you seed money if you want, if the insurance isn't fast enough; but damn it all, you have to make up your mind, on your own or discuss its feasibility with your confidants. And by tomorrow."

David looked at his mother, "Did you know about this?"

She shook her head. "But I feel he was thinking of us a lot, dear. The least you can do is to consider it."

David pushed his chair back.

"I'll pass on lunch with you two. Thanks Uncle Peter, I bet that wasn't easy to say. I'll be in touch with my decision before noon tomorrow."

David took a cab back to the house and changed for a run. His mind was awhirl. Once again his father grated like cold air on a sensitive tooth. "What did he mean about no goals? Was it my fault that External Affairs suddenly stopped the process for me; was it my fault that I couldn't land anything permanent in teaching?"

If he was honest with himself though, teaching was a stop gap. What had his father said? "Those who can, do; those who can't, teach." Even though Des was trying to be funny, David had responded quickly and defensively, "And those who can't teach go into sales." That was always the way, sparring.

But then there were these other facets, newly found: the literati, the memorial visitors bearing witness, and now the cache of diaries with the lure of travel. All of a sudden his dad was piquing his interest. Then it struck him that he, David, had no close friends to confer with, as Peter had suggested. He had some working buddies and sailing and skiing mates, but no confidants. He had girls in his life but that was the problem, too many of them and no one special. At least, not since Lydia left his life. "Damn, here I am in my mid-thirties and no best friend, no money, no career, what a miserable shit! What did Dad say? You're hair's receding; you're getting older but not maturing." But rather than feeling sorry for himself, he was actually buoyed by the possibilities before him.

He thought, "Why couldn't I do both? Yes, why not take the long-term offer to teach history with my own class, see if I like it; and then take the 'Des Dare' starting in March? Why couldn't I commit to both? I would have to run that by Uncle Peter but why not?" He finished his run with a sprint.

Later around the kitchen table, Meg was having a vodka tonic and David joined her with a scotch.

David asked, "Mom, were you ever happy with Dad?"

She gave that sidelong, shy look. "Once, when we were first married and after you were born. He loved you Davey; he loved us both. But something happened after a trip he took. He must have gone to an Eastern Bloc country because he brought home one of those matrioshka dolls for you, the kind where there is one inside the other. You were about four or five. Do you remember?"

David shook his head.

"Anyway, after that he seemed to freeze me out. He was tough on you too. He never hit you or anything but he wasn't as kind and gentle."

"Did you ever think of a divorce then?"

"Oh no, sweetie. The Lord will forgive many sins but not that. I had tried to talk to your father, even said it was ok if he had, you know, been with another woman. But he just glared at me and growled 'You don't understand the first thing about trust', and went away. We pretty much lived separate lives after that, you know, our own bedrooms and all."

"That must have been difficult. I felt he was always picking on me."

"Did you dear? Well his work took him away a lot more after that and maybe it was just as well; it made it easier somehow, didn't it?"

"What do you think I should do with Dad's dare?"

"Oh that's up to you dear. I was hardly part of his life really and I don't want to be now. But you, David? You'll have to decide for yourself. He did take care of us in his way though. The house, your education; just not always with kindness or a lot of communication. He was a bit curmudgeonly really."

"Yes, he was pretty grumpy usually," David agreed.

"You know I asked him to take me to England for Charles and Diana's wedding in 1981, a little holiday and pre-retirement trip. To be in London, the sights, the atmosphere. I just wanted to see a city draped in bunting. But your dad just brushed it off. Anyway maybe I'll go now. What do you think?"

"Looks like Dad wanted us both to make up our minds about what we want to do."

It was New Year's Eve. David called Peter and asked him to come over. Meg was in bed by nine, in fact David helped her to negotiate the stairs and she pecked him a Happy New Year kiss on the cheek. Peter arrived by ten.

"Uncle Peter, I came to a decision today but I need your approval. I want to take Dad's option but I was hoping to commit to the teaching job too. Could I start the odyssey at the end of March? That way I can put aside some money, get my passport in order, tidy up my loose ends, so to speak."

"I don't see a problem with that, Davey. I'll need time to set up the trust fund anyway; and you will have the insurance money by then to get started. I always said it was an unusual behest that your father was proposing but he was pretty intent on it. He called it a means to get to know him in this world while he was in the next, always with a chuckle. So what changed your mind? You were pretty adamant about not wanting to do your father's bidding."

David grinned and sipped his scotch. "I guess this week has had more of an effect on me than I realized. It started with clearing out his things; you know the books, and then those guys at the Chateau. It threw me for a loop. Who knows, maybe it's being near the Senate and sober second thoughts and all." He smiled sardonically at Peter.

"Seriously though, while I was running, a few things came to me. If I really am an historian then I better practice it. Here is new evidence about Dad, so maybe I should investigate, even if it changes my bias. Maybe personal history is where everyone should start. Also there's nothing like a death to make one reflective. I guess Dad's truth was beginning to hurt. No close friends by me, the one person I'd really like to talk to; well I let her get out of my life a while ago. Dad never said I was a loser but I'm starting to wonder. Also you got me thinking, was my defensiveness simply a self-justification thing that I do? I don't know, maybe it's time for some introspection."

They both sipped and gathered their thoughts. David began, "Uncle Peter, do you remember that big blowup Dad and I had around the time of Franco's death?"

"Oh Davey, how could I forget. That was a terrible row you two had. I got no thanks for trying to mediate."

"I know, I can't remember if I ever said sorry to you but that was the last straw really between Dad and me. I recall that I was home on a Christmas break from my job with the World Federation of Democratic Youth and Dad was getting ready for another road trip. I don't remember how we got onto it but probably it was me. Franco had died that November, 1975 I believe, and I had said good riddance to him. Dad didn't disagree but he was grumpy. 'What the hell do you know about Spain and fighting that bastard? Good riddance yes, but let the ones who fought him have the celebration and retribution.' And soon we were off. Me calling him a bourgeois fascist and he dismissing my anti-imperialist, student protest beliefs as so much pap. It wasn't long before he called me an idealistic wet one; what did I know about democracy beyond students' mincing marches, and why didn't I do something useful. I remember thinking to myself that if that is what he thought of me, then I was done with him; 'I despise you', I yelled."

"Yes that was something; discussion topic to hissing poison in one fell swoop. Such tempers you two."

"And then there was that warning about disdain and cynicism in the will; it struck a chord. I have been pretty holier-than-thou lately. So, I'll pick up this gauntlet he's thrown, a toast to the journal journey, Des's Dare, and my introspective odyssey." They clinked glasses.

Peter said, "To Des, to you, and to what the New Year may bring. And these are yours." He handed over the closet keys.

While driving home, Peter laughed out loud, shook his head and shouted to Des. "You old goat, you got him and you got him all by yourself. Good fishing!"

After Peter left, David took the legacy keys and went to the closet. Turning the light on, he saw the wine rack and the cedar boxes. He pulled the one marked the 80s out to the kitchen and opened it with the small key. Inside was a cluster of five other keys, labeled one for each box. Opening the last page of the last journal he took out an envelope addressed to him. Inside was a note neatly folded. He read:

To David:

If you are reading this you are truly acting as my son by taking on this challenge. I couldn't share much with you until now, as you know. As I reveal these admissions of mine, you will see that I did not lead a perfect life and some of what I did may not be forgivable.

I converted to Catholicism when I married your mother. One lesson that stuck the most was the story of faith, hope and charity. And of the three virtues, the last one, love was the most important, the priest said.

I didn't always practice those, I'm afraid. I overlaid my own interpretation on that parable and believed more in the virtues of trust, loyalty and commitment. Sometimes love lost.

But as you begin this odyssey, ironically in pursuit of Me, I do believe that it's better to put Other before Self. A son needs to, has to, leave the father, but it isn't as easy for the father to leave the son. Remember that I always wanted what was best for you.

From your Father, with love.

David thought as he went to bed, "Well Dad you had the oddest way of showing it."

Ottawa was still cold, -10 C., and it had snowed a bit. David was taking a cab to the train station. He needed to return to Hamilton today, his term job was about to start. He had called his contact to confirm he would take the teaching position, and now carried the suitcase and the wooden box stenciled with *The '30s, Property of Desmond Dilman*. He had promised to call his Mom on Sundays and now he sat to finish reading his holiday book, musing that he was kind of hitchhiking a ride into his father's galaxy. When he got to Hamilton, it was that messy faux winter weather, almost freezing and sleety. Tossing his finished book onto a station bench for any passerby's amusement, he resolved to focus on non-fiction for the foreseeable future; the real world of classes and research, including his dad's world.

Fortunately the two realities meshed. Three of David's classes were Grade 10: *Canada and the 20th Century*. He would have to teach World War I, The Roaring 20s, The Dirty Thirties and a good chunk of World War II by March Break. Another assignment on his timetable was a senior enrichment class on Latin America. As a result, most evenings were busy preparing lessons, trying to stay one day ahead of the students. He gave himself Friday night and Saturday to unwind, occasionally skiing with his mates; but other than that he surprised even himself with his resolve and discipline. Sunday morning he dedicated to reading his father's journals before returning to marking and lesson preps in the afternoon and evening; and a call to his mother.

Those calls were more and more duty-bound. His mother was often inebriated, and when he upbraided her once, Meg replied quickly. "God forgives my sins Davey; I don't need you to do that nor to judge me." She often begged him to come to Ottawa for a visit, that she was lonely and drank less when he was around. David suggested she come to visit her sisters-in-law but Meg was not receptive to the idea. In the end, David said to her that it was only ten weeks until his teaching term and the winter were over and he would see her then.

One weekend, he and a few mates went to ski at nearby Ellicottville, New York. At dinner, he tried some serious talk about work and relationships. He loved his teaching and wanted to let them in on it, but beer and chicks and jokes to guffaw at were more their style. That got David thinking about who he used to be able to talk to. Like Lydia.

He had met her in 1968 in Sofia; Bulgaria. He was in his bearded radical phase then, a curly ginger beard set off against his dirty blonde hair. They were among student reps for their respective countries, Canada and Brazil, at the week-long Youth and Student Festival that summer. The slogan theme was 'For Solidarity, Peace and Friendship'. Many of the participants had marched against the Vietnam War and had been involved in the global May Day student marches that spring.

There were seminars on organizing protests and study groups on topics like Saul Alinsky's book, *Rules For Radicals*. David had referred to the guru in a discussion, using the line, "Machiavelli wrote so the haves could keep power, but Alinsky writes so the have-nots can take power." It was glib, a paraphrase of something he had read in a magazine but Lydia gazed at him with those piercing green eyes and he was smitten.

Soon they were discussing the merits of Brazilian coffee among other things over cups of watered-down cafeteria java. It was early August and David persuaded Lydia to skip a day of workshops and go on a picnic to Vitosha Mountain and the Rila Lakes, smiling that it would allow them to focus on the friendship part of the festival slogan. His eyes took in her long tanned, lean legs and tight bum in her hiking shorts as she sometimes walked ahead of him around the lake path. He found he wanted to caress a handful of her light brown curly hair while she pointed out mountain views.

They talked about everything: upbringing, beliefs, goals, pursuing post-graduation degrees, like admissions freely given while hitchhiking, not expecting to see each other after the festival. But she meant more than a fling to David and they wrote to each other more than occasionally afterwards, he even promising to teach her to ski one day.

They hatched a plan to apply for jobs with the World Federation for Democratic Youth or WFDY, a rather idealistic organization dedicated to promoting youth unity, peace, freedom and independence and eliminating want and frustration everywhere. Lydia now had a Masters in Political Science and thought of teaching eventually. David had just received his Masters in History and had failed in his bid to get hired by External Affairs. Both at loose ends, they thought the work would solve their apartness and put practice to their ideals.

The job required fund-raising and planning the festival that was to be held in Berlin in 1973, the 10th World Festival of Youth and Students. They were expecting over 25,000 participants from 140 countries under a new slogan: 'For Anti-Imperialist Solidarity, Peace and Friendship'. David was pretty much anti-everything authoritarian these days and Lydia just wanted to share her ideas with others.

Renewing their friendship was bliss but the peace and solidarity not so much. David was certainly vociferous about fascist pig Americans and Watergate break-ins. Lydia had been listening to David rant about the reasons to equate anti-imperial with anti-America over coffee, her chin cradled in her hand.

Lydia thought it was more anger than principle and she confronted him on it.

"Dahveed, you are good at pointing out the mistakes of Americans but very forgiving of others. Sometimes I think you have blindness on."

"I think you mean blinders, and I believe that Americans are the root of imperialism and war in the world." He had started growing his beard again, ginger and curly; and he looked the radical part.

"But others do violence too, no? You wrote to me after Sofia that you admired that Black Power Salute at the Mexico Olympics, snubbing the Americans; but I think you admired the theatre more than what they called human rights injustice? After all, those black athletes did take all the American support they could to get to the podium."

He stopped to look at her, a bit confused at the challenge. "A means to an end, that's all that was."

"And was the massacre of the Israeli athletes or the victims of IRA bombing only a means too? Are you proposing violence now?"

"Of course I'm not *proposing* it but you can only push people so far and they fight back. Remember it was American soldiers who shot American students practicing democracy at Kent State."

"Well I *propose* more of the methods Gandhi used. If the British coal miners can get a settlement by a peaceful strike and if the Americans can pass the Equal Rights Amendment with democratic voting, then certainly reform is possible without violence."

"I *could propose* to you too when I see those flashing green eyes," and he leaned over the table to kiss her but she pushed him back.

"Não sei, Dahveed. I don't know."

They were often separated in their work, and organizing for over 1,500 lectures and workshops kept them busy. The setting in Berlin was drab, a socialist grey, even with a refreshing paint job. The city still looked shabby and the colour of festival flags and posters could not hide that fact. They had got Black Panther, Angela Davis as guest speaker, but her message seemed to gloat about the goals of Palestinian terrorism, which Lydia didn't agree with. Claiming largesse and success didn't make it so. She was not impressed when the Communist and Stasi news agencies claimed three times the actual number in attendance. And when the closing festival party was praised for the East Germans' 'openness', and the Stasi called the party Red Woodstock, as if aping America, but Communist-style, Lydia just shook her head.

Not caving to cynicism though, she decided to stay with WFDY because the next festival would be in Havana in 1978 and she thought Latin America could be a better venue. David however seemed to relish the bravado of the Berlin event, and signed on for another term because he had nothing better to do and wanted to be with Lydia. But their attitudes clashed more and more.

Their relationship got somewhat complicated because another worker from Canada, Mike Giordano, serious about community coalition politics and food banks, started spending some time with Lydia too. Mike was a bit younger than David and they had known each other as members of the New Left and Canadian Union of Students from university days. They had even attended a solidarity event for homophilic societies in 1969, called ECHO (Eastern Coalition of Homophile Organizations) as part of their "radical" inclusive politics. Now they had paired up in Havana with WFDY.

Mike was a very likeable guy. He had an open face, quick smile under a wispy moustache and a sensitive side, expressed in deep brown eyes. However he was more practical than David, focusing on the art of the possible. Lydia liked his company too.

To garner support for the Havana festival, David remembered suggesting a foray into gay rights and pushed to canvas the homophilic movements in California for support. That state had just legalized homosexuality, especially in San Francisco where Harvey Milk, openly gay, had been elected. Mike was a bit uncomfortable with the strategy and called it bandwagon stuff but David countered that homosexual money was as good as anyone's. These differences of opinion bubbled whenever Lydia entered the conversations.

"Dahveed, are you just using those people like a fad, maybe?" Lydia sometimes had a better measure of David than he did of himself. "How do you say, a lark? You are always looking out for yourself and fun. Why can't you be serious about young people like Mike is, getting them jobs or better education or fighting poverty?"

"What do you mean, Lydia? I'm working so that youth can be FREE from fascists and imperialists. Why not tap into a ready source of funds? C'mon, homosexuals are very aware of what being colonized and unfree can mean."

"You do know that in the Soviet Union, an author can't even write about homosexuals. You don't say anything about that. I think you're so one-sided; you're only against the American imperialists but you say nothing about the Soviet kind. And now they keep testing nuclear weapons, my god."

"I'm not one-sided, I'm single-minded. And you can't disagree that the U.S. messed with Chile; would you rather the Soviet Union didn't provide arms to Cuba or Peru? Don't you think it's a kind of self-protection?"

Lydia threw up her arms. "Such a snake you can be, twisting all the time."

"Here, have a bite from my apple said the snake; it comes from the Tree of Knowledge," joked David but Lydia knocked his apple from his hand, the tension increasing rather than lessening.

"Dahveed, I like you less when you are like this, and I am losing my love, no!"

"Lydia, this is becoming a grind. Why do you keep raining on my parade?"

"Because it isn't your parade to begin with. It's about youth and the festival."

And so it went. In any event, Lydia and David's relationship was turbulent and by the end of the 11th Festival, they were no longer an item. He did miss her though and had to admit jealousy that she might be with someone else, Mike or anyone.

When he recently received a card from her forwarded from Ottawa and postmarked from *Angra dos Reis*, south of Rio in Brazil, David was chuffed that she remembered him. She was teaching at a private school near there and wondered how he was doing. Maybe he would try to reconnect.

In the meantime, he communed with his father. Reading the 1935 journal was like a primary document while he prepped lessons and taught the Great Depression to sixteen year olds. They were only a few years younger than Des had been at the time, but a whole world apart.

The journal hooked David. Des began his story with the Regina Riot in July. David's jaw dropped when he got to the point where his father was arrested, for murder.

PART TWO: THE QUEST IS AFOOT

CHAPTER 7.

A JOURNEY OF A THOUSAND MILES BEGINS WITH A FIRST STEP (Lao Tzu)

Ottawa/ Regina, March, 1985

Regina, June, 1935

David looked out the window as he sat on the train that was whisking him from Hamilton to Ottawa at the end of term. He noticed snowmobile tracks cutting through the melting fields, the packed snow lingering like slow-to-leave guests. It was the Monday after the March Break, students were back to school and travel was less congested. He had finished his long-term teaching assignment and was on his way to discuss details with Peter about the first leg of the 'journal journey'. It also made sense, he reasoned, to visit with his Mom and deposit the '30s cedar box. Then the plan was to retrace the train route that the On-To-Ottawa Trek leaders took from the capital city back to Regina in June, 1935.

He reflected on the last three months with a certain self-satisfaction. The principal, department head, and students had all given him glowing evaluations for being innovative, thorough, reliable, and straight-forward. He also felt that he had thrown himself into his work like never before, including being a volunteer on two school skiing trips. He amazed himself at how good it felt to treat both students and colleagues as genuine persons, even as equals rather than 'not-worthies'. Now that the term was over, he was looking forward to some quiet moments on the three-day train trip out West to consider some of his changing attitudes.

Where had he developed his usual disdain for high school populations in general and where did it fade to on this teaching gig in particular? Was he embracing teaching or was it a passing fancy like so many other phases of his life? What would be the plan and next steps after Regina for his bequeathment? And there was one other element that needed clarifying too.

He had written Lydia, but with some trepidation. He told her about his father's death and some details about the strange quest he was taking on. He also told her about his sense of fulfillment during his recent teaching term, but wondered if it was because he could see the light at the end of ten weeks that helped fuel him or whether the glow was real. He asked about her work in the private school and hoped she would write him back. Hence the nervousness, he supposed. Would she write back and where did he hope any renewed communication might lead?

David put his head back on the railway car seat, closed his eyes and began to see in his mind's eye the diary information he had read and re-read several times over the last weekends. Des had back-filled the period before his arrest with details of the Trek. Salient episodes popped up for David, such as the élan of the men after leaving Golden on June 8th, 1935. The locals there had welcomed the strikers with open arms. They set up trestle tables with freshly baked bread, and there was a bathtub filled with beef stew over a fire. The almost 2,000 men were able to rest under shade trees and be tranquil for a bit before re-boarding and making the train look like it had spiked hair with all the silhouettes of men on the tops of boxcars. The men were talkative and Des copied down stories, researching to be a writer like Hugh Garner, he said.

Des continually asked his fellow Trekkers for their Depression recollections and was told stories of eating gophers, surviving on skimmed milk and potatoes in the many jungles on the edges of towns; and the welcome soup kitchen fare in the bigger towns where they got two meals, porridge in the morning and beans and wet bread in the evening. The amounts were meager enough to make the transients move on rather than stay though, always under the vigilant eyes of spic-and-span Mounties. Eager to fit in and be part of the inner movement, Des also attended so-called seminars where some of the Trek leaders gave lectures that sometimes resembled revival meetings.

One of these speakers was an older guy, Slim Evans. He was tough. He had spent time in jail for organizing mining strikes and walked with a limp from a bullet he received striking in the States, shot by scabs in Colorado when he was 23. Now he was 45, a member of the Communist Party and talking about proletariats and bourgeoisie and socialism.

Before the main speaker started, Des chatted up another fella who was younger. Bobby Jackson, 21, had called the northern BC camps slave camps. Des asked why and Bobby told him about crowded bunks in tar paper shacks in the wilderness, eating army rations, getting 20¢ a day and working for 6½ days every week. He too was a member of the Young Communist League. He said Slim would be more 'theoretical' than he was. Then they hushed when Slim began to speak.

"The goddam system in Canada makes you believe there has to be a better way than fuckin' capitalism", Slim started out loudly. "That millionaire Bennett sits on his fat ass in Ottawa and tells his Mountie goons to stop us. But ole Iron Heels ain't gonna stop us, is he boys?"

A shouted "No" went up.

"No sirree, boys. Now a few of yuz can make it in the capitalist world, but only a few. Like our brother Turk Broda. Yep Turk did okay. He was workin' the relief camp in Riding Mountain, over Manitoba way. Like you boys he played hockey in the winter too; damn good goalie. But the hockey bosses put a limit to what a good goalie can make. Signed him for $7,500, the maximum. Oh Turk will do okay, but the bosses will do a damn sight better off him, selling tickets to the Gardens. It's the system boys. They have the power. So what are we poor workin' stiffs gonna do about it? Well we're startin' by goin' to Ottawa and protestin' for our rights, a living wage and better working conditions. It's like the song about the runaway train says, 'the runaway train just blew and blew; a donkey was standing in the way, and all they found was just his bray'. This On-To-Ottawa train is gonna knock those asses off the track. As long as we keep workin' together, right?"

And the crowd echoed back, "Right".

That night, Des wrote in his journal that the speech was spellbinding and he wanted to be a bigger part of the Trek. When Des had told Bobby that he loved reading and wanted to write, Bobby had said don't go see Slim or he'll get you reading *Das Kapital* or the *Communist Manifesto*. But Doc Savage was someone who always needed help; he could use an egghead to write and deliver notices and posters and stuff. And that was how Des met Doc.

Robert Savage or Doc was only five years older than Des but had leadership qualities well beyond his years. He was already head of Division #3 of the Relief Camp Workers' Union, which was pretty militant. The origin of the name 'Doc' was vague; some said he was dubbed when he came to the medical aid of a worker in the camps but others said it was because he was heroic like that new comic character, *Clark 'Doc' Savage*, an adventurer who was a blend of physical and mental prowess. At any rate, Doc was a good organizer with an eye for detail.

He was especially helpful in Regina where the Trekkers stopped on June 14th. They were forbidden to get back on the train and all exits to the city were closed. While camping out on the Exhibition Grounds by the CPR tracks between the RCMP Depot and downtown, the air was rife with rumours, including one to put all the Trekkers into a new relief camp north of Regina. Doc put Des to work, writing brief practical broadsheets for the Trekkers, like where soup kitchens were being set up; dos and don'ts of polite behaviour to practice with the Regina townspeople; dos and don'ts of hygiene, and so on.

Doc, Des and a few other volunteers used an old Gestetner mimeograph duplicator in a small dusty office near the grounds that was donated to them. Des had been sitting long hours pecking at a typewriter onto the stencil masters, sweating buckets and loving his job. But his backside had been getting more and more painful and he was starting to squirm beyond tolerance. Doc had been dictating, and perspiration was rolling down Des's back and wetting his underwear. Finally he couldn't take it anymore and jumped up.

"You're a doctor, can you see something wrong with my ass?" he asked Savage, and began pulling down his trousers.

"Whoa there fella, we hardly know each other," Doc chuckled. "What seems to be the problem? Is my article causing a pain in the butt?"

"No, it's just real sore on my bum cheek. Can you see anything?"

Doc bent over to have a look. "You've got a boil, it seems. I think it should be lanced and a hot cloth put on it."

"Can you do that? It's killin' me and I can't concentrate anymore."

"Well, each according to his needs and abilities I suppose. Sure, stay bent and I will heat up a needle."

Just then another volunteer entered the office. Harry Blask was a small, olive-skinned man who had been involved with mining strikers in Drumheller earlier and was now "cultivating acquaintances", as he put it, among the Trek leaders. He had a hint of an accent, seemed to ask too many personal questions, and tarried a trifle long while looking over things; but Savage used him from time to time. Des was friendly but didn't want to be a friend.

"This is lookin' innerestin' boys. Am I innerruptin' sumpin'?

"Fuck off Blask; can't you see I'm operatin' here?" Doc said with a grin.

"Juss sayin', Herr Boss", he raised his hands up as if surrendering. "Got any posters to deliver yet?"

"Not yet, come back in a half hour will ya?" Doc approached Des, after holding his lighter to a needle.

The lancing done, a plaster put on the boil and Des sitting on a cushion, they continued their broadsheet work before calling it a day.

Later, Blask sauntered up to Des and Doc who were having a beer at the cafeteria tent on the Exhibition Grounds.

Doc asked, "Got all the posters set up like I told ya, Harry?"

"Yep! Did the operation go okay?" Blask leered and winked to other groups nearby.

"Button it Harry, there are enough rumours around here without you insinuatin'"

"Juss sayin', Herr Boss," and he put his middle finger into a hole made by his index finger and thumb.

Des frowned and cuffed Harry. "You don't know nuthin'. Bugger off."

"Ha, bugger's the right word, Mr. Writer." Those nearby laughed at the joke, and Des blushed.

"Okay, that's enough." Doc warned, and the guys went on to chat about the upcoming football season's odds for the red and black clad Regina Roughriders, who lost the Grey Cup last year to the Sarnia Imperials. There were plans for new playing and practice fields called Taylor Field, just down the road from the Exhibition Grounds, and it was generating some sports talk.

Time was beginning to weigh heavily on the Trekkers after two weeks camping out on the grounds. Recently they had voted for eight leaders, Doc among them, to ride on to Ottawa and negotiate with Prime Minister Bennett, but it had amounted to nothing and the guys were getting restless. Doc told the story again of Slim Evans calling Bennett a liar for claiming that Evans had filched union funds, which later Evans had admitted to doing, but only to feed starving workers.

"Name callin' and blusterin' fiasco, a waste o' time", Doc had said of the Ottawa meeting. Now it was stalemate in Regina and the boys wanted some action.

That happened soon enough. Des wrote about the big event, the weekend of the Regina Riot. It was the Dominion Day long weekend, Monday July 1st. It seemed the Mounties and the Regina police, with orders from Ottawa, had a scheme to pluck the Trek leaders out of the crowds at a peaceful rally in Market Square that Monday. Many of the boys had been watching friendly baseball games before wandering over to Market Square where the leaders were addressing a smallish crowd, augmented by many citizens and their families. It was mainly fund raising since the Trekkers' sources were dwindling and their cause was stalled. Des was there that afternoon, feeling kind of spiffy in a clean white shirt, sleeves rolled up over his elbows, dark blue trousers, brogues shined, and a brown tweed poor boy hat pulled jauntily to one side.

Suddenly all hell broke loose. There was a shrill whistle and from four large vans at each corner of the square, Mounties emerged with baseball bats and tried to squeeze the gathering strikers in; some Mounties even had got onto the stage and were taking the speakers away. It was awful, heads were cracked and bloodied, people fell screaming; but the Trekkers among the crowd recovered and there were yells to make barricades. In the donnybrook, they overturned cars and picked up whatever they could to fight back with. Out of somewhere the Mounties or the police tried a horse charge. But the boys were ready. Two lines of men formed up; when the horses were in range, the first line threw their rocks and then crouched, then the second threw. When their supply of rocks was gone, they all retreated behind the barricade.

Des was part of a group who squirted behind the Regina Bottle Exchange picking up planks or cordwood and bottles as weapons. There was Doc, Harry and an older guy, Nick Schaack, among a few other strikers in this sortie. Des wrote:

"We were cursing as we passed out makeshift weapons and I noticed a little dust devil was blowing grit in the middle of the yard. Just then some police came around the corner, yelling at us. They called us Reds but we saw red ourselves and went at them ferocious-like. In the scuffle, I saw one cop hit Shaackie with a bat and he fell backwards. I heard a smack and then a thud as Schaackie hit the ground, the air knocked out of him with a whoosh, and then all the noise became muffled, except for Schaackie's moan and one piercing scream..."

...Des went to help Schaack and looked back to locate the cause of the scream. That's when he noticed blood spattered on his face and over his clean white shirt. One of the police had fallen face-first in the dirt with a halo of red spreading from him, near Nick. One of the Trekkers, bug-eyed and ashen, threw down a piece of bloodied wood. Just then two goons roughly grabbed Des and Shaackie, pulling them to their feet. The fallen cop was still on the ground, a pool of blood around his head. All the other Trekkers had scattered back into the Market Square melee. Des remembered Shaackie moaning and being woozy and then all was blackness. He figured he himself was clubbed and put into a paddy wagon because when he came to, he was in a cell, alone.

"Where am I?" Des asked, gingerly touching a lump on his head.

"You're in a guard room at the RCMP Training Depot, asshole", growled a burly Mountie. "Now that you're awake, we got some questions." He manhandled Des to his feet and tugged and pushed him, shoving him onto a chair. Des felt nauseous and vomited onto the floor, splattering his brogues.

Just at that moment a tall, thin, mustachioed Mountie came in and unknowingly stood in the vomit, befouling his own polished brown leather riding boots. "Fuck…you're in a shit load of trouble, buddy."

"What for? Vomiting on your boots; you walked into it, idiot."

The Mountie backhanded Des for the backtalk. "No, scum, you're in it. We're gonna charge you with murder."

Just then Harry Blask entered the room.

"Hey Harry, tell 'em I didn't murder no one. I was helping Nickie."

"Is this the one, Detective Staff Sergeant, sir?" asked the Mountie.

"Yep, that's him. Get him cleaned up, and then take him to Room B."

Des was baffled, but Blask set him straight in a hurry. Harry, with no obvious signs of a dust up about him, was sitting behind a table in the interrogation room. He was wearing a blue tunic with four gold arrow-tipped stripes on his sleeve. Des's mouth dropped.

"Yep, I'm a Detective Staff Sergeant with the RCMP but I work undercover. Actually, they know me around here as Operative # 1. So now that you're in the know here, Des, I wanna make a deal with you."

Des shifted uneasily in his chair. Blask continued.

"Listen, you're in a lotta trouble here. We're gonna charge you with the murder of a policeman, Regina detective, Charles Millar. I could argue that you were only an accessory to it but, with the weapon nearby and the blood on your shirt, I dunno."

"Shit Harry, you were there; you saw. I didn't clobber that copper."

"Sorry Des, I was goin' after Doc and didn't see it all; anyway Doc escaped. We have to pin it on someone, ya see."

Des raised his voice. "No I don't see; you're framin' me for something I didn't do."

"Well, we gotta lot on you, Des. There's the possible murder, sedition you wrote in those broadsheets, being a Commie, and then the perversion."

"I'm not a Communist, you're makin' that up, and the other things too. What perversion?"

"Indecent exposure for starters. But I could spread it around that you're a queer. You know, offering your backside to a fella."

Des growled, "Ah you bastard, Harry. You know that's all bullshit."

Harry raised his voice and slapped the table top. "It ain't, if I say it ain't. Shut up and listen. I especially hate commies and faggots and you could be both. So here's the deal. I've been watching you; you work hard, you follow instructions, you fit in well with the guys. So you come work for me and I'll drop all the charges, whaddaya say?"

"What do you mean, work for you?"

"Join the Mounties, train at the Depot here, and get some extra training in a special branch. You agree to that and I'll see that all pending charges are dropped."

Des was between a rock and a hard place. His head was spinning. "You're not jokin' are you? Jesus, can I think about this, Harry?"

"I'll give you a half hour, no more."

Des asked for a coffee and a cigarette. He ran his fingers through his hair, felt a sticky scab forming, and then held his head in his hands, elbows on the table.

"Damn", he thought. "This is some kinda checkmate. Blask is throwin' me under the wagon here. I got no options really. The Trek is finished; and I don't wanna do jail time. I don't have any prospects for a job, but shit, this is blackmail."

It was more than the blow to the head that was making him confused. Friendless, homeless, jobless, goal-less, in a mess. Whatever world he had before had suddenly collapsed. Feeling trapped, Des could see no other way out; he would have to do what Harry proposed.

Finally he lit the cigarette, inhaled deeply and blew out the blue-grey smoke. He sipped some black, weak coffee.

Des said to himself, "Okay, I can do this. They might have me by the short and curlies but they won't own me. I'll play their little game, but they won't defeat me."

And with that inner private pledge, "they have me but they don't own me", like a mantra chanted, Des agreed to join the Mounties and submit to Blask's tutelage in the Security Service. He filled the rest of the 1935-1936 journals with information about the Trek's aftermath and his early training. Des clearly was upset by some things and merely observant about most. David felt the writing was powerful and was impressed by what his father put to paper.

For instance, while Des was in training, a Mountie circular came out, a poster promising $2,000 leading to the arrest of whoever murdered Millar. It came out the same day that Nick died, on October 18th. Des felt the irony of that one, a good Trekker ignored as a footnote and more time and effort investigating for a dead cop. He also inwardly fumed over the inquiry, the conflicted testimony that Nick had died first from a scratch, then a tumour, and finally pneumonia. When the Regina Riot Inquiry Commission said that only the strikers caused the riot, as if the Mounties and police and horsemen were onlookers, Des realized that anything could be made to look like whatever you wanted, especially if you held the power.

He had learned the first major lesson in his new craft; be a dissembler. Hide what you feel; hide what is real; keep your secrets. Two could play the game of being loose with the truth. Be a hypocrite to them, but be true to yourself....

David let out a rush of breath as the train pulled into the Ottawa station. He saw his uncle on the platform and greeted him. Dinner at home was simple fare; Meg had managed salad and pasta, cozy food. Her pre-dinner vodka did not interfere with the process and the table talk was amiable.

"I'm so glad the teaching term went well David. I bet those students had crushes on you, dear."

"Mom, really! I worked hard on getting them to like history. It was fun; especially imagining they were working with a 1930s budget, using 1931 Winnipeg grocery prices and Eaton's catalogues."

"Phooey dear. I always learned best from a good-looking teacher. Those girls might have looked like they were paying attention but they were day dreaming, trust me. Anyway, imagining the Depression couldn't be anything like the real thing."

David and Peter exchanged glances. Peter asked her, "What do you mean, Meg?"

"Well, times were pretty tough, weren't they? Kids might try to imagine it but it won't be the real thing. I remember that Trek nonsense, I was fifteen. But we were more interested in finding fun."

She began somewhat wistfully.

"For example, it was more fun to play miniature golf. For a dime you could play and it was the cat's meow to stay out under some coloured lights on a warm summer night, mooning with a guy with a putter. Sometimes we would go to a movie which was a break from sitting around the radio at night. My favourites were *Mutiny on the Bounty* with Clark Gable and *39 Steps*, the Hitchcock thriller. I would work in my father's garden on Saturday for 25¢ and have enough to go to the movie theatre. So times were poor but things didn't cost a lot either. Bread was 4¢ a loaf and milk was 6¢ a quart. I remember some girls leaving school to work and there was talk that Western Canada was really hard hit, a charity case really; but we didn't read much about it, or pay much attention to it on the radio, or think about it much. We just got on; nothing special. How was it for you Peter?"

Peter looked at her seriously for a moment and took a deep breath as if deciding to give something up.

"It was different in Poland, in Krakow. I was 21 in 1935 and studying pre-law at university. When I had some spare time we would go to jazz clubs. I remember Henryk Gold's band was very good. But the country was poor and confused. Marshall Pilsudski had just died and modernization was slow. We only just got a railway between Warsaw and Krakow. There had been a terrible flood near us in 1934, which killed a great many people. But you have to remember that Poland was mainly agricultural and food prices were very low. The peasants, yes, don't look so surprised; we had peasants and they were very poor. Unemployment was high; the army put down radical protests and killed many more than the one person who died in Regina."

"Two," corrected David.

"You must have had lots of girl friends though," Meg insinuated.

"Just one," and Peter went silent, gazing distantly into his wine glass.

"Mmm, well I will leave you boys to talk your business while I clean up. How long will you be staying, dear?"

"Just a day or two, Mom. I have to work out some plans with Uncle Peter and then I'm off to Regina for a week and a half or so before next steps. I must be about my quest, you know."

David topped up Peter's glass and his own with the 1982 St. Emilion Bordeaux from the closet under the stairs. Peter had reminded David of his father's wish for them to sample a vintage wine from Des's cache each time he returned to Ottawa. They clinked and smiled.

"So your research went well and you want to go to Regina by train and spread some of Des's ashes there. What are you learning about your Dad?"

"Well it looks like he was hoodwinked into his career. Did you know that?"

"Not really. I knew that he brushed me off whenever I asked him how he got into his job. Said something about *'me rompar las pelotas'* in Spanish. I thought he was saying 'don't bother with that', but later I understood it meant that they squeezed his testicles. But Des never elaborated."

"Ha, they certainly did bust his balls. If he didn't join the Security Services, they would have thrown the book at him on trumped up charges. Why he stuck with them, I don't know. But he went through the training and apparently did quite well."

"Well your father, in his somewhat vulgar way, also had another saying, 'Don't shit where you eat'. They paid him well so he was tied to them. Maybe it was as simple as that."

"He might have felt he had to do his work, but I don't understand why he believed in it so much. It seems he became a real Commie-basher."

"Well we all hated Communists back then, allies in the war but brutes and manipulators too. Maybe your dad felt abandoned by his Trek friends after his arrest. I'm not sure, but I do know that he fumed against Communists from time to time, calling them faux-intellectuals. He said you could hardly call yourself a thinker if you just followed what Stalin and party hard liners told you what to do. I guess you have more digging to do. So come to my apartment tomorrow. I'll have the ashes in a vial and we can go over your account details."

"Another thing, Uncle Peter. I have forwarded all my mail to your address, if you don't mind. Just didn't want to tempt Mom with opening my stuff. And there may be a letter from someone named Lydia on the return address, just so you know. Plus I am going to take a few more volumes of the journals; I want to re-read his Depot time in Regina and maybe get a sense of where Dad went afterwards."

"No problem," Peter said. "Until tomorrow. The wine was very good tonight David; it helped to loosen our tongues and thoughts, I think."

So David boarded the train in Ottawa and left on a 3-day journey to Regina. He travelled lightly, packing his duffle bag for a week or so. Peter had given him a copy of *The Fourth Protocol* by Frederick Forsyth, a current best seller that he knew David would never buy on his own as a hard copy. "Something light to help you pass the time. Well, light reading anyway." Winter was not willing to let go just yet. The last week of March hovered around zero and winds blew wisps of snow across fields, from Northern Ontario to the Prairies. David looked out the train window from time to time catching glimpses of lakes, endless forests and rolling prairie; but mainly he read, dozed, and thought. Some of Des's entries flitted by like the telephone poles on miles of prairies.

David recalled what Des had written about some of his training at Depot, a sprawling area of buildings and parade grounds at the western edge of Regina. Apart from the usual fitness training, some martial arts, firearms, and criminal investigation classes, he also undertook specialized training for tasks that Blask had called 'secretive undercover work'.

It included a farrago of lessons. Des learned how to tail someone without being detected, to use disguises that helped him to blend in, such as using facial hair, hats, and glasses, but not to make him look too distinguished; to use a 'trailer' to spot whether the follower himself was being watched; and to send coded and secret messages. For instance he was trained to dissolve six paracetamol tablets in water, then using a clean fountain pen to scratch the invisible message on paper where when ironed, the information was revealed and read. He also learned techniques for dead and live drops, where messages could be passed without giving away one's security. Des liked mastering these lessons. He had no real inhibitions, no references to ethics; the skills were merely means to ends. He enjoyed practicing on the Depot grounds and sometimes even in the city itself. It was a game to him.

On the night before arriving in Regina, David went to the dining car and recognized someone sitting alone.

"It's Robert Savage, isn't it? I'm David Dilman, Des's son; we met at his memorial service in Ottawa."

"Oh yes, how d'ya do? It's Doc actually. Will you join me?"

"Sure thanks." David explained that he was doing some last will and testament duties and Doc said that he was just returning from the Trek anniversary planning meetings.

"The planning for the commemoration took longer than the actual Trek," he mused.

"I know what that job can be like; I used to plan five years for a 2 week conference."

"Oh ya, when was that and who for?"

"After university, I worked as a fund raiser and planner for the World Federation for Democratic Youth."

"Really? Wasn't that a front for Soviet money and ideology, peddlin' propaganda?"

"There was some rumour to that effect, but," David smiled and changed the subject. "You know my dad mentioned you in his journals, how he worked on your team during the Trek and how you two got separated during the Regina Riot."

Doc was picking at his meal and put down his fork and knife.

"Did he? That was a long time ago but I do remember that weekend. It was some rough. Your dad and me worked hard at gettin' out posters advertisin' the meetin' in Market Square. We were standin' there when all hell broke loose."

"Yes, he wrote that you and he were getting ready to fight the police when someone hit an undercover cop."

"Ya, sumpin' like that. Your dad was always a good Joe, always helpin' someone, and then we got separated. I got lost in the crowd and then hightailed it out of the city, made tracks north from the campgrounds, hidin', and makin' my way back to the coast. Then I shipped out on a freighter. Later I ended up in Quesnel, in B.C. Like I said, I never saw your dad again."

"Do you know anything about my dad being a Communist?"

"Nah, he wasn't that; me neither. That's one reason your dad and me got along. Your dad had a head on his shoulders and could think things through. We never bought all that class revolution crap, and 'workers of the world unite' bull. Hell, it was tough enough just gettin' reforms. We both knew that organizin' those Trekkers for a cookout could be like a trip for biscuits, so unitin' workers of the world wasn't gonna cut it. Nah, neither of us ever signed up for the Party."

"Trip for biscuits?"

"Ya sorry, sometimes I stay in the past, an old expression. Means going nowhere."

"Can I ask you another question, a pretty personal one about my father?"

"Sure, shoot."

"Did you ever hear of my dad being a homosexual?"

"A gunsel? No I never figured Des for a queer, why?"

"He wrote that some Mountie was going to cite him as a pervert, showing his backside to guys."

Doc hooted. "That would be old Blask, I bet. I figured Blask was a snitch for the dicks, but you know sumpin' funny?"

Doc leaned in over the table. "You know at your dad's memorial, that Mountie commissioner was showing us a picture of that other Mountie, Frank Zaneth, the one that wanted a medal for your dad. Well, I took a good long look and I tell you that Zaneth was the spittin' image of the guy we all thought was Harry Blask."

"Really, that's a coincidence. That means Blask or Zaneth was really this Operative #1 that recruited my Dad, or tricked him really. Say Doc, you have a few hours layover tomorrow morning don't you? Could I buy you breakfast in Regina in exchange for you showing me the old haunts like Market Square?"

"Sure Dave, I haven't been there in a while. Let's call it a deal and now I'll say a good night."

They took a cab from the train station to a decent restaurant near the former square. Doc was a bit discombobulated because he couldn't get his bearings for Market Square; Regina had redone its downtown starting in the 1970s and although there were refurbished and designated heritage buildings, things had changed. David asked the cabbie to take them to a half decent breakfast place and he dropped them off at the Copper Kettle on Scarth.

Doc looked at the front of the building and said, "Ya know, next door to this place used to be the Mac and Mac Ltd. clothing store. Your dad dragged me here and he bought a good white shirt. He joked with me that the Army and Navy store was too low class and Marxist for him.

He liked to dress up when he could and was lookin' real snazzy that Monday."

Later they tried locating some spots around the old Market Square. They found some plaques dedicated to the riot, tucked away in a hallway by the Ritz Café and by Victoria Park away from the original site. The new downtown had some old heritage buildings with new corporate occupants who didn't know, or didn't want to be reminded, of their history.

"So it isn't the same as you remember eh, Doc? I guess the Bottle Exchange and your office are gone now."

"Ya, I don't see 'em. There are some I can figure out, like the old newspaper building and the library. We used to spend time there researchin' and tryin' to get the reporters to give us some good coverage, but mostly it's different. Ironic isn't it, only the police station and justice building are on the old sites. But winds of change blow don't they, Dave? The boys are gonna have problems with their memories when they show up here for the commemoration."

David waved Doc off at the train station and as he turned away, he had a thought, as he braved the cold spring day in Regina.

"So it was Zaneth who set my father up. He must have felt guilty for a long time to make those requests to give Dad a medal. And it was good to get some perspective from Doc, but stopping here in Regina must have been hard on him. I guess you can never go home again, as the saying goes. Winds of change for sure and this one is a cold one."

David was glad for his scarf and gloves and huddled down against the wind as he walked the streets of Regina. Finally he took a cab to the RCMP recruitment and training site known simply as the Depot. It sprawled on the western edge of the city.

David began to place Des's time there in context. His father would have been ensconced here about a year, six months on the campus and six months on probationary assignment in the field. There were a dozen buildings or so, with various functions, ranging from residences and classrooms, to a chapel, a library, a gun range, a gym and drill hall. And beyond the Depot, the Prairie, windswept and seemingly flat for as far as the eye could see.

David walked out onto that frozen Prairie expanse about 800 metres and turned to face the Depot and the rising cityscape. Out of his pocket he took a small blue vial with a stopper, not unlike an antique medicine bottle. He opened it and let the ash contents get taken by the west wind, drifting over the sod and towards the site of Des's deceptive recruitment and training.

"So Dad, this is where you got started. Your ashes are part of Regina now, but only on the edge of it. Like you said, they might have you but won't own you. I wonder where the next scattering will be.

CHAPTER 8.

THE FALSE PROMISE

Ottawa/Barcelona, April 1985,
Spain, April-May 1937

David and Peter were discussing the Regina trip at Peter's place during an early spring evening. David had brought a Spanish Rioja from Des's closet cache, a 1978 Marqués de Cáceres Gran Reserva. Its brick red colour and tobacco bouquet went well with some *queso Manchego* that David bought at the Byward Market. They were sitting in the living room of Peter's modest but open-concept penthouse where they had views of the illuminated roof of the Library of Parliament.

Peter's living space was as uncluttered as he was, sleek teak coffee table in front of the fireplace, matching honey-coloured teak dining table and chairs, and one book case showing eclectic spines, perfectly in line and interspersed with some framed photos. The few paintings and carvings were tasteful, notably an Inuit soapstone of a Mother and Child and a serigraph of Alex Colville's 1955 painting, *Family and Rainstorm*, the mom ushering two kids into the car before a storm. Peter placed two wine glasses from his Riedel Sommelier 1973 collection on the table and David poured.

"This wine looks significant, David. Are you giving me a hint about what's next then?"

"This is to tell you that Spain will be the next destination for Dad's ashes, Uncle Pete."

"Is that so? Mmmm, this is very tasty isn't it? If I'm not mistaken, the cheese is made in La Mancha. The cheese and the wine were paired nicely. Are you planning on tilting at windmills?"

"Ha, I don't think so, tilting that is. But yes, Spain is on my radar. It seems that Dad's first big assignment was providing information about the Mackenzie-Papineau Battalion that fought in the Spanish Civil War. He had been part of the security team tailing the Canadian Communist Party leader, Tim Buck, after Buck's release from jail in 1936. But then his journals tell me that he went to Barcelona as a war correspondent; at least that was his cover."

"Interesting, I didn't know your dad until 1944. He was a bit vague about his life before that. He did mention though that he knew Fascism first hand from Hitler and Mussolini's little practice war in Spain. We were being bombed ourselves in Italy that night when he told me."

Peter held up his glass and admired the colour in the candle light; his gaze and voice trailing off. After a moment, David watched Peter come out of a reverie.

"Yes, your father hated fascists even more than he did communists."

"Yes, I'm learning that he would write people off pretty quickly, sometimes because of ideology but more often when he felt that he had been used or betrayed. At the same time, he could carry on with something even though he didn't believe in it necessarily."

"That's an interesting observation. Any examples or evidence, after all you are a historian and should back up your claims." Peter was smiling.

David sipped some wine. "Well, on ideology, I've just been skimming journal entries so far but it seems that he had no use for Canada's Prime Minister at the time, Mackenzie King. Dad fumed over the fact that King's grandfather's name was adopted for the Canadian volunteers when King himself tried a lot of devious ways to thwart those guys going over to fight Franco and the fascist Nationalists."

"Go on."

"Well this is partly my research and partly Dad's journal. It seems that most of the volunteers were Communist members or sympathizers. From July 1936 most of them joined other existing International Brigades, mainly the American Abraham Lincoln Battalion or the British one. Then Prime Minister King started making it really difficult for the volunteers. First he passed the Foreign Enlistment Act in April 1937 which made it illegal for Canadians to serve in any foreign army or for anyone to help them. Dad thought the Liberals were just being stooges of the other non-interventionist countries.

He especially condemned the Liberal embargo on arms to the Republicans. He said it was like tying the hands behind their backs of those fighting Franco. Later when the civil war was effectively over in 1938 and the brigades disbanded, King refused money for the Canadian volunteers' passage back. Dad wrote it was like an authoritarian parent making up some damn rules as he went along, you know, like setting hurdles along the course while the race was on. Jump because I say so."

"Hmmm, sounds like Des should have read his own journal from time to time, wouldn't you say?" Pete chuckled.

"I never thought of it like that," smiled David. "Anyway, at the time, Zaneth wanted to target the Canadian Communist Party. He was pretty sure they were breaking the new Liberal law and so he used Dad to spy."

"Really, how did that happen?"

"Well the CCP was the main recruiter for Spanish volunteers in Toronto. From there, men would go to Montreal or New York for passage to France before going over the Pyrenees or on a freighter to Republican Spain. The recruiters' screening was very tough at first, not accepting drunks and adventurers or anyone that didn't have legitimate left leanings. When the recruiting went underground after the new law in 1937, Dad was sent to New York to ferret out information about third class passengers on the Cunard White Star Line and to give those names to Zaneth. Then on April 24, 1937, he booked passage himself as a war correspondent or researcher for the *Toronto Star*, sailing on the Dutch liner S.S. Volendam.

Maybe Zaneth was able to pull strings with the Liberal-oriented newspaper owner, I don't know. Anyway, there were enough Canadians in Spain by the summer of 1937 that they were able to form their own battalion, the Mackenzie-Papineau, *Los Canadienses*, and it seems Dad was there."

"Fascinating. You've found out a lot. When do you want to go?"

"I thought I'd spend a few more days in Ottawa, visit with Mom, read some more about Dad's time in Spain. Does that give you time to make arrangements? You know, book me a flight and a room large enough for a writing desk in a modest central hotel, say for three or four nights."

"Yes, I should be able to. Maybe I can get Nancy to help."

"Oh before I forget, can you also transfer some money to my account, and get me another vial of ashes? I'll need to rent a car to visit the battle sites and Dad spent time in Madrid too, but I can arrange those hotels as I go."

Peter's eyes widened at the flurry of requests. "You have certainly gotten business-like with your plans."

"I find I'm getting really excited about following Dad like this."

"I'm sure he would be pleased. I am too. By the way, here is the mail that came here for you. But don't go just yet; I have a book that you might find interesting for Spain."

David put the envelopes into his satchel to read later and Peter went off to his office to fetch an old copy of George Orwell's *Homage to Catalonia*.

Peter handed the thin paperback to David. "I remember when I first read this. My impression was that it was a hard time, very confusing and disappointing for Orwell. It was like the hope for a Republican Spain was a false promise of a radiant future. He got frustrated with the many smaller games within the larger match. I talked to your father about it, and he said Orwell got it right. It was just like kids fighting over desserts and who got the bigger piece of cake, even though the cake might have gone stale.

They clinked glasses again, each lost in different thoughts of Des. David saw the rather dashing figure off to spy in the Spanish Civil War; Peter saw the suffering man scarred and cynical in the Italian trenches seven years later.

At home alone later and nursing a scotch, David was going through the 1937-38 journals and memorabilia in the cedar box. There were some newspaper clippings, one about Norman Bethune's blood transfusion unit in the Madrid and Guadalajara battles; a front page reporting the Fascist bombing of Guernica in April 1937; a 'Special To *The Star*' article describing the thousands of Spanish war orphans and the Canadian fundraising used to set up two orphanages near Barcelona; and a *Toronto Star* report of 10,000 people greeting 275 returning volunteers at Union Station. Then he lifted up the iconic *Life* magazine cover photo of Robert Capa's *Falling Soldier*, capturing a Republican militiaman at the moment he was shot. David's jaw tightened. It was a passionate and brutal time; sobering thoughts to finish his scotch. Then he turned to his own mail.

There was a pay cheque for his last month of work, about $2,400, some junk mail, and one from Lydia. He was as nervous as a school boy when he opened it, realizing it would be another ending or possibly a new beginning with her. He read it very carefully.

Dear David:

It was so good to hear from you. My sympathies to you on your father's death. I remember you did not get along so well with him so I hope you and he had made amends before he died. My English is not so good as it was, so I am hoping I am conveying the proper sentiments.

You asked about my work. I am teaching girls and boys at a municipal school on Ilha Grande. You can reach the island by ferry from a town south of Rio, Angra dos Reis. I think you would translate that as Bay of Kings. The school is called Monsenhor Pinto de Carvalho but do not jump to conclusions thinking it is religious. This island is very beautiful, with sandy beaches, jungly mountains, and the children so eager to learn. I have obtained some business partnerships so that I have resources to teach science very well. I am sure you would like it here. I am glad also that you have enjoyed some teaching yourself.

You are probably wondering why I have sent a postcard after so long not seeing or communicating with you. It is because I still think of you and still carry some fondness since Cuba. Perhaps we have both changed a little since then, no? Also you still owe me skiing lessons, a promise from you I would like to collect.

I would like it very much if we could see each other again. But it is good to begin to write also.

With affection, Lydia.

David leaned back in his chair realizing that he had been tensed up and let out a sigh. He almost wanted to whoop, but his mother was sleeping. He blew his breath out with puffed cheeks. Could it be that he might see Lydia again? His hopes were high. For now he would savour the excitement; later he would write back, but not until he was calmer. He started thinking of rendezvous possibilities to see her though; he thought about her with too much affection to let this opportunity slip by. Affection was her word too, wasn't it? He read the letter again.

David flew the nine-hour overnighter into Barcelona, arriving during Easter Week to brilliant blue skies and 20 °C. He had read most of Orwell on the flight and got a sense of what a mess those ideologies of the late Thirties put people through-communism, anarchism, democracy and fascism. David remembered from a university course he took that even Orwell had given 35 names of suspected communists to British Intelligence before he died. If Orwell could do that, then why couldn't his father do something similar for the Canadian government? Maybe it wasn't so easy to keep a black and white moral compass.

He was tired on his cab ride to the hotel but found enough energy to keep jetlag at bay and explored a bit. It was an inexpensive 4-story hotel near the Parc de Joan Miró, quite central really. The eucalyptus fragrance and modern art in the park belied that it was the former site of a now-forgotten abattoir for *corrida* bulls. Perhaps Spain and the city were trying to cover up an ugly past, but David was open to its charms nevertheless.

The next morning, he made sure he sent a postcard thanking Peter and Nancy for the perfect arrangements. He had already sent a postcard to Lydia from the Ottawa airport saying he was in Spain for a few weeks, asking her to write her schedule of holidays to Peter's address.

Naturally Barcelona was a changed city from Des's time there. For starters, David noticed the dailies were full of news of a different breed of internationals now. Instead of the international battalions, now the headlines jumped out about the football club, Barca, managed by an Englishman, Terry Venables, and the recent transfer of Argentine Diego Maradona to Naples. In 1937 it would have been different for his father. The papers would have screamed about Franco and the Nationalists or the fact that the ruling elected Popular Front was trying to centralize their army and quell fellow anarchists and socialists. The politics of the civil war were very miasmic and the farrago of factions confusing.

Des would have noticed several different battalions of militia, each with different goals and with sometimes conflicting strategies. He landed in this quagmire to investigate those Canadians fighting a most uncivil war. David, on the other hand, when he took breaks from reading to explore, found the city both pleasurable and most civil.

Des was in Spain on a deadly mission in a devastated Spain, with several bombed and ruined towns instead; such as Belchite which was left as a ghostly reminder to the war on Franco's orders. David was in Spain, not on a lark exactly but more akin to that. On one of his walkabouts, David visited the *Poble Espanyol,* an amalgamation of buildings typical of old Spanish villages, a holdover display from the 1929 International Exhibition. It evoked a more peaceful and traditional time.

David enjoyed being a tourist, strolling along La Rambla, sampling cafes and bistros. Once he went to the Plaça de Catalunya where the languid statue, *La Deessa* (The Goddess) by sculptor Josep Clarà, was reflected in a pool. The figure reminded him of Lydia, the open oval face and the hair in a bun before she undid it and beckoned him to join her. Des, on the other hand, would have seen anarchist women dressed in blue denim overalls called *monos* wearing an array of armbands, mostly red with various insignia including the hammer and sickle. Today there was Tourism; then it was 'The Cause'.

David planned to read the journals, research some Civil War histories, and tour Barcelona's sites for a few days before renting a car to travel to places Des wrote about. Sitting at a tapas bar on the Plaça de Catalunya, a sweater draped over his shoulders on a pleasant spring evening, David was sipping a house wine and reading Des's entries from April, 1937, same month and almost 50 years later. From his father's words and his own delving, David was able to extrapolate what he called Des's 'Spanish phase'.

Spain was a baptism of fire for many young men and David's father was no different. Sure, his assignment meant travel, meeting high-ranking diplomats, volunteers, celebrities and a beautiful courier. But the experience also shook Des to the core emotionally and psychologically, not to mention physically and ideologically.

At first David read only the excitement and early flushes of adventure, especially his father's account of a trans-Atlantic crossing, befriending volunteers like Taffy Stockdale, and being seduced by Margareta Gross. David smiled when reading this account.

"Why, you Lothario, Dad." He sipped some more wine, looked around, and realized that actually he could be sitting somewhere near where his father and this other Margaret had been meeting almost fifty years before. He stretched and felt like wandering down to the harbour and mulling over what he had been reading. The Columbus Monument was only a couple of kilometers down La Rambla and he fancied some periwinkles or *bigaros* from a seaside vendor. That and a glass of Spanish cava blanco would cap the day nicely.

Near the docks and seated at a wobbly table, David chuckled to himself and admitted, "Well Dad. I really am enjoying this; reading about you while I get to travel in your footsteps. Thanks for this."

He speared another periwinkle and sipped his sparkling wine. Then an observation struck him. The biggest argument and tipping point with his father happened over the announcement of the death of Franco near the end of 1975. Why did that cause such rancor?

Then, David was a brash twenty-seven year old and thought his Dad was just a stuck-in-the-mud locks salesman. Now he realized his father had been seeing a lot of the world first hand, meeting ambassadors, cloak and dagger with a pretty woman. But something must have happened here in Civil War Spain to cause Des to dismiss David with such disdain and anger that night in Ottawa when David lightly said good riddance when Generalissimo Franco died. David slowly began to realize that something in Spain caused the depths to which Des would plummet.

Wanting to find a clue in the journals, he paid his bill and walked back to his room. David's feet were sore after walking five kilometers in his roped-sole *espadrilles*, so he propped himself up in his bed, reading more of the diary.

Monday, May 17, 1937

After a week of getting my bearings in Barcelona and practicing my codes, I decided that I should get to where the Canadians were training. Margareta is sure swell. She took me to a bar, Els Quatres Gats, not far from La Rambla. It's frequented by artists and, at one time, Pablo Picasso used to go there. She also told me she heard the famous painter was working on a giant mural to commemorate the bombing of the Basque city Guernica last month. She moves easily among people and knows tons. I invited her again to tour with me and she accepted this time. We took the train to Valencia where there was evidence of recent bombing by the Nationalists. "No matter," she said, "we have our picnic basket still." Slowly the train moved south-west and we arrived dirty and tired in Albacete. We spent a good chunk of time here; it was hot in the sun but cool in the olive and lemon groves where we would take breaks from interviews and picture-taking, often to grope and picnic, in that order. That is until I re-met Taffy Stockdale...

...I had been doing so-called interviews for the paper, learning who was a Commie or not. Margareta was taking photos. The Canadians were training, marching, singing the *Internationale*, and even helping with the local grain harvest. The guys, down to the drill sergeant, were good-natured. When he barked that the boys were "Useless! Youze guys would starve in a grocery store," no one was offended. Another guy, Jack Lawson, a crusty Scot from Vancouver, took one peasant's hand sickle and crossed it with his rifle, saying to the lads, "This is what that fucking armband means, you tossers." The Canadians were fairly well-disciplined and proud of the fact that they had so many volunteers in their own designated battalion now, plus their own company in the Abraham Lincoln Battalion. They even had a bugler for reveille, well that is until the Yanks crushed the annoying instrument.

I hung out with Jack a lot because he had the job of finding the whereabouts of every Canadian volunteer so he could get addresses to help folks back home send personal packages to the boys. There was a group called *Friends of the Mackenzie-Papineau Battalion* and they wanted to send money, food and clothing directly to the volunteers. Also Jack was asked to let the *Friends* know when wounded volunteers were returning to Canada so they could be met at the stations. I helped Jack shunt packages to various volunteers and was able to collect those wounded returnees' names for Zaneth too.

But back to Taffy. Margareta and I were in the canteen and I had been stroking Margareta's inner arm, that soft smooth skin on the inside of her elbow. She looked tantalizing with her long shoulder length hair, lightened by the sun; her tanned arms in a white blouse; I was even toying with the idea of saying I loved her. But she got impatient with my attention and sent me to get drinks. I was ordering some sangria at the bar when Taffy entered, large and loud and tanned, with a blue beret jauntily placed on his big head. He gave me a boisterous bear hug, lifting me off my feet. When he eyed Margareta over my shoulder, he jabbed me in the ribs.

"Wow, she is one sweet patootie. Is she your filly, Barry? "

"Nah, not really. We're just working together for the paper. You know, me doing research and she, taking pictures."

But I was lying, trying to sound cool. I was head over heels for Margareta. Dissembling to Taffy proved to be counter-productive.

At the table, Margareta held out her hand and Taffy took it in both of his.

"Well introduce me, will ya."

Over several glasses of sangria and tapas, Taffy regaled us with tales of good luck. The coastal freighter they took from Marseilles, the *City of Barcelona,* had been torpedoed off the Spanish coast.

"That tub was carryin' about five hundred of us and went down in a hurry. About fifty boys never made it. A local fisherman picked me up and got me to Barcelona. Like I told Barry here, stick with me, Margareta, I'm lucky."

"Who were some of the ones who bought it? Anyone I know?" I asked.

"Karl Francis was one for sure."

Later, as Taffy and I were about to go to the 'loo, Margareta said, "You know Taffy you have a nice face; could I photograph you sometime?"

"Sure kitten, anytime."

Outside I pushed Taffy on the shoulder. "What the hell are you doing, moving in on my girl?"

"Whoa buster, what's this *MY* girl? You gone all bourgeoisie on me? You don't own her, or anyone for that matter. Since we're here fightin' for democracy, maybe you oughta let her *CHOOSE* who she wants to be with."

And he pushed me back hard against the wall. I went to punch him but the sangria and my lack of skill were no match. Taffy parried and caught me with a punch to the side of the head and then an uppercut. When I came to and returned to the canteen, nursing a sore jaw, bruised cheek and split lip, I noticed our table was empty.

The next day, I went off alone to the lemon grove with my satchel, carrying notes and some blank pages, a canteen of water, a candle and a tin plate. I mixed lemon juice and water and used a cotton swab to print a message on a page. When I waved a lit candle behind the apparently clear page the words appeared in brown. Satisfied with the simple method that Zaneth had taught me, I began printing names of guys that I had remembered would not be receiving Lawson's care packages. Karl Francis drowned when the *Ciudad de Barcelona* was hit; Thomas Beckett died at Jarama defending Madrid, as did Joe Campbell, the 41 year old French Canadian, and Fred Lackey, one of the first from Toronto to be recruited. There were easily 25 names. Then I bundled the pages neatly in a manila envelope and located Margareta who was photographing some peasants in the field.

"You have a swollen face, what happened?" she asked.

"Taffy and I had a bit of an ideological disagreement. Get enough pictures? Hope so, because I need you to get back to Barcelona and courier this package."

"Aren't you coming with me?

"No, a change in itinerary for me. I have to go to Madrid and meet the newspaper's feature writer. I got a feeling you can manage on your own anyway. I'll meet you back at the studio in about a week. Don't wait up."

Margareta bristled at the sarcasm and reached for my arm but I pulled away.

"Don't worry; I'll still keep an eye out for someone to help you get to Australia. I'd be careful of Taffy though; his boats sink."...

David was dog tired and closed the journal. He felt vaguely ill too and his stomach was cramping. Falling back on the pillow, he turned out the light and tried to sleep.

Suddenly he shot up and bolted for the bathroom. Falling on his knees before the toilet bowl, the nauseous feeling gradually passed. The porcelain rim felt cool against his cheek. When he stood up, he felt dizzy immediately. The nausea returned and he felt himself swaying in the small cubicle until the sense of vomiting forced him to lunge down to the bowl again. He puked repeatedly and sweated through his tee shirt and underpants.

Thinking that a shower would help, he stripped down and stood under the lukewarm stream. Then he felt another wave with a griping stomach cramp that doubled him over. Suddenly he was voiding a stream of vomit and diarrhea. He was on his hands and knees in the shower and could see the foul effluent draining away. How long he lay this way he didn't know but gradually he felt the wave pass and he used the walls to guide himself back to bed.

Aching as if he had done way too many sit-ups, he lay in a fetal position on the bed and dozed into a sleep of delirious dreams. Espadrille rope soles became snakes that he tried to kick off; he was trying to hold onto a broken spar in the stormy sea but his hands kept slipping off; he kept trying to gather lemons to his lap but they turned into Taffy's punches, pummeling his gut. Then there was his father, Des with a bright light behind him and he was pulling Taffy away. David woke himself with a shout, "Dad, is that you?"

He opened his eyes quickly, squinting in sunshine and blue sky out of the window. His bed was soaked in sweat, the sheets twisted and wet about his legs. His stomach hurt and he began to remember why.

"Fucking periwinkles," he croaked from a dry mouth and thick tongue. "Oh damn, I'm going to be sick again."

Food poisoning especially from shellfish was nothing to trifle with. As well as the nausea and diarrhea spells, David's lips felt a bit tingly. Hapless, helpless and a trifle disoriented, he managed a call to the front desk and asked for a doctor and for cleaning service; it didn't matter in what order they appeared. Then he called room service to send up some tea and toast; that much he remembered from motherly nursing.

Clad in a clean tee shirt and running shorts, he sat slouched in a chair, feeling wretched and a little sorry for himself. He closed his eyes and again he saw the vivid dream vision of his dad pulling Taffy off him. It seemed so real in his delirium and now it offered a certain comfort. He couldn't remember the last time his father offered him help.

CHAPTER 9.

SUFFER THE CHILDREN

Barcelona, April 5-9, 1985;
Madrid, June 1937 and the Aragon Front, Fall 1937

It was 3 p.m. on Good Friday and David felt like he had already been crucified. The concierge had recommended a doctor who in turn recommended lots of bottled water, Pepto Bismol and a BRAT diet (bananas, rice, applesauce and toast). David was between troughs of waves, so to speak, and decided to pop into a Telefónica exchange to call Peter. Sitting in a cubicle *locutorio*, like a confessional, David briefly explained his personal 'stations of the cross'.

"Hello Uncle Peter, yes, the room is great. But I just came down with some food poisoning from a local vendor last night. Feet are sore from city walking, gut churns regularly, and head is pounding. Ha, yes, my crown of thorns. Yes, I've seen a doctor but I'll probably need a couple of days to rest here in Barcelona. No, I'll be able to extend my room and no, I can manage on my account, thanks. We can settle later if need be. I just wanted to give you an update. By the way, has there been any mail for me?"

There was a pause before Peter returned. There was a post card from Lydia and David asked him to read it. Peter relayed the brief message, "Just had Carnival and no holidays until July," and a phone number.

"Can you give me that phone number again, Uncle Pete? Thanks, and say hi to Mom. Tell her I remembered her antidote for an upset stomach and it worked. Enjoy your Easter dinner together. *Adiòs por ahora.*"

Next David placed a call to Lydia. It was 10 a.m. in Angra. The connection was not brilliant but David was thrilled to be talking to her again.

"Lydia, it's David. No, I'm not in Canada right now, I'm in Barcelona. Well I'm in Spain for a week or so doing some research and following some of my dad's footsteps in this crazy quest. Yes it is going well; it's interesting. I was hoping that if you had holidays you might like to join me for a little road trip in Spain but I just got the postcard message that you don't have any time off.

Man, it's so great to hear your voice too, even though it's breaking up a bit. Listen, I'm a little under the weather right now, nothing serious, but I can't talk long. I was wondering if you could see yourself spending some time with me in July. If you could just think about it and let me know. Here in Europe would work but I'm flexible. Brazil or Canada or even somewhere else; don't worry about the money. I came into a bit when Dad died. Okay think about it. Could you hear all that? Good. And Lydia, it's my turn to write. *Hasta pronto.* Oh right, *áte mais tarde.*"

David paid for his two calls and then hurried the few blocks back to his room; he was moving to a crest of a wave again and felt like heaving. Following the doctor's orders he rested through the Easter weekend and read. He didn't feel like his own resurrection occurred until Sunday afternoon. But on the productive side, he had been able to read Des's details in the journal and also get more context of the civil war by skimming parts from Hugh Thomas's 800-plus page tome, *The Spanish Civil War.*

He learned that by June 1937, the Nationalists under Franco were in a stalemate with Republican forces around Madrid. However they were pushing the Republicans back in a northeast line from Madrid to Zaragoza. This was the Aragon Front. Des had spent time briefly among the training troops of the Mackenzie-Papineau Battalion near Valencia and then visited Madrid for a few days in the summer of 1937 as part of his cover. In the fall of 1937 he was embedded with the Canadians along the Aragon Front near Zaragoza. David had read about this time in Des's diary and pieced together this phase of his father's next six months in Spain.

Americans and Canadians recently had been fighting at the Battle of Brunete, southwest of Madrid, desperately holding the Nationalists at bay. Des and Margareta had seen some veterans of that battle recovering in Albacete. They were emaciated, eyes running with puss, suffering from dysentery, and so shell-shocked that they didn't want to talk.

The Abraham Lincolns had gone into battle at Brunete with 2,500 men and came out with only 600 fit to fight. Des wasn't sure if Madrid had fallen or was still fending off Franco but he had received a coded message from Frank Zaneth to go there and meet with *Toronto Daily Star* writer, Frederick Griffin. Griffin was a left-leaning correspondent; had written sympathetic dispatches on the Regina Riot in 1935 and a book about the Soviet Union in 1932, entitled *Soviet Scene, A Newspaperman's Close-ups of New Russia.*

Before leaving Canada, Zaneth had discussed briefly with Des about the possibility of getting Griffin to supply information against Canadian Communists while Des was in Spain. Zaneth had sent a coded letter from 'Harry Blask' to Barry Desmond and it sounded like a fruit salad recipe: *2 grape figs 'n 4 floral in da 2 mango dried.* It meant, two letters of grape and fig or 'grfin', and four letters of floral so 'florinda', and two of mango so 'madried'. Reading between the lines, Des understood he was supposed to see Griffin at the Hotel Florida in Madrid. It wasn't brilliant code but Des and Zaneth had discussed the method before he left.

Madrid was a mess; Franco had been bombing it relentlessly from the north and west. Rubble and ruins, broken glass everywhere, even on the main thoroughfare, Gran Via. But the élan of the city's defenders' was high and infectious; for instance, the workers were proud that the post office had no windows left but was still open. The Hotel Florida was less than twenty blocks from the front line and was bombarded at least once a day. The place was the preferred residence of many literary giants too.

David read that Des met Fred Griffin, a jaunty Irishman, in the battered Hotel Florida bar. When Fred pointed out and said hello to up-and-coming photojournalist Robert Capa, as well as authors John Dos Passos, Martha Gellhorn and Ernest Hemingway, Des was agog.

...*In fact Hemingway shook my hand, noticed I was a bit bedraggled from my stint at Albacete and offered me the use of his shower to clean up later and invited me to rendezvous at the bar.*

"Right then, let's be off to the Telefónica, I have to file a story," Griffin said. "Maybe Papa can autograph that hand later, the one that you probably won't wash," and both men laughed.

We walked quickly, hugging the walls and stepping into doorways from time to time as a precaution. The Telefónica was a few blocks away and the tallest building in Madrid so, in effect, a lightning rod for Franco's artillery. After filing the story we went to the nearby Hotel Gran Via and its basement grill for lunch...

..."So you must be a cub reporter if you've never been fired by Harry Hindmarsh. Hell, he fired Morley Callaghan five times and fought with Hemingway. You better say you've been fired at least once if you want to sidle up to Papa. So what do you need with me?"

"Well Mr. Griffin;"

"Fred, for Chrissakes."

"Right, well Fred, I've been collecting notes on the civil war from the Canadian side's point of view in Barcelona and Albacete. Mr. Hindmarsh wanted me to feed you some of my research on the new Mackenzie-Papineau Battalion and also on an orphanage in Barcelona supported by the Canadian Committee to Aid Spanish Democracy."

Griffin looked over Des's head and recalled, "That committee is headed by Salem Bland, I believe. He's anti-war. I've seen him around the *Star* office sometimes. Not my cup of tea really. I'm not too interested in Bland writing. Listen, I'm heading back to Canada, today actually; why doesn't the great Harry Hindmarsh get you to write those pieces?"

"Hmmm, maybe because I'm a cub?"

"Well you gotta cut your teeth sometime, young fella."

"There's something else, Mr., uh, Fred. You know about left causes and the working stiffs, right?"

"Ya sure, I suppose I have some credentials. I've travelled throughout the Soviet Union and I've interviewed Premier Gardiner and some Trekkers for the *Star* when I was doing a focus story on Saskatchewan, why?"

"Don't get defensive on me but I gotta ask you something. Do you ever get nervous about Communists in Canada?"

"Ok, boyo, what are you getting at?"

"I stumbled onto something fishy; it seems the Canadian volunteers have had their passports taken in France and some in Canada are worried that passports of dead boys are being used illegally. Have you heard anything like that?"

"No, I haven't and I don't really care. I'm not a Red if that's what you're asking; not that it's any of your business. But I write my stories about people, real people. I try to capture their view of things; it sells papers."

"I'm not talking about writing style or journalistic objectivity exactly."

"Then what, exactly? Seems to me the Communist Party is trying to help make a better world and some in our government behave more like fascists, though they'd never admit it. In my experience, you go after a story from all angles and truth will come out. But some angles are better than others; be personal and give the real deal. Anyway, if you're trying to make a better world, then what are a few dead men's passports?"

"If you knew some of our boys were doing something illegal, you wouldn't feel it'd be your duty to, you know, would you blow the whistle on them?"

"Shite, man, they're all doing something illegal just by being here, according to that jackass King. Look if you think you have a story here, in my opinion, it'll only hurt the volunteers. My advice, drop it. Write your story about the boys training hard and the orphans in Barcelona; raise some money for the poor sods. Anyway, I have to go. But wait. I'm thinking my room at the Florida is paid up for two more nights, why not take it and hand in the key when you go. It'll make Harry happy."

"Harry?"

"Ya, Hindmarsh. Who'd you think I meant? We're saving the paper some expenses. Look, nice meeting you, and go for the good, real people stories. Leave that legal shite for the lawyers and the Mounties."

We shook hands and left the grill; Griffin was probably feeling good about helping a rookie. I was a bit shaken that I almost blew my cover. For a minute I thought he meant Harry Blask and I was close to asking him how he knew Harry. Whew, got to stay focused! I figured there was no way that Griffin would turn in volunteers, Communist, dead, or whatever; so I decided not to invite him to give names away. I guess it's not so easy to turn someone if you haven't got anything on them. I'd try to remember that fact. Anyway I picked my way carefully back down the Gran Via towards the Hotel Florida.

Griffin's room was one of the darker, shabbier ones at the back of the hotel but safer from bombardments too. It had no bath or shower so I stashed my bag and was attracted to the noise downstairs. The front hotel lobby was gay and festive, writers and journalists swilling beer and wine. Hemingway, who was working now for the *North American Newspaper Alliance*, was at the centre of a group and holding forth about both Republican and Nationalist war strategies. Martha Gellhorn, a war correspondent for *Colliers*, long light brown hair in a bandana, cigarette in hand, looked at Hemingway affectionately and with mild amusement. Just then Hemingway noticed me in the lobby and called me over.

"Hey, Barry. Come on over and have a drink. What'll you have?"

I took a glass of sangria and Hemingway, looking at me more closely, noticed the bruise on my face. "Did Griff smack you?"

I smiled abashedly, "No, I was on the losing end of a punch the other day."

"Well hell, all you need is a lesson or two. C'mon, clear out boys. Barry, take your shirt off and spar with me a bit. I'll show you how to avoid a punch. "

I had heard that Hemingway liked to prove individual courage but this seemed bizarre. He began with open handed slaps to the side of my head.

"You have to weave and bob, Barry. Get your hands up and your elbows in."

I began to shuffle around, trying not to think of the absurdity of boxing with the great American author in a bar in Madrid.

"Keep your hands up so I can't slip a punch inside. That's it, keep parrying my punch. But you gotta punch back too."

Suddenly he slipped a jab between my hands and caught me on the nose. My eyes watered and I fell backwards on my ass, blood dripping onto my lap.

"Sorry Barry, sometimes that feeling that I gotta win takes over. No hard feelings?"

I heard a woman's voice say, "Jesus, Ernest, isn't there enough blood out on the streets; you don't have to shed it in here!" Martha was angry with him and her eyes flashed.

"Here, kid, take my key and use my shower to clean up."

Hemingway had a suite at the front of the hotel of course, more dangerous because of the shelling. After showering and changing my clothes, I looked around the room. On the bureau was a hard copy of *A Farewell To Arms*. Just as I picked it up to look at, Hemingway came into the room.

"Sorry again for the jab, Barry. Now you look like you've gone ten rounds." And he laughed heartily. Seeing me with the book, he said, "I'm just working on the proofs for my newest book, *To Have And Have Not*, due out in October. But you're welcome to have that book if you want."

"Oh geez, that's generous, thank you."

"So you must be a volunteer; who are you with, the Abraham Lincolns or the Mac-Paps?"

"Neither really. I'm working for the *Toronto Star* and they asked me to contact Fred Griffin for an article idea. I'm just a researcher and scheduled up to the Aragon Front next. Sorry if you thought I was a fighter, or even a boxer. I would like to be a writer though. I read your book, *The Sun Also Rises*. It was fantastic."

"Did you ever meet Morley Callaghan at *the Star*? He and I used to box in Paris; the kid decked me once, could never forgive him; helluva writer though. Get that sonofabitch Hindmarsh to let you write; and don't be afraid of getting fired. He's fired us all, lots of times."

"Thanks for the advice Mr. Hemingway."

"Call me Papa. And let me inscribe that book for you. You got spunk kid, but keep your hands up."

Back downstairs at the bar, I saw a woman I thought I had seen before. Her accent, Australian I thought, and her self-reliance attracted me.

"Pardon me for interrupting. Did I see you in Albacete recently?"

"Could have, mate, if you'd been there too. I'm Aileen Palmer; and your Tony Canzoneri right?"

"Uh? Oh, you saw me and Mr. Hemingway, eh? Nope, I'm not a boxer but I guess you know that. I'm Des, er, Barry Desmond."

"Glad to meet ya, Bare. If you're not a fighter, are you a lover? What're you doing here?"

"I'm researching stories for a Canadian newspaper; what about you?"

"I'm with the British Medical Unit; I was in Albacete helping the wounded from Brunete."

"I saw some of those guys; they were in pretty bad shape. They looked like they had been to the edge of hell and certainly needed taking care of. Are there many like you here?"

"That's a funny question; you mean women, nurses, or Aussies?" She had a forgiving rather than challenging smile and I appreciated that.

"Sorry, that wasn't put very nicely. All three really, I guess."

"There are a few Aussies on both sides but Australia is more anti-communist than pro-republican. I was here travelling with my family last fall and decided to stay. My oldies and sister support The Cause but went back and I volunteered with the BMU."

"Listen, I'd like to keep chatting but I'm starving. Want to have dinner with me? One other thing I wanted to ask; I have a friend here who would like to go to Australia; is that difficult? "

"You seem too nice a bloke to use the old 'I've got a friend' line. Is that how Canadians try to have a naughty? Sure, let's grab a bite. I could bog into some tucker; that'd be great." She had a husky laugh, like Barbara Stanwyck in the movie, *Forbidden.*

We spent an enjoyable few hours, translating slang and getting tipsy on house wine. I thought of getting back at Margareta by trying a fling with Aileen. We were just having fun and I liked her too much to use her like that though. Call it respect; or stupidity, more like.

I left the next day, taking the train back to Barcelona. I had to get Margareta to courier some messages. It was tense between us but she did give me a note from Zaneth, aka Blask, asking how the fruit salad went and also that the lemon-tree bore fruit. I told her that I had met an Australian woman working for the British Medical Unit and that she gave me some information about emigrating. Aileen had said her parents would sponsor someone who was an artist but especially if that person was helping the Republican cause. I suggested that Margareta and I visit one of those Canadian-sponsored orphanages; it might help her credentials with the Aussie patrons. She wasn't sure.

I told Margareta a few days later, "I learned some things about the orphanage. The committee back in Canada has raised $10,000 in one month to help Spanish kids. The founder there, Rev. Salem Bland, said the money comes mainly from Canadian workers and immigrants too, at $5 a month to support one child. That Australian nurse, Aileen, said that these kids are in bad shape and need a lot of help in their *colonias infantiles.* Apparently there are thousands of orphans, kids moved from the front and major cities and they need shelter, clothing, food, medical care, and help from trauma. Some are from Guernica; some have seen their parents executed. It makes me angry and sad at the same time. Some photos could help their situation for fund raising. If you want to get to Australia, Margareta, I suggest we visit the *orfanato.* What do you say?"

"I'm not so good with kids, Barry. Besides why are you helping me? After all, I did leave with Taffy?"

"As Taffy said, I guess you had a right to choose. Anyway I

promised to help you get out of Europe because of helping me, not because of, you know."

"You are sweet." Margareta reached across the table but I withdrew my hand.

"When Aileen was telling me about those kids, I figured your photographs could drum up lots of support. I'm going to do some research so I can pitch a story to my editor at the *Star* and you can give your spiel to help the committee. Let's go tomorrow."

"I suppose; if you're coming too and this Aileen says it will help me emigrate then, I guess I can face it."

We hitched a ride on a supply truck taking milk and other foodstuffs and came to a dusty stop in the courtyard of an 18th century former convent. What ensued there, at least my reactions, totally surprised me. As Aileen would say 'well, stone the crows'.

There were some children standing shyly at the edge of the courtyard. I saw two girls in dresses and aprons, one in espadrilles, the other barefoot, standing on cobblestones and leaning against a low wall in the sun. God help me, they looked like they were standing before a firing squad and I wanted to collect them in my arms and protect them. The parts in their dark hair were so neat and straight; they were so presentable on the outside but their wary faces belied horrors on the inside. Margareta had her camera out and was shooting photos, but I took her by the elbow and we went in search of the head matron.

We found ourselves in a black and white tiled dining room with tall pillars and a wall mural of happy children playing ring-around-the rosy. It was noisy with about forty children eating and sitting, six to a card table that should have held four. There were six ladies, dressed in starched white nurses' outfits and light blue aprons, serving and minding the kids. The din stopped when they saw us, some chairs scraping but wary eyes all looking upon us.

One of the nurses, the head matron, approached us. We introduced ourselves and stated the reasons for our visit. I left Margareta to enquire whether she could stay for a few days to take photos and that the committee could use the pictures to help raise funds. The head seemed to think it was a great idea. I offered $100 to offset Margareta's room and board, and then excused myself while the matron showed Margareta around.

Back outside in the glaring sun, I shaded my eyes looking for the girls. They weren't there but two young lads were standing by the supply truck. They may have been six or seven years old; the shorter one was barefoot, wearing a long sleeve white shirt that was too big, and short pants that went down below his knees. His hair was tousled like he just got out of bed. The taller boy had a shapeless suit jacket and trousers with huge knee patches and was wearing the ubiquitous espadrilles. His shirttail was knotted at the front to offset its oversize and both boys had ropes to hitch their trousers up. There they were standing with their hands in their pockets, staring; the tall one with a hesitant smile, the short one just looking, accusatory and judging. It struck me like a spear and left a pang, "What have we adults done to the children?"

All of a sudden I was overcome with emotion. I went to the low wall, slumped to a sitting position, knees up, elbows on them and buried my head into my hands. Such sobs. It was like sorrow being pumped out of my depths. I couldn't stop; my body heaved, my crying was guttural. I cried for the orphans who saw parents shot, who had bombs rain on them; I cried for my lost childhood too, banished from home. I cried because Margareta didn't choose me. I was a blubbering mess in the courtyard. Then I felt a gentle hand on my shoulder. I tried to wipe snot and tears from my face as I looked up into the matron's kind face.

"Are you feeling alright; can I help you?"

I sniveled, choked and croaked in a voice that I didn't recognize, "Uh, uh, no thanks. I think I'm fine now. Don't know what happened but thank you; and especially thank you for taking care of the kids. They break my heart."

"They do us too; and it makes them more precious. I have come to tell you that your friend asked if you could come back in three days for her."

"Yes, of course." And I sniffed.

"There is another supply truck coming then. We've been very

fortunate this month." She put her hand on my arm, "And thank you for your donation. The driver is ready to go now."

September/October, 1937
Fuentes de Ebro

The Ebro River zigzagged southeast from Zaragoza through harsh brown landscape, cut with ravine *barrancas* and interspersed with stream bed *arroyos*. The two opposing sides were digging in along a front, Fuentes de Ebro and Quinto forming one arm along the river valley and back southwest to Belchite along the main road. The Nationalists had fortified towns in anticipation of a Republican push.

The Republicans didn't disappoint, planning a two-pronged attack up the valley and over the mountains to try a pincer on Zaragoza. It was another example in war that "the best laid plans of mice and men oft go astray". It was punch and counter-punch for two weeks around Belchite until there was a standoff; then another attack at Fuentes until the Republicans spent themselves. It was a recipe for disaster and my list of dead Canadian volunteers was growing. The war was beginning to curdle my blood.

Margareta and I had hitched a ride to the front and arrived at Belchite towards the end of the first week of September when that part of the fighting was waning. The Mac-Paps were being used to support attacks and replenish the ranks in the line. I recognized some of the guys from the earlier battle at Brunete but no one felt like talking to a reporter before a battle.

One night we found ourselves in an olive grove, cut with gullies, the ground hard and rocky. Suddenly there was a downpour and although we were under tarps, the *arroyo* flooded and took supplies off in a rush of water, dinner plates, ammunition boxes, shoes. Some of the guys started singing "Every Time It Rains, It Rains Pennies From Heaven". During the day, like dogs fighting over a bone, the guns growled endlessly around Belchite. Buildings were in ruins, sides missing and showing empty rooms like a child's doll house. The church was pockmarked from shelling and the tower stood out erect, like a middle finger saying "Fuck you" to both sides.

Casualties mounted. I knew Aileen was helping here and we happened upon her at a makeshift hospital near the town. She told me that Paddie O'Neill, a former Trekker under her care, had died from wounds that morning. I introduced Margareta and left them to exchange information, my end of the bargain done. The scene outside the tent flap was bedlam. Another shelling of the town was underway and the bursts of orange and yellow reminded me of autumn colours back home, except that, instead of the sweet earthiness and savoury marjoram scent of fallen leaves, wafts of pungent cordite pinched my nose.

There was some talk going around about six guys who had run from the fighting by stealing the only Mac-Pap ambulance. They were stopped while heading for the French border and were before a commissar tribunal now. Our men, all volunteers of course, were discussing in their down time the ethical dilemma, whether they should be held to the same soldierly rules or whether they could 'unvolunteer'? Some wanted to execute the six as deserters but most were of the sentiment that the Mac-Paps should just keep the 'meat wagon' that the six had stolen and let the twits split. The commissars didn't think it was that simple though. Maybe they were worried about keeping morale up and the men on the straight and narrow politically. Or maybe they reasoned that by taking an ambulance the lives of other wounded volunteers could have been jeopardized. Anyway the incident got up the men's noses and no decision was going to be a good one.

There was a lot of commotion suddenly; trucks in muddy ruts were moving men north for a planned push. They were being transferred about 10 miles to Quinto for the run at Fuentes and we managed to squeeze in among 40 men and gear. The Fascists held high ground, and the Republicans, to get at Fuentes, had to crawl along a communication trench through flat ground overlooked by enemy machine guns. An *arroyo* surrounded Fuentes like a castle moat. We were settling in, waiting for orders to get to the gully when impulsively Margareta wanted to get some pictures closer to the action.

I had been trying to interview men as they moved to the rear and wasn't too happy about getting nearer to what these men faced because of her impulsivity. These guys looked horrible, bloodshot eyes, suffering from lice and dysentery, more like remnants of a medieval army camp.

While Margareta and I were arguing, Taffy showed up.

"Well hello you two, are you here for the show?" His teeth smiled white against a grimy face.

"Margareta wants to get some action pictures. I said it was too dangerous; maybe you can talk some sense into her."

"Why not come with me? We're scheduled to move up and I hear some Russian tanks are going to help us up to the *arroyo.*"

I couldn't believe what I was hearing. "Use your blinkers you two. Isn't the sight of the men who've been in action enough for you Margareta?"

"C'mon kitten, put on this backpack and wear this helmet. Barry, you can do the same unless you wanna be a crumb."

I gave in. "Oh shit, Margareta, this is nuts. Put mud on your helmet then. The guys said they do that so the glare doesn't give 'em away to snipers."

"He's right and the backpack saves your pretty ass when you're crawlin' in those trenches."

I challenged him. "Why are you wearing only that beret then, Taffy?"

"Cuz I'm lucky, remember?"

We crawled along a shallow, rocky trench to our side of the *arroyo* ridge. My hands and knees were bloodied from my traversing like a crocodile. Then we huddled for what seemed like hours in the hot sun. My tongue was thick and Taffy offered me some water with a smile, warning me to keep low. I was sure if some commissar found out a reporter and a photographer were there, we were going to get sent back to Barcelona, if we survived.

Even I could tell that our artillery and airplane bombings were ineffective. The Nationalists still kept raking us with occasional machine gun bursts. Finally we heard the engines of our tanks as they screeched and clanked, about fifty of them. They stopped behind our trench and delivered an ear-bursting salvo before charging over the trench toward the town. I swear Margareta was smiling as she saw a tank demolish a part of our trench and crush two soldiers, all the while photographing. Taffy shouted for us to get ready. Beside me, and I didn't even see it happen, a young Spanish boy was clutching his blood-soaked stomach and moaning, "*Madre mia, madre mia.*"

Just as Taffy stood up to run, he stopped erect, something smacking his beret off; he threw out his arms as if on a cross; and flew back into the trench, flinging his rifle aside. Bits of goo struck my face as I was gripping Margareta's waist to hold her down.

"I got it, I got it." She sounded strangely jubilant somehow.

"You got hit? Where?"

"No, I got it- the picture; that was perfect action!"

"Jesus fuck, are you crazy; that was Taffy for chrissakes!" I was shouting in her ear and holding her down.

Had the world gone mad? Men going over the top were being cut down in droves. Tanks were burning. There I was holding a slender woman's body and she was exulting in death around her like Medea, taking photos. To my left I saw Commissar Joseph Dallet, as if on a hike with his pipe and walking stick, encouraging the men, until bullets thwacked into his flesh. Men caught out in the dry *arroyo* scrabbled in the hard earth with their dinner plates, whimpering and trying to go to ground and find a semblance of safety. Finally evening fell and we were able to scurry from the action like rats in a runnel.

"What the hell, Margareta, are you possessed or something?" We were back at the collection area, with blankets wrapped around us and sipping something like coffee. Her camera lens had been shot and she was more worried about her film than her person, or anyone else for that matter. "Didn't you care that Taffy was killed?"

"Yes I suppose, but we were all just doing what we wanted to do, what we had to do. Even you got your names." She was petulant.

"I don't get you."

"Oh, you are such a naïf. Just because you had me in bed doesn't

133

allow you to GET ME, you know. C'mon, let's go back to Barcelona and the studio and just do our jobs."

December, 1937.

The wind from the mountains blew cold as the year was ending. I was sitting alone in the Els Quatres Gats drinking a cava to celebrate my 20th birthday. Some celebration! I was mulling over the last few days. Margareta had returned to Poland to get her papers in order. Her plan was to move to London and start the immigration process to Australia. The day before she left, I had stolen something from her that I wasn't proud of, but not contrite either.

While she was packing upstairs, I was browsing in her studio and saw some photos hanging along with the proofs. I particularly noticed the one of Taffy being shot and decided to take it and the proof. I was damned if she was going to use Taffy the way she used me to get ahead. It was better for Taffy to give back to the many rather than the one, I reasoned. I tucked them in my satchel and left without saying goodbye.

There was a group drinking and discussing art at the bar. Unexpectedly, I noticed Robert Capa among them, showing some photos and making points about photography as art.

"If your pictures aren't good enough, it means you weren't close enough," he was explaining to some local artists.

"Robert!" I interrupted. "What are you doing here; I thought you were in Madrid."

"Hey, it's Barry the Boxer. I'm just in Barcelona picking up some supplies before shipping out to Belchite. The Nationalists are there in force again and are about to bust through. That's where the action's going to be, Barry. That's where you want to be if you want to get a story."

He left the group to join me at a table.

"Ya right. I tried a story like Griffin suggested but my boss turned it down. It was about an orphanage. The editor called it too soft, wanted more brutal life. Said even if he used it, I wouldn't get a byline anyway."

"You've got to keep trying Barry. If I quit after my first rejection, I'd never get anything sold."

"Ah it doesn't matter." Then I had an idea. "Rob, how close to the action do you have to be to get a good picture? Would the point between life and death be close enough?"

"Hell that would be perfect."

I reached into my satchel and slid the photo of a falling Taffy across the table. "Would this be art then?"

"Wow, that's great; all the big magazines would pay a lotta dough for this shot."

"You can have it, on one condition."

The next day, Capa and I drove in his car to the *orfanato*. When he handed the head matron $1,000, I gave him the picture. "Merry Christmas, ma'am, or sister," I said, and we left...

David was still exhausted, mostly from the food poisoning and also from reading of his father's experiences. But he felt stronger on Monday so decided it was time to rent a car and leave Barcelona on Tuesday. Choosing a red Seat *Ibiza*, he exited the urban cluster for the countryside.

David's plan was to take a meandering route away from the Mediterranean Sea, a slow 400 kilometres drive inland and he was happy to take his time over a few days. It more or less followed, in reverse, Franco's plan of 1938. In that offensive, the Generalissimo, using forces that outnumbered his enemy five to one, wanted to split the Republicans' north and south armies with a wedge down the Ebro River that would take him to the sea. On the front seat David had his maps, Des's journal, and a picnic lunch, simple fare to be on the safe side, some cheese, bread, water and a banana.

There was some prettiness on this road trip, spring wildflowers, Romanesque churches and even a romantic view of a peasant cultivating his vineyard with a burro. But mostly it was dramatic or forbidding; such as the dry Montserrat range near El Bruc, looking like knobbly arthritic fingers reaching up from the earth. After 200 kilometres that first day he reached the town of Móra d'Ebre and decided to stop. It clung to the river side and had a graceful, arched bridge. But the ruined castle fortress, still exhibiting shell holes from its use as a defense in the Retreats, brooded above the main village.

David had purchased some of that flimsy blue airmail writing paper and an envelope, and now sat in the hotel bar with a club soda ready to write a longer letter to Lydia:

Dear Lydia, I'm following the route of the Retreats of 1938 in the Spanish Civil War, in reverse. As I wrote you earlier, my father left me a challenge posthumously and I took him up on it. I have some money and his journals as an entrée into his life in hopes that I would come to understand him some. And you know, I think it's working.

I've learned that he was hoodwinked into joining the RCMP and recruited to be a spy of sorts. I visited Regina where his journals started in a riot in 1935. Next Dad had to spy on volunteers who went to Spain to fight Franco and fascism. It seems that under these circumstances, he suffered with the soldiers and was hurt in love, but he also got to meet some incredible people. Ernest Hemingway was one of them! I might even be getting closer to understanding why he was so dismissive of me; a little closer anyway. It's all quite a revelation; I had no idea about this past, of course.

I've sort of cut loose from any former addresses in Canada while I'm doing this travelling autobiography of my father's and my Uncle Peter is my temporary post office. Driving through the countryside here today, I thought how nice it would be to be hiking in the mountains with you; having a picnic, catching up. I would love that.

So why not agree to meet me for a summer holiday; somewhere neither of us have been; somewhere new. At first I thought it could be connected to this thing I'm doing for my Dad's will, like a road trip in Spain. But now I think it would be best if it were just something for you and me. We could meet in Europe, but not Sofia or Berlin please. Like Thomas Wolfe said, "You can't go home again." It could be Rome or Geneva or Salzburg, you name it. One week or one month, your call. I will pay for your flight and we can share after that, if you insist. Please say yes.

And Lydia, I still have affection for you. It's a good place to re-start, don't you think?

Yours, David

He folded the letter and licked the envelope flap, trying to remember the taste of Lydia's lips. But then he gave his head a shake and grinned a self-warning, "Not too fast." However he did let his hopeful excitement induce him to try some Spanish paella for dinner, the rice, chicken and chorizo sounded appetizing; he would pick out the shrimp. Then he retired early to his room to read more about the Retreats.

Whether it was the shellfish-tinged paella or merely a continuing tentacle of food poisoning, David had one relapse left, a fitful sleep of Des-filled delirious dreams.

CHAPTER 10.

A GOOD RETREAT IS BETTER THAN A BAD STAND

Catalonia and Aragon, Spain, April 1938;
Barcelona and Ottawa, April 1985

David suffered dreams of phantasmagorical proportions that night at Móra d'Ebre. When he awoke, he rationalized an explanation for his nighttime delirium; the paella possibly and he had been reading Des's journal so that his recurring feverish dreams were seeded with the horrible ordeals during the Retreats of 1938. In the cool reality of morning though, David still actually felt he was like Jacob who had been wrestling with the angel. It all seemed so realistic as he recalled the nightmare. He sat on the edge of the bed, both it and he were disheveled and the images came back vividly.

It was a grey dark dusk. David was in his running togs with a group of four men crouched over and running. They were brown, dirt-faced, muddy-uniformed; he noticed fingerless-gloved hands grasping dun metallic rifles; and the men were stinky, like the sulphuric foundry smell of a marathoner hitting the wall.

They kept running and the ground went yellow dusty with bullets pocking; they dodged and dipped around endless hills, past town signs they saw in the black river valley, Caspe, Maella, Gandesa and Móra d'Ebre. And still they ran; they were hungry, thirsty, and ducking bombs and bullets from behind and overhead and beside. Finally they slouched behind some boulders, gasping for air and giggling at having escaped a gauntlet, if only for a moment.

David had a chance then to look more closely at his comrades. They introduced themselves, Canadians all. Tom Mallon was a machine-gunner, his shoulder wounded and bleeding badly; Red Walsh was older and out of breath, a commissar, and carrying a satchel; Sam Witczak, tall, lanky, in his late twenties, fumbling with a cigarette he knew he couldn't light; and another guy in a hooded robe, like a monk's cowl. This one stared at David, put his forefinger to his lips, and said he was Barry Desmond.

"What are you dressed like that for?" Tom Mallon grimaced as he asked David.

"I was just out for a run and then all hell started breaking loose." They all giggled some more.

Sam Witczak said, "Somethin' like that happened to me too. I was readin' the *Daily Worker* in Toronto one day and look where it landed me."

This time guffaws.

David was shocked to see his Dad as a young man. David started shivering and the one named Barry Desmond draped a great coat over his, David's, shoulders to keep him warm.

He said to David, "Awful things for guys so young to see, aren't they?"

Sam had a stupid smile on his face as he said "You mean like those women back in Gandesa, throwing themselves on their children when that fucking Messerschmitt Bf 109 strafed them?"

David's Dad answered, "Ya, that and those Spaniards who had no ammo. The idiots ran at the enemy with rocks until they were mowed down."

Red asked, "Did you see that stupid bugger blow his brains out before the fascists got to him?"

Barry Desmond pointed at Tom. "What about Tommy here? He can't run anymore."

Tom grunted, "Leave me a grenade and clear out while you can."

Then Red said to make a litter of their arms and they started to carry Tom but the terrain was torturous and he was yelling in pain. They left him on a ledge over a *barranca* and started running for their lives again. Ratatattat from all around and Franco's men laughing, mocking them with the International Brigade's own motto, "No Pasarán…They shall not pass." They had been running for hours it seemed. They were all breathless and then they heard someone moaning.

It was Tommy on the ground. "Shit, we've run in a circle," Sam said. His eyes were wide and white and he started to grapple at Red's' satchel. "Give me a grenade Red, I'm gonna end this now."

Red pushed him away. There was a thud and Sam hit the ground hard. "Oh God, Oh God, I'm hit. Finish me!" and he started weeping, his face in the dirt. Then there was an explosion and Red clutched his stomach, falling to his knees. Shrapnel had hit him and his guts were exposed.

Barry Desmond tackled David to the ground; his arms over David's shoulders and they were staring at each other. When there was a lull, David's father got up, grabbed Red and him by the arm and led them away from the ridge and down into an *arroyo* that wound away from the maelstrom. The stench was awful; David couldn't tell if it was Red's bowels or if someone had crapped but it was sickening. Red reached up and put a bloody hand on Barry Desmond's face still in the cowl's shadow. "I can't go on Barry. Here, look in the bag. Leave me a grenade and take my pistol. Inside are some passports, six of them; you have to promise me you'll get them to Freddie Rose back in Montreal. He'll know what to do with them. Promise me. Passports, Fred Rose, Montreal, got that?"

"Ya, sure thing, Red." With that Walsh lay back moaning.

His Dad looked at him and said, "Stay right on my tail, David. Follow me." They ran crouching. Next they were peering out from the fortress at Morá d'Ebre, the river inky below them. Barry Desmond cupped his palms over David's cheeks and looked straight into his eyes, forcing him to be calm.

"I'm trying to help you David. I can get you out of here but I can't protect you through life. Now do you see? Life is not a goddam lark; it's filled with suffering. So many of us are much too young to witness what we saw tonight. If you've suffered with me, I'm sorry; but too many kids hurt, way too many. Every kid should get a chance to grow up, David; I need you to grow up."

"But Dad…" Just then Barry Desmond raised the pistol towards David and began to pull the trigger. David yelled, "Dad!" There was a bright light and David's father vanished. He looked behind and saw a Nationalist soldier fall...

With the noisy thud of that sight, David awoke. The recollection was all so vivid.

David's bed looked like it had been in a dormitory fight. His books had been swept off the side table along with the lamp; the sheets were twisted and wrapped around his shoulders; his right shoulder was sore because he had been sleeping with his arm cocked over his head; and worst of all, he was embarrassed. In his sweating delirium he had an accidental bout of diarrhea. Apart from all that, he felt surprisingly well, like a wave had passed. Still, the vision of the wartime episode with his father seemed so real.

First he dealt with the immediate reality though, stripping the bed, throwing the bedclothes and his shorts and tee shirt into the tub. He rinsed everything thoroughly and then showered himself. Apologizing and explaining as best he could to the desk, saying *desculpe* several times, he then tucked into a couple of mugs of coffee and croissants, ravenous. Then he asked the kitchen to pack a lunch, cheese, bread, grapes and a bottle of wine. Settling up, he went to continue his road trip.

The sun was just rising on a cool morning and as it hit the hoar on the castle ruins, the rising vapour looked like smoke from a recent shelling. David involuntarily shivered and drove on.

He decided to stop at some of the places the Mac-Paps retreated to that spring in 1938. Retreat? It was more like a rout. The Republican government already had moved from a threatened Madrid to Valencia, and then in 1938, from a threatened Valencia to Barcelona. For their supporters it was a crumbling and humbling experience; for Des, his father, it was no different, according to the journal entries.

David passed through Gandesa, Maella, and Caspe. He had read about them, experienced the names in his dream and was now visiting in person. Such sweeps of the river, red and yellow soil being plowed, abrupt cliffs and mesas cut with those dreaded *arroyos* and *barrancas*. After driving 150 km to Fuentes d'Ebro along the Ebro River, he stopped to have his lunch in an olive grove. Under the dark green leaves with creamy white clusters of fragrant blossoms, it seemed perfect, idyllic almost. Nature and the countryside, like paint, were trying hard to cover up flaws in the human canvas.

But these were the very places that men screamed, were pierced and crushed; those lovely town squares with white-washed churches were the ones where mothers and children were strafed. His father ran with the other Mac-Paps, fleeing for their lives, making suicidal stands at bridges along that winding river. David's mood remained sombre.

He drove on toward Belchite looking to book a room. There was a guesthouse and restaurant, *Nuestra Señora del* Something, just outside of town, unpretentious and near a gas station. Since David was hoping to be relatively private, it was an acceptable arrangement. He was settled in by mid-afternoon with sufficient time to do what he wanted to do.

Belchite *nuevo*, a rebuilt enclave of roughly 1,500 people, was just west of the actual Belchite *viejo*, the battle site. David had no inclination to drive to the new town. The mainly rural countryside was filled with pink blossomed almond trees and cream blossomed olive groves, soon to be virgin olive oil, a Belchite specialty. But quite frankly, David was sick and tired of Aragon. He parked at the ruins, a Franco legacy; and began walking, taking only his satchel with the vial of ashes, the wine, and Des's journal.

He looked atop a rocky hill and saw the ruins, stark silhouettes standing against the blue sky. The Romans had been here and a medieval knight called Alfonso the Battler, but none were as vicious as those fighting the civil war. David scrambled among the rocks aiming for the landmark rubble of the *Iglesia de San Martin*. The ruins were phantasmal, like a testament to the living dead, a ghost town; and it made David's nightmare more surreal. He decided to sit in one of the arching alcoves of the nave, his back to the eastern wall and feet stretched out in the grass. He pulled out Des's journal and began to re-read the entries that he was sure had caused his dream.

Wednesday, March 9, 1938:

Zaneth had sent a letter addressed to Margareta's studio. I still had a key and checked once or twice a week for instructions. After Teruel fell to the Nationalists, he asked me to go to the Aragon front at Belchite once more, the last time, because he suspected there would be casualties and maybe errant passports to get during a Republican retreat. It's a bitch here. We could hear the crump of bombing getting closer as we moved up the line in the freezing pre-dawn. I was carrying cognac, to ease the cold I told myself, a pistol and my notebook in a carry bag when all of a sudden Billy, the guy behind me, grunted and fell in the trench, dead. The sniper probably had me in his sights but Billy walked into the bullet. Fucking luck...

Friday, March 11, 1938:

...Thought the day was foggy but it was only the dust being thrown up by bullets. Today I was helping carry stretchers at Caspe. My legs and back were killing me, running crouched over and carrying what often amounted to dead weight. Sometimes I felt as big as a barn door and the hairs on my neck bristled expecting to be shot. At least I was helping out and also it gave me a chance to get the names and search for papers of the casualty, I mean the fucking human being, the volunteer, the Canadian I would be happy to have a drink with. What a hell-hole!

Thursday, March 17, 1938:

Caspe fell today. It seems that the Nationalists are breaking through everywhere and turning our flanks. No lucky four-leaf clovers today. Where is St. Patrick to drive those fascist snakes away when you need him?

Wednesday, March 30, 1938:

For three weeks since Belchite we've been making relatively orderly withdrawals down the Ebro River valley. A couple of times we were bunched into trucks to retreat but mostly we have slogged over 95 miles on foot, the line crumbling after Maella and Gandesa. One guy said he was tired of retreating, that he was going to stay behind a boulder at the head of a narrow *barranca*, smoke a few cigarettes, and fight the fascists all by himself. We just left him there.

Monday, April 18, 1938:

Yesterday was Easter but it doesn't look like any resurrection is going to happen here soon. We were outnumbered and fled as best we could, scattered in groups of four or five. One guy in my group was Red Walsh, a commissar now. He was good at scrounging us some food although he nearly got himself shot for it. Do you believe the lines are so mixed up and confused that we actually followed some German soldiers to the Ebro? All the bridges had been destroyed but we managed to cross under cover and made our way to the old castle at Morá d'Ebre. There is a lull here now but rumours abound! One has the Nationalists breaking through further south and reaching the Mediterranean; another says that if Franco moves further against Catalonia, France will intervene. The worst though is that the Communist leader, Marty, is shooting Communist officers who retreated or failed an order. Have the *Rojas* gone completely fucking mad?

Tuesday, April 19, 1938:

If it isn't resurrection, at least it's respite. It seems this Aragon Offensive of the Nationalists has sputtered out. It's gone quiet here. Today I was a stretcher bearer again and as I was helping Walsh to the ambulance, he gave me his satchel with six Canadian passports and made me promise to give it to some Communist politician in Montreal, a Fred Rose. Anyway, right now I'm angry at the world. Zaneth has left me here too long. I feel like an undertaker for him. And everything has gone topsy-turvy. The Republicans have executed volunteers, and now like Cronus, the Communists are eating their own sons. And Franco is no better, bombing civilians and leaving so many children. Agghh, a curse on both their houses. I don't know, I feel like throwing some discord among them somehow; to start getting back in my own way. Remember, they may have me but they don't own me...

David closed the journal. It was now late afternoon. Shafts of sunlight entered the pock-marked ruin and David was caught in one like an actor on a stage. His dad's journal had depressed him. Still he felt this was the time and the place to fulfill the will. Walking out of the church, and among remnants of other war ruins, he searched for some grass, anything that possessed life. Keeping his back to the sun which was now descending to the west beyond the new Belchite, he took a long swig of the wine as a toast to his father and then poured the remainder onto the grass.

"Like you Dad, I turn my back to the light; I will not gaze on the new town Franco wrought; and I pour this wine, like blood, to remember all the blood spilled on this hill and on so much of Spain."

Then fishing in his bag, he took out the mini-urn, the vial of ashes. He cast the dust over the grass and it mingled with the yellow earth and red wine.

"There Dad, this country, and its war, gored you and others like you. Exactly how it affected you, I'm not entirely sure; but it shaped you and was part of you, just as you are now part of it."

David went on to Madrid and visited sites but was ready to return to Barcelona and to leave Spain; just as his Dad had been. Both had had enough. David returned to the same hotel, booked the same room for two nights and arranged to fly back to Ottawa on Sunday, April 14th, two weeks being plenty. He could read more of his Dad's last entries in Spain while sipping *cafecitos* and soaking up some sun in several plazas. That was his plan.

But his father was about to carry out a more complicated plan before leaving Spain and now David read about it in more detail.

First of all, Des went to Margareta's studio to fetch any mail or messages. There was one letter for him from 'Blask', timely even if it was another hokey recipe, called "Cure for Hangovers". It read-two coconuts, two melons, 2 honey tbsp., one mint sprig, one nectarine, one orange, one water. Des quickly deciphered, co-me-ho-m-n-o-w; or 'come home now'. Feeling he was at the end of his assignment anyway, it came as welcome news to Des. Writing an unencoded answer on a post card, "making arrangements now", he went to the brigade branch post office in the city to mail the card, but also to arrange a meeting with one Lucien Tellier, who was working there.

Des had met Lucien Tellier in Albacete after the Battle of Brunete. He was slightly younger than Des, only 19 at the time, but he had experienced a lifetime's worth of shelling, bombing, and machine gun fire. Tellier was shell-shocked, feeling the waste of life and lack of purpose after three-quarters of his troop had become casualties. Des was able to break the ice with him because Lucien was also a Trekker and welcomed the familiar contact. Later, after a relapse on the Aragon Front, Tellier was reassigned, fit for non-combatant duty only, and sent to work in the post office.

Lucien's older brother, also a Trekker, was a Communist and already using a false identity after Regina in 1935. Des was guessing he had convinced Lucien to join the Young Communist League and that Lucien knew Communists in Canada. At least that was what he was betting on. He invited Lucien to join him for a coffee on his break.

Lucien's eyes were constantly shifting, dark bags underneath. He was fidgeting with his spoon and often stirring his *cafecito* to distraction. Des played his card.

"Look Lucien, we both know the Republicans are finished here. You've got to start thinking of yourself and how you're going to survive back home in Montreal."

"I dunno nutteen 'bout dat. I wanna go back home, me; but I got no *papiers* and no *pesetas*."

"Well that may be where we can help each other. You remember Red Walsh right? Just after he was wounded, he gave me two passports and made me promise to get them to some Joe in Montreal, a Communist politician, name of Fred Rose; do you know him?"

"Maybe yes, I dunno, why?"

"The guys who owned these passports may be dead, you see. So if you can get to France, you can use one passport, pass yourself off as," (he gazed at one passport), "Tom Mallon, say, to get back to Montreal. I bet Fred Rose would be happy to get two passports for him or the Soviets to use. I also bet he'd be willing to help you with a job too. What do you say?"

"Maybe, I dunno, why you helpin' me anyway?"

"Because I'm sick of this fucking war as much as you are and I feel badly for what the fascists here and at home did to you. Do you want to go home? Will you do this for me and Red, and for the Party? We'd all be grateful."

Des slid the two passports, one Tom's and one Sam Witczak, in a brown envelope across the table. Lucien looked at it, looked away and then took it.

"Hey Lucien, merci. Et bonne chance, eh."

The next task on his list was equally audacious. He had read that one of the two communist cabinet members in the Republican government, Jésus Hernandez, had just been appointed the Head of War Commissars in the Spanish Republican government. Formerly he was the Minister of Education who was responsible for both propaganda and children's literacy. Des, under the guise of interviewing him for an article in the *Toronto Star*, arranged an appointment.

Hernandez was not a tall man but looked aggressive with short wavy curly hair, wire-rimmed glasses and jutting chin which he had a habit of thrusting outward. Des was a bit obsequious, thanking the minister for seeing him and congratulating him on his new assignment. Hernandez was impatient and circled his finger forward indicating to get on with it.

"I have two connections or angles to my interview, sir. One is to help the literacy program at a nearby orphanage supported by Canadian workers' funds; another is to fulfill a promise made to a commissar with the Canadian Internationals. "

"*Si, si,* go on."

"The one supports the other, as you will see."

"And so you have my attentions, comrade."

"You may or may not know this sir, but the Soviets, through the Canadian Communist Party, have been receiving Canadian passports of deceased volunteers. I have managed to get two of them from a Canadian commissar who was wounded at Morá d'Ebre. I thought you might be interested in having them, for a price, to help with any arrangements you might need after the war. On the streets they say you have Soviet NKVD connections and having the passports might assist you in, shall we say, relocation, if you need it. By the way, how is the war going?"

"I suppose as a *periodista* you need sources anywhere you can get them for your stories. There is so much rumour going around, *sí?*" And he leaned back in his chair. "But you do offer me something practical, *Señor* Desmond, no? What did you mean 'for a price'?"

"Well sir, the money wouldn't be for me but for an orphanage. I will sell the passports to you for $1000 each but first you have to donate the money, in your name if you wish, to the *orfanato*. The publicity would be good, don't you think? Then I will give you the passports."

"How can I trust you? *Más importante*, how can you trust me? I could take the passports now, no?"

"True, if they were not hidden; and I've registered this interview appointment with my newspaper. They will investigate if anything goes wrong," Des bluffed. Hernandez gave a slight shrug of understanding and compliance. Des continued.

"I'm not trying to bleed you sir. Here's the low down. Why don't you go out to the *orfanato* tomorrow with a photographer and *periodista*; take a picture of you handing the $2,000 donation to the head matron there; show the picture afterwards to the bartender at the Els Quatres Gats; and you will get what you want. Two Canadian passports, one Tony Babich and one Bill Keenan, both killed at Belchite."

"It is, *Señor*, how you say, scratching each other's backside?"

"Yes sir, exactly." Des smiled.

And so Des kept two passports himself, one belonging to Steward O'Neill, who everyone knew as Paddy, and one belonging to Jim Wolf of Vancouver who died during the battle for Belchite. He wasn't sure what he would do with them yet but he felt justified that he had kept his promise to Red Walsh and that he had made sure that the sacrifices of some of the Mac-Paps would actually help some of Spain's future citizens.

Afterwards Des made his arrangements to get to Paris then Liverpool where a second class ticket was waiting for him on the Cunard-White Star liner, *Aquitania*, bound for New York. Although not as bad off with wartime trauma as Tellier and other surviving Mac-Paps,

Des was suffering his own neurasthenia and needed time to recover.

David on the other hand was reading the *Montreal Gazette* on his return flight. It seemed that U.S. President Ronald Reagan wanted to request $14 million to aid Nicaragua's rebels, the Contras, who were fighting the elected leftist Sandinista government. Reagan had already imposed a trade embargo against the Latin American country. David thrust the newspaper down onto his lap and looked out the window at a carpet of clouds below. In disbelief he thought, "Christ, it sounds like Spain all over again, fascists, democracy, anti-communism, and embargoes. The Spanish volunteers were fighting for progress, to stop bullies and here we are at it yet again. What a fucking merry-go-round!" He too closed his eyes and needed rest.

It was springtime in Ottawa when David landed. The tulips were blooming; grit-encrusted snow banks were all but gone. However he was not feeling the perennial hope of spring; in fact he felt a certain ennui since his return. Part of it was the letdown after exciting travel; another was the lack of routine that he missed; but mainly he was feeling depressed for his father and those volunteers who seemed to have sacrificed for ideals that amounted to nothing. Furthermore, his mother's coddling didn't help. In fact, it made him impatient. So he took long runs along the canal to ease his tension and to think. When Peter was free mid-week to come over for dinner, David was ready for a more pertinent conversation.

Meg had made a pot roast for the occasion; the aroma in the kitchen was cozy. Peter had brought over a bottle of Chateauneuf du Pape, 1983.

"It's a bit young yet but I thought you might like a change from the Spanish wines. This should go well with that wonderful meat and vegetables, Meg."

"Oh Peter, you're always so thoughtful, thank you."

David said, "Don't open that one Uncle Peter, I recall that Dad had an older one in the closet, a 1976 I think, so it will be perfectly aged, right?"

"Perfect," said Peter and he rubbed his hands. "I'm looking forward to this evening, lots to talk about and no meetings to attend."

"You and that closet, David. You're just like your father," Meg clucked.

"You know Mom, it wasn't that long ago I would have chafed if you said that. But now it's not so bad being compared to Dad."

Margaret and Peter looked at each other with raised eyebrows.

David continued, "He went through a lot over in Spain and he'd just turned 21."

"Sounds like you went through a great deal too. Neither of us knew him then and you've had the benefit of his journals; is his life over there meant to be a secret?" said Peter affably.

"Not exactly a secret but I owe it to him to be discreet somewhat."

"Oh do tell, dear; everyone likes to hear the scoop."

David bristled a bit. "Mom, Dad's life is not some celebrity gossip. Maybe I'm feeling a bit protective, which is odd don't you think?"

Peter said, "I think it's admirable, David. Tell us what you want to, when you want to. In the meantime, I think your mother has something to announce to you."

"Oh Peter, it's no big deal. Oh well, maybe it is. I'm going to do something that your father suggested in his will; I'm going to go to Britain later in May. Peter helped me plan what I wanted to see and he even agreed to accompany me at the start, as my escort of course." She looked up from her plate and flashed Peter a sidelong glance.

"Really, Mom? Hey that's great. Tell me about it."

"I'm going to spend about a week in London. I'm so excited. We've booked tickets to see *Cats* and Agatha Christie's *Mousetrap* at St. Martin's Theatre."

"Remember you'll have to keep the ending a secret, Meg," Peter warned. "I suggested a two week bus tour as well so she gets to see as much as she can. I'll accompany you in London and then leave you to your own devices on the tour."

David asked, "Have you been to the U.K. before, Uncle Peter?"

"Yes, just after the war. I studied law at Edinburgh. I did go down to London by train a few times. I haven't been back in almost 40 years though. Anyway, I thought I might try some golf while your Mom's touring. They have some lovely hotel and golf deals in Sussex."

"So Mom, you're finally going to travel. How long will you be away?"

"Three weeks dear. Peter says I should be able to see Buckingham Palace and St. Paul's and lots more. Plus, I don't want to be away too long since I haven't done this before. Peter suggested three weeks to see if I like being a tourist. Imagine, me being a tourist, at my age. Turning 65, my goodness."

"Oh Mom, you'll do fine as a senior citizen," David teased.

Meg fumbled a bit trying to refill her wine glass and David got it for her. He and Peter still had plenty. She exclaimed, "Well damn, that oven is sure throwing out a lot of heat." She was flushed and her face was a bit puffy. David gave Peter a questioning look.

"Did Des travel in Britain?" Peter asked, taking the attention away from Meg.

"I know he transited through Liverpool but no, nothing yet about spending time there. Just looking ahead in the journals, he spent time in Italy though."

"Journals, journals. I swear you have your nose in those books more than, well you seem to have more time for your dead father than you do for your living mother." Meg's voice got a bit shrill.

David glanced at Peter again and said. "Are you upset about something, Mom?"

"No, no, forget it. It's just that, well, you're the only one around this table that knows about your father in his twenties. I didn't meet him until he was 30, and he never told me much about himself before then. It's like he's taking you away from me." And she began to cry. "Oh excuse me; I don't know what's got into me. You two chat and I'll go freshen up."

After his mother had gone upstairs, David said, "She must be sneaking drinks Uncle Peter; she's only had one glass of wine and look at her."

Peter was concerned too. "I think she is drinking more, David. Often when she calls me she's slurring her words. I just put it down to her going through a rough patch, with your father's death, you travelling and working on the project, and she's now officially a senior. I was hoping the U.K. trip might help. But I don't know."

"Yes, that's good of you to help her get that trip going and to spend some of your time with her."

"Well only some time David. I don't want to give your mother the impression that I'm any more than just a good friend."

David nodded and tightened his lips, almost apologetic. Peter cocked his head and looked at David with querying eyes.

"David, you never have to be ashamed, not with me. I'm here to help, remember."

He took a sip of wine, then asked. "You know Davey, I was wondering. Do you think you might be going to Italy next on your father's journey?"

"It makes sense, Uncle Pete. I did want to give myself a bit of a break, collect myself, but yes. I was thinking of going there in mid-June and then hopefully meet up with Lydia in July. Why?"

"I was wondering, if it wouldn't be an intrusion, if you would allow me to join you for a time in Italy. I suspect you'll find that I enter your father's journal sometime around the Battle of Monte Cassino in 1944. You would be doing me a favour if I might share that part with you; and I may be able to help you too, so you don't have to face it alone. Spain was hard, wasn't it?"

"Yes, it did become difficult although I enjoyed Barcelona. Uncle Pete, if you and I could rendezvous in Italy, that would be great. But what about you and Mom in Britain?"

"The plan was for your Mom to return alone. My ticket and time are open-ended; it was going to depend on golf." Peter half shrugged. "I don't want to plan your itinerary but I could join you in Monte Cassino."

"Yes, I mean, for sure, I would be honoured."

"No Davey, I'm the one who would be honoured. You'd be doing me a huge favour. You see, I really miss Des too." And he put his hand on David's shoulder.

"I see you two are still friends anyway," said Meg returning.

"We're always friends here, Meg."

David said, to change the flow, "Did you know that Dad actually did get published once. In the *Toronto Daily Star*. He cut the article out and it's in the '30s box. There's no byline on it, but I know it's his piece. It was on the orphans caused by the Spanish Civil War and one orphanage in particular."

"How do you know?" Both Meg and Peter asked together.

"Putting two and two together from the journal. The editor said that Dad wouldn't get a byline, no recognition if the paper used it. Anyway, the paper only knew Dad by his cover name and it could've blown that, I suppose."

Meg said, "Your father always had a soft spot for kids. I remember once when you were four, you wandered off with an older boy. It seemed you were gone hours and we were frantic, looking for you high and low. I found you playing two streets over. I was so relieved I just wanted to hug you. You were pleased to be doing something new and on your own and that the nice lady fed you soup. I squeezed you close and then started shaking you, telling you never to do that again. Just then your father came up, told me harshly to stop, and picked you up. He carried you to that lady's door and thanked her for taking care of you and on the way home he scolded me to never shake you again. He was so unfair, I thought, but really he just hated anything bad happening to kids."

"I had never heard that story before, Mom"

"It's not a story, it's true," she replied, picking idly at her beef with her fork. "So I suppose you're going to be off again soon?"

"Actually I'm going to stay a couple of weeks. Thought I'd research Dad's next decade and then make arrangements to go to Italy. Dad was there during the war. Then Uncle Peter and I are going to rendezvous, after you return from Britain."

"Really? So aren't you flying back with me Peter?"

"No Meg, you'll be a seasoned tourist by then." He smiled but Meg pouted.

"Say Mom, why don't you and I take in a couple of movies before you fly; if you can find the time from your packing and prepping?"

"That would be nice dear," she perked up a bit. "I'd really like to see that Robert Redford one, *Out of Africa*. It just won the Oscar for Best Picture, you know."

The rest of the evening proceeded on an even keel. When Meg had gone to bed and Peter had left, David poured the rest of the wine into his goblet. He wanted to re-read the last of the '30s and begin a perusal of the '40s. Des's entries were much briefer for 1938 and 1939, as if he had very little to say after his Spanish assignment, and that style continued into the '40s.

Frank Zaneth was still chasing his theory that the Canadian Communist Party had conspired to recruit and send boys to Spain and wanted to prosecute the bunch of them. Apparently the RCMP brass didn't see the same conspiracy. So they set him a new task of tracking safe blowers and bootleggers and promoted him to the Criminal Investigations Branch in Ottawa in July 1938, where he debriefed Des. He kept Des under his wing, saying that Des was like a son. Maybe he realized that Des was fragile now, and in part it was his fault for sending Des to Spain so inexperienced.

Zaneth still sent Des on anti-communist assignments though. Des travelled to a couple of cities to make notes on the returning volunteers. The biggest one was in Toronto, in February, 1939; an estimated 10,000 gathered to cheer 300 veterans. Rev. Salem Bland had addressed the crowd and Des had written down a line from Bland's speech, "You have done one of the most gallant things done in history". Des added the comment, "What a load of crap!"

In 1940, Zaneth was promoted again, this time Coordinating Officer for the three western provinces and he took Des with him, giving him low key investigations of safe cracking, as if he was trying to ease Des back. Then in 1942, Des relocated again with Zaneth who was placed in charge of the Montreal Sub-Division.

Des was assigned to watch and report on young French-Canadians who hadn't registered yet with the home forces under the National Resources Mobilization Act or NRMA.

Frank Zaneth called Des into his office in the summer of 1943 and said, "Des, you're one of my best-trained men now and I need you to do a job for me. One catch, you report only to me. There's a Commie Polack in Cartier riding who's trying to get elected for this new Labour Progressive Party, which is just a front for the Communist Party. Changing the name doesn't change the leopard's spots, son. I want you to start following this guy and build up a portfolio on him. But he's a shifty bugger, Des, so be careful. His name is Fred Rose."

CHAPTER 11.

WITH HEAVY HEARTS

Ortona, December 1943
Ottawa, May 1985

Meg heard David say goodbye to Peter at the front door but she didn't notice subsequent footsteps on the stairs.

"He must have his nose in those journals again," she said to her face in the mirror. She was sitting at her make-up table, sipping vodka with a slice of lemon in her water glass. "It's true," she thought, "my face is getting a bit puffy. Mind you that crying didn't help."

She wondered what prompted her to tell that episode of shaking young David. Maybe she got caught up in his enthusiasm, but she really was getting a bit tired of David gallivanting after that stupid 'getting to know me' stuff that Des put in the will. She knew that she'd rather he focus on a career or marriage. She'd love a grandchild and David wasn't getting any younger either.

If her revelation of David's childhood was the result of the booze talking, she would have to cut back substantially; but then she smiled at herself, knowing that wouldn't happen. Besides she was only drinking because she wasn't particularly happy and she'd much rather be happy. She read somewhere that alcohol could raise the libido in women. Shit, she would have to be more careful; getting maudlin was one thing, but she didn't want to lose control again with Peter. On the other hand, a couple of drinks wouldn't matter, really.

So far there was nothing sinful, unless one believed that catechism idea that you could sin whether it was thought, word, or deed. Hell's bells, if even thinking about it was a sin, you might as well do it, she giggled to herself. Oh Lord, there would have to be a lot of forgiveness going on for old Meg.

Hah, old. She didn't feel old. She didn't look old either, she observed, just that damn puffiness creeping in. Her big blue eyes were still fetching and she cared enough to keep her hair coloured and coiffed, not like some other dowdy old frumps at the church.

She was already beginning to puzzle over the problem of vodka supply while she was travelling in Britain with Peter. Hmm, Peter, such a gentleman. They were both widowed now. Surely Peter could notice she was flirting with him. Why did he have to go off with David instead of flying back from the U.K. with her?

She put her hands under her breasts and uplifted them. Not too saggy. What man wouldn't want to nuzzle these girls? She giggled again and remembered the first older man, not boy, to fondle her. It was her first real job, personal assistant to that new Member of Parliament, Fred Rose.

She was 23 and had been working for him for about six months; a meticulous fellow in his mid-30s with a sense of humour, his shirt collar and tie up tight under his chin, his fuzzy-topped head and moustache made him look a little like a peach. But he noticed her, treated her well and even tried it on, touching her breasts through her blouse, almost like he was asking a favour. His little moustache tickled her neck when he leaned over her typing but she dared not laugh. She also remembered reading in the paper that he died a year or so ago back in Poland; when she mentioned it to Des, he glared at her and went out for a walk, slamming the door.

Whew! Her head was so ticky-ticky busy; Des would say she was addled. And she felt so tired now. Getting into the middle of the queen-sized bed she let her hands wander to her breast and then her clitoris. Hmm, that felt good and she thought of pleasuring herself. But it was only thought and not deed; Meg fell asleep with her hand on her crotch.

Downstairs, David sighed deeply as he explored the contents of the '40s cedar box more fully. There were the newspaper clippings, mainly of wartime, some by a *Toronto Star* journalist, Greg Clark, with bylines from Ortona, Italy and one about Canadians and Poles breaking through the Hitler Line; a couple on the elections in the Cartier riding in Montreal won by Fred Rose in 1943 and 1945; one on Igor Gouzenko with the white cloth hood over his head looking like a ridiculous Ku Klux Klan member; and one on the jailing of Labour-Progressive Party organizer Sam Carr in 1949. There was one other artifact, it looked like a war ribbon, mauve with bronze swords crossed over a bronze vertical bar and light blue vertical bars at the borders. It was clipped to a dark blue velvet backing with an attached label, *Brązowy Krzyż Zasługi z Mieczami.* He thought *krzyż* was 'cross' in Polish. He would have to ask Uncle Pete about that. There was also a marriage certificate for Margaret Tanner and Desmond Dilman dated October 24, 1947; and a copy of David's May 12th, 1948 birth certificate.

David did some counting on his fingers. "Hmm, so Mom was two months pregnant when she got married."

Altogether they seemed like disparate clues to another eventful decade for Des. David sighed again, getting ready to tackle Des's next segment of recorded life.

David had offered to make dinner the night before Peter and Meg were to fly to England, so they could focus on packing. Also he wanted to cover some arrangements with his uncle about Rome before they left. He had decided on something a bit 'dorm' for his culinary effort, spaghetti Bolognese, a variation on his Mom's recipe which pleased her. The effort worked.

"See Mom, I'm perfectly capable on my own. No need to worry."

Peter asked him how his research had been going and if he was all set for his next phase.

"Yes, thanks again for arranging my flight to Rome. It looks like I'll meet you there in early June. I have some addresses in Ottawa to check and maybe a side trip to Montreal before I go, but I'm good money-wise for that. I'll be leaving Ottawa on Saturday, June 1st, and arriving in Rome on Sunday. Anything you want me to say to the Pope, Mom? "

Meg shushed David and started remonstrating again about feeling badly that she would be leaving on his birthday.

David joked, "Don't worry Mom, it's the best 37th birthday gift you could give me. Just kidding."

Then to Peter he added, "You'll have to call me long distance here with your particulars so I can meet you in Rome. Are you sure you're going to be okay with whatever accommodation I choose for us there?"

"Of course, of course, as long as it isn't slumming. So our itinerary together will include a bit of Rome and then off to Monte Cassino, is that right?"

Meg piped in, "Well I think it's silly you two running off like a couple of school boys and leaving me stranded."

"Mom, it's not school boy stuff; you call it 'male bonding' now. Besides you won't be stranded; you'll be taken care of, like royalty."

"Oh fiddlesticks, you two."

"Mom, is that your antediluvian swearing? You're sounding more and more like a senior."

"Behave, David."

"Speaking of behaving, Mom, are you okay if I ask you a few things about what I've read in Dad's journals."

"I guess so," Meg answered but she seemed wary. "Why?"

"Well you start to show up in Dad's entries, as early as the summer of 1943, did you know that?"

"No I didn't know. All good, I hope."

Peter smiled at her, "Now Meg, why wouldn't it be good?"

She crunched her nose at Peter. David said, flipping through some pages, "Yes, here it is, Tuesday, August 17, 1943. 'Saw a beautiful young lady coming out of Rose's office. Asked Lucien about her; not his dame he said. New personal assistant for Freddie; must follow this one up."

Meg blushed a bit. "Oh that must have been the Member of Parliament, Fred Rose. He set up his office on 30 Beechwood. Poor man, he never got a Parliament Building office at first after winning the by-election on August 9th, so he established one in his apartment. Such fusspots some of those Ottawa people, so prejudiced. You know Mr. Rose could walk around Stornaway and Sussex Drive but those snobs would never accept him living in their neighbourhoods, even as a Member of Parliament. So your father remembered seeing me, eh?"

She fluffed her hair and added, "Funny that your father wrote that; I had coffee with him a few times, nothing serious. We only started dating for real in the summer of 1947."

"Who was Lucien?"

"Must have been Lucien Tellier. He was a young guy, mid-twenties, who did errands for Fred, I mean Mr. Rose, between Ottawa and Montreal, his Cartier riding."

"What did you do at that job, Mom?"

"Oh, odd things: type letters, mail, make phone calls. It was a new political party, the Labour Progressive Party, and Mr. Rose was new in town. A friend of my father's had asked him if he knew anyone that could be a Girl Friday for a new MP."

Peter interrupted. "Meg, wasn't Fred Rose the M.P. who was arrested and jailed for running a Soviet spy ring?"

"Yes, I believe he was. He was arrested in February, 1946 but I had quit that Christmas. My father told me to give my notice because he knew there were shenanigans going on."

"You knew nothing about what Fred Rose was up to?" David asked incredulously.

"No I didn't Davey, and don't speak to me in that tone, please. I was twenty-three when Mr. Rose hired me and I gave my notice when I was twenty-five. I worked hard, did what Mr. Rose asked me to do, didn't snoop or ask questions. After work I volunteered at the church, knitting and filling ditty bags for the troops.

"But a spy ring of maybe twenty people, Mom; didn't you notice?"

"He didn't involve me in any of that. There were some shady characters around sometimes, like Sam Carr. He wrote for their party paper, the *Clarion*, I think. He asked me to do some typing from time to time. Stinky pipe smoker, if I remember correctly. Tried to get fresh sometimes, saying I was much prettier than those women who went into uniform. They were 'unwomanly' he said. He didn't like Rosie the Riveter types or lumberjills either. But after Christmas in 1945, my father got me a job as a Girl Friday for Archbishop Vachon, where I worked until your father and I got married."

"Well you were some looker Mom; Dad noticed you."

"Oh there were boyfriends, dear, although the pickings were slim during the war."

Peter asked, "What was your father's business with Fred Rose, David?"

"It was anti-Communism really. The Labour Progressive Party was just another name for the illegal Communist Party apparently. So Dad's boss, Zaneth, wanted him to tail Fred Rose and company, find out what he could and report back. I think he got Lucien Tellier to spy on Rose from the inside. Dad kind of ran him. Dad knew Tellier from the Spanish Civil War and Unlucky Luke, his nickname, owed Dad a favour."

"Did your father uncover the spy ring then?"

"I don't think so; that was Igor Gouzenko really. But Dad passed on some information to Zaneth who passed it on to Norman Robertson, the Under Secretary of State for External Affairs, something about the passports from Spain."

Meg pushed back her chair. "Well this has been lovely David, but I'm getting tired and still have some packing to do. The pasta was divine, the wine tasty, and the conversation nice. I hope you liked stirring up the memory pot."

"I did, Mom; I thought it was neat to see an entry about you. Good impression you made, Mom, good night."

Peter and David stood as Meg retired, re-filled their glasses with the last of the wine, and moved into the living room.

"Before you ask, my packing is done; and I know there's more you're not telling," Peter began and smiled.

"You're right. For starters, it was Dad who asked Zaneth to find a new job for Mom, that she was in some danger. Zaneth talked to Archbishop Alexandre Vachon who then warned Grampa Tanner, who told Mom to give her notice to Rose and work for the archdiocese."

"So your mother really didn't know what was going on around her."

"Not much has changed, has it?"

"Don't be unkind David. It sounds like your mother didn't go in for whisper campaigns; she just got on with her job."

"You're right, sorry. It seems Dad had some rude awakenings too. At the end of the Spanish debacle, he sold and bartered some passports from dead volunteers that he got when the Republicans were retreating. I think he learned that there are unintended consequences to the best of intentions."

"Yes, that's a hard lesson to learn. Explain please though, I'm fascinated."

David sipped some wine and then began. "When Dad was fleeing with some guys in Spain in 1938, one of them, Red Walsh, a wounded commissar, gave Dad some passports and made him promise to get them to Fred Rose of Montreal who would know what to do with them. Dad fudged the promise a bit. He gave two to Lucien Tellier to help him exit Spain, hence the favour owed; and sold two to a Spanish Communist Party official to donate money to an orphanage. Those were the good intentions. Then complications developed."

"They always have a way of doing that."

"Dad found out from Lucien, who overheard Rose and Sam Carr crowing about it, that one Canadian passport that the Spanish official bought, Tony Babich's, was used to get a false identity for a Spanish Soviet agent. It seems that they were able to renew a passport using Babich's information for someone named Frank Jacson, who was really Jaime Mercador, an NKVD agent. Mercador used his false identity as

Jacson to gain access to Leon Trotsky in Mexico and assassinated him in 1940 with an ice pick. Those two Stalinists, Rose and Carr, were chortling about the deed, according to Tellier. Dad never let on, of course, when Lucien told him but he was pretty devastated in his journal."

"Yes, I see how he would be."

"There's more. Rose went on to say that a passport belonging to a Sam Witczak which he received from Lucien, he sent to the Soviets and it was used to get an agent into the United States. His real name was Litvin and he was lecturing at the University of Southern California; can you believe it? This was in 1942 and the FBI were investigating."

"What did Des do?"

"He passed on the information to Zaneth but not his own involvement. It must have sickened him though because he started badgering Zaneth to let him volunteer for overseas service. He had registered already after the NRMA in 1940, but Zaneth claimed, and convinced Dad, that he was exempt from service because of his security role. But you know Uncle Pete, I think Dad was still feeling the effects of shell shock from Spain, that and the good he thought he did turned to evil; it all worked on him and he itched to do his part, almost like a penance. He felt like a counterfeit, especially when Zaneth congratulated him on his good work. Zaneth was able to pass Dad's intelligence on to External Affairs, which they appreciated, and it probably helped Zaneth's career too, I bet. No wonder he wanted to do something for Dad later."

"But when I met your father in 1944 he wasn't with the 1st Canadian Division fighting; he was doing some 'flunkey job' as he called it, batboy for the Dean of Canadian War Correspondents, he told me."

"I'm just getting to that part in his journals now. Apparently, Zaneth relented eventually to Dad's requests to join up but only on RCMP terms. There was a *Toronto Star* reporter, Greg Clark, a captain from W.W.I, too old for service in WWII, but a brilliant writer and war correspondent. Anyway, Clark was short of stature and in his early fifties, traipsing around Italy with the 1st, so Zaneth suggested to his cronies at the *Star* that Dad become Clark's aide-de-camp. He persuaded Dad that this way he could be with the troops and pick up some writing tips. Dad agreed just to get to Europe, Private Desmond Dilman, no cover required."

"So he wasn't working on assignment for Zaneth then."

"Nope, he was on leave to do his part for King and Country; Zaneth just tried to keep him as safe as possible, that's all."

"Hmm, so did Des say how he ran an insider in Rose's office?"

"Yep, he did describe it actually," and David flipped through some pages. "Here it is.

Wednesday, July 14th, 1943

I was reading the paper on a bench opposite the Montreal LPP office on Esplanade, casing out who went in and out. It was muggy and their office window was plastered with the upcoming election stuff, just like my shirt was glued to my back. There was Fred Rose of course looking dapper in his fedora at a rakish angle; and Sam Carr, wavy ginger hair and goatee, smoking a pipe; some toughs in leather jackets, the idiots, in the heat; and then someone I recognized. Lucien Tellier...

... I kept sipping a coffee and eating a bagel and cream cheese while browsing the sports section yet again until Lucien came out shortly after, looking at a piece of paper and obviously on an errand. I folded the newspaper and followed him up to St. Viateur, where he entered a bakery. It was busy and noisy and hot from the open oven, but aromatic. I grabbed him by the arm and steered him to a street side table, ordering each of us a coffee. He looked nervous and tried to pull from my grip but relaxed when he recognized me; we chatted up old times and I asked how he was making out job-wise.

Okay he said, not much pay and running errands for the Jew-boys, but okay. He said they use the French-Canadians like lackeys in spite of all their talk of workers of the world uniting. He said he had to go with his coffee and bagels order soon but I leveled with him. Told him he owed me since I got him out of Spain and obviously my contact to Rose got him a job. He squirmed at that so I turned up the heat, said that I knew he hadn't registered yet with the NRMA and that he had been roughing up some opponents of the LPP during the campaign.

His eyes widened but I put my hand on his shoulder as he started to get up; forced him back into his seat; and showed him my RCMP badge. He slumped; I had him. Told him I wanted to meet him for coffee every now and again and I wanted him to tell me what Rose, Carr and the commies were up to. He could earn a little extra dough and I wouldn't report him. I helped him carry the coffee and bagels back towards the party office and showed him a brick garden wall along the way. When one loosened brick was just so, I wanted to meet him at the bakery. He nodded that he understood. So Unlucky Luke was mine…

David summed up, "So that was in Montreal and then Dad moved back to Ottawa in August when Rose won the election. That must have been when he spotted Mom."

"Quite the interesting life your father was leading, David. He grew up fast didn't he? He would have been only twenty-five that summer."

"Yes, Uncle Peter, but I can't help thinking it was wearing on him. I mean he was a bit rough on Lucien and all the while pushing Zaneth to let him go overseas. I get the impression Dad was under some strain, maybe even depressed."

"You may be onto something David."

"Oh yes, before I forget." David went to the closet and came back with the military ribbon. "Do you know anything about this or what it means?"

Peter seemed lost in thought for a moment while he held the ribboned medal artifact on blue velvet. "It means Bronze Cross of Merit with Swords; it's a Polish award for deeds of bravery in perilous circumstances. Your father won that at Monte Cassino," and Peter got up, "but I'll tell you that story later. I'm going to have to go; it's getting late."

David got Peter's spring jacket for him and Peter reached into his coat pocket. "And here's another mini-urn for you in Italy; I'm looking forward to an interesting reunion for Des and me and you, on Italian soil." They clasped hands and hugged.

"See you in *Roma, ciao.*"

The next day David saw his mother and uncle off in a cab to the airport and decided to go for a run, of the long slow distance variety. Daffodils and tulips were beginning to bloom along the boulevards; tulip time meant the city would be hosting the 11th Ottawa Marathon soon. One day he would like to train for a marathon, but right now 'Des's dare' seemed to be marathon enough. He ran down Glebe, past Central Park to the path along the Rideau Canal. He crossed over to Colonel By Drive just to sample some of the marathon route, before wending northerly towards Major's Hill Park and Sussex Drive, past 24 Sussex, and past the Governor-General's residence with its busloads of tourists, before turning southeast onto the trails of New Edinburgh Park. He was running with an easy pace, breathing well, but he noticed his legs were tightening as he passed Porter Island, understandable after about 20 km. Finally he turned north onto Beechwood and stopped in front of number 30. He bent over, suddenly spent, a reality check after running the equivalent of a half-marathon.

He thought, "So this was Fred Rose's apartment office; Dad could have been here when he first eyed Mom, or over there leaving a signal for Tellier."

Arms over his head to grab more air into his lungs, David scanned 360 degrees. He wondered, "This feels odd being here, running in a pleasant neighbourhood where a young man first eyed the attractive woman he would marry. It's almost like I expected I'd be caught in a time warp or something. I mean in a way, my life history started here."

The cars whizzing by jolted him from his reverie of historical baggage. Walking back south over the Rideau River to St. Patrick's St., he blew out a cleansing breath and waved for a cab.

A few days later, and David was alone on the weekend. He had just finished a bachelor's dinner of scrambled eggs, beans and a beer and thought of unwinding by watching some sports on television. The Montreal Expos were playing the San Francisco Giants; that could be a possibility. There were none of his favourite hockey teams playing. The Quebec Nordiques had knocked the Montreal Canadians out of the Stanley Cup playoffs early and then lost their next series against the

Philadelphia Flyers. Now the Edmonton Oilers were playing the Flyers in the finals, so maybe catching Gretzky and having another beer would round out his Saturday night. Just then the phone rang.

"It's David speaking. Lydia? Wow, hello. *Boa noite*. Yes, I'm much better, fine actually. It was just a stomach bug for a few days. How have you been keeping? How's work? Tell me about your teaching."

Lydia sounded confident and professional in her rich mezzo-soprano voice but also a bit hesitant.

"Dahveed, it's not so good to take time talking about work especially on the weekend, no? I was hoping you were not out."

"No, I'm in. A middle-aged bore, drinking beer and watching hockey. Canadian eh on both counts."

"How does it go, your venture for your father?"

"It's been pretty amazing really. So much he never told me when he lived; now he's revealing it after he's dead. I know I don't want to be like that, uncommunicative that is. There is so much to tell you about. Do you think we'll be able to have some time together?"

"I am thinking lots about your suggestion that I come travel with you this summer and;"

David interrupted. "Yes, say yes, please, I meant the offer sincerely."

Lydia let out a deep-throated laugh, releasing some of her tension. "That is one thing I wanted to make sure about. I thought you meant it, but almost a month has gone by. So, yes then, I would love to do some travelling with you. That, we can talk about no?"

"Great, where to, how long?"

"Well, I break for two weeks starting Saturday, June 29th and I have to be back at work on Monday, July 15th."

"Hmm, I'll be in Italy in June and could collect you in Rome, if you want? We could spend a few days in Rome then do some sightseeing by car; maybe some hiking, a complete getaway with some physical activity and picnics? How does that sound? Have you been to Rome or anywhere else in Italy?"

"No, I haven't been outside of Brazil since our time in Cuba, *não acredito!* I can't believe it, seven years. But I can't afford so much."

"I was serious, I can pay for it."

"No, it's generous, your offer, but no."

"Ok, you pay for your flight, and I'll arrange the rest, if you agree; or I pay for your flight and we share the rest. You decide."

"Could you buy my flight and we share the rest? It's not so easy to save on a teacher's salary in Brazil."

"Of course, I'll send you a money order for your air ticket with my next letter and make reservations for hotel and car. Do you want two rooms in Rome or a room with two beds? Lydia this is amazing, *Que saudade!*"

"I miss you too, very much. But I don't know about the arrangements; maybe two rooms, or at least two beds, for the start, no?"

"Whatever you're comfortable with. I fly to Rome myself at the first of June and then I'm doing some research and touring with my uncle south of Rome on my venture. But I'll meet you in Rome at the end of June. I'll send you the fare and a letter and any arrangements I can make next week and I'll call you next Friday around seven o'clock. Can you have your flight information by then?"

"Yes I can do that. And perhaps two beds in Rome is fine, ok? *Querido*, sweet Dahveed, ciao. "

"Yes, ciao bella."

David hung up and let out a whoop; and it wasn't because Edmonton had scored.

The next week was a whirlwind. David busied himself with preparations for a longer stay away and arrangements for two separate agendas. Knowing Peter would prefer his creature comforts, he arranged an upscale hotel near Piazza Navona and a 2.0 liter Fiat Argenta for comfort and speed, rationalizing that it was part birthday present for himself and, whether it was spending his inheritance or quest money, it didn't matter. He also booked them into a hotel in Monte Cassino for four nights with a view of the hilltop monastery. But for Lydia and himself, he was more conscious of expense for both their situations which meant humbler digs in Rome's Trastevere neighbourhood and a smaller car like a Fiat Uno. And instead of Tuscany and its touristic expenses, he learned that the region of Abruzzo's Parco Nazionale offered wonderful hiking and a 'far from the madding crowd' experience.

Those necessities out of the way, David also applied himself to Des's journals. By November 1943, Des had shipped out and joined war correspondent, Greg Clark, with the 1st Canadian Division. The troops were rested and up-to-strength with a new division commander, Major-General Chris Vokes, whose assignment, along with British, New Zealand and Indian allies, was to push the Germans back over several river valleys that cut across Italy's Adriatic coast; break the defensive Hitler Line; and eventually help liberate Rome. It was early December when Des met Clark, a diminutive man with a wispy moustache and lovely laugh lines.

...."Why do they call you Tommy, sir?" Des asked Clark who was in hip-waders and sporting a fishing rod. He had just spent a couple of hours in the Sangro River, which the Allies had crossed at the end of November.

"Look at my size, sonny; I'm five foot, two; it's a damn sight better than calling me Elf. They called me Tom Thumb in the Great War. But don't be fooled; I punch above my weight. So, you're my aide, eh? Seems the *Toronto Star* felt I needed an assistant. Am I babysitting you Dilman, or are you babysitting me?"

"I hope you don't see me as an insult, sir. It was the only way to get my boss to okay me enlisting."

"Well let's start by you calling me Greg or Tommy; and I'll call you Des, unless you do something really stupid; then I'll call you asshole."

"My orders, sir, er, Greg were to be your bodyguard against

Germans when you're getting your stories, keep you out of harm's way, assist you with anything connected to your war corresponding, which includes getting you cups of tea when you want them."

"Ha, a real flunkey then. It's true that I've covered some bad spots in this war, the retreat from Dunkirk, the massacre at Dieppe. But let's hope our luck is changing, eh. Where did you get your qualifications for this posting?"

"Saw a lot of shit in Spain sir, I mean Greg, filed a story myself for the *Toronto Star* once, know my way around a camera shoot, and did some stretcher-bearing. I can shoot a gun pretty well too, if I have to."

"Well I do like to get as close to the action as I can without getting in the way. Okay, enough jabbering; let's not be bumblefucks; time to move. Get my gear together and see if you can commandeer a jeep for us, otherwise we'll both be slogging to the next push."

It seemed to be a workable arrangement. Des threw himself into his assignment rather recklessly. He wasn't exactly suicidal but he didn't seem to care what might happen to him. He never flinched about putting himself in harm's way so that Greg could get great stories, such as exposing himself to German fire in order to take unusual photos, assisting sappers to push anti-tank guns into position while Greg interviewed them, or stepping carefully on uncleared paths so Greg had a route to follow to a story or vantage point. He even wrote some rough drafts so Greg could go fishing and 'the dean' would comment on writing style later. They were a good team as they covered the advance of the 1st Canadians over the Moro River and into Ortona.

Yes, over the Moro and into Ortona sounded so straightforward but it was three weeks of hell that didn't help Des's mental state. He helped Clark get a few particular stories that gave *Toronto Star* readers vicarious war experiences, but the price was telling. Des couldn't seem to shake his morose moods. It was a wet and cold December and after crossing the Moro River in early December, the Canadians were facing German crack troops on a slight ridge above a gully before Ortona.

Greg and Des had a nose for some good stories of brave acts as they pushed into Ortona. One occurred on the line's left flank at Casa Berardi where the Royal 22nd Regiment, or Van Doos, held off the Germans and a Canadian captain was awarded the Victoria Cross. Another happened after some intense fighting at the centre of the attack at a village called San Leonardo.

Des tracked down a young guy to interview. His name was Mitch Sterlin, a lieutenant with the Royal Canadian Regiment. He had performed heroically at a villa near the village, now nicknamed Sterlin Castle, because of his efforts to gain a foothold in glutinous mud and to turn the German flank. He was only twenty-two, a science graduate from McGill and Des used his own Montreal familiarity to chat him up.

Des was impressed by this young soldier's serious demeanor in spite of his youthfulness, his helmet tilted up, how the cigarette clung lightly onto his full lower lip, and the tiredness in his voice. But his smile was bright through his grimy face when Des told him about the smell of the bagel bakery on St. Viateur and how the Canadiens were winning it big with 'Rocket' Richard, Elmer Lach and 'Toe' Blake scoring often. Des broke the ice and Sterlin agreed to talk to Greg afterward. Sadly, one week after that interview, they found out that Mitch had been killed in action.

Another story was gleaned at a bombed-out church in Ortona on Christmas Day. The troops had been in close combat with the Germans for five days already, house by house. To avoid the murderous streets and snipers, the Canadians developed a street-fighting tactic called 'mouse-holing', where they blew a hole in the wall, threw in grenades and cleared out a house of Germans, floor by floor. But it was slow, bloody, and tiring. One British reporter that Des was talking to at the church told him about five or six Canadian soldiers who found some old women and a half dozen children huddled in a room of one of those rubbled houses. The Canadians were engaging the Germans from that room, and every time an anti-tank round was fired the kids hugged a soldier's leg out of fear. It conjured up a picture and Des hoped to find one of those soldiers who had the wherewithal and compassion to take care of children in this killing zone.

The Brit pointed out a young guy sitting and laughing with other Seaforth Highlanders at a makeshift dining table in the church nave. The staff had scrounged the essentials for a special Christmas meal for the men to eat in shifts—there were white table cloths, chinaware, beer, wine, roast pork, applesauce, cauliflower, mashed potatoes, gravy, chocolate, oranges, nuts, and cigarettes. Des squatted beside the Seaforth Highlander and introduced himself, asking the young soldier about the episode. It turned out that Eric Sellers, only a year younger than Des, hailed from Vancouver, and he agreed to talk to Clark later. When the meal and the interview in the church were over, Eric was ordered back to the fighting while someone on the church organ played *Silent Night* in the background. It would be Sellers last meal.

The Germans cleared out of Ortona on Dec. 28 and Greg filed a story "Ruined Ortona Behind Canadians' Drive North" with a lead that said, "Dead and debris fill tomb-like streets…." In the now-quiet town, he and Des were sharing a cup of tea under a tarp.

"What's up Des, you're looking pretty sullen. Our boys won, don't you know?"

"I know, Greg. But what did they win? I feel like I just got to know a few lambs before they were sent to slaughter."

"It's pretty hard to remember the cause we're fighting for when you see the mess we're making, isn't it? But you have to keep believing; otherwise, as an old shepherd, you'd want to throw in your crook. You know my oldest boy is fighting too; I can't afford the luxury of thinking it's all a waste."

Des confessed, "When I was back in Montreal, I was tired of watching on the sideline. Quebec wasn't exactly pro-war and my job was pretty much tattling on the dodgers who wouldn't even register for General Service. When the Feds jailed the mayor for publicly opposing conscription, I was glad. I knew guys younger than me were dying and I felt like I wasn't doing my part, even though my boss said I was doing valuable work. I felt I had to do something more positive; it was eating me up. But now after a month of being 'in action', I wonder if those Quebeckers are smarter to want to stay out of it."

"Let me tell you a little about fishing, Des. You can't catch trout with dry trousers; you gotta get wet, get into the stream. If you don't want Hitler, then you gotta fight him. It's that simple. And if the country needs you, you have to put those needs above your own. You may not like it but that's how it is, like salmon swimming upstream to die so others will live."

"I see your point but I can't help feeling bitter. Young soldiers trying to calm children hiding from guns and later those very soldiers dying for it while others at home don't want to do their part. Maybe I'm just a little confused and depressed."

"Want some scotch in that tea?"

"No thanks," but at least Des managed a wan smile. "So what's next Greg?"

"Call it the fatherly side of me, Des, but I want you to take a break from this work. Seems to me the 1st are going to keep butting heads with the krauts up the coast here. My sources tell me the next big story is going to be further west of here, at Monte Cassino. So why don't you go do some 'aide' work there, case it out for me, get us some digs, figure out the lay of the land. Call it pre-story research or just a change of scenery. Take a week or three while I square it with the newspaper and the military and then I'll meet you there. But just reconnaissance, you understand. And Des, remember 'carpe diem' doesn't mean fish of the day. Be safe. There, that's my Polonius to you; look it up, writer-boy."

Neither Greg nor Des could foresee the crucible that Monte Cassino would be.

CHAPTER 12

THOU PARADISE OF EXILES, ITALY!

(Percy B. Shelley)

Monte Cassino, 1944
Rome and Monte Cassino, 1985

David met Peter at Rome's Fiumicino airport and they quickly caught each other up as they taxied to the hotel. David asked how his Mom and Peter's time in England went and Peter's reportage was factual rather than explanatory. Meg was impressed by the topiary entrance and tea at Fortnum and Mason's; she was out of breath shopping along Oxford Street especially at Liberty's with its faux-Tudor architecture and scarf prints; and was agog at Harrods's opulent displays. Peter said their Sloane Square Hotel was perfect and central and he also enjoyed a few days alone on his East Sussex golf holiday, Dale Hill near Royal Tunbridge Wells. However, he got more reticent when David asked further about Meg's behaviour.

Eventually, Peter sighed and said he didn't want to be tattling, but yes Meg's idiosyncrasies flared up a couple of times. Once at the theatre her hand rested on Peter's inner thigh. He removed it, at first just putting it down to girlish exuberance at fulfilling a lifelong dream to be in London; but when she did it again after the intermission he had to remonstrate with her and she sulked. Then, on the eve of their parting before Meg's bus tour, Peter and she were leaving the Rivoli Bar at the Ritz, a goodbye treat from him, when Meg seemed to stumble from the curb and twist her ankle. She clung to Peter's arm and limped to a cab, immediately imploring Peter to give up his golf and accompany her on the tour.

"When I said I wouldn't, she walked unescorted to the elevator with a toss of her head and without a limp. Before the elevator door closed she glowered and said, 'Go do your male bonding, then'. She has to realize I'm a friend and nothing more."

"Oh Uncle Pete, I'm sorry."

"It's not your fault, David, and those were the only two scenes, so to speak. I try to show compassion for what ails her but I'm afraid your mother misinterprets. Sometimes, especially when she's drinking, she sees more than I intend; she confuses compassion for passion, I think."

David shook his head, disappointed in his mother and sympathetic with his uncle. "It's too bad Uncle Peter, and it does make things uncomfortable. Why do you think she's flirting? Did she do that when Dad was alive or do you think it's still part of grieving?"

"Oh I don't know David; we'll get through it though. Oh fantastic, look at this view; I vaguely remember this area," he added with pleasured surprise, looking out the window.

They had been driving along the Tiber River and had just glimpsed *Castel Sant'Angelo* looming on the opposite bank before they turned onto *Corso Vittorio Emanuele II* toward *Piazza Navona*, which some Romans called the centre of the city, even the centre of the world. Their hotel was old world, no elevator and fewer than thirty rooms, albeit with modern amenities, but not outrageously expensive. After checking in, they strolled the couple of narrow blocks that opened up onto the beautiful piazza built on the ruins of Emperor Domitian's ancient stadium. Choosing an outdoor café near the *Fontana dei Quattro Fiumi*, Bernini's baroque work depicting four major rivers of four continents, they sat on chairs with caning - no plastic here.

"What civilized culture to have coffee by, Uncle Peter." David was looking around the open space, ornate fountains and obelisks, ecru Verona umbrellas sprinkled like cocktail stir sticks about the plaza edges amidst mingling promenaders, colourful flower sellers, and portraiture artists; it was both abuzz and leisurely.

"*Na zdrowie*, David, cheers; so all this," he said with a wave of his arm, "we were liberating from the *Fascisti*; it's what we were fighting for in World War II, wasn't it?"

"Cheers, Uncle Peter. And thanks for battling for all of this. I think the Pantheon is near here and the Trivi Fountain too."

"You're right. But one thing your father said to me, remember that beauty's cousin is blemishes. You need ugly to know beauty."

176

"That's pretty deep, were you guys talking about the arts."

"Not just art, life really. Des used to say that it takes suffering and ugliness to appreciate its opposite. You can't have good without evil, or happiness without unhappiness, and he said it seems to be in the same proportion as diamonds are to coal."

"Yes, I could hear him saying that; it's cynical enough. Did you agree with him?"

"Sometimes. This square for instance was the site of an arena built for foot races and athletics and maybe 20,000 spectators watched. But three times as many people would attend the Coliseum, not far away, where they cheered for blood and violence. And just over there, the church to St. Agnes. She was martyred for her Christian beliefs. One legend says she was condemned to be dragged through the streets naked but she miraculously grew hair which conserved her modesty. Her skull is supposed to be preserved in the church, if you want to see."

"No guff? No, I think I'll pass on that. But it does give new meaning to the term 'hair shirt', doesn't it? Or is that 'hirsute'?

Peter smiled, "See, you like to play with words, just like your father. Anything to get a laugh. Seriously though, there is a place I would like to show you tomorrow that might show what Des meant."

The next morning was bright and springtime warm; they enjoyed the walk, Peter tall and elegant in a sports jacket and silk scarf, David with his sweater draped over his shoulders and hands in his pockets. They walked in the direction of the Forum for roughly fifteen minutes, zigzagging until they reached the river near Tiber Island. Peter pointed to the Great Jewish Synagogue of Rome across the street. It was a huge monolithic structure built in 1904 and it dominated the corner.

"This was the entrance to the Jewish Ghetto, David. Come let me show you how beauty and ugliness can mix together."

They passed some turnstiles that impeded easy access, strolled beyond the synagogue entrance and past parked bicycles, and headed toward the squeal of school children playing at recess.

"These planter boxes are actually anti-car bomb barricades. There was a suicide bombing a few years ago, I believe in 1982, that killed one and injured over thirty. There wasn't much about it in the news. But come along, let's walk."

They wandered by the school entrance and the guards, past kosher bakeries and delis. Peter guided David to another street past a music school. A beautiful fountain was trickling in front.

"It's a Bernini work; delicate isn't it? The Turtle Fountain. And just behind here are the ruins of Marcellus' Theatre, circa 13 B.C." Peter led David down a small alleyway.

"But amidst the beautiful art is a plaque, see here. Largo October 16, 1943. The Nazis ordered gold to be collected here or else hostages would be taken. People piled their gold, Jews and Christians alike. The Nazis took the gold and then on October 16th they took the Jews anyway, thousands of them. We didn't get to Rome until almost a year later, until after June, 1944. We were too late to help these Jews. So you see, beauty often has a sullied side; that's what your father meant."

It was late morning and both men were subdued as they packed the car and headed off, taking the ring road out of Rome and the A1 *Autostrada* southeast. For about 100 kilometers the valley motorway followed the Sacco River and the Liri River, with rolling mountains on either side, the Apennine spine of Italy on the left, the Alban Hills and rounded craggy Aurunci Mountains on the right. At the exit to Cassino, the skyline was dominated by an abrupt and aloof tor topped by the monastery abbey, Monte Cassino.

In 1944, the Allies had been pushing the Germans back from Naples up Route 6 but the enemy dug in along the Gustav Line, and a bottleneck formed at Cassino. War correspondents said that fighting here was so fierce that the waters of the Liri ran red that May.

David and Peter checked into their hotel. Cassino was a sprawling town, with a university now. It had been completely rebuilt from rubble within a decade after the war. The newish, family-run hotel provided a balcony view of the abbey sitting serenely on the tallest of several precipitous humps overlooking the town. Looking up, David said, "Jeez,

Uncle Pete, how the hell did you guys take that mountain monastery?"

"It wasn't easy, David, but we had to."

Peter requested time for a nap, so David took his Dad's journal with him to a shaded seat under a courtyard plane tree where he read the entries for that battle in 1944.

Monday, January 31, 1944

I sent a dispatch to Greg telling him not to come to this hell-hole yet. It's cold and wet and it's all jammed up here. Allied troops have come the 50 miles from Naples up Route 6, but are stuck at the Gustav Line defended by the Germans. The remnants of Cassino town are connected to the old fortress abbey by a winding road but there are ravines and goat tracks all over, and the Germans hold all the high ground. The French had tried to move through the mountains to the north of Monastery Hill but were repulsed. Shit, they were North Africans sent into winter conditions with one blanket each. They came back with frostbite, if they came back at all. The Yanks tried attacking up the Liri Valley and around into the town but they were turned back too. The Germans are really dug in with barbed wire, machine gun placements and thousands of land mines. I overheard one Yank say they went into battle with 184 guys and only 17 answered call after two days. He called it mass murder and the rumour is that the Germans have some of the best troops here, the 90th Panzers and 1st Parachutes. Looks like they want to stall the march to Rome, but really, both sides are exhausted...

...I've managed to make a nest for myself about 2 miles southeast of Cassino in a Catholic parish church, *Parrochia San Bartolomeo Apostolo*. It's like a bloody League of Nations here: New Zealand Maoris, Americans, French Algerians and Moroccans, Indian Gurkhas, and Brits. I go for walks in the rain through scrubby gorse sometimes, no fishing though. I play poker sometimes to kill time and won a pair of reading glasses from a British Special Operations bloke. He pulled me aside afterwards and gave me special instructions to go along with my winnings, speaking of killing time. Also I did manage to get a book on works of Shakespeare from an American 1st Lieutenant who wants to be an English teacher after the war. Bob Waugh is his name and he serves a mean cup of coffee. Read *Hamlet*, and boy, that Polonius speech to his son; Shakespeare's not a bad writer. Wrote Greg about it; that should give him a chuckle.

Friday March 3, 1944

Still winter gloom, icy, wet, rivers still swollen. Well the month that celebrates Valentine's Day is over and I swear there is no love left in the world. Don't know if it can get worse. My Yank friend, Bobby, tried to explain it was like Dante's seventh level of the Inferno, the one for tyrants and warmongers he said. I asked what level the soldiers who just follow orders would be in. He hoped it would be the top levels of limbo or purgatory, he said, getting to the mountain to see paradise. I only see one mountain here and it leads to hell, no matter the level.

Got asked some questions about my status here; thank goodness I have my orders with me, so they accepted me as a war correspondent, 'warco' as the Yanks say. Been helping out where I could, loading mortar shells and supplies. They also told me to be careful walking in the gorse. The Jerries had sprinkled land mines all over as they retreated northwards.

It is a war of attrition along here. The French were saying it's like Verdun in WW I; lucky them, they have some historical context. For the rest of us, it's bloody madness. Bobby and the Yanks were moved out after 80 per cent casualties. New troops in the line now. Kiwis mainly. Again they tried the 'right hook' approach over the mountains east and north of the abbey. They actually got to a hill just below the abbey and heard the Germans talking, but that was as close as they could get before counter-attacks. I was helping with a mule-train; do you believe it? Mules with supplies of food and munitions to so-called jump-off points to help out the guys pinned down below the abbey.

The abbey is an imposing walled monastery that St. Benedict started in the 6th century. It was beautiful to behold in the mists or the setting sun. But it's ancient history now, pulverized by American bombers on Feb. 15. I was returning with the mules and heard the guys below cheering. Whether the Germans were occupying the monastery or not is debatable, moot really. They're in there now, in the ruins, and more entrenched than before. Their artillery is deadly from that observation post.

Two days AFTER the bombing, the Kiwis, Brits, and Gurkhas from the 1st Battalion of the Royal Sussex Regiment tried a frontal attack over the river into the town and support from surrounding ridges of the 'right hook', but they lost so many officers, twelve out of fifteen, the Sussex Tommies told me. Another attack utterly failed. The Kiwi commander, Maj.-Gen. Kippenberger, stepped on a land mine today and both feet were blown off. That just about sums up the whole strategy, I'd say.

Wednesday, March 22, 1944

It's been raining for a week again. Continuous noise from our artillery barrage. Some success! The train station has finally been taken but there are German snipers galore in Cassino town. I was talking to some soldiers about how we dealt with snipers in Ortona. Understandably they were pissed; said if I was so brilliant why wasn't I commanding; or why don't the Canucks come on over and show us how to do it. These guys are exhausted, three battles in three months and still in the bottleneck, no further ahead. Let's hope they get a breather; better yet, some reinforcements.

Monday, April 24, 1944

Got a message from Greg saying that he was coming, needed a story on the famous abbey. Heard that no Germans were killed in the American bombing at the end of February, but a couple hundred Italian peasants hiding in the monastery died. Six monks apparently wandered out of the bowels of the crypts. He wondered if I could find a way into the abbey; I laughed out loud at that one. Also heard a different language this past week. Fucking Polish!!! One said to me, "*Dzień dobry* or do I say "goot morn ink"? Is it just me or is the whole goddam world fighting the Jerries? Seems troops have been transferred here in dribs and drabs over the last few weeks, secret bolstering for a new offensive maybe.

Thursday, May 4, 1944

Just back from a sortie of sorts. A few days ago I met this Polish 2nd Lieutenant, Peter Nowak. He's tall and thin with a wispy moustache and has a woebegone, sad look about his eyes. His English is pretty good although his accent is thick. Learned English at Yaggie-something university in Krakow. Anyway, we've been hanging out together in our spare time, chatting, playing chess and drinking that café Americano. The story of the Poles getting here is remarkable, from Siberian prisons to

Iran to North Africa as part of the British Army strategy, and now here. They've recently transferred over from the Ortona area. They do look a bit odd in their four-cornered caps, the *rogatywka*, with the white eagle badge. I call him Rug when he wears that cap. They even have a bear mascot they got in Syria, called Voytek, who helps them lift the seventeen-pound mortar shells.

So a few days ago, Peter was saying he wanted to do some reconnoitering. He understood that I knew some of the mountain paths that led around to the north of the abbey and asked if I would show him some routes that we took with the mules. He said he wanted to give his platoon every chance of succeeding against the Nazis, and of coming out alive.

Off we went at dusk, the 'Rug' following me, both of us with blackened faces, dark woollen turtlenecks, pistols, knives, food and water for a night or two. We worked our way slowly scrabbling around gorse and over rocky outcrops, always moving toward a ravine called Death Valley. It wasn't called that because of our 20-mule team supply line though. There were German bunkers and machine gun nests all over the ridges. Beyond it was Phantom Ridge and a couple of knobby hills, Hill 593 and *Colle d'Onofrio*, over to the left toward the abbey. Peter was especially interested in those. Jesus, it was *molto freddo*, colder than a witch's teat up there.

In the dark, I told Peter to stay in a sangar, one of those excuses for a foxhole, rocks piled up to make a bit of protection. I scouted up ahead for a bit then heard a grunt behind. Crouching and scurrying back like a rat, I saw a *kraut* with his rifle butt raised, ready to crack Peter another one. I lunged at the German, knocking him off balance and onto the rock wall of the sangar. There was some clattering as his helmet hit and his rifle fell away.

Shit, we didn't need any more noise so I jumped on his back and put my hands around his neck tighter and tighter, and squeezed the life out of him. Then just to be sure, I took out my knife and silently slit his throat. I gulped and it felt good to swallow and feel air, knowing that the *kraut* couldn't. My hands were sticky bloody and I wiped them on his uniform as I rolled him aside, seeing his eyes white in the night. I took his papers; you never know what Intelligence can do with the information.

Next I went to Peter. He was out cold and bleeding from a gash over his ear. I waited a bit in silence, expecting the *krauts*, but heard nothing more. Then I wrapped some gauze around Peter's head wound, pulling his 'rug' over it to hide the white. Slinging him over my shoulders, I started down the path.

After what seemed hours, Peter was coming round and groaning so I put him down, gave him some water and rested. Day was breaking and, although we were probably out of danger, to be safe I cut some gorse and put it over us. I thought of sleeping but Peter was woozy and had a headache. I remembered something about not letting someone sleep if you suspected concussion, so I tried to keep him talking.

There were the rumblings of earth-shattering artillery further up the valley where we had been, so I presumed the Germans would stay in their bunkers and not search for us. I asked Peter how a good kid from Yaggie University ended up in a shit-hole like this.

"You know, it would be okay if you left me here to die, Des."

"You're not going to die, you stupid Polack, you just have a big bump; your head's too thick anyway."

"*Tak*, so a lot of good my university is doing, ya? You ask how I got here. It's a long story."

"Perfect, we got all day."

"I was just starting my law practice in Krakow. My wife Anna and I had been married two years when war broke out. Because I was lawyer, my family was picked up by the Soviet NKVD and sent to Siberia camp in 1939, after Nazis and Stalin make pact. Me, Anna, my young son Aleksi, Anna's mother and father whom we were living with, all of us jammed into rail cars in winter. Anna's father died on train on way and his body was just thrown off. We went to gulag. It was hard, me cutting wood long hours in the cold, but we managed. Anna worked in bakery and her mother kept young Aleksi. We built barracks, ate fish soup and bread every day, picked mushrooms and berries in summer. Then in 1941, after the Germans attacked Russia, Stalin declared amnesty for us.

General Anders was given permission to form a Polish army. The Russians crammed us back onto livestock trains, with little food, and hole in the centre of the floor for toilet. Terrible for us, for over 25 days to Krasnovodsk, town in Turkestan on Caspian Sea. My mother-in-law died on that trip and her body too was thrown off the train. Brutal beasts! But me and Anna and Aleksi, who was four and a half, we survived."

"Well that's good then; now we just have to make sure we come out of this alive."

Peter laughed, grimaced and coughed. There were tears forming in his doleful eyes.

"Buck up Rug, are you hurting?"

"Not where you can see. They didn't survive."

"What? Who didn't?"

"My wife and son. There were thousands of us Poles at Krasnovodsk, men who wanted to be soldiers, like me, other civilians, including families, and orphan children too. I joined Anders' army and we trained a bit and were given meagre supplies. I still remember getting British wool uniform though. Aleksi found it too rough when I hugged him. Stalin wanted us to fight in Russia but eventually agreed to send us to British who could train and feed us better. In April, 1942, we soldiers decided to march around the shores of Caspian Sea into Iran and join with British while women and children were put on boats to cross sea. Ships were filthy. Rust-pails, you say?"

"Rust buckets," I corrected.

"*Tak*, just so. Russian ship so dirty and bad no one wanted to touch anything, didn't even want to lie down but stood the whole three-day voyage. We marched hard to meet the ship on time but my Anna and Aleksi weren't on it."

"Whaddaya mean not on it, for chrissakes?"

"Cholera, they got sick fast and died and bodies were thrown into sea."

184

"Oh Christ, Peter, I'm so sorry."

"After that, I train hard, fight hard in Egypt, and now here."

We were quiet for quite a while after that. Then Peter spoke softly.

"I miss them great deal but my Anna said before I march off, 'Always take care of others and yourself. Don't get *wredny, kochanie*; how you say, nasty or mean, sweetheart'. She was so kind and generous. It's not an easy thing she make me promise, ya? So I won't die today, okay? Want me to carry you a ways now?"

I laughed. It was darkening so I threw the gorse off, put his arm around my shoulders and we trudged down the mountain track, brothers- in-arms, with the thundering artillery behind us...

Just then Peter came out to the patio, two cups of coffee with him. He looked refreshed after his nap.

David accepted the thoughtfulness. "Let me guess, café Americanos, right? I was just reading about you and Dad meeting here in May, '44. Going on reconnaissance patrol, and the story of you and your wife and son. I had no idea, Uncle Pete. I'm so sorry."

"That's what your father said too. A long time ago, David, forty years."

"You and he were just coming back from reconnoitering and you had a concussion."

"Oh, it wasn't that bad really although I still have a little scar." Peter showed a white mottle on the hair line above his right ear.

"Will you tell me what happened next?"

"About Monte Cassino? Of course, over coffee. About Anna and my son, later over wine perhaps."

"Deal."

They each sipped their strong brew and then Peter began.

"Your father, um Des, he helped me back along the rocky tracks and across the flooded Rapido River, like a St. Christopher he was. He sat by my cot in the camp hospital and was telling the doc that I should be kept out of the line. I laughed because the doc simply looked at him and said, 'I think you're the one outta line, buddy.' Later I told my Commanding Officer what happened and he said 'We must honor that bloke somehow.' Bloke, ha, that Polish commander was sometimes more British than the Brits. 'Any soldier who saves Polish soldiers should be honored.'

Your father, when he heard about all that, blather he called it, he just slipped away for a day or two. When he came back, I was just about to be discharged and rejoin my platoon. Des said that if I ever needed anything after the big show was over, anything at all, that I could contact him. He wrote down his name and two other contacts in Canada if I ever needed help, and he put it in a big book, Shakespeare, I remember. He said to wear it under my rug to protect my head and maybe some of the English words would sink in too."

"So I guess at some point you needed some help then?"

"Yes, I certainly did. It was a few years after the war though, in 1949, when I decided to immigrate to Canada."

"So what happened to you when you went back into the line?"

"We went back to the gorge, Death Valley, our jump-off point, on the night of May 11th. We were part of that right hook again. So much artillery blasted on the Germans. We took Hill 593, the Germans called it Mount Calvary and it really was a place of crucifixion. For five days it went back and forth. The Germans attacked us so ferociously and then defended like madmen when we counter-attacked. I remember my platoon crawling into a hole looking for coverage and the crater was filled with dead bodies. It didn't matter; we just kept burrowing in deeper, trying to find protection.

But because there were Allied breakthroughs elsewhere, the Germans were in danger of being cut off. On May 17th they just disappeared from the ruins and the next morning we were able to take the abbey. We were exhausted climbing the last bit to the monastery and planting our flag; the victory was bittersweet, so many dead. I tried hard to take care of my platoon but it was very rough. "

"What a horrible experience, Uncle Peter. You and Dad went through a lot of shit. Are the reminders difficult for you?"

"No, I've been anticipating these feelings, but it's good to be here with you. And with Des again." Peter patted a vial of ashes in his pocket.

"Don't you think we should go for dinner soon?"

During the meal, Peter was pensive and David conscious of not prying too much, but between the last of the wine and the arrival of espressos, David did ask, "Can I ask you some things about your family during the war, Uncle Peter?"

"Of course, but you know, I haven't shared any of it really since that time with your father."

"We can stop anytime. How old were you and your family in the war?"

"I was twenty-five when the war started, just finished my law degree that spring. Anna was a year younger, my childhood sweetheart and we got married in February, 1938. Actually, we had to get married and her parents were very kind and generous about it, letting us live with them while I stayed in school, and accepting us and the baby with so much love. For a year and a half we lived a lovely life but then it just collapsed, like so many others, when the Germans attacked and the Soviets arrested us. We were all devastated when Anna's father died on the trip, but her mother, Genia, was very strong for us. She took care of little Aleksi and Anna in the barracks when I was off in the forests cutting timber."

"It must have been very hard trying to be a family and raise a child in the gulag?"

"It may sound odd to you but we were very happy, as happy as we could hope. Anna could sneak some extra flour to our barracks sometimes and Genia would make pancakes. Aleksi squealed with delight when Anna would have flour on her nose. He had such a laugh. We were so proud when he said his first words and learned to walk. He loved berry picking with us. I loved being a father, the way his hand went in mine, so trusting; Anna and me telling him stories of what a busy day we had and what we would do when the war was over. Sure it was hard to keep him calm on the train to the Caspian but we made it an adventure. "

Peter let out a huge sigh." Oh such memories, David. Are you alright with them?"

"Yes I think so, but I don't know if I could be as composed as you."

Peter shrugged, "I may be composed, but only just; I've cried many times for them and for me."

He looked at his watch and said, "*Która godzina?* What time is it?"

It had been an emotional and somewhat cathartic day. They retired for the night, David reading some last entries before turning out the light.

Friday, May 19, 1944

Greg, all five foot, three inches of him, arrived a couple of weeks ago with the Canadian 1st, but we'd been forbidden to write any stories until now. We saw the Polish flag fluttering on the ruins yesterday morning atop a treeless mound of rubble that stretched from the town to the abbey. Greg thought it would be appropriate to 'go to church' this morning so we trudged up the pocked and winding road to the ruins. God, I hope Peter made it; there were so many casualties. I did whisper a hope and a wish, close to a prayer I suppose, under my breath...

...The ruins were appalling, twisted and fragmented. We picked our way past rocks, metal, and blackened tree stumps. One corner of the abbey was semi-intact showing four stories of blasted window frames, looking like gaping cavities and missing teeth. We entered the courtyard, heeding make-shift signs warning of German landmines. We noticed a beheaded statue, presumably of St. Benedict. The monks believed that St. Benedict ascended into heaven from this spot, but the headless statue looked pretty rooted to me. There were some arched cloisters and stairs remaining that led to the shelled dome of the church, but it was too dangerous to wander around.

We looked down the hill onto the Liri Valley and ruined town of

Cassino. I said "What a fucking mess we've wrought here, Greg. It hits home when you realize we've destroyed a part of civilization, even if it was a 6th century monument to cloistered men."

He answered, "Yes, but the road to Rome is open now; keep your eye on the prize, Des. We can't lose our future to history, can we?"

Then Greg told me a story about his own father back in Toronto after World War I. He wanted Greg and his brother to walk the long way home on Howland Avenue, avoiding the view of neighbours who might be looking out their windows. "You see, he was proud of us Des, but we were the only boys to survive the war on our street. He was happy we were alive, but he felt compassion for those neighbours who weren't so lucky. Life's a funny mixture."

Then he added, "Being up here doesn't make me grateful to God at all. You know I forgot the Lord's Prayer at Vimy Ridge, burying my buddies in 1917. But damned if I can't help myself; I still pray for my own son's safety. Yep, life's funny."

The Liri Valley was beautiful, red poppies in fields of new greenish wheat, and orchards with blossoms. But miles up ahead, the ridges are bristling with German soldiers and their deadly defenses again. Intelligence tells us the Germans have dug in about eight miles away at Pontecorvo in a defensive line called the Hitler Line.

Friday, May 26, 1944

What a difference a week makes. My war is over, it only lasted six months. A week ago I was looking for Poles to interview for a story but they had moved out of our sector already. On Sunday, Greg and I were catching a ride north on Route 6 after the mines had been cleared. By Wednesday the Royal Canadian Regiment had taken Pontecorvo, reducing it to a heap of rubble. The German defenders were dazed and surrendered, and one crazy Canuck had even climbed the church tower to ring the bell in celebration. But Greg told me all this from my hospital bed.

I remembered going out pre-dawn on Tuesday with two guys and a water truck. We were going to pump fresh water into the tank from the Liri River so we could cool off our field guns. It seemed safe enough, and a good story too, but we took a wrong turn. We were chatting about pushing to Rome when all of a sudden we must've hit a mine.

Greg told me I was pretty lucky; the front of the truck had been sheared off but all three of us had been thrown clear of the cab. When the dust cleared, Buzz, one of the guys, was bleeding from his leg but managed to pull me to the ditch. The other guy, Stan, got shot in the shoulder and dropped to the road. Buzz managed to duck and zigzag among trees along the road until he reached a Canadian outpost. When it got dark again, a rescue party of infantry came out and found Stan and me. Apparently I was out for 48 hours in a coma, concussed, broken ribs, shattered collarbone, and a collapsed lung which the doc called trauma pneumothorax. Because it could recur, the doc is sending me to the rear for bed rest for a couple of months. When he saw the word, 'warco', on my charts, he said I probably could be more help as a war correspondent back in Canada. Call it a ticket home to raise war funds, I guess.

Greg wished me all the best and was glad I was alive. I asked him if he got an interview with Buzz and Stan and he said yes, he got the story. "Then it was worth it." I said...

At breakfast the next morning, David told Peter about Des's last entries of the war.

"Interesting," said Peter. "He was right of course. The Polish II Corps had moved out. We fought beside the Canadians again at Piedimonte San Germano, breaking the Hitler Line there on May 25th, but Des was injured and wouldn't know."

"Did he ever tell you how the war ended for him?"

"Yes, in his way. He said he was out looking for water and fell into the deep end. He was in over his head unable to tread anymore, so they sent him home. You know how your father could be vague when he wanted to be. But I pressed him and he told me what happened, more or less."

"I don't remember Dad ever having lung or rib problems, do you?"

"No, except to say he couldn't swing a golf club."

"Mmm, or ski or shoot a hockey puck. Maybe that's why he never played with me. I wonder why he never said so? So what do you want to do today? Explore a bit?"

"Sure you drive up that winding road and get us a parking spot before the tour buses arrive."

"Ha, we can be like St. Benedict; let's get closer my Lord to thee."

It was a warm and clear day, the morning mist had burned off and the white fortress-like walls of the behemoth monastery beckoned like a beacon. Peter was relating some information from a brochure he had picked up at the hotel.

"It only took ten years to rebuild the monastery and the town on their original sites. The Allies weren't the only ones to destroy the abbey apparently, but we're up there with the Lombards and Saracens of the Dark Ages. And Nature too; there was an earthquake in 1349. During the last reconstruction they found the original bronze doors and used original plans to redecorate the interior with Byzantine mosaics. Two Germans officers anticipating a possible destruction transported most of the archival manuscripts to the Vatican in October 1943. Hmmm, returning historical manuscripts the same month as taking gold and Jews, fair exchange for civilization?"

He looked up as they entered the parking lot, thoughtfully. "You know, I believe it would've been simpler and cheaper if we had just offered the Germans the money to leave."

The abbey felt surreal, the restored peaceful arched cloisters, the St. Benedict statue with attendants holding him up, the elegant stairs leading to the basilica with its recast bronzed doors. The basilica was opulent in renovated mosaics of gold and blue, and the archway over the stairs down to the crypt was awesome with gold stars in a deep purple and blue sky of tesserae. It was beautiful. However, Peter nudged David that he wanted to get some air. They walked back out to the courtyard balustrade and looked down at the topiary cross sculpted in the Polish cemetery below.

"You guys fought from down there?" It was precipitous and David was agog.

"It was like hell back then. Shall we descend, David?"

Walking along the treed avenue, they entered the solemn stepped Polish cemetery, with red pennants, red votive candles, and rosaries draped over crosses, including General Anders, who was buried there in 1970. Reading epitaphs, David came across a line, '...Mid death, and to their anger stayed true!'

Peter saw it too and said "Well, that was certainly not my sentiment, David. There was a great deal to be angry about, but not to let it drive you. No, the world needs more compassion, not anger. Sow not in anger; that was the torch my Anna passed to me, and even your father believed it sometimes. "

"My Dad?"

"Yes, remember what he said in his will. It's not easy but, in my view, anger will eat you up inside. Love is a gentler motivator, but a motivator nevertheless. Maybe the Beatles had it right in their song, *Love Is All You Need*. Come, this is where I'll say goodbye to Des again."

They walked out of the cemetery and up the avenue of poplars. Then they scrambled up a small earthen bank into the trees. Peter took out a vial of ashes, unstopped it, and poured the contents on the cool dark earth.

"Good bye once more, my best friend. David and me, we're spreading some of you on the ground where you and I met and became brothers. We fought the good fight at this place, and here we are again in hopes for a better future, especially for David."

He pulled out a flask from his breast pocket and took a drink. "It's scotch, Glenlivet, whose motto claims to have 'started it all'. It's appropriate for the occasion, don't you think? And it makes a connection to Scotland where I went after the war and from where your father saved me again." He passed the flask to David who took a generous swig. Then Peter poured the rest onto the ashes.

Peter then said, "Now let's go finish talking about this past, shall we? Let me buy for a picnic and I suggest we eat at the Commonwealth War Cemetery."

CHAPTER 13.

WHEN ONE WAR BEGETS ANOTHER

Monte Cassino and Ortona, June, 1985
Ottawa, 1944-49

Back in Cassino, Peter and David stopped at a *salumeria* for salami, cheese and bread and at an *enoteca* for a bottle of 1984 Ruffino Chianti Classico.

"This wine has just earned an upgraded rating so let's try it. Your Dad and I always had a soft spot for Chianti," Peter explained. Their picnic purchased, they followed the signs directing them to the Commonwealth War Cemetery, where over 4,000 soldiers were buried. It was a trim and uniform final resting place replete with a reflective pool and a black-and-white mosaic deck in geometric designs around it. The breeze was picking up, from the north, from Monastery Hill, so David and Peter sat on the steps in the lee of the cenotaph cross for shelter. The sun was warm, the pool dark and unfathomable, and the reflected tops of the surrounding poplars seemed like bony fingers reaching into the depths.

"You know, Uncle Peter, I don't think I ever heard how or why you came to Canada. You were just always there, my uncle."

"Actually I saw you soon after you were born on a visit to Ottawa. I tried to visit as often as I could but the law courses took a lot of time. You must have been six-ish when I moved from Toronto to Ottawa in 1954. You know, being with you was like getting my Aleksi back."

"Really? I loved having you around and doing fun things. So, I know Dad was back in Canada in June of 1944. What happened to you between then and 1954?"

"Let's see. I took the option in 1945 that the British gave the Poles to go to resettlement camps and take education in the U.K., instead of taking paid passage back to Poland. Then the British managed to insult the free Poles when they were organizing the 1946 Victory Parade in London. All the wartime Allies were represented except the Soviet Union, Yugoslavia and Poland. Almost a quarter million Poles had fought for democracy with the British against the Nazis but we were denied the opportunity to march with them. Why, you ask?

Politics. The British invited the Soviet government in post-war Poland to represent us, but the exile Polish government still in the U.K. complained. The British solution was not to invite any Poles. I remember, in spite of my promise to Anna, being astonished and angry at the British betrayal. It was a final straw for me. It was as if that one shameful act tossed everything that happened to me since 1939 into my face like a cold breaking wave."

"Why didn't you leave Britain then, why stay for a few more years?"

"It's a good question. If I was to do good in the world, I could not live in a country that played so loose with me and my comrades. I know of great spiritual people who keep unkind people around them so they might practice patience, but I wasn't one of their number, I'm afraid. So I used the British benefits while I could and then I left them."

"Used them? How so?"

The British, maybe from guilt, offered the Poles many benefits in 1947 when they passed the Polish Resettlement Act. I arranged to get a stipend to re-qualify my law degree in Edinburgh, always with a view to immigrating to Canada, which I did in 1949. Des was very helpful with references to get me into Osgoode Law School. One of them was Greg Clark."

Peter took a bite of sandwich and a long sip of wine. David let him swallow before asking, "And how did my Dad get that Polish ribbon of honour?"

"Ha, that. Well my Commanding Officer was true to his word. He commended your father for his courage and General Anders himself actually awarded the ribbon, *in absentia*. By that time, Des had been discharged and was back in Canada. He wore it when he met me at my arrival in Montreal and said it was a symbol of our brotherhood."

"And I'm glad you came to Canada, Britain's loss and our gain." They laughed and shared the bottle of wine.

"Did Dad ever call you Rug again?"

"No, he never did. Maybe it reminded him too much of the first man he killed with his bare hands. Or maybe because I never wore my Polish cap again. I'm not sure."

After their picnic, they ambled among the many Commonwealth grave sites and when they bent down to read names, they could peripherally see the abbey, always above their sightline at the top of the stone markers. It was late spring and the individual floral arrangements of red geraniums and yellow roses at each grave, although pretty, were paltry considering what they covered.

Private Umpherville, aged twenty-two, died May 17, 1944, Hastings and Prince Edward Regiment. "Into God's hands," they read.

Private John, aged twenty-one, died May 12, 1944, Royal Canadian Regiment. 'May your sacrifice not have been in vain,' on his grave stone.

Private Forsberg, aged thirty-two, died May 23, 1944, Loyal Edmonton Regiment. On his marker, it read, 'To the world he was just a soldier; to me he was all the world.'

In a sober mood, Peter asked, "So where are you now, Davey, and where are you going?"

"You mean once I get used to how lucky I am to be alive? Hell these guys were young. I suppose I'll return to Rome with you tomorrow. Then I have a bit of time until Lydia arrives. I thought I would visit Ortona, finish the couple of '40s journals I have left, and spread Dad's vial of ashes somewhere. Also I want to check out some arrangements for hiking in the Abruzzo National Park before Lydia arrives at the end of June."

"That's good that you have a plan, and I hope I get to meet Lydia one day. But what I really wondered, if you don't mind talking about it, what are your thoughts and feelings now about your father?"

"Mmm, I have been giving that some thought, you know. I feel as if I've been affected by his journals a lot. Sometimes I even empathize with his depression or post traumatic stress or neurosis or melancholia, I don't know really what to call it. In fact I sometimes get to the point of feeling it myself, more than vicariously I think. I certainly know more about him, but it's like peeling an onion, lots of layers and it can make you cry. There's plenty I don't understand yet about his anger, or mine for that matter; and I have this feeling that, I don't know, that I'm starting to like him but he's going to let me down again."

"That's interesting. Do you think you're anxious because you're not sure about Lydia either? Are the feelings connected?"

"Oh Jesus, Uncle Peter. That's a lot of introspection for me. Are you suggesting I need a therapist rather than a journal?"

"Ha, David, no, not at all. I guess all I'm saying is that it's important to take time to know yourself as well as your Dad. Although, one thing I can tell you with certainty, Des never let me down; he was always my best friend. But maybe I didn't demand so much either."

"Certainly I feel more sympathy for him so far. But I also feel like I'm seeing a mirage and hoping there's an oasis. I'm not sure. And I suppose I feel the same about Lydia. We're taking another chance on each other too, really."

"When the prize is love, always stay hopeful. At least you're taking and making opportunities; it's much better than never knowing, yes?"

"I am hoping, Uncle Peter. Tell me, why didn't you ever remarry, you know, pursue love again?"

"Ha, like your father, you like to turn the table, don't you? You know Des asked me that too. I guess I gave all my love to Anna and Aleksi, then to you and your family. Besides, I think I was cursed."

"Cursed? How so?"

"There's an expression, 'May your first love be your last love'. I suspect it was true in my case. And the next part of my question; where are you going? I don't mean in Italy; I mean with your life. Your father's quest won't last forever."

"Oh ho, a bit of parental concern mixed in with the avuncular, eh? I've been giving that some thought too, but so far it's like wandering in a desert. I know I have to start putting out some feelers for my future, and I'm trusting that the beach at Ortona might help."

"Okay, I've done my duty. By the way, dinner is on me tonight, I insist; and tomorrow a fast ride in the Argenta back to the airport. You have no idea how much I've enjoyed this time with you David."

"And me too, Uncle Peter."

After David dropped Peter off in Rome for his midday flight, he was anxious to go east toward Pescara and the Adriatic coast. He aimed for the A-24, wanting to make time. But navigating through the city before he got on the *autostrada* ramp was fraught with traffic, and tour buses around Tivoli and Hadrian's Villa slowed him again. He was forced to stop halfway to the coast in L'Aquila, the capital city of Abruzzo.

This city was a like a welcoming inn to David. It resonated. Having recovered from an horrific earthquake in 1703 (there were memento plaques on rebuilt buildings everywhere), it also had a historical reputation for being a forward-looking town, often in the thick of European geopolitical intrigues from the 13th to the 19th century. Maybe it was a sense of that ambient radicalism that made David feel at ease here.

He took a room at a hotel across from a Spanish castle and close to the city centre, with its *Duomo* and market. When leaving the hotel for an exploratory walk, David caught sight of a view of the still snow-topped Gran Sasso in the distance, aesthetically framed in a fountain out front, the *Fontana Luminosa*, of two gracefully arched and nubile women holding a jug of overflowing water.

David wandered this city of hills, its steep stairs and winding narrow streets, cloistered walkways, and beautiful churches. His mind went back to Lydia. He tried to picture the two of them here. Could their relationship be rebuilt like this city, with charm and grace?

In the waning golden light, he came upon a church, the Romanesque *Basilica Santa Maria di Collemaggio* on the town's periphery, which housed the mausoleum of Pope Celestine V. David read that Celestine of L'Aquila was both an independent thinker and a forgiving ascetic who became a pope. The atmosphere inside the three naves, with hues of ochre red and white, was breathtakingly airy.

The ambience of the fading earth tones of 15th century frescoes depicting Celestine's life seemed to enfold David. Whatever it was, David felt it matched his frame of mind. The church seemed to welcome, awe, and inspire him all at the same time in some sort of spiritual connection. It was an odd admixture that David put down to a co-mingling of Peter's questions about his future, the next steps of Des's quest, and the anticipation of seeing Lydia again, of life beyond now.

Deciding on an espresso before turning in, David sat at a table near a memorial stone. He read that it was to honour the 19th century homosexual and gay advocate, Karl Heinrich Ulrichs, who was buried in L'Aquila. A line from his eulogy was on the rock, "I will look back with pride that I found the courage to come face to face in battle against the spectre..." Was that what he and his father, even Lydia for that matter, were doing? Fighting ghosts and confronting memories in the shadows? His confidence in the future waned a bit like the cold damp mists arising. He needed to sleep.

Refreshed in the morning, he drove on to Ortona. David planned to visit the specific places that Des wrote about during his time in that WW II battle. He took a hotel for a few days near the Lido Riccio, a wide expanse of sandy beach just below the town. That way, David rationalized, he would have easy access both to the rebuilt coastal town on the bluff, the sites connected to his dad, and some reflective time for himself by the sea.

The town wasn't particularly pretty but then again it grew from rubble. The next day in a light rain, David drove through town and took the coast road, SS16 south. He turned right along a ravine road signed for Villa Rogatti, San Apollinaire (battle headquarters in 1943) and San Leonardo (west of where Mitch Sterlin held off German counterattacks). The road narrowed and wound under the *Autostrada Adriatica* A 14, through the Moro River valley, unflooded now. It was lined with bamboo and olive trees like sentinels, pergola-style vineyards and prickly pear cacti, almost warning one to enter at one's peril. All hints of war were gone now of course, just riparian clutter; Italy had moved on. So David drove further along and up, looping back along the ridge road toward Ortona where he found Casa Berardi.

It was an uninhabited two-story manor, squat and square, like an early medieval fortress, made of brick and flaking stucco, with symmetrical high windows above and a stone stairway to an upper story side door. Like a lesser lord, it was situated on a country track overlooking the ravine. There was a huge rusted iron front door and a balcony above. The walls were pock-marked with bullet holes and shell craters still.

David parked by a waist-high privet hedge and a path that led to a small fleur-de-lis monument, commemorating the role played here by the Royal 22nd Regiment. There was also a plaque on the *casa* wall dedicated to Captain Paul Triquet, who had won the Victoria Cross for his courageous actions here.

David walked to the back of the house and looked down into the ravine. It didn't seem that steep until he began to descend a bit. It was steeper than he anticipated and he slipped down, wanting to see what the soldiers would have encountered while they attacked. He had only gone about 20 yards or so when he realized the light rain had turned the soil to a thick porridge-like goop. He turned and saw that the roof of the casa was just visible. He had little traction and globs of clinging glutinous muck glommed onto his trousers and his shoes; he was a mess but also appalled by what Triquet, who would have been David's age, had to fight in.

Breathless and disheveled, with glop like sticky rice on his shoes, trousers and hands after scrabbling back up the slope, David clomped toward the car, his shoes having grown thick geisha-like soles from mud and pebbles picked up along the way. He sat by the monument and tried to flick the muck off his shoes with a stick. It was near impossible. When he brushed off his pants, he just smeared more muck.

He laughed ruefully. "Ha, maybe war memories are like this stuff, not so easy to get rid of. Walk a mile in a man's shoes, eh? I barely made fifty yards and there were no bullets whizzing at me."

He retreated back to his hotel for a hot bath, room service to clean his clothes, and some time to rest and read the journal.

The next day, David thought he would go to the church where the

Seaforth Highlanders had their Christmas Day dinner, *Santa Maria di Constantinopoli*. He drove to the main square where the police station was, hoping to get directions. It was closed but a couple of older men where sipping coffee at the edge of the piazza. One asked in perfect English if he could help.

David tried some Italian. "*Si, grazie,* but I don't know many more words. I've been driving all over trying to find a church and I can't seem to locate it."

"*Mi scusi, mio zio,*" he said to the older companion, his uncle, and then to David," I've known this town for a long time. What church?"

David smiled, gratified that this fellow spoke English. He checked his map and notes. "*Santa Maria di Constantinopoli.* It's on *Via Don Bosco* but, *non lo so,* I don't know."

"You're in luck my friend. My name is Bruno. My car is here and, if you follow me, I can show you."

David, not sensing any ruse or danger, followed. After a bit of twisting and turning down streets, Bruno veered and parked. There was no church. Bruno saw David's puzzled look.

"Ah yes. The church is no more but it was on this site. It's a private home now." David looked a bit incredulous.

"*Si, si.* I was a boy during the war. We used to kick the football in the yard by the church. Then my family went into the hills when the Germans came. After Christmas we came back, and me and my buddies, we found cigarettes and cutlery in the ruins. They rebuilt a lot of Ortona but not everything."

"Oh, I see," said David a bit disappointed. Then he looked at Bruno, short and jaunty, nattily dressed in trousers and sports shirt, not the baggy suit of his uncle back in the piazza. "You speak very good English."

"I should. We moved to Boston when I was a teen. I come back almost every summer to visit old friends and relatives. Came a bit earlier this year since your Canadiens knocked out my Bruins in the first round of the Stanley Cup." He had fun laugh lines, likeable.

David rejoined, "And it doesn't look good for the baseball season either. Both the Red Sox and the Expos aren't doing much so far this year. Can I buy you a coffee?"

"Thanks but no, I have to get back to my uncle in the square."

"*Molte grazie*, Bruno from Boston," and Bruno, almost like an apparition, said *ciao* and disappeared. David was left in the growing heat.

"So much for recreating history," he mumbled to himself. "Let's try the cemetery then."

The car's air conditioning was a welcome respite from the humidity. David drove south out of town and continued towards *San Donato*, a town less than five kilometres away, to the Moro River Canadian War Cemetery. There were ominous dark thunder clouds billowing over Ortona and the Adriatic which made the tidy green grass and tall white cross stand out starkly against the black backdrop. The monument proclaimed, "Their name liveth for evermore", with all the identical gravestones standing to attention, looking like dried upright bones.

There was a guest shelter on either side which David noted in case he needed an escape from the gathering storm. He wandered up and down the rows, finding both Eric Sellers, the twenty-five year old who died Christmas Day after the Seaforth Highlanders' dinner, and Mitch Sterlin, who died on Dec. 19, only twenty-two years of age.

Because those boys moved his dad to tears and depths in 1943, David decided to pour some ashes on each grave, by the red roses planted there. Then the skies opened driving the ashes into the earth with a powdery eruption. David sprinted to the nearest shelter and sat down to wait out the storm.

The rain tossed up an earthy aroma, the wind swirled, and David closed his eyes taking in the sounds and smells. His mind worked out a reckoning.

"Well Dad, I guess Italy comes down to this for you, some ashes where you chatted up some Canadian boys for Greg Clark's articles and some ashes where you met Uncle Peter. I know a bit more about you, of course, and I got to see a side of Uncle Peter I didn't know before. I'm starting to see some causes for your general resentment. But I still can't figure out exactly why you were so angry with me for most of my life.

You know, it's very difficult capturing the past that you were in, but you probably knew that would be the case. It's the historian's challenge after all, trying to do justice to the past. I feel I'm still up to the task. But now I'm going to take a break. Lydia's coming to Italy and we have you to thank for the tryst."

David opened his eyes as if coming out of a meditation, feeling calm. The storm was ending so he drove back to the hotel for a light lunch of Caprese salad and a glass of local Montepulciano d'Abruzzo, a nap, and some time for the beach.

There was an on-shore breeze lightly flapping the rows of umbrellas that looked like mushrooms. The *Lido Riccio* was a crescent of white sand five kilometres long and abutted by hotels and railway lines. The sun cast long late-afternoon shadows as David walked, journal in hand. The breeze buffeted his hair and made his t-shirt cling to him. At the apex of the crescent, he came upon a lone lounge chair and decided to sit and read.

Monday, August 28, 1944

Hard to believe it's been three months since I was wounded. Met with Zaneth last week in Montreal and he wants me to case out Fred Rose's office again. Zaneth is re-marrying in September and said a good woman makes a good man better. He even recommended it for me. He was like a school kid really, not appropriate or entirely professional, but hell, let him have some joy. My job is to run Lucien again if I can. Seems Rose and the LPP might be causing trouble over conscription...

...Lots of casualties in Europe since D-Day, and the federal Liberals want to send those registered cowards, the Zombies, over to fill the ranks. So Quebec is belly-aching again. I said to Zaneth that it would be better if the Allies freed our prisoners-of-war held by the Germans in Europe and used them as reinforcements. Anyway, it's war and what do I know? So, here I am running for Zaneth between Montreal and Ottawa.

Friday, Sept. 1, 1944

Finally saw Lucien at the bagel bistro and cornered him. Asked him if he had registered for the war yet and he gave some malarkey that Rose got him out of it. I just about lost it, fucking coward. It was the smirk that got me. I tried to shame him with accounts of the Van Doos at Ortona but he shrugged and said "How much you gonna pay me this time for spyin"? The smarmy bugger.

I grabbed the collar of his jacket but the pain from my collarbone made me wince. He noticed and seemed to enjoy my pain. I passed him an envelope of money which seemed to satisfy him. He told me some things about Rose's strategies, including that he was not going to join the anti-conscription *Bloc Populaire* of dissident politicians because Canada is allied with Stalin. Seems Rose's Communist needs trump the Quebec ones.

I'm in the same boat. My livelihood and Zaneth's desire for information trumped my disgust for dealing with Lucien and his type. Not sure why I still warned Lucien to keep his head down because the RCMP would be looking for deserters and shirkers. Never mind, somehow I'm going to make him Unlucky Luke again.

Wednesday, Oct. 18, 1944

I was reading a newspaper by the bus stop down the street from Rose's office when I saw the pretty secretary leaving. Beautiful sunny autumn day, a breeze blowing golden leaves from the trees. Followed her to Kresge's on Rideau St. and, as luck would have it, asked if I could sit on the unoccupied counter stool beside her. She was having her lunch.

Lovely fragrance of perfume and shy glances my way with those beautiful big blues. I ordered a BLT and coffee and we chatted. Found out she works half day on Wednesdays and likes to come for a lunch before catching the bus home. She was proud that she was working for a Member of Parliament.

She asked why I wasn't doing my duty and I explained that I already had. She gushed with sympathy and apologies when I told of my discharge, and I have to admit it felt good that she was concerned. She wouldn't let me buy her lunch but agreed to have coffee sometime and gave me her phone number. Trusting type, and I like her.

Friday, Feb. 23, 1945

Haven't done much writing lately, so time to catch up. One thing worth writing about was that I had coffee with Margaret Tanner on my birthday in December, nice present to myself. Easy to talk to but I won't let myself get like Zaneth who is more talkative and revealing since he's married again. Does love do that? For instance, Frank told me there's a big raid planned in Drummondville on the weekend to round up deserters and anti-conscriptionists. If he tells others as easily as he did me, then there are bound to be leaks.

Anyway I did a nasty. Met Lucien for any updates that afternoon. I said that if he's going to be in Montreal over the weekend then he might want to wear his good threads and go to Drummondville on Saturday, there was going to be a big hoof. I couldn't go because I had to stay in Ottawa but it should be fun, lots of girls, and dancin'. If he takes the bait it should be a real 'bash'.

Tuesday, Feb. 27, 1945

Met Lucien again at the bagel bistro this morning. He had stitches over a black eye. I said I hadn't seen him like that since Spain and asked him if he tried to hustle someone's dame. He was grumpy and narrowed his good eye at me. "Bay maudzee", he said, "Dare was a partay ok, but dare were lots of coppers too. You didn't know nutteen 'bout dat, did you? Dare was a riot when da police dey try to take some guys and I got hit."

I played dumb of course. He did say something interesting though. Not about conscripts, but about Rose and Carr in cahoots with Russians, trying to help get some Soviets into Canada and the U.S. I passed him his envelope of Judas silver and told him to keep his eyes and ears open.

Thursday, May 3, 1945

Saw Margaret for a burger and coke today. Knew it was her birthday tomorrow so I wanted to see her. Not really a date because I 'bumped' into her by the bus stop. Bit of luck really because she left work early today. She said that Rose and Carr closed the office early because they were meeting with a Toronto doctor.

I asked if someone was sick and she said no but she saw Mr. Carr counting out several hundred dollar bills to put into an envelope. I said maybe it was payment for some kind of medical procedure, and asked if she remembered the doctor's name. She said it was Sobalot or Soboloff and that Carr said it was a good pay day for just a signature. Anyway she was glad to get the half-day off and thanked me for remembering her birthday. She was flattered and said I was sweet. I enjoyed mixing business with pleasure.

Friday, August 31, 1945

Kept back some of Lucien's money for myself. Spent it on Meg since she's been giving me as many leads as he has. Seems Rose has been speaking Russian in the office, especially to a Colonel Z about radio X or something before closing his door. I passed this on to Zaneth and he gave it top priority. Something's astir.

Monday, December 3, 1945

Called Meg and met her for a Chinese today. It was a birthday present to me I said. My, my, 28 years old. Remembered a Latin phrase Greg always used, *tempus fugit,* time's a movin'. I had passed on information to Zaneth that both Lucien and Meg had mentioned more talking in Russian happening in the office. I asked Zaneth for a BIG favour, to contact Meg's father and get him to get Meg to quit working for Fred Rose. It's too fishy there; something's going down and she shouldn't get mixed up.

Anyway, on our date, over coffee, I reached over the table and put my hand over Meg's. It was smooth and soft and I squeezed gently. "You know Meg, if you want to give me a birthday and Christmas present rolled into one; if your Dad should give you some advice in the near future, please follow it. See it says so in the fortune cookie, 'wise advice will come your way'." I crumpled the paper slip quickly, raised her hand and kissed it. I think I may be fallin' for her...

David looked up at the scudding clouds and realized it was dusk. What he was reading seemed to put Des squarely in the center of the Gouzenko Affair, an event that was the putative beginning of the Cold

War. David recalled from his history classes that Igor Gouzenko, a Soviet cipher clerk working at the Russian Embassy in Ottawa, sought asylum early in September, 1945. Eventually Gouzenko's revelations spilled the beans on Rose and Carr and others for conspiring to get false identifications so the embassy could set up a spy ring.

A Toronto physician, Dr. Sam Soboloff was implicated for signing passport applications for $3,000 each. Prime Minister Mackenzie King listened to aides, slowly realized it was serious and, true to form, established a Royal Commission to get to the bottom of it. David remembered that Fred Rose was arrested in February, 1946, put on trial and convicted of espionage.

A co-conspirator fingered Rose for dealing with a member of the Soviet's main military intelligence, the GRU. It was Colonel Nickolai Zabotin, the same Colonel 'Z ' that Meg overheard. They were conspiring to give the Soviets information on the high explosive, RDX, a code for Research Development Explosive being experimented on at McGill University. It was more powerful than TNT.

David whistled lightly and thought to himself, "So, Mom must have been over-hearing these plans, and gossiped to Dad about 'Z' for Zabotin, Dr. Soboloff and 'Radio X' or RDX. What an amazing incidence of coincidence. Dad realized what she was into, even if she didn't, and he wanted to protect her."

In the end, Rose was ejected from Parliament and jailed. He was released in 1951, when he returned to Poland. Sam Carr on the other hand, David recalled, went missing during the RCMP round up of Soviet espionage suspects on Friday, February 15, 1946, until he was discovered in 1949 and jailed.

David marched back quickly across the sand to the hotel. He wanted to eat quickly and return to the journals. His father was apparently at the epicentre of the quintessential Cold War event in Canada. But it was equally important to David to get glimpses into his parents' early relationship. Some details were niggling at him. David picked up the thread again after dinner.

David learned that Des had been reading back copies of *The Clarion*, of which Carr was the editor, a working-class rag that supported the Labour Progressive Party. Des was hoping to get some insights into the man he was trying to catch. The assignment had his father checking out seamy apartments in Manhattan where the RCMP thought Carr was hiding out for some time.

There were leads and connections but no prize. Des followed a woman with henna hair for days, who they believed was somehow connected to Carr and who left the buildings regularly, but then she vanished. Once Des feigned friendship with a postman, buying him a beer and chatting him up.

When Des described Carr, the postie said, "Oh you mean Mr. Lewis. I often deliver postcards to him. I have one now." Des said the guy named Lewis was his friend and offered to deliver the mail to him. It was postmarked from California with the message, "Go west old man", and signed 'L'.

Frustratingly, Des lost Carr while tailing him in Central Station but followed that lead to the University of Southern California, where Litvin, the Russian infiltrator on one of Des's Spanish passports, had been a lecturer. But no Carr. Des always seemed to be a step or two behind. Then there was a lead that a Joe Lewis, aka Sam Carr might have returned to Canada via the Eastern Townships. Zaneth told Des to come back to Ottawa; it was mid-August, 1947.

All this time, Des wanted to send a postcard to Meg from time to time to keep himself in her mind, but thought better of it for security's sake. She was on his mind but that was as far as he allowed himself to go.

David got back to the specific story.

Tuesday, August 12, 1947

One of those hot humid days with a wind picking up in the evening and thunder clouds looming. I had decided to look for Meg at the Archbishop's Diocesan office on Kilborn Place off Banks St., a pleasant neighbourhood just south of the Rideau River. I was intending to ride the bus home with her after she got off work, but what actually happened, I couldn't predict in a million years...

...I didn't know where I stood with her but I wanted to explain my absence somehow and hoped she might still have a spark for me. I stepped out of the shade, my fedora protecting my eyes, to greet her. Meg immediately put her white-gloved hand up to her cheek but not before I saw a purple-black lump there, a black eye, and a cut on her lip. She let out a gasp, put her face into my chest and let herself be hugged.

She started sobbing and I waited until it ebbed before speaking. Her hair was fragrant and clean and I kept inhaling deeply through my nose, not being able to get enough of her scent. My arm around her shoulders seemed to calm and protect her, like a wounded sparrow.

"What happened?"

"Oh I'm just so happy to see you, what a lovely surprise."

"No, your face."

"Oh that, it's nothing, I ran into the door frame at work yesterday. Clumsy me."

She dabbed her puffy eyes gingerly and asked if we could walk a bit instead of getting the bus right away. We wandered toward Heron Park and she put her arm through mine. I told her I had been on a special travel trip, selling security systems in the States and meant to write. I thought of her often. She said she thought of me a lot too and kissed me on the cheek.

Just then it thundered and big raindrops began to fall just as we reached a covered pergola along the park path. We huddled against the passing storm and I asked her how she liked her new job and if she ever saw the folks from the old office. She laughed, "Hardly, I mean Mr. Rose was in jail, but maybe you didn't hear." She said she loved her new job with the archbishop but how did I know? I tried to keep tabs I said and mumbled something about Lucien.

Anyway she looked at me squarely under that pergola, the fresh smell of rainfall on hot earth, put her arms around my neck and pressed her body against me, round soft breasts and hard hips. After a long kiss, she said, "Welcome home, I hope I'm going to see a lot more of you." My knees almost buckled. The rain stopped just as suddenly as it began, breezy and cooler now. Not wanting to let any ardor cool though, I asked her to a movie for tomorrow.

So it's a date, we're going to see that new movie, *Crossfire* with Robert Mitchum, about a murder investigation of suspected demobilized soldiers. I don't know whether I'll be able to follow the plot but who cares.

Saturday, September 13, 1947

What a fantastic night! Meg and I have been seeing each other a lot over the last month. Movies, miniature golf, and even an Ottawa Trojans football game. Tonight we went to dinner at The Prescott Hotel, a good Italian joint in Little Italy. The 'P' serves those large glasses of beer for a quarter and we had a few before eating. That plus a bottle of house wine. Meg was rubbing her nylon-covered toes up my pant leg under the table and it aroused me.

Whether it was the booze or the flirting I don't know but we were both a bit tipsy after dinner. I had recently bought a used car, a 1941 Olds sedan, so we drove to a spot down by the Gatineau River. Kissing turned to petting and then groping. The windows were fogging when Meg unbelted my trousers and unzipped me, hand on my erection. She slurred something about teaching her how to handle a stick shift. Then she hoisted her dress and straddled me face on. Our tongues darted in each other's mouths and my hands were on her smooth bum as it rose up and down.

I thought I would faint when I quivered and buried my face in her breasts. Suddenly consciousness broke through, "Oh shit, Meg, I didn't use a condom." Her eyes were bright in the moonlit night and she laughed light-heartedly, "Too late now, mister." God, I love her.

Monday, October 20, 1947

Meg and I are getting married. She told me on Thanksgiving that her period was late and the doctor confirmed last week that she's pregnant. We agreed to tell her parents and have a civil ceremony but they were none too happy. The Bishop soothed things though when he agreed to marry us at a small ceremony, so on Friday we will be Mr. and Mrs. Des Dilman. I told Zaneth who congratulated me and gave me a week off for a honeymoon. So after the wedding, Meg and I will drive to Niagara Falls and then it'll be house hunting I guess...

David paused and thought for a minute. Then he flipped ahead in the journal to his birthday, May 12, 1948. There he read that he weighed nine pounds, a big bouncing baby boy.

He read that Des had been incredibly proud and said to the nurse who was holding young David in the nursery, "Not bad eh, for being premature?" The nurse looked at Des quizzically as if he were mistaken or naive at best.

"This baby isn't premature; if anything he's overdue." Des, a new father with a little knowledge, inwardly disagreed with the frumpy nurse and offered her a cigar, mumbling, "Maybe there's a man in your life, sister." Later he mentioned the story to Meg who pooh-poohed the incident as doctor error and inexact science, before gushing over her baby swaddled beside her.

The rest of the journal was filled with a record of happy family life, Christmas together in their new home on Glebe, Meg happy with the baby, house decorating and furniture purchases. Des went to work each day in Ottawa except for two 'sales' trips to New York. David skimmed some more and an entry, dated just before his first birthday, caught his eye.

Monday, April 11, 1949

Well, we finally closed the case against Sam Carr. I went to New York in January when we got a lead that Carr left Mexico for NYC and might be in a basement apartment. I cased it out and sure enough, there was the henna-haired lady, who we now knew was his wife, Julia. I tailed her and overheard the grocery cashier call her Mrs. Lewis. So I tipped off the FBI before coming back to Ottawa. Then in February, Zaneth and I went down to verify that the FBI had captured 'our man' and we brought him back to Canada...

...He was cool as a cucumber I have to say, no emotion, telling the reporters he had a good breakfast on their taxes. Zaneth and I flanked him when we arrived in Canada with a lot of photographers' flashbulbs going off. Speaking of which, Zaneth knew the papers would be there, so he warned me to buy new threads on his expense. I felt pretty good in my new navy blue overcoat and dapper double-breasted navy suit. We were pretty photogenic, I must say.

In court, Carr lost his jauntiness. He was arraigned without his props, no pipe and fedora, and no folded newspaper under his arm. He's still a youthful-looking man in his early forties, slick wavy hair combed back from a high forehead, Charlie Chaplin moustache now, and a slightly cleft chin. He was nicely attired in a double-breasted brown suit, but less cocky for sure. The trial was short; he was found guilty on all counts of conspiring to commit a forgery, breaking the Official Secrets Act, and making false statements to get passports.

Lucien testified that Carr tried to use a passport from a dead Mackenzie-Papineau soldier and that sealed the conspiracy charge. I did overhear something odd when the guilty verdict was returned though. Carr glared at the Crown counsel and said, "Don't look so smug over there. Your Mounties and G-men couldn't catch a cold. You all know I would've been long gone two years ago if I had been able to get that passport off the Bishop's broad."

The security guards took him away but he looked over his shoulder and sneered at Zaneth and me, "Ya, I beat her good for her trouble, just like I'll beat you when I'm out." Then he raised his fist, "Workers unite."

It sure got me thinking. Was Meg the Archbishop's broad? His braggadocio in the face of justice was like he had rained on the parade. What the hell did he mean?...

CHAPTER 14.

GET BACK TO WHERE YOU ONCE BELONGED

Abruzzo and Rome, 1985

David leaned back on his pillow in his Ortona hotel room after dinner and furrowed his brow. Was it Sam Carr who had bruised Mom's face that day when Dad returned to Ottawa? What would she have to do with passports though? And although Mom was pregnant when she married, was it one month or two?

David thought of a childhood poem from Lewis Carroll, *The Walrus and the Carpenter*. "The time has come, the Walrus said, to talk of many things: of shoes and ships and sealing wax and cabbages and kings." He had so many things he wanted to talk to his mother about when he was back in Ottawa, especially the journal revelations. He wondered if she would divulge anything.

Subconsciously he ran his fingers through his hair but there was no discernible curl, and the thought that Carr might be his father flitted away. Anyway, it could all wait. He shook his head slightly; now was the time to put Des and the '40s away and concentrate on Lydia and the present.

David took the winding route from Ortona back to Rome, from Ortona, via Guardiagrele, catching views of vineyards and vistas above the Moro River, then through the *Parco Nazionale della Majella*, before stopping for lunch in Sulmona. It was a lovely town of antiquity and the birthplace of Ovid, the Roman poet who penned "The Art of Love". David checked it off as a possible day trip to explore with Lydia. It wasn't far from Scanno, a mountain village central to hiking and the preferred site for a week's lodgings.

Confident that he had reconnoitered enough of Abruzzo to guarantee a fun time after spending a few days in Rome, he drove to make his rendezvous with her. Continuing on through winding mountain roads, he noted the light filtering through leafy overhangs which hinted at hidden glades, and made him dream of isolated picnics. He was getting more excited about seeing Lydia with each kilometre.

David dropped off the speedy, comfortable Argenta and arranged to get the smaller Fiat Uno later in the week, booked a small flat in Trastevere, description acceptable, sight unseen, before getting a taxi to the airport. At international arrivals, he hoped to make a good first impression for the second time. It had been seven years since they had seen each other and he so wished that she would approve of him. He was casual on the outside, wearing a yellow golf shirt, blue blazer, denim jeans and loafers without socks but nervous on the inside. David saw Lydia first and he could feel a rush in his chest. He was smitten all over again.

Leaving the luggage carousel, she stood out and above in the crowd. Looking early morning rumpled and chic at the same time, she was wearing a white sleeveless blouse with a baggy blue sweater over her arm, a denim skirt cut just above the knees, and white tennis shoes displaying a Tretorn swoosh. Tall and graceful, she seemed regal to him. She was scanning over the heads of the crowd, a wee furrow of concentration on her brow. Her light brown hair, thick and fuller in the current style, was a bit frizzed and pulled back with a turtle shell clip. She looked tired from the long red-eye flight but her eyes flashed green when she espied David.

Her face suddenly crinkled into a smile. The white teeth contrasted attractively in her tanned face and her sweet, shy, single wave melted David. He hugged her tightly and kissed her on both cheeks, before taking her jam-packed knapsack, and put his arm around her waist to whisk her away to a waiting taxi. He felt like a prince-charming protecting his princess, but knew he had to eschew such romanticism, and quickly.

David heaved Lydia's bag into the taxi, gave the address to the cabbie on a slip of paper, took both Lydia's hands as he sidled beside her, and searched her face again.

She said, "It's good you sent me a photo of you without your beard. You look younger and I like that little cleft in your chin."

"This is like a dream, Lydia. I can't believe I'm here in Rome with you, in person." He almost had said 'in the flesh' but again was conscious of letting libido and id get ahead with Freudian slips. "Let me look at you. You're a vision, you haven't changed at all."

A single deep laugh burst from her. "Dahveed, you are sweet. But I am 36 now, middle-aged no? And terribly tired. You may see a vision, but I think I must look like an apparition. Come, let's go."

The taxi windows were open; loud traffic and wind made it difficult to talk. They held hands and smiled but mainly took in the scenery as they sped along. Lydia pointed out names she recognized, the historical ones like Leonardo da Vinci airport and *Via Christoforo Colombo*, and she smiled excitedly when the cabbie answered her question, "Tiber, *si, si.*" They also sped by product brand names such as Gucci, Ferrari, and Cinzano. At the last one, she squeezed David's hand and he smiled remembering that night they drank vermouth from the bottle and got tipsy on the last night of the conference in Sofia.

David remembered sitting on a bench by the city's artificial Lake Ariana near Sofia University, sipping and necking and promising to write. He wasn't so good at keeping that promise and he inwardly winced. When the cab passed the monolithic Jewish synagogue, he said that they were close; Trastevere was on the left. The taxi turned over a bridge and entered very narrow streets, honking and swerving. Lydia's eyes widened and she said it reminded her of Rio Centro. They clattered on cobblestones and stopped in front of a huge wooden gate fronting a non-descript stuccoed building.

"*Si, si, numero settanta cinque, Via della Scala,*" the cabbie nodded as he ushered them and rang one of a half dozen door bells on the wall identified as #75. It was about 3 p.m., quiet on the window-shuttered street. Soon the big gated door squeaked open and a slim, efficient, older lady led them into a cool passage. It opened onto a shadowed courtyard surrounded by three stories of apartments, some with laundry hanging on tiny balconies. They climbed a stairway up two floors and the agent opened a thin door onto a small bed-sit that fronted onto the street. She affably turned on water taps, demonstrated the two burner hot plate on a counter by the sink, and started up a window air conditioner. Smiling, she handed over the keys, and left with a curt "*buongiorno*".

Lydia said she needed to rest a bit, and shower, so David went out to explore the area. The streets were labyrinthine but all seemed to lead to a huge piazza dominated by a fountain and church. He read on a poster stuck to one pillar of the 12th century *Basilica di Santa Maria* that live music was scheduled later that night. There was a plethora of restaurants, with outdoor tables in the ready for evening strollers. Graffiti decorated the walls of the pocked and faded buildings with swirled colours of street art, and there were niches high up the walls of some buildings with statues, one a Madonna, like urban grottoes.

He explored a steep street that went up to a statue of Giuseppe Garibaldi, the Italian Unification general, and it opened onto a huge green space called *Gianicolo*, giving great views down to the old streets and the River Tiber below. At last he focused on finding a little *alimentari* where he purchased some breakfast things like coffee, sugar, tea, cream, bread, peanut butter, eggs, and some fruit, plus essentials like toilet paper. Carrying the sum of his husbandry in a plastic bag he returned to their little *appartamento*, having given Lydia a couple of hours of respite.

Lydia was sitting on her bed under the window wearing a long white tee shirt, slightly hanging off one shoulder, and her hair was turbaned in a towel.

"Feeling fresher?" he asked, glancing around the small room. She smiled, hands over her head tousling her wet hair. "Mmm, much. What have you been up to?"

"Just checking out the neighbourhood; I think it might be hopping tonight. And here are some supplies for the morning."

"Thank you Dahveed, you're being very kind, and helpful, and considerate, and; are you feeling a bit nervous and awkward too?"

They both laughed then. "Lydia, I feel like a schoolboy on a first date. But at the same time I'm so happy being here with you."

"Me too. But let's just take it slowly. Let's give us some time; we need to catch up, no?"

"Yes we do; we have a lot of talking to do. Let's get ready to go out on that 'first date' then."

He showered and changed to a white shirt while Lydia looked

stunning in a black cotton dress with cap sleeves and slightly stuffed shoulder pads, pearl studs, and open-toed sandals. Her perfume, *Paris* he thought, wafted up to him as he followed her down the stairs and out into the Roman dusk. "Duty-free," she smiled over her shoulder when he complimented the fragrance. They were both tanned and fetching and Lydia took David's arm as they strolled.

The night air was warm and velvety. They got to the piazza as the band was setting up and they sat at a bistro table near the fountain where other couples were gathering on the steps in anticipation. They ordered a bottle of Chianti and brought their heads closer together to chat.

"Tell me more about this quest of your father."

"Okay. You know it began a little like a déjà vu of our argument in Havana. Remember you told me to grow up and get to know myself? It seems my Dad was seeing me in the same light. When I was out on a run, it struck me that he may be right. No future, getting more angry and cynical; and I realized I had no one to talk to for advice, no one since you. I thought of how much I missed you, I thought of you a lot actually. When I skied, I remembered promising to teach you; when I sailed, I wished you were in the cockpit beside me; when I finished a run, I wished you were there to say, 'get away, you're too sweaty'. I don't know if there's such a thing as ESP, but dammit, that was perfect timing when you sent that postcard to my house, an incidence of coincidence if ever there was one." He took a sip of wine and looked into her face from over the rim. "You know you haven't changed a bit. But I digress."

"Yes, you do, and you haven't changed much either except there is more room on your face and forehead." She tousled his hair and gently flicked her thumb on his cleft. They laughed about receding hairlines and crow's feet beginning to show.

"So my Dad offered me a chance for travel and some spending money if I took possession of his diaries and paraphernalia and tried to get to know him posthumously, and," he paused and took another sip, "maybe learn something about myself too. He knew he was a lousy father and hoped that I might understand, if not forgive, our relationship, and maybe not repeat his mistakes."

"And have you?"

"It's too soon to judge the mistakes part but yes, I've been learning. I've travelled some, to Western Canada, to Spain, and here in Italy. I just visited Monte Cassino and Ortona where Dad served for a while in World War II. So far, I've learned that he had a tough start to his life, being around a lot of violent events; and that he really loved my Mom, in the beginning. But somewhere, somehow, shortly after they were married and I was born, things changed.

That's where I'm up to now, starting the '50s. And in the process, I'd say I've also learned that things aren't always what they seem, that one should cast a wider net of tolerance around others, be less judgmental, grant that motives and values might be different without being wrong."

"Whew, it sounds like a modern pilgrimage. Are you enjoying it?"

"Well it's brought us back together, and that makes me happy. But I must admit that sometimes I've felt depressed with his life and the twists and turns he had to make."

"Is that so different from any life? Are you actually becoming more empathetic because of this task;" she teased, "is it changing you?"

David smiled but stayed serious. "Mmm, good question. It's affecting me for sure, but changing? I feel it is, sometimes."

"Your father wanted to do something good for you, I think. Parents always want the best for their offspring. But often, when they give advice, they want you to follow it, not just consider it."

"Perhaps. When my father gave suggestions and I didn't follow them, he just turned his back on me or belittled me."

"My parents always wanted me to be independent. But then they were sad when their wish came true. I went away to school and got a good education, I worked overseas and traveled, and now I work on an island while they are in the mainland city. I guess one has to be careful of what one wishes for; results can't always be predicted. Like, how do you say, the one who grants wishes, the genius in the bottle?"

David smiled, "Gee, I love talking with you again. It's genie in the
217

bottle, by the way. No, I think it's a bit more of an age-old pattern. I think my father got buffeted by winds he couldn't control, tried to protect me but didn't know how, and in the end, hoped I could navigate better, that's all."

David looked at her as the music started, and smiled. "Well this conversation is getting a bit heavy. On the other hand, I just realized my father's wish from the grave has brought us back together, so maybe he was a genius in a bottle, after all."

He squeezed her hand and shifted his chair to look at the band.

The middle-aged rock band was making a valiant effort on the piazza stage, including covers of the latest summer-time hits, and they were appreciated by both the strolling crowd and restaurant-goers. The set had popular Italian tunes and they threw in a few North American ones, like Cyndi Lauper's "Girls Just Wanna Have Fun". Some couples were up and dancing. Lydia and David were sipping their wine, conversation on hold, when the group played Billy Joel's "Just The Way You Are".

David leaned to Lydia. "Do you remember this song?"

"Oh yes, the World Federation dance in Havana, our last date, no?"

"Would you like to dance to that tune again now?"

"*Certamente.*"

They stood just beyond their table, the amber light from candles and basilica lights casting shadows. David held Lydia lightly, left arm out and they smiled, blue eyes on green. "Nice song; not so nice a result last time."

"Same song, different time and place; history doesn't always repeat itself, *meu querido*," and she held his stare with confidence. Then he pulled her closer to him and smelled her hair. Their slow unison on the cobblestones left them both a bit flushed.

The set was over, the square was less noisy, and they sat to finish their wine before moving on. A chill was rising from the river. David wrapped his blazer around Lydia's shoulders and kept his arm there as they ambled along.

"I noticed a restaurant on the next street. Shall we go there; it won't be a far walk home."

"*Sim*, I mean yes, that would be perfect. I don't know if it was the wine or jet-lag but I'm feeling very tired again. I may need you to take care of me tonight."

"At your service, ma'am." David squeezed Lydia's shoulder and leaned to smell her scent; a combination of disbelief and not getting enough of her.

The restaurant was abuzz. There was a table on the street leaving room only for couples to walk, or bicycles and an occasional Vespa to pass. The eatery served as a sports bar too and A.S. Roma was playing on the screen. Someone at the bar sneered as David passed, "*maladetta Inglese*" and tried to jostle him. David quickly replied, "*No, siamo Canadese.*"

It seemed passions were still high after the Heysel Stadium disaster a month before when 39 Italian fans died in a riot in the match against Liverpool. The owner felt badly for David and Lydia being accosted and gave them a half liter of Merlot on the house when he delivered the two thin-crust pizzas. They felt they must drink the wine so as not to offend, but it was not savoured.

Afterwards, David ordered himself an espresso and Lydia carried on with water, but she was flagging. On the stairs to the *appartamento* he pushed on her hips from behind and guided her up the steps. As he was opening the door, he turned to her and said, "Lydia, I've had a bit to drink and..." At the same time she said, "Dahveed, I don't want our first night to be wine-induced. I want to be clear-headed." They laughed at the synchronicity. David said, "Well that's a good start, being on the same page. You use the bathroom first."

When he came back to his bed, Lydia was already asleep in hers. He gazed over to her contentedly; just being with her again was bliss. Then he picked up his 'holiday reading', a paperback by Robert Ludlum, *The Bourne Identity*, a current top spy thriller. He smiled as he cracked the spine "A spy genre, Dad, and that's as close as I'm going to get to you for a couple of weeks." Before he had finished a page though, he reached up to turn out the light.

Both wanted to explore the city after sleeping in so they had a quick coffee and toast and left. It was getting hot and muggy. The streets had been washed down and flower sellers were out as David and Lydia walked hand in hand. They crossed the ancient Roman bridge, *Ponte Quattro Capi* or Bridge of the Four Heads, over the *Isola Tiberina* and strolled towards iconic ancient Rome.

They absorbed the old city on foot, meandering over to the Piazza Venezia and the Monument to Victor Emmanuel II with its giant equestrian statue. Descending the stairs behind the grandiose and ornate structure, they slowly strolled among the ruins of the Forum, recalling history of the Senate House and Julius Caesar's pyre, feeling the relief of shade among the pine trees on the imperial Palatine Hill, and eavesdropping on the many guides with their groups of tourists.

Later they kept to the shadowed walls in the Colosseum, avoiding any picture-taking with ersatz Roman legionnaires. Footsore and in need of sustenance, they left the hubbub of Rome's historic center in search of a quieter, leafy spot to share a prosciutto sandwich with salad and two cold beers.

"I thought being on my feet all day teaching would have conditioned me, but my feet are killing," Lydia said as she stretched her legs out.

"We don't have to go flat out; we're here for a couple more days. Here, put your feet up on my chair." He undid her tennis shoes and began to massage her feet. Lydia moaned appreciatively.

"So, do you play tennis now?"

"Some, mainly after school and weekends. There's a clay court in the town. And do you still run?"

"I try to get out a few times a week but my routine has been messed up lately."

"It's good to stay active, no? You know, I was interested in your comments about enjoying your last placement. Will you look for a teaching job next?"

"I've been thinking about that; what to do once this quest is finished, which it should be by Christmas or so. I really liked teaching high school History but I'm wondering about something where the kids are more needy or focused. My Dad wrote that he learned from a Frontier College mentor when he was younger, so I thought maybe something like literacy or Independent Studies. But that's mainly volunteer work and I need something that pays. I also thought of the United World Colleges; there's one in British Columbia. Or I could stay with high school in Ontario, I just don't know yet. Education yes, but where and how? I'm not sure. How do you like your teaching?"

"I love it, teaching on *Ilha Grande* is very isolated but the kids are like family. And working in Brazil is better for people of left leanings now; more promising since the military government ended and we have elected a new president."

"I remember you saying how it wasn't easy for university students in the '70s. Was it hard for you to get a job after leaving the WFDY position? That couldn't have been good for your résumé," David smiled.

Their food orders came but Lydia was reluctant to move her feet. "Just a bit more massage, *por favor,*" she implored and carried on.

"No, the WFDY was not so much a good reference for me. But I was not a big activist at university. You remember how we differed about fighting the 'imperialist enemy'. I was more a community organizer, like a Saul Alinsky, an urban radical more than an urban guerilla, remember? When I went back to Brazil, I just wanted to get a job teaching and help the young in small ways. My father helped me a lot. He was a journalist and had contacts. Also he, how do you say, flew under the radar always, and advised me to do the same."

"Oh yes, I remember those differences of opinion with you. I'd like to think I was just an idealistic youth but I also remember you saying I was self-centred and one-sided. You hit close to the bone, as I recall."

She smiled ruefully and reached for her beer, "We weren't on the same page then, were we?"

"No we weren't." He gently put her foot down and swigged some beer, a cold Nastro Azzuro. "But I'm hoping we're turning a new page," as he eyed her over the rim of his glass.

"You know," David said, after chewing a bite of sandwich, "it's not just my Dad making me think about my future; it's also my past with you." Lydia looked away and David thought it best to change the subject; maybe he was moving too fast.

"Tell me more about how your father helped you in Brazil. I can't remember my Dad helping me with anything since I was about four."

"At first it didn't seem like help exactly. My father, Gregorio; it means 'watchful' in Portuguese, no? Like his name, he is very protective even though he also wanted me to be independent. He had been working for the *Jornal do Brasil*, finding appropriate copy to re-publish from English international papers. It was a leftist paper that the military left alone. In 1967 the *Jornal* sent him to Havana to cover a conference, but his report was not complimentary. So the newspaper suggested he go work for the conservative newspaper, *O Globo*, which he did.

This was when I was 19, the summer you and I met in Sofia. My father and I had an argument before I went to Europe. He said an American in the hotel at the Havana conference had been asking him too many questions about the Brazilian guerilla, Carlos Marighella, also university students, and where I went to school. It scared Papa. He wanted me to be very careful in Bulgaria and not get mixed up with *malucos*, crazies, as he called them.

Actually he wanted to forbid me to go, but knew I wouldn't obey. He said it was time to wrap oneself in the country's new motto, 'Brazil, love it or leave it'. I said I could not do that until I had learned more about the world. Anyway at the *Globo*, he had more conservative and Catholic contacts. So when I returned to Brazil, he pulled some chains to get me a job in a Catholic school outside of Rio."

David chuckled, "You mean he pulled strings, the expression is to pull strings." Lydia smiled at the tease and threw a cherry tomato from the salad at him.

"General Figueiredo was assuming the presidency then and he was more tolerant of opposition parties. Still my father was careful and wanted me to, how do you say it, smart guy, be a small vegetable? He wanted us all to stay like small vegetables."

"Oh you mean just like small potatoes; that was probably smart. I bet he wanted you to be closer to home in Rio too."

"*Certamente*, but I visit when I can."

They decided to return to the air-conditioned room for a bit of relief from the heat and to venture out again in the cool of the evening. After their rest, David suggested they do an evening promenade, typically Italian, and not venture overly far. Lydia was amenable. This time they turned right on Via della Scala wandering towards the river and *Ponte Sisto* which took them to the wealthy chic *Piazza Farnese* and *Campo di Fiori*.

They gazed upwards at the opulence of the Farnese *palazzo* and French embassy bathed in the amber spotlights. Without pausing long, they passed into the *Campo di Fiori* beyond, into the hubbub, the odors and colours of the soon-to-end Sunday market. There, the fish, fruit and flower sellers were tidying up, as couples arm-in-arm moved toward the surrounding restaurants and cafés, the Verona umbrellas offering solace and service. The hawkers and walkers were joyous, oblivious to the ancient history of this built-over medieval meadow, a former place of public execution.

A statue of a victim of that fate, the Dominican friar/philosopher Bruno, overlooked a corner, a giant hooded, brooding bronze. He had denied several Catholic beliefs in his day, such as the Immaculate Conception and the Trinity, and was burned for his troubles in this square in 1600.

"Let's go to another part of the piazza, please Dahveed. I don't think I can take him scowling down at us," said Lydia.

They settled on sitting al fresco elsewhere and ordered a salad and pasta. "Wine tonight?" asked David.

"Mmm, just one glass perhaps," and she lowered her eyes but not her smile.

David bought a rose from a passing girl. Lydia asked, "Are you being romantic and gallant, *meu cavalheiro?*"

David laughed. "No, just appreciative. That you made the effort to write me after all those years, that you came here, that you're with me tonight."

"*Muito obrigado.*" She bowed her head and smelled the rose.

"Lydia, can I ask you about, you know, others in your life, you know, men?"

"But *meu querido*, you have been asking about men. Remember you talked about my father today? Who else?" she asked innocently.

"I deserved that."

With his elbows on the table and chin on his folded hands, he took a deep breath. "You know, I've thought about you and us so much. Sure, I've been with other girls, but they could never compare to you. And when I thought of you with other guys, at first I'd get mad with jealousy, then so morose that I'd been stupid to lose you."

"Ah yes, I remember how you used to clench your jaw when you saw Mike Giordano and me talking and joking. You know you never had to be jealous. We just talked and laughed." Then she leaned back in her chair and pointed at him. "Ha, you just clenched again."

David smiled and rubbed his jaw.

She put her two fingers to her lips and then reached to touch David's. Eyes averted, she said, "The truth, Dahveed, is that you never lost me. We just went separate ways. Me too, I've had dates, but no 'relationships'," and she searched his blue eyes for signals. "It seems you were my benchmark, no? Once my father asked me about boyfriends and I tried to explain about you. He said that, in his experience, opposites attract and then you spend a lifetime dealing with it. So, *meu amor,* I guess you are my opposite."

David leaned back in his chair, as if stunned, then got up. He leaned down to Lydia, took her face in his hands and kissed her. "I love you. If love means your insides are all atremble and about to burst, then I love you."

She laughed and shooed him back to his seat, and the restaurant patrons nearby smiled and took up their conversations again.

Lydia and David basked in his recent declaration as they walked past Bruno and the few blocks into the nearby *Piazza Navona*. It was filled with milling couples. At the Egyptian obelisk and Four Rivers fountain, David steered Lydia into a side street and meandered until he brought them to the back side of the Pantheon. They walked along the sheer, high curved walls until they came out front onto the *Piazza della Rotonda*. People were walking slowly and looking up in awe to the pediment atop eight mammoth columns awash in yellow light.

David said, "The inscription says Agrippa made it, but really it was Hadrian. It's not always easy to get to the truth in history."

"No matter, it's brilliant, and I see possibilities for a science and math project. How did they build that?" replied Lydia. "I would love to see it in the daylight, when it's open."

"No problem. But come, there's one last part to our walkabout."

They finished their circumnavigation and retraced their steps back towards the *Piazza Navona*. He scanned and spotted the restaurant, *Tre Scalini*.

"My uncle Peter told me about this place and said we'd have to try their famous chocolate gelato *tartufo*. He said the café had been here since 1815, licensed by the Vatican, and it was featured in the 1960 Fellini film, *La Dolce Vita*."

The dessert was a secret house specialty, a concoction of 13 varieties of Swiss chocolate ice cream topped with whipped cream and a wafer. Costing twice as much to eat at a table, they opted for take away, and shared it while sitting at Bernini's fountain.

"Mmm, this is delicious. I hope all our walking and hiking will burn this off, " she said.

After savouring spoonfuls, David said, "It's so decadent. And that concludes my idea for a promenade tonight. You can plan tomorrow's.

Shall we head back?"

"Speaking of tomorrow, I promised my father and mother that I would see the Vatican and send them a postcard. Are you fine with that?"

"Lydia, my sweetheart, I'm happy just being with you, wherever it is."

Back at #75, David let Lydia have the bathroom first again. When he finished his toilette and came back into the tiny bedroom, he noticed Lydia's bed was empty.

She was lying on his bed, naked save for white panties, her hair cascading on the pillow, her hands on her belly forming a frame around her navel and her fingers splayed toward forbidden fruit. David sat down beside her. Gazing at her eyes, he cupped and caressed her breast, then leant down to kiss her softly but long. Lydia reached around his neck and pulled him down for a harder embrace, tongues exploring.

David traced one side of her body, from the soft and smooth cheek, to shoulder, along her arm, pausing on an erect nipple, bending to kiss it, before continuing to trace down her stomach, hip and leg. He never got to trace her other side. Lydia shivered a bit and raised her pelvis. David slipped her panties off, stroking her Mound of Venus and probing gently with his fingertips, always amazed at the contrast from smooth skin to coarse and crinkly pubic hair.

Lydia moaned softly and parted her legs. David lay facing beside her and Lydia placed her thigh over his hip. His fingers stroked her tight muscular buttock and he clasped her to him.

Their love-making was gentle at first, re-discovering what they had missed, and then it became a kind of devouring, making up for lost time. Later, they rolled away from one another, glistening with sweat despite the air-conditioning.

"Do you think we worked off the *tartufo*?" she asked and they both laughed huskily before she fell asleep in the crook of his arm.

When they woke next morning, Lydia realized David had moved to the other bed.

"My arm fell asleep and I didn't want to disturb you," he said over his shoulder while getting coffee.

Lydia started poring over the map of Rome and said, "I missed your body this morning, so for penance, you'll have to follow my plan today, ok?"

"You still want to be in control, like last night?" he teased her. She lightly cuffed him on the way to the bathroom.

It was turning into a steamy day again. David suggested a treed walk to the Vatican if possible. Lydia checked her map, guiding him up the stairway from *Via della Scala* to the *Oro Botanico*, a green space overlooking Trastevere. This was the Romans' Janiculum Hill, dedicated to the god Janus who looked both ahead and back, as well as deciphering auguries to tell the future. They passed several busts of Garibaldi's idealistic Redshirts, who died for Italian independence, and who now formed a gauntlet on plinths along the walkway.

"You know, Janiculum is a perfect place for us to consider where we've been and where we're going, don't you think? I mean, besides the Vatican," he grinned. Waving at the busts, he said, "Seeing these guys makes me wonder about past causes and idealism. I know my causes have changed in the last decade. How about you, Lydia?"

"Oh no, you won't catch me that easily. You first. Are you saying your ideals have changed, or disappeared?"

He went to sit on a bench under a plane tree with its wide-spread branches like an umbrella, and Lydia joined him. "When we met and were part of those WFDY conferences, we were promoting, what was the slogan, 'For anti-imperialist Solidarity, Peace and Friendship'. Seems a bit flimsy compared to these guys. Now they were real radicals, laying down their lives for nationalism. Even my father was caught up in real fights, conflicts against fascism and communism. Me, I don't have the same fire in my belly, if I ever did. When I think about it, I was more talk and street theatre than real action. In fact, you said that to me, I remember. Now my aim is not so lofty. All I want is a job that pays and lets me help kids, that and a desire to make you and me happy."

She squeezed his arm. "Ah *sim*, my goals have changed a little too. I remember I was quite naive in Sofia and Berlin, but you were more, *eu não sei*, I don't know, like you used the organization to make some fun. I loved some of the fun and it made me question some of my approaches. But maybe knowing what was happening in my country, and even some fear perhaps, made me more practical. I still believe in justice and equality, but I can settle for just more fairness in the world now."

David nodded, "I get that. I think I'm more ready for fairness than angry protests and grandiose theories. Some of it may be the influence of my Dad's journals too. I don't want to be so angry and intolerant anymore, like he was."

Lydia nodded, "I am glad to hear that. I find that nowadays I take small steps and am happy with tiny victories."

"I'm not saying I stopped being a leftie, you understand, I'm just saying that I expect less. I'm not so sure. And you?"

"*Eu também*, me too. Does it make you sad not to be the rebel?"

"Not sad exactly, just wondering if I was a fraud before."

She laughed throatily. "We better go before you start feeling self-pity. Maybe we're just growing up, *meu querido*?" They smiled at each other before walking on hand in hand.

David asked her, "So have you become Catholic again? Is that why you're taking me to the Vatican?"

"*Não seja idiota*, don't be an idiot. I haven't capitulated entirely. No, my mother asked me to see the Vatican and to tell her about it; that's all."

The opulent wealth of marble and gilt actually offended them. They even snickered about the fawning acolytes around a red-capped cardinal, and about the Malvolio-esque striped costume of the Swiss guards. But Michelangelo's *Pietà* affected them profoundly.

"She looks so heart-broken, his mother. It's the mothers who pick up the pieces after the causes are fought for, no? And it's always the innocents who suffer," said Lydia. "*Bastante*, let's go where there is some lightness of being, *por favor*."

David tried to calm her. "My Dad wrote that one needs a blemish or two to appreciate beauty. Maybe all that gaudy stuff made us appreciate what Michelangelo wanted to convey. Anyway, right now, I'd settle for a cool drink," replied David, wiping his perspiring brow.

She led him away from St. Peter's Square without looking back. They came back to the river, passed Hadrian's Mausoleum, over the angel-adorned causeway of the *Ponte Sant' Angelo*, and kept to the umbrageous side of the river walkway. Looking at her map, she took them across *Ponte Cavour*, past a street of high end shops, such as Armani, Versace, and Cartier, which tempted some window-shopping but also offended their socialist values.

David joked, "Come the revolution, I'll have some of those." At the end of the street, Lydia found the graceful sweep of the Spanish Steps which they ascended and carried on to the Trevi Fountain. The afternoon skies were darkening and as the gushing reverberation of the Baroque water feature beckoned, a clap of thunder competed with the noise.

"No time to toss coins; hurry," shouted Lydia and they ran with the map over their heads in the beginning rain to the Pantheon, reaching the portico as the heavens opened. They entered the graceful, cavernous edifice, noticing the waterfall of rain from the open hole in the roof, the oculus.

"Do you remember the oculus in Havana? asked David. They had been on a city tour in 1978 when they went up the elevator of the Havana attraction. David had taken the opportunity to have a stealthy grope to which Lydia responded in kind.

"Yes, but just one kiss this time," she smiled at the memory. A tourist harrumphed, saying they were in a church after all.

They finished their embrace regardless and then David asked, "You see that tomb and marble plaque there, the one to Umberto and Queen Margherita? The pizza is named after her. Basil, tomatoes and cheese, the colours of the Italian flag. I could go for one now, and I know a place."

The rain had abated. He led her to the *Piazza Navona* again to the *Antico Caffè della Pace*, recommended by Uncle Peter, a celebrity haunt for the likes of Madonna and Sophia Loren.

"To peace and idealism, wherever it went," David toasted, as he and Lydia clinked glasses of Nastro Azzuro and relished their slices of Margherita pizza.

"To friendship," replied Lydia.

Tired and footsore again, they returned to the room after a long day of touring. Lydia said, "Dahveed, I'm not sad that this is our last night in Rome. I think I'm ready for some open spaces and some hiking with you; I'm afraid I've had enough of the big city."

"Sure, if that's all it is; is anything bothering you?"

"No, *meu amor,*" as she put her arms around his waist and pulled him against her, "I just want you without these urban distractions, and I think we need the open sky to talk about how we make this relationship work, no?"

"Well I have an idea on how to make it work. We simply have to create memories for the times we're apart." And, as he forced them off balance, they tumbled onto the bed with laughs and stifled squeals.

That night they wandered Trastevere street mazes one last time, sashaying arm in arm. And by noon the next day, they left Rome in the rented Fiat Uno, singing loudly, "*When The Moon Hits Your Eye Like A Big Pizza Pie, That's Amore*". But they both knew that their euphoria was limited; a long-distance relationship would not be easy.

CHAPTER 15

WHICH WITCH HUNT?

Ottawa, July-August, 1985

David landed in Ottawa on Sunday, July 17, tired but eager to continue his work on Des's next storage box. Uncle Peter met him at the terminal and David virtually proclaimed without solicitation that he was reinvigorated to finish Des's dare, to make renewed efforts to arrange for a teaching job, and that there might be a future with Lydia.

Peter pursued the idea when they got to the car, "Was it a good summer holiday with Lydia then?"

David confessed, "It was fantastic, if truth be told. We had a great time seeing Rome from Trastevere, and thanks for the tips about restaurants, by the way. Abruzzo was exactly what the doctor ordered."

"Doctor? Were you sick again?" Peter looked sidelong at David.

"No," David smiled a little sheepishly, "Unless you mean lovesick."

Peter laughed. "Ha, do tell." He punched David lightly on the shoulder.

David told Uncle Peter the general drift, that they drove into the gnarly Apennine chain of rounded mountains from Lazio to Abruzzo, which perforce meant circuitous navigating. They loved the hill town of Opi where they had *pasta carbonara* for the first time; they really liked hunkering down in Scanno, with a routine of hiking mid-morning and returning exhausted to a hot bath, an espresso or prosecco on the balcony, and the smell of wood fires in the cool mountain evenings. Also they managed a day trip to Sulmona, and a side trip to Aquila on their way back to Rome and their leave-taking.

"And is that it?" asked Peter. "No future plans?"

"That's all I'm going to tell you," laughed David. "Future plans are a work in progress. I've decided to apply to teach at Pearson College in Victoria; try to see Lydia at Christmas somewhere, somehow; and finish up with dad, so to speak, also by Christmas or thereabouts. You may think it's ironic, but Lydia and I promised to write a daily journal and mail it weekly to each other. How's that for communicating in a long-distance relationship? Now Dad's got us writing journals too," he said with a smile.

"I'm really happy for you David. I hope to meet Lydia one day soon. I'm sure your mother will be glad too."

"And how is Mom after her return from England?"

"I'll let you judge; we're going there for dinner. She insisted."

Meg greeted them effusively with bear hugs and kisses, having imbibed sufficient vodkas already. The table was set for a summer lunch, cold meats and salads. David brought out a bottle of prosecco, plus a local virgin olive oil for his mother, and a bottle of Montepulciano d'Abruzzo from a new winery, Masciarelli's.

"I stopped there on my way back from Ortona. Gianni Masciarelli inherited the acreage in 1978 and is developing a great wine to rival Bordeaux, he says. Anyway, it went into production in 1981 and I bought one of the last bottles of that vintage."

"Sit! Sit! Let me look at you! Tell me about your travels. I haven't seen you for so long!" Meg emoted.

David recounted an abbreviated version of what he had told Peter, and then wanted to ask about England before venturing into journal details. Meg said demurely, "Great Britain was fine but travel is over-rated. Really, Davey, when you've seen one castle, you've seen them all. Peter says you two had a fabulous 'bonding' time," emphasizing the word.

"We did Mom, each of us got a chance to say goodbye to Dad in Italy, once in Monte Cassino and once in Ortona."

"How many of those stupid vials of ashes are you going to dump around anyway?" she said verging on shrill.

"Four so far and, depending on the journals, maybe another four or five. And speaking of journals, I came across some puzzling entries. I was hoping you might help clarify them for me."

"Well it didn't take you long to get into that stupid journal stuff again. Ask away, if you must, but really David, I don't like it," and she thrust her wine glass out for more prosecco.

"Thanks Mom, it was some comments Dad made around the time I was born and a court trial." Meg seemed to sink more into her chair. David tried to be tactful, "There seems to be some miscalculation about whether I was premature for one, and for another, Dad had some doubts about an accident you had."

"David dear, we have company, mind your manners."

"Mom, Uncle Peter is family, not company! Surely we don't have secrets."

"Yes of course, but; oh very well, what is it you don't understand?"

"Dad and you got married in October 1947 and he wrote that you were one month pregnant then. When I was born he was proud of my weight, considering I was one month premature. The nurse told him it was nonsense, that if anything I was overdue. So that would have meant you were really pregnant in August, not September."

"Well David, honestly, you're raising some very indelicate topics. What does it all matter now?"

"Because it was memorable. Dad remembered your first night of sex in September. He also remembered something Sam Carr said at the end of his trial about the Bishop's girl. Did Sam Carr beat you up in August; were you the Bishop's girl?"

"My goodness, David, am I on trial here? What are you insinuating?" Meg huffed. "Now if you'll excuse me, I've had enough. Suddenly I'm quite tired and need to go for a nap."

"What were you driving at, David?" Peter asked, after Meg had exited.

"Maybe it's not important, Uncle Peter, but Dad began to have doubts about his and Mom's relationship. I think Sam Carr played some disruptive role in the Dilman family life."

"I think that's something you and Meg will have to iron out together then. Or you'll figure it out from more research in the journal. It's never straightforward with Des, is it? I'm going to go now; why don't you have a nap too. Both you and your Mom will need a breather, I suspect."

Meg lay down heavily on her bed and sighed audibly, "Des, you and that geedee journal, what a hornets' nest you're stirring up for David, and me. Damn you."

She closed her eyes and remembered back to that August evening before closing up the Archbishop's office.

I was working late and had heard some scrabbling outside the office window. I put it down to the wind blowing the branches of the heavily laden rose of Sharon bush against the wall. In hindsight it must have been that fugitive, Sam Carr. I remember tidying up the desk before leaving, when I smelled a vaguely familiar, pungent pipe tobacco odour, Amphora it was. I was putting two and two together; Sam smoked that brand and used to stink up the parliamentary office. Suddenly, a rough smelly hand clasped my mouth and an arm pinned me around the chest. A gruff voice, Sam's, spoke into my ear and a blast of foul breath hit my nose...

..."Just stay calm and quiet and you won't get hurt," he said. "I need something from you." So I nodded and he let me go.

He was a bit disheveled, a few days growth of beard, some stains on his shirt and suit jacket. "Not as dapper as the last time you saw me, eh? But you still look good." He was ogling and I looked away.

"Listen Margaret, I know that Freddie left his documents in your care. Lucien said so too. He had a couple of old passports. I need one now."

I remember saying he was an idiot; Mr. Rose was in jail and I quit before he was arrested. "Bullshit," he barked and I jumped a bit. "Fred told me you took those really secret things to a safety deposit box at the bank." I told him he was crazy, I only deposited certain envelopes that Mr. Rose said were special riding donations to the safety deposit. When I said I didn't know anything about passports and that I didn't have a key, his backhand came from nowhere, smacking me on the cheek. I fell back against the desk. I remember feeling blood on my lip. He pulled me by the hair to my feet and when I insisted I knew nothing, he pushed me

234

hard against the door frame.

When I came to, he was on top of me on the desk, grunting like a pig. My eye and head hurt something fierce and I moaned. He leered over me, mistaking my moan for pleasure because he said, "I knew you'd like it. I said I needed something, didn't I? No passport, but pussy will do." Then he left. It was horrible.

Thank God, everyone had left the Archbishop's office that day. I remember rolling off the desk and falling to the floor, aching, and I almost retched. My dress was ripped and my bra was smudged and pulled up by my neck. He had emptied drawers and cupboards in his search, paper was strewn everywhere. I started to cry and tided myself, the room, and the desk up as best I could before going home. By then it was dark and I could sneak past my folks up to my room.

I had been praying hard in bed that night and when I saw Des waiting for me the next day, it was like God had answered me. I knew I wasn't going to let Des get away again, and I didn't...

She smiled mischievously and then began to snore lightly.

In the meantime, David was on the living room sofa, trying to nap, with the unopened '50s box beside him on the floor. He was remembering his last week with Lydia, and he too had a smile on his face. He was daydreaming about a hike they took mid-week, from Scanno to a mid-mountain hut, called *Stazzo del Carapole*. They were intending to go up another thousand feet or so to see *Le Ciminiere*, a mountain outcrop looking like a Paleolithic monument. It had been hot going and the *stazzo* was in a lovely meadow with a breeze, so they decided to stop for refreshment before pushing on.

The air was cooler up there with a slight breeze at our backs, making us feel our sweat. The meadow was beautiful, with wild flowers: blue and purple gentian, also the pincushion flower with its long hairy stem topped with mauve-tipped petals and white-centred heads like needles in the middle; and purple and white valerian, meant to be all-healing and relaxing. We had already seen the fabled chamois, that antelope-goat with the black on its face, like running mascara, and grand views of Lago de Scanno *far below...*

... "Let's not go in the hut, let's stay outside and picnic in the woods above the stazzo," I said and Lydia answered, "Has that pincushion stem given you ideas? It has me."

We spread our little picnic towel on a bit of an incline, the closest to level we could find, sunlight dappling through the beech branches above us. I had just popped an olive into Lydia's mouth and was cutting some cheese and salami when she started to undress. I quickly matched her even though I said she was a shameless hussy.

Crackers and condiments were hastily brushed aside and she wrapped those sinewy tanned legs around my waist, heels on my buttocks. Her darkening nipples were hard and pressed into my chest while we kissed. "Do me," was her breathless command and wish. Oh god, it was fantastic loving her that way, my nose rubbing her fur, my tongue licking, her hands on the back of my head, urging me on.

But the ground was too uneven and stubbled with beechnuts that acted like ball bearings. I was sliding down the hill ever so slightly, but enough that I was conscious of having to scrabble my fingers and toes into the rocky ground for purchase. As my fingers dug deeper, hers kept kneading my head deeper on her. Finally she came, and I, on my knees below her, surveyed our love-making flotsam - olives, crackers, cheese, salami, unopened bottle of wine, all on the edge of an erotic trail.

We started laughing quietly; my knees were scraped red, and her bum was dirt-smudged. Just then we heard other hikers below us, out of sight by the hut, and we shushed. I threw my shirt to her for cover and we sat clutching and silent. We were like co-conspirators. While the hikers went on, we stayed catatonic until their sound ebbed.

"Your turn," she said, and I couldn't have loved her more. I slipped into her like a boat into its mooring; it felt like home. Afterwards, we ate what we salvaged and sipped wine from the bottle, sitting naked and talking sotto voce.

"Where are we going to go from here, Dahveed?"

"Down I suppose; I don't want to go up to Le Ciminiere now. It would be anti-climactic, don't you think?" I looked over at her with a smile.

"Not the hike, *idiota*, us. When will we see each other again?"

"As soon as we can, I hope. Christmas time for sure."

"It won't be easy, *meu querido*, me in Brazil, you in Canada."

"I know but, I love you Lydia, I'll do anything to make this work."

"And I you. You know, I said to myself once that I would not be able to marry until I knew that you had; only that would release me."

"Well I haven't married. I sure am ready to, with you; but I don't have any prospects yet. I'm still getting myself sorted out, remember."

"Yes, but being with you, it's like we have rekindled a spark, no? Do you feel the spark can flame up and keep itself, sustain itself?"

"I don't know Lydia, but I'm willing to try. Let's agree to keep our own journals while we're apart, entries every day, letting each other know what we're doing, our thoughts, our feelings; and let's send those diary entries to each other every week. Do you think that will help keep us in touch until we get together again?"

"I'm willing to try, *meu amor*, and I expect a Christmas gift too, no?" She smiled and we kissed.

When Meg came back downstairs, refreshed after her nap, David was sifting through the cedar box contents. He had just finished reading an RCMP letterhead dated 1950, assigning Des to the new intelligence Special Branch dealing with counterintelligence, and that he was to report to the Officer in Charge of the Special Branch, Charles Rivett-Carnac.

Strewn on the floor were newspaper articles. There was one on Fred Rose being released in 1951 and going to Poland in 1953, one on Carr being released in 1956, and some others on Igor Gouzenko. There was also a boarding pass for a flight on Trans-Canada Airlines, to Heathrow and another for British European Airways, to Berlin, both dated 1957. There was a book review of Hugh Garner's *Cabbagetown*, the abridged 1950's edition, and David remembered his father's collection of inscribed books. He was just picking up what appeared to be a gold wedding band, when Meg put her hand to her mouth and gasped.

"My Lord, that's your father's wedding ring. He told me he lost it on one of his trips, in Poland I think. What's it doing in that box? I told him he probably took it off his finger so he could go with some tart over there, some *babushka*, most likely." David stared at her.

"Mom, can you fill me in here? Dad must have had a reason for not wearing his ring and putting it in this box. Did you two agree to a separation or something?"

"Heavens no! I don't know exactly what happened, David. I accused him of being unfaithful when he got back from that trip to Poland and he said I was the pot calling the kettle black. It was outrageous for him to accuse me of course, and it was never the same between us after that."

"I was about nine then and I vaguely remember you two fighting. It was pretty tense around here. Wasn't that when Uncle Peter taught me to golf and ski and took me to ball games? I think you sent me to summer camp too? I felt like you didn't want me around then."

"I always wanted you around, Davey. But your father turned mean and Peter was so kind. It was like he knew that your father and I were going through a rough patch and we thought it best to help get you out of a poisonous situation."

"Yes it was toxic. So, Mom, what about that discrepancy in my birth date? Was I overdue or premature? "

"Oh that. Your father must have miscalculated and blurted nonsense. You know how he could be. He latched onto that like a dog on a bone. I just said you were a healthy boy so what did it matter."

"And what about Carr claiming to have beaten up the Bishop's girl?"

"That must have been gallows' humour; after all he was on his way to jail, so why would anyone believe him anyway. I'm going to sit in the back garden for a spell. Want to join me?"

"No, I'm going to keep on working. I want to get going on the next decade here."

"Oh Davey, I do wish you'd get your nose out of the past, literally, and think about the present and future."

"Oh I am, Mom, but I've promised to deal with the past too." And to himself he thought, "I wish you'd deal with it too Mom."

After a while, David made some tea and joined his mother in the back yard, teapot, cups and some cookies on a tray.

"That's sweet, Davey."

"Thought I'd join you for a break. Iced tea might've been better; it's pretty humid, isn't it? So you think you're finished with traveling for the time being, eh? Not your cup of tea?" as he poured.

Meg smiled. "Thank you. No I don't think I'm cut out for travel after all. Not unless I have companions like you or Peter. Oh by the way, Peter said you did some traveling with a girl in Europe. Was she Italian?"

"No, she's Brazilian. A woman more than a girl," he smiled, considering how much to tell and paused to look at a brilliant cardinal caught in the late afternoon sun.

"I met her almost fifteen years ago and we worked together at the World Federation after graduating. We're just reconnecting, and very fond of each other."

Meg looked at him sidelong over her teacup. "Is she special?"

David laughed out loud, "Oh yes. But we're not rushing anything."

"Well the clock keeps ticking for us all, you know. I so wish I could be a grandmother."

"Ha, look who's rushing. But seriously, if you were going to be a grandmother, you'd have to cut down on your drinking. A lot."

Meg turned red but, with an effort, bit her tongue. Then she said, looking at him squarely. "I'll make you a deal. You make me a grandmother and I'll stop drinking. Until then the subject is taboo for both of us, ok?"

David bit the inside of his cheek, thinking a moment. Then he said. "I'm concerned about your drinking, Mom, so is Uncle Peter. I really wish you'd control it because I think you have a problem. But okay, it's a deal."

He shook her hand, once firmly, kissed her on the cheek and went back to the cedar box and work. Des had not done entries for every day so David skimmed. Some key words caught his eye and it was like entering a portal to a different world. He read.

Monday, January 23, 1950

The January thaw continues, hovering around freezing and sunny. We're having one of the warmest Januarys and I'm going to a meeting about the so-called Cold War. Drove out to RCMP Headquarters tucked in Vanier this morning. It was a pleasant drive down Rockcliffe by the Rideau River, along diplomat row. Zaneth said it was very hush-hush. Since May, Frank had been Assistant Commissioner for the whole organization and Director of Training, not bad for an Italian-Canadian he boasted. Also he said he had tapped me for a special assignment.

We met in a seminar room with Zaneth; Commissioner Stuart Wood; Chief Intelligence Officer, Superintendent Charles Rivett-Carnac; Sergeant Cecil Bayfield, who had followed the Gouzenko suspects for five months and coordinated the raid in February 1946; John Leopold, a rabid Commie-hater and baiter who dogged Tim Buck, the Canadian Communist Party leader; plus a few others I didn't recognize. Now we're called Special Branch instead of Security Service but there's still only a couple dozen across the country. Manpower is still tight, and here we are, half of us at this meeting...

...Frank introduced us and then Wood took over. He said the government's working group, code-named *Corby*, had decided that we were in danger from Communist infiltrations and crypto-Commies. They wanted us to investigate and compile a list of Communists and their sympathizers who may be more loyal to the U.S.S.R.; in other words, traitors to Canada. They wanted a top-secret list.

Rivett-Carnac then stood up and said he would be in charge of an operation called PROFUNC. It stood for Prominent Functionaries of the Communist Party. They needed this PROFUNC list so they could round up and intern potential enemies of the state in case of a national emergency.

Afterwards, I had coffee with Zaneth. I hate it when he's buddy-buddy, but I keep it under wraps. Because of my experience investigating Communist Mac-Paps and Rose and Carr, he wanted me to co-lead with Bayfield on this assignment and Rivett-Carnac had agreed. The investigators would work independently, loosely in two teams, reporting directly to Rivett-Carnac; but Zaneth wanted me to teach them some maneuvers, so to speak.

Frank was now conducting classes on conspiracy and interrogation in Ottawa and Toronto to senior officers and he ordered me to attend as a main operations conduit on the PROFUNC team. He said he was planning on retiring next year and that this was setting me up for a brilliant future. Of course that meant promoting me to Sergeant. I had earned it he said.

Fucking right, I had earned it. He thinks it's a favour, or maybe he's still guilty about blackmailing me into this job in the first place. I tugged my forelock of course, but I'll work this one to my benefit somehow.

Friday, February 24, 1950

Zaneth's courses didn't teach me much although he re-emphasized the benefit of one strategy. He suggested using a trailer when following someone to make sure that you yourself weren't being followed. But I believe in being careful, working alone. I'll mention it to the others but that tactic doubles our manpower and expense. I don't know why I'm concerned about saving them money though.

Decided since I was in Toronto anyway, I'd check in on Gouzenko for leads. He and his wife Anna and little boy were now living in Clarkson, a Toronto suburb, under a new identity. His new handle is George Brown. Some gall, choosing a Father of Confederation and Globe newspaper writer.

What a bastard, our Igor is! Here is this Soviet snitch who wanted to be middle class in Canada instead of being purged by Stalin, living off taxpayers money in this cozy nest, and he's already written a lumpy book about it a couple of years back. He called it *This Was My Choice*, as if he were courageous instead of running scared.

Anna asked if I wanted tea but Igor was rude and sent her from the room, the fucking inept cipher clerk. Now he's writing another book about his 'ordeal', he calls it, this time fiction. And he gives interviews wearing a stupid pillowcase hood. I'd put a pillow over his smug face if I could.

I asked him about other Communists in Canada and he whined that he had already given thirty-nine suspects' names to the RCMP, 'sleeper agents' he called them, but the Mounties were only able to convict eighteen. He said something about his job being done and it was our work now. I bit my tongue and kept up the apple butter, flattering him and saying we still needed him. Anyway, I got a few more names from him and started the list. Fred Rose and Sam Carr of course; and Richard Boyer, the atomic scientist at McGill University; Henry Harris, a Toronto optometrist; former Postmaster General Ernst Bertrand; and a few others who Igor knew the Soviets were trying to recruit, like David Laxer, another Labour-Party organizer; and Al King, a Trail union worker who did something with heavy water production.

It seemed the spy ring tentacles were everywhere, operating in front groups for the Communists, such as the National Research Council, the Canadian Association of Science Workers, mathematician Israel Halperin at Queen's University, even External Affairs and the U.S. Treasury apparently. I jotted them down, thanked him and wished him luck, dissembling all the way.

Monday, March 6, 1950

I'm back in Ottawa now, spent a lovely weekend with Meg and David. He's really mobile now, really sturdy, and we had fun in the snow in the back yard, building a snowman. It's been colder than usual, well below freezing but spring will be here soon. My list of names to investigate is growing. Rivett-Carnac wants a whole profile: appearance, age, where they work, residence, even possible escape routes we should be aware of, and to update any changes over time. Lots to keep us busy. Bayfield and I are working our teams hard. We've got such a backlog;

there are over 37,000 cases we're looking at. Ridiculous, with so few investigators!

I did have an interesting dénouement to my couple of weeks in Toronto though I reconnected with Hugh Garner at a book signing at the Royal York before I caught the train to Ottawa. His book *Cabbagetown* was just published and he was signing some copies. He had a bottle of scotch in front of him and was smoking a cigar when I approached. I said I'd met him once in Calgary in 1935 and he had encouraged me to write.

"Hell, we were wet behind the ears then, weren't we?" He laughed and starting coughing as he offered me a chair. There was no one else waiting, so we chatted, mainly about unions and Spain and the war. He was a bit inebriated and offered a bunch of opinions. Of Spain, he said, "Well, we were all victims in that one." About spy rings, he said, "The government's overplaying this communist crap. Shit, they're even going after folks that write with their left hand, for chrissakes." When he asked if I had written anything, I shrugged diffidently, said I had written a couple of articles but no, not really. "Well you don't score any goals if you don't shoot at the net, boyo." He was getting loud and my train was due so I asked him again to inscribe my copy. He wrote something about it's hard to escape your history. Anyway, we shook hands; it was good to see him again.

Hell, maybe we are all victims, after all is said and done. It's true that some of these leftie punks we're fingering have just been in the wrong place at the wrong time. But shit, we're all dealt different cards, and it's our job to play 'em the best we can. Besides they chose to join those Commie-fronts, no one forced them.

Friday, May 12, 1950

Davey turned two today. Boy he's a great kid; I could hug him to bits. Meg and I agreed that he could have his own cupcake today, a chocolate one with icing and sprinkles. We laughed as he grabbed it in his hand and ate, smearing it all over his face. Meg got a little upset at the mess but I said to let him be, he's having fun and we can clean up in the bath later. We gave him a little pull toy, a duck on wheels that clacks behind him. He pulled that thing all over the place and wanted it in bed with him. I love that boy.

Tuesday, October 31, 1950

There seem to be Communists coming out of the woodwork everywhere. Senator Joe McCarthy and the House of Un-American Activities Committee is ferreting them out like crazy. Alger Hiss, with the State Department, was convicted of perjury and being a Communist. An American grand jury indicted Ethel and Julius Rosenberg for passing atomic secrets, and Klaus Fuchs was arrested in Britain for atomic espionage. We have our own shit too.

Bruno Pontecorvo, one of our atomic scientists at the Chalk River nuclear plant, fled to the U.S.S.R. The *Financial Post* reporter, Ron Williams claimed there were over 50,000 card-carrying members in the 'red union roster'. He called them Stalin's North American troops. Speaking of troops, the Korean War continues with the Chinese Communists now involved! Weren't we fighting a war just five years ago? Oh hell, are the Red goblins out celebrating tonight?

Friday, January 12, 1951

Gotta tell Bayfield to rein in that bulldog Leopold. The idiot says there's a red under every bed. It's nuts! We've got ACTIVE files on 20,000 names and over 2,000 organizations we're checking out. Not many of those will end up as espionage, if any. Some might be subversives, maybe. We're getting more recruits but not enough to deal with this crazy backlog. Looks like I'll be working another weekend. This Commie search has ruined my Christmas holiday with Meg and Davey. I'll have to figure a way to get it back.

Tuesday, May 8, 1951

Jeez, haven't written much since January. This process has been pretty zealous. For every hundred screened, we find maybe one security risk. And it's not always political. Now we even look at guys who might be vulnerable to Soviet influence because of loose morals or even debt. It's not just civil servants either. The Security Panel has us looking at the

Electrical Workers, the National Film Board and the Great Lakes seamen. Talk about fishing. There was a bombshell on the wires today. Two British diplomats, Guy Burgess and Donald Maclean, had gone 'missing' and now it's confirmed that they defected to the U.S.S.R.

By the way, Fred Rose was released early from jail. Seems he returned to Montreal and he's not very healthy. I wondered about tailing him myself since he had been my case, and after all he is a real Communist. But R-C said it was taken care of. Apparently he put that bulldog, Leopold, onto him. The strategy is to let any potential employer of Rose know that he's dealing with a traitor. Maybe there is justice.

I've got a holiday planned this weekend to celebrate Davey's 3rd birthday, want to take him and Meg to Niagara Falls on the train. That is unless Rivett-Carnac gets the jitters, or the zorros as some of the younger recruits say, and we have to work again.

Monday, May 14, 1951

Sure enough the Security Panel called a meeting for Saturday. Pissed me off but I forced myself to look keen. I had to cancel our trip though. Meg was sure disappointed. Instead, we took David to a carnival at Landsdowne Park on Saturday and he had his first cotton candy. Made him sticky and excitable, but he seemed to really enjoy the carny barkers and bright lights. I won Meg a kewpie doll and she held my arm on the way home. Who needs the Falls?

Thursday, November 1, 1951

More and more I feel I'm part of a witch-hunt. It's like we're standing in a shadow cast by the Americans and I'm getting tired of the lack of light. It's the Mounties' Redcoats against the Commie Reds; are we guardians or goons? It's all getting pretty muddled. We denied security clearance to eight scientists who were part of a Communist front group, the Canadian Association of Science Workers. One young couple got caught up in the sweep, the Jones', and they got a raw deal, I think. He was an idealistic, leftist engineer, just thinking that scientists should consider the human consequences of their research, and he wrote some articles in their rag newsletter. He worked for an electronics firm and they withdrew him from defense contract jobs because we didn't give him a security clearance. They didn't fire him, but his wife lost her job.

Thursday, February 14, 1952

Got into a huge shouting match with Rivett-Carnac today. Seems a 1950 RCMP report I had done on a Department of External Affairs diplomat, Herbert Norman, had been passed to some witch-hunting senators in the American Senate Internal Security Subcommittee. Is this fucking information sharing or what? Rivett-Carnac ordered me to conduct a second investigation. "Why?" I demanded. We're having enough trouble investigating people once. Norman was already exonerated."

"Several reasons," R-C coldly answered, "one of which is because I'm ordering it. And another is that the new Commissioner Nicholson is under some pressure from the Yanks. Let's face it, Norman is suspicious."

He skimmed the report, looking over his reading glasses and said, "Attended Cambridge University with those British traitors, member of a Commie front organization, the Institute of Pacific Relations, and recently was fingered by a witness at the American Senate Subcommittee. And those namby-pambies over at External keep giving him important jobs, Japan, the United Nations. Shit, Dilman, you yourself saw him meeting with that traitor Israel Halperin. So investigate again!"

I remembered Norman. Nice guy, proper and cultured, nattily dressed, piercing blue eyes behind owlish wire-rimmed glasses. An academic diplomat if ever there was one. But I could find nothing on him except circumstantial evidence, not that that would save him. So I sighed and went through his file again. Those Americans have got us sniffing like bloodhounds after coons...

David looked up and was surprised to see the sun was setting and realized his Mom was upstairs. He rubbed his eyes and his knees cracked as he unfolded himself from the floor. He called his mother but there was no answer, and went to the kitchen to fix a sandwich. There was an empty vodka bottle in the bin and a lime half-cut on the counter, no doubt in the same condition as his mother, he mused.

He thought about what he had been reading. Jesus! The so-called bland decade of the Fifties, of rock and roll, Elvis Presley, and buttons for 'I Like Ike' and 'Ban The Bomb'. They all seemed like some kind of Kafka nightmare. Such fear and innuendo.

It must have been so depressing after the sacrifices and idealism of the war, having to live with bogeymen everywhere at your work and in your neighbourhood. His dad seemed overworked and sounded like he was getting depressed again.

David made himself a coffee hoping to get through another of Des's years before going up to bed and writing his own journal for Lydia. He noticed that there were fewer entries in his father's journal, the tone being somewhat flat and monotone, recording on the fly or being perfunctory . Then there were several in a row, more upbeat ones, that caught David's eye.

Wednesday, September 30, 1953

I had to come up with a plan. Daylight Savings Time ended on Sunday and it seemed like the light was fading on me too. Work has been getting to me. I know I said they wouldn't own me but now I wonder if they're consuming me. It's not getting any better either. It's like a danse macabre of 'one step forward and two steps back'; some good news and double the bad news...

... Stalin died in March and then the Yanks executed both Julius and Ethel Rosenberg in June; the Korean War ended in July and then Soviets tested their first H-bomb in August. Over 2,000 died when the North Sea flooded Holland. No wonder some jerk predicted the world would end in August!

Davey has been in kindergarten half-days, a big step for him, but he's doing fine. Seemed a good time for me to take a break and I told Meg I had to go on a bit of a sales trip for a few days.

So on a couple of hunches, I planned to track down an old contact, Lucien Tellier, in east-side Montreal. My plan was to use him again. Surely it was more important to get real Communists rather than sympathizers and lackeys. Maybe Lucien could help.

Thursday, October 1, 1953

At first Lucien said I had nothing on him, but I said that Carr was in jail for passport tampering and I could tell *les flics* that Lucien had given a couple of Mac-Pap passports to Carr. He knew I would lie to get my way. All I wanted was some *bona fide* Communists, not suspects. Also, I could pay him again for his services, more than the last time. He said he could get me two names, and then we were done. I agreed.

The next was more difficult. I met Herbert Norman at a bar in Hull. He was uncomfortable, dapper among the working stiffs and looking a bit pouty. I said to him that I had a proposal. If he could get me the names of two Communists who were in External Affairs, I would make sure he wouldn't be investigated again. He tapped his fingers on the table. I could tell the stress of investigations was wearing on him. He said he would get back to me.

Friday, October 2, 1953

Today I went into the office, ready to tell R-C my plan, to cut to the chase and get real Communists; but R-C told me to sit down, that he had a new assignment for me, a bizarre one.

It appears that the London-based Polish government-in-exile had squirreled some royal treasures out of the castle in Krakow before Hitler took Poland, and the goods had somehow been hidden in Canada for safekeeping during the war. Canada gave asylum to a Polish-in-exile representative who is currently working at the Catholic University of Ottawa. Now the Communist government of Poland wants the treasures back. We're in an awkward position; Canada recognized the new Communist government after the war but we're obviously anti-Soviet Communist now. My new assignment is to find out what's going on and report back as soon as possible. I had trouble hiding my smile and relief; away from the desk and working on something specific. Lucien and Norman will be Plan B for the future.

It was pure joy at home tonight. I played 'fort' and 'rasslin' with Davey after dinner, and Meg and I did some wrestling of our own after Davey's bath and bedtime.

Tuesday, October 6, 1953

Norman let me know that he wasn't playing; he wasn't a Communist and didn't know any in External. He would have to live or die with Special Branch Intelligence investigations about his security risk status.

But Lucien said he had two names for sure and an interesting suspect. I also found out that the exiled Polish representative here, Stanislaw Szczęny, on his own authority transferred the Polish crown treasures to the Hôtel-Dieu convent in Quebec City. Clearly I had some things to be grateful for this Thanksgiving weekend. A fascinating new case and two out of three nibbles on the never-ending assignment to identify Communists. The hooks are baited and it's time to cast the lines...

CHAPTER 16.

A BETRAY OF TRUST

Ottawa, 1954-1955, 1985
Kraków, Poland, 1955, 1985

Lydia swayed in her hammock slung between the palm trees in the yard by her digs on *Ilha Grande*. She was reading a slightly thick packet that had come from David, smiling over his stories of running early in the morning to avoid the humidity, or his asking for a picture of her because he could remember her body parts but not her face. There was some news too, of applying to Pearson College near Victoria, British Columbia, one of six World Peace Colleges.

David gave some sketchy background about the school operating under the International Baccalaureate for about 200 students and he'd let her know any results of the application as soon as he heard. He also said that he might be going to Poland, perhaps with his uncle, for a week in September because of information in his Dad's journals, but nothing specific. She observed that he told her of what he saw or thought but rarely of his feelings. She knew that emotions were in there; like a vitrine of curios, you could see them but not touch them. She would have to ask him specific questions, she realized. All he wanted to know from her was about her Christmas holidays.

It was mid-August and David was taking a break in his back yard. His iced tea was refreshing but his mother's seemed to be having a different effect on her, if mild slurring was any indication. He had just finished reading a package of mail from Lydia, and Meg, like a yenta, pried for information. David showed Meg the picture of Lydia in her school attire wearing a white blouse, and sweater draped over her shoulders, sweet smile, and full head of hair held off her face with a mauve ribbon. Meg hummed and clucked, but there was also begrudged approval.

Lydia wrote that she had a *recesso escolar*, a break from teaching, which would last from Christmas through all of January until after Carnival in February, approximately eight weeks, and slyly inquired why he wanted to know. Work and family were fine but she missed him terribly. He smelled a whiff from a few drops of her perfume on the letter and smiled, making a note of giving more details about feelings to her in the next bundle. But his recess was over and he returned to the '50s journals. Back inside, he continued reading.

Wednesday, January 20, 1954

I returned to my assigned Polish file this week. Winter is not always the best time to travel in Quebec, but I'd managed to arrange an interview with the Mother Superior at the Hôtel-Dieu Convent in Quebec City and had to go...

...I'd found out that Stanislaw Szczęny, a mathematician at the University of Ottawa, had transferred the Wawel Castle treasure out of Ottawa with the Polish ex-curator's connivance. I interviewed Stan early in the New Year.

He said the Polish government-in-exile snuck out the valued Wawel treasures in cargo chests in 1939 on the Polish liner, the *MS Batory*, and stored them at Ottawa's Experimental Farm which had fire-proof and temperature-controlled facilities. The Mounties themselves escorted the crates, he added.

Then after the war, when Poland was betrayed by Britain and Canada who accepted the Communist rule of Poland, he decided to move them to the only Catholic and anti-Communist place in Canada, namely Premier Maurice Duplessis' Québec. What a bizarre scenario!

The Mother Superior was cordial but cold. She had a nervous tic of constantly pursing her lips which accentuated her upper lip wrinkles and made the hair follicles on her chin twitch and scrape along her starched wimple. Yes, she had the crown jewels and more; no, I couldn't see them; and no, I couldn't have them. They were under her safekeeping.

I showed her pictures and a list of what we understood she had. Yes, she confirmed she had the two-handed coronation sword, called the *Szczerbiec*, two jewel-encrusted crowns, two orbs, and some letters from Chopin as part of the cache.

Then she admitted that the Communist Polish government had sent some very nasty and demanding letters to her so that she felt compelled to enlist the aid of Maurice Duplessis himself. No, she would not change her mind and let the Canadian government handle it. Instead of losing my temper, I complimented her on her sang-froid. When I added that really it was a federal matter between nations, she rapped her knuckles on the desk and said, *'Mais non, monsieur. C'est une affaire entre mon Dieu et moi.'*

Sometimes flattery gets you nowhere. Maybe Québec is the best place for the Polish royal treasure. But the fact of the matter is that Duplessis will make political hay out of this, thus proving his claim of being the defender of Catholicism who has no truck with the Communists.

Tuesday, February 2, 1954

The Wawel Castle file is somewhat dormant. I reported to Rivett-Carnac who said the politicians are dealing with it now. Then Lucien contacted me so I went to Montreal to meet him at our favourite bagel bistro. He was surly and wary as usual. I told him that I heard Fred Rose had gone back to Poland and he mumbled that it was good riddance. Going on a hunch, I asked him if he ever met up with Carr when Sam was on the lam. He looked away, said maybe once or twice, and slurped his coffee.

"I got doze names, here in dis envelope. Now we're done, *n'est-ce pas?*"

"What's your hurry? So if you saw Carr, you were aiding and abetting a criminal. That's bad, Lucien. What did he see you about?"

"He wanted a passport to get out of the country. I told him I doan have one. Then he asked who did. I doan know but said maybe the secretary, I dunno, me."

"You told that monster that Rose's secretary might have a passport? Did you know where her new job was?

"*Oui* (which he pronounced *way*), I told Carr that she was a good Catholic girl working for dat Archbishop Vachon after she quit Rose."

"But she didn't have any passports, did she? You bastard."

"Take your names and give me my money."

I squeezed his wrist as he pushed the envelope towards me. Then I forced his hand back and he writhed. "*Maudit, chalice!*"

"Settle down you creep; you're drawing attention. Let me look at those names, you snake."

I read and looked up, squinting threateningly at Lucien. "There's only one with a check mark and two with question marks. What's this shit? Are these the real deal or not? "

"*Bien sûr*, of course. Gérard Fortin. He's a Communist organizing a bush workers' union out dare in the boonies. Pierre Trudeau? He's dat young intellectual dat doze priests accused of being a Red after he visit Russia last year. Remember he was writing pro-worker articles in dat Asbestos Strike a few years back? He's one dat Duplessis wanted to get with dat Padlock Law; you know, lock him up and paint him Red for writing Commie propaganda. So he might be one."

I growled at him in a low voice. "Fuck, Lucien, we have thousands of 'maybe's'. I want 'for sure'; that was the deal."

 "Well, dis one could really interest you," he said pointing at the name Trumpet. You guys are running a double-agent out of duh Soviet Embassy, it seems. My sources say duh Soviets dare doan know who it is except for a code name maybe, and would pay *beaucoup* to know." He said this rubbing his forefinger and thumb together.

"I don't know anything about us running a double-agent and if I did I wouldn't sell him out."

"Well one of your guys has been asking around about how to contact Communists; maybe he wants to sell dis agent out for duh money and you can catch him, *peut-être*. So we are *finis*, okay?"

"Your sources better be good, Lucien, because I know where you live if these are bum leads. Yeah, we're finished, and this is for sending Carr to my wife." I took his coffee mug, spat in it, and left.

Friday, May 14, 1954

We're all very excited. Peter has finished law school in Toronto and is moving to Ottawa this weekend. He's going to start his law practice here. Tomorrow he'll be here for dinner and wants to give Davey a belated birthday present, a nice touch for him to remember. It'll be good to have him around.

On the work front, I had told Cecil Bayfield a while ago that I heard we had a very important double-agent running out of the Soviet Embassy, that I'd learned the code was maybe biblical, something about a 'Trumpet', and that the spy might be in danger of being revealed. Bayfield knew nothing about it.

I kept my eyes and ears open and nothing came up until a week ago. A low-life dandy with the counter-espionage surveillance team, James Morrison, invited me for coffee out of the blue. Morrison was an odd one. He drove a new flashy red Buick Roadmaster convertible and wore shiny pants and a loud cream sports jacket with shiny black stitches patterned throughout. He bragged it was the new Dacron material, as if it mattered to me. I sure don't know how he does it on his salary though.

Anyway, he warned me off any questions about 'Gideon'. I put two and two together and realized this was the guy Lucien was talking about and the code name was Gideon, not Trumpet. The idiot got under my skin so I pulled rank.

Who the hell did he think he was; didn't he know I was his superior? He warned me to stay off his turf. I challenged him, "You and who's army, the NKVD? He laughed sarcastically at me and said that, if I was such a big shot and 'know-it-all', why didn't I know it was KGB now? I glared at him, "Look asshole, if you need money for your fancy duds maybe you could do a deal with the NKVD, the KGB, or the CBC, if you have the balls." Oh, he had the balls he said, and that if I went nosing around anymore, I better watch my back, or better yet, watch my family's.

The unveiled threat bothered me a lot. I mentioned it to Cecil but the strange thing is he said Morrison wasn't on any Soviet Embassy staff duty. Should I go to Rivett-Carnac? Something fishy is going on...

David needed a break and a shift in his focus. He decided to write to Lydia. He was sitting at the kitchen table, pen in hand and sipping a coffee but the journal's revelations kept entering his thoughts. He was only seven then and didn't remember anything unusual but he sensed some danger for Des and his mom and himself from the journal.

He put those thoughts on the back burner while he wrote Lydia. He told her of his arrangements for his own Kraków trip, his picture of Lydia lying by the thin blue airmail paper. They were keeping up their daily diaries more or less and sending them in small packet-missives but sometimes a summary letter was needed.

Monday, August 12, 1985

Hello sweetheart:

We're having some humid weather and thunderstorms here. Hopefully it will clear the air a bit. How I miss you. I've been busy most days with the journal and research except for a couple of times when I played golf (rather badly) with Uncle Peter. My days go something like this, as you probably gathered.

Run five to ten miles early to beat the heat of the day. Home to shower, then coffee and read the newspaper. (What do you think of this new Soviet leader, Gorbachev? He wants more openness or glasnost he calls it. Could be opening a can of worms, don't you think?) Anyway, then it's Work. Lunch. Work. Dinner. Bit of work. Write to you. And so it goes.

I heard back from Pearson College yesterday. They included some brochures that were very appealing; I have put one in this package for you. They don't need anyone right now but were impressed with my résumé. My international experience, plus my ability to teach sailing and cross-country running, were very desirable, they said, since they don't focus on team sports and competition. They asked if they could keep my application on file. Lydia, it's a place and a style that I think (and feel) I would really like to work at, kids from several countries on grants, the teachers promoting tolerance and peace issues. The site is right on the ocean and in the woods too. So I wrote back thanking them for their consideration and yes, please keep me on file. It's a poker in the fire.

I'm looking forward to experiencing some of your life in Brazil but also would love for you to share mine in Canada some day. And yes, I remember my promise to teach you to ski. You do realize it will be cold? But I can teach you about après ski also ("wink, wink, nudge, nudge, say no more"). By the way, what do you think of me coming to Brazil to holiday with you in January?

I took my mom to see the acclaimed new film, Kiss of the Spider Woman, last week. She said she heard it was about Brazil and it would be good to know a little about that country if I was going to be serious about you. Of course, I'm serious about you but I don't know if the movie gave my mother a great sense of Brazil or feelings for it.

It was a brilliant movie but the prison conditions with the torture and homosexual scenes, I could see her worrying about me if I went there. William Hurt was tremendous as Molina; go see it if you can.

How did I feel during the film, you might wonder (you asked me to include more of my feelings, right)? I missed you like Raúl Juliá missed Sonia Braga. I worried about you and all the police torture; I would go mad if you were caught up in that situation. Brazil may be better than it was but it's still in an iron grip, however benign. Really I had this urge to go to you and hold you right away. You must think it's all talk since I'm going to Poland and not Brazil, eh?

Poland is on my agenda for several reasons. In my Dad's journals, he says he was requested to accompany the Polish in-exile representative to Kraków as security while negotiations for the Wawel Castle treasure continued in 1955. Dad also took the opportunity to visit Fred Rose, a personal nemesis of his. But, this was also the time when my father's behaviour changed towards me and my Mom. I hope to find out more clues about that and want to meet with a shady character from Dad's past, a Sam Carr who is still alive and living in Poland. My Dad's writing went sporadic and vague in the diary so I'm hoping that this trip might fill in some blanks.

Uncle Peter will not be coming with me. I proposed it over lunch the other day. He said he had faced his demons and didn't need, or want, to return to Poland, that I was more than capable of facing my and Dad's ghosts now. He said he wasn't abandoning me, but it did make me feel more alone somehow.

Anyway I leave next week, August 19th, with another vial of ashes, on a junket to Kraków, with double motives; one for the quest and one for my own curiosity. I'll be back in Ottawa a week later.

I'll write you a long letter after my trip.

Love you, David.

David finished and went to bed. He wanted to complete these journals before his trip and gird himself for what lay ahead if he could.

But he was tired and was only able to read one more entry before drifting off.

Tuesday, September 20, 1955

It's getting harder to keep secrets away from Peter and Meg, even their question, "How was work today?" puts me on edge. This security work is like the Hydra, no sooner do I cut one Communist down when two others grow...

...Lucien's tips were mixed. We got Fortin; we got nothing on Trudeau; and James Morrison and Gideon were a complete puzzle. Cecil Bayfield invited me for lunch and said that R-C and External were all hush-hush and aflutter; Gideon has gone missing. I wonder if Morrison sold Gideon out finally. Damn, if he did! It would be partly because I caved to his threats and let R-C and Bayfield handle it, not carefully enough apparently.

It's going to be a long trip with Szczęny to Kraków but good to get out of Ottawa for a spell. My assignment is to keep an eye on Stan and protect him from vindictive Poles or KGB, but I also hope to see an old 'friend'...

David was on his own flight now to Poland and he was thinking about the similarities to his dad's trip. It was almost thirty years ago to the day that his father took this very trip, David thought. Back then it wasn't British Airways but a forerunner, a British Overseas Airways Corporation (BOAC) flight from Toronto to London and a British European Airways hop to West Berlin where he took a train to Kraków. Des's journey took many more hours than David's.

Shortly into David's own flight, he closed his tired eyes and seemed to enter a hypnagogic state, somewhere between a daydream and a wakeful sleep, a psychological state of transition where a person feels like they are 'seeing' more clearly and interpretively. Des's journal came alive for David in his fluting state at 35,000 feet.

David remembered what he had read and dreamily seemed to accompany his father in Poland, as if he were actually there with Des in Kraków.

Des had described the royal Polish city of Kraków in some detail and David had researched it too. Kraków had escaped much of the WW II damages even though it was the capital of the German Occupation. Its medieval architecture which emanated around a spacious cobble-stoned square in the Old Town was untouched. These were ancient and historical buildings surrounding the old square or *Rynek Główny* as it was called.

The two most prominent structures were the Renaissance Cloth Hall with graceful arcades, and the red brick 13th century Gothic basilica, St. Mary's, known as *Mariacki*. It had two uneven towers, the taller one where the fabled bugler warned the city of invaders from the east so long ago, and where present-day buglers still commemorated the event every hour. There were also many other old brick palaces with cellar pubs and restaurants, none more famous than the inn *Wierzynek*, the graceful symmetrical, grey-green plastered building that hosted royal weddings.

Just beyond the centre, there was a unique green park buffer, the *Planty*, circumnavigating the Old Town where the medieval walls used to be, enfolding the 14th century Jagiellonian University on the west side, and Wawel Castle on the south, near a bend in the Vistula River. It was a city of attractive facades and hidden nooks.

The Jewish suburb to the southeast, *Kazimierz*, was not so lucky. It used to have over a hundred synagogues and prayer houses for over 60,000 Jews but, by the end of the war, all remnants of Jewishness were gone. Kraków was only beginning to re-build the main Old Synagogue when Des visited, ten years after the war's end.

David, still in his dreamy fog, was sitting at the café table with Des and Stan. It was at the ornate *Szara* Bar with the fluted ceiling, decorated with brown and floral designs and black wrought iron. They had a view past the bronze Adam Mickiewicz Monument, Poland's great Romantic poet, to the Town Hall. The sky was blue with a few puffy white clouds and an occasional dust devil swirled paper and grit and leaves around in the near-empty, early-morning square. Szczęny was sitting opposite Des and David.

Stanisław had receding hair that made his dark darting eyes look even more intense. He was fond of sitting backward on a chair, his chin resting on his arms folded on the back of it, sleeves of his white shirt rolled up, staring at you as if he were constantly challenging.

Dad was speaking. "So what time is your meeting with the curators at the castle?"

"They said ten. We may be there over lunch. Just be vigilant."

"I will, I will, relax. Listen, I'm arranging to meet someone too, this afternoon; so keep that in mind with your meetings. We'll need a break for an hour around 3 p.m." Then Des read from a phrase book, "*Czy pan rozumie?* It means, 'do you understand'?"

Stan laughed, "Your pronunciation is terrible. Yes I understand."

"That's okay; the guy I'm seeing speaks English." Des grinned; Stan and he were easy with one another.

They walked together down *Grodzka* Street, the Royal Route to Wawel Hill, admiring the crenellated wall which enclosed the castle, its cream and red brick looked quite stunning along the river. An usher escorted them into the castle.

They passed through several state rooms, rich with tapestries, along checkered marble floors and wooden ceilings, all ornate. They reached the Crown Treasury Room and ascended some stairs that wound around a cream-coloured central pillar called the Hen's Foot, passing through Casimir the Great's room, their shoes echoing on the ecru marble floor. It was meant to impress and by the time they got to the 14th century Jadwiga and Jagiello's Room, they were duly impressed. There was a table and four chairs and two dour men awaiting. At the head of the table, an empty glass case resting on two marble pedestals almost cried, "J'accuse".

After introductions, Alfred Majewski, the head of the castle's restoration, began the negotiations by pointing to the empty case and saying the coronation sword of Sigismund I, the *Szczerbiec*, belonged in that case and that Canada and Pan Szczęny must return it. The other fellow was stolid, sitting in a baggy, wrinkled blue suit, his eyes puffy and half closed all the time.

Des looked at David and nodded to confirm he suspected KGB.

The conversation went back and forth in Polish until a break for lunch. Des made sure he was always between the rumpled stale-skinned guy and Stan. More conversation, sometimes the elevated volume echoing in the empty room, and then adjournment at two o'clock.

As they rose to leave, Alfred said, "We recovered the *Mariacki* altarpiece of Veit Stoss from the Nazis when loyal Polish prisoners-of-war said it was hidden in Nuremburg, and we'll get our Wawel Treasures too."

Stan spoke in Russian to insult Alfred, "*Da, nyet, navernoe*", yes, no, maybe."

Leaving the castle grounds, Stan said the negotiations went well, that the bottom line seems to be that they want the treasures back not only because they're Polish, but also he guessed because they wanted them to celebrate the 1000th anniversary of Poland being Christian, which was slated for 1966. He had wiggle room to negotiate, he smiled.

In his mind's eye, David envisioned them retracing their steps back to the *Grodzka* Street hotel where Des told Stan to lock the door and let no one in, until he returned and used the password, which he wrote down in case the room was bugged. Des changed his coat and hat in an effort to confuse anyone following and they departed, knowing he would be tailed.

They (Des and David) entered the Old Square and went into the Cloth Hall market, the *Sukiennice*, which was now teeming with people. He raced ahead, removed his hat and burst through an exit leading to the *Mariacki*.

The church was full too, with people wanting to see the stained glass and famous altarpiece, almost forty feet high with richly painted panels depicting the life of Mary, the Mother of Jesus. There was also a line of tourists waiting to climb the stairs of the tower just as the hourly bugle began, signaling 3 p.m.

It was easy to hide among the throng and leave via a side door, since all eyes were focused upward. There was plenty to distract anyone trying to follow them and Des was adept at backtracking on narrow side streets until they got to the *Planty* near the university grounds.

Slightly out of breath and running a bit late, Des put his hat back on and rested by a tree, lighting a cigarette and casually looking around. Then they walked briskly to the statue of Copernicus by a red brick college, flanked by two plane trees. A depressed-looking man was sitting on the pedestal step wrapped in a dark overcoat too big for him.

Des walked up and said, "Hello Fred, long time no see. Thanks for agreeing to meet me." Des looked up at the statue of Copernicus, who was gazing down onto a ringed astrolabe in his hand, and remarked, "Seems like he has holes in his world too, Fred."

Fred grumbled, "You're late. I would have left but you promised me a meal, not sarcasm."

With a quick look around, Des took Fred by the arm and led him to a cellar restaurant nearby, taking a table so they could see the legs of passersby through the casement window.

"I'm not hungry, Fred, but you go ahead and order. I just need you to answer some questions. How's the import-export business going?"

He looked up from the menu and said, "You guys have ruined me, harassed me, jailed me, taken away my citizenship, and now you want to put the knife in again? 'If you prick us, do we not bleed?'", invoking Shylock's speech.

"Settle down. I'm more interested about your past, not your present or future. Do you remember your personal office secretary while you were an M.P.?"

"Sure I do, Margaret Mary was her name, I think. Sweet young thing. She quit at the Christmas holidays, just before I was arrested. Said her father wanted her to work for a Catholic, not a Communist, so she was giving her notice to be a secretary in the Archbishop's office. Why?"

"Do you also remember Lucien Tellier, your gopher?"

"Yes, of course, and again, why?"

"Lucien told me he sent Sam Carr to see Miss Tanner at the Archbishop's to try to retrieve a bogus passport so he could get out of the country. Do you know anything about that?"

Fred had finished his borscht and was now devouring his breaded pork cutlet. He finished chewing, swallowed and said, "I do recall some news in jail that there was a manhunt for Carr but that he eluded you guys until he was caught in New York. What's this got to do with me?"

"Someone messed up Miss Tanner. I just wanted to know if Carr was involved."

Rose put down his knife and fork. "Sam Carr was a brute and a bully, very good qualities in an organizer. He could be pretty mean if he didn't get his way. I never gave Margaret Mary any passports to conceal but if Carr thought she had one, he could be rough. I heard that he bragged about hurting her at his trial's end. That was bad of him."

"Did you ever hear if Carr raped Miss Tanner?"

"No, nothing for sure. But Carr was capable of it. There were rumours about him in the constituency but I ignored them. Sam was too useful and dangerous to confront."

"One thing more, Fred. Did you ever try it on with your secretary?"

Fred blushed, "Once or twice but nothing more than an office squeeze. Nothing serious."

"Okay, thanks Fred." Des laid enough *złotys* on the table for a week's worth of meals and they left.

Des was very contemplative on the walk back to the hotel. David was disturbed. Had his mother been raped?

At the hotel, Des knocked on the door and said, "*Rozumie!*" , the password. Stan opened the door shaking his head and chuckling and they left immediately for dinner.

"I want to treat you to dinner, my expense account, Stan. Let's go fancy."

They walked to the Old Square, turned right and entered the *Wierzynek*, a 14th century palace, the site of a twenty-day wedding feast of King Casimir the Great's granddaughter. Up the plush stairs there were thematic dining rooms, one with antique clocks, another a knights' armoury, walls with ornate paintings, friezes and garlanded wall paper, antique mirrors reflecting golden candle light, wooden-paneled ceilings, and floor-to-ceiling windows with views to the lit buildings of the *Rynek Główny* . Stan's eyes widened but Des seemed unfazed.

"You know, Stan, you Catholics are lucky. You can sin and get fully forgiven. Me, I can't confess or get forgiven. Maybe that's why I can't forgive others their trespasses so readily."

"But Des, don't you realize, it's God that forgives."

David laughed, "That's a good one, Dad. See, you're not God after all."

Des ignored him, naturally. "Let me ask you something, Stan. What would you do if you just couldn't trust someone anymore, like your wife?"

"Unfair, Des, I'm not married. But once trust goes, it's really hard to build up again. I had a best friend who stole my girlfriend once. All I can say is that I tried to forgive and trust again, but it was never the same. I guess I'm not God either."

They were looking at the menu. It was going to be expensive, really expensive, almost a week's wages for two meals and wine, but Des didn't care. If it was costly, it was also rich food; you knew what you were getting for your money.

Des fancied wild fare, and ordered saddle of roe deer and quail in currant vodka sauce served with pear chutney and dauphinoise potatoes; Stan went moderate and typically Polish, dumplings with sausage and lard to start, and lamb cutlets and cabbage for his main. Des also ordered an aged Grand Cru Pinot Noir from Burgundy, as much as the meal cost. David whistled under his breath at both the decadence and the ambience he was sensing, almost like a clairvoyant.

"Des, are we celebrating something I don't know about or is something bothering you? You're acting differently since returning to the room."

Des answered thoughtfully after appreciating a sip of wine. "A bit of both I guess; the end of our assignment and a bit of grieving, I suppose. Something in me snapped during my meeting this afternoon; I learned I can't trust someone I thought I could and my universe is falling apart, ironic in the city of Copernicus, isn't it? So tonight it's eat, drink and be merry, because you never know when you'll be able to again."

Stan had second thoughts, "I know my expenses won't cover this, are you sure we want to be doing this?"

"Yes, I'm sure; I'll recoup the cost somehow."

"Do you want to talk about it?"

"Not really. I have a friend who's like a brother at home, who I may confide in, but right now I just want *carpe diem*, as they say."

Over dessert and almost at the bottom of another bottle of wine, Des sighed and said, "I'm going to tell you something I've never told anyone, Stan. A memory from when I was a kid that reminds me of the way I'm feeling tonight.

There was a creek through some woods near where I lived. We used to play along the path, throw sticks into the stream to see whose could go the furthest in the current. One day my friends and I came across some older and rougher boys from another street. They had caught some garter snakes and were pinching them behind their heads to open their jaws wide and then forcing sticks down their gullets. Horribly cruel and awful to see, especially since I didn't like snakes anyway.

I must have looked shocked and scared. They noticed us and one boy ran at me with a newly stiffened snake. I turned and ran, hating those bullies, but also hating myself for being a sissy. I vowed I would get back at those sadists somehow and never show my fear again. I'm afraid it means that I bear a grudge. I can sense my heart just kind of freezing over. That's the way I feel tonight."

"Did you ever get back at those boys?"

"In a way. I told my school principal that I knew about a gang responsible for vandalizing. He called the police and the police investigated. The bullies got hassled and were frightened. I do work at getting my own back, even if it's fudging an expense account," he laughed. "But I don't know if getting back is going to work this time."

Des gulped the last of the wine. David grit his teeth and thought. "Snakes, sadists, sissies and shame, that's a bit of a sibilant memory, Dad. But why did Rose's account make you freeze out Mom and me? Rose didn't really have conclusive evidence so why did you jump to the worst of conclusions? Why did you want to believe Mom let you down? Why was I a disappointment to you?"

David woke out of his reverie as the plane was landing in Kraków It was Tuesday, August 20th. He had booked into a hotel in the *Stare Miasto*, the Old Town, on the *Planty*. Claiming to be a freelance writer, David had arranged beforehand to interview Sam Carr two days later in Kazimierz, the former Jewish district. Carr had returned to Poland upon his release from jail in 1956 and had been writing, not for the Communists, but for a left wing progressive Jewish organization's magazine, under the pen name of George Lewis.

David spent the first day taking in the sights that were connected to Des and was amazed at how real they were to him. But he also wanted to tour Kazimierz prior to his meeting. He bought a bagel sandwich, smoked salmon with thin-sliced *golka* cheese, from a yeasty plump lady with a blue street cart before taking a short walk south from Wawel Castle into the old Jewish suburb.

It lacked the colour of the other touristy parts of the city; then again its history still cast a pall. Beginning In March, 1941 the Nazis rounded up the Jews of Kazimierz and transferred them to a ghetto across the river further south, in Podgorze. David was reading a book about these events, *Schindler's List*, winner of the 1982 Booker Prize by Thomas Keneally.

David stopped into Izaak Synagogue, both sobering and cavernous, where Jewish artifacts and historic pictures from the 1940s gave testimony to the event. A few blocks away, he also found the red brick wall surrounding the 19th century New Cemetery. It was dank, overgrown with trees, with brown dead leaves from past autumns littering the paths and rough gray gravestones scattered higgledy-piggledy, no Jews left to tend them.

One headstone commemorated Róża Berger, who died in 1945. She had lived in Kraków's ghetto; survived Auschwitz with her prisoner number 89186 tattooed, and then was shot in an anti-Jewish pogrom in Kraków at war's end. Understandably dispirited but still anxious, David made his way back to the rendezvous, the Ariel, a happy little white stucco restaurant, with a red mansard roof and gabled windows. He espied an old man sitting at an outdoor table, reading a magazine, smoking a pipe and sipping a coffee.

Sam Carr was seventy-nine now, his pate bald but with gray longish tufts tinged with wispy reddish curls by his ears. His brown suit fit a bit large and his white shirt cuffs had grime stains. His full moustache was a dirty ginger and he held his briar pipe in his discoloured teeth to one side. David also noticed the slightly cleft chin.

"Are you Sam Carr, or do you prefer to be called George Lewis now?"

"Sam will do," he said looking up, bloodshot blue eyes and saggy skin, with prominent dark bags under his eyes. "Are you the young freelancer, David Desmond?"

"Yes, would you like to order something to eat, on me?"

"Well, if you insist, the food here is typical Yiddish. May I recommend the matzo ball soup or gefilte fish? So tell me more about this article you're researching."

"Next year will be the 40th anniversary of the Gouzenko Affair and the subsequent uncovering of the spy ring in Ottawa. In my queries to Canadian magazines, I'm proposing to write a 'whatever happened to' or 'where are they now' piece. I know I missed interviewing Fred Rose who died in 1983 but I was hoping you might provide some information on him and on yourself, of course."

David ordered a *Żywiec* beer and Jewish dumpling while Sam asked for both the soup and the fish with a glass of house chardonnay.

"I try to keep my memory sharp but it's a long time since writing for the *Clarion* and helping elect Fred. What would you like to know?"

David took out a notepad, trying to look professional, and began asking some general questions. Then he moved on to Carr's own arrest.

"You were obviously very clever because you eluded the Mounties for a long time, almost four years, before you were caught. There were manhunts for you in three countries, but you always slipped away, that is until 1949. How did you do it?"

Carr seemed to puff up a bit; David didn't think he was sated with lunch, so it must have been pride.

"I was too smart for those guys. And I used connections. My wife would always go out on errands during the day and she could change hair colour or wear wigs. We moved around too, but always in big cities, like New York or Mexico City. And the Communist Party would send me money. Once the Mounties almost got me in Ottawa but I was too slick for 'em."

"When you say you used your wife, do you mean you used people, used women?"

"Of course. As a Communist and working stiff, you always had to get an advantage on the bourgeoisie somehow, by hook or by crook, as they say. Sometimes we had to use muscle, sometimes threats, sometimes lies, whatever persuasion would work."

"Did you ever have to hurt anyone?"

Carr put his soup spoon down and stared at David. "What are you driving at, kid? The capitalists were always using us workers and sometimes beating us. It wasn't right, but they did it, and so did we. What was good for the goose was good for the gander, right?"

"There was a report," and David looked as if he were checking notes, "Did you have to hurt someone in Ottawa, trying to get a passport?"

Carr leaned back in his chair, and relit his pipe. "Oh yeah, I yelled that at some Mountie stooge at my trial, didn't I? Turns out some secretary I had to see was his girlfriend, so I rubbed it in a bit."

"What did you do to her?"

"I could tell you but it would have to be off the record. Do you really want to know?"

David laid his notebook and pen on the table. Carr continued, "Like I said, I needed a passport. We used to have some extra passports from dead Canadian volunteers in the Spanish Civil War. The Soviet Union was eager to have phony documents for their agents and we were able to supply them from time to time. This time I had to get my hands on one to get me and my wife back to Europe; we couldn't be fugitives forever.

Fred was in jail so I had to ask around who might have kept the stash we had. A connection of mine thought a former office secretary might have one. I cornered her in her office one night after work. She was quite a dish but didn't go for sweet-talking. So I tried my usual heavy-handed stuff on her because I'd had it with her stalling and brushing me off.

Yeah, I beat her up a bit. Now I'm not proud of this, but in the new world, after the revolution, we each will give according to our ability and receive according to our need. She was pretty and showed some lovely legs. Fred used to cuddle her from time to time. That night my need was greater. We were workers and we united, if you know what I mean? "

"You mean you raped her?"

"Let's just say she would have given her consent, if I had given her more time," he smirked.

David was flabbergasted and shocked. "You raped my mother, you bastard."

The wizened senior looked at David squarely, smiled wryly, touched his cleft and pointed at David. He said, "On the contrary, I think that makes you the bastard, son."

David thought he was going to be sick. He went inside the restaurant looking for the washroom. After splashing cold water on his face, he looked into the mirror. He saw maybe a slight resemblance to Carr, only the little cleft chin that Lydia liked to trace. And blue eyes, but Meg had blue eyes too; and Des had the receding hairline. Then he remembered that his own beard had been a curly ginger one, different from his light brown hair. He couldn't be Carr's illegitimate offspring, surely!

Back on the street, Carr was gone. David left enough *złotys* for two, plus tip, and walked in a daze, heading toward the Vistula.

At a bridge over the river, David stopped and took in the city. The Wawel Castle loomed and barges were moored on the river bank. He was feeling slightly vertiginous after the roller-coaster experiences in Poland.

He thought, "This is a sick place, Dad. I know this river runs by Auschwitz, some 100 kilometers upstream, just west of here. So much hatred and inhumanity ran along the river, to this city and beyond. Even Oskar Schindler couldn't save his workers in this hell-hole. The city is beautiful but it has so many horrible stories inside. Just like us, I guess.

Sure, Carr confirmed what you suspected from Rose, but you left here with your mind made up, and even Uncle Peter couldn't soften you when you confided in him. You hated Mom for not being honest with you, for not being trustworthy anymore. But it spilled over onto me. Why? Because I looked a little like Carr? I was your son, dammit. Like Mom said, why did it matter as long as I was healthy? Why did you freeze me out too? Shame on you, Dad. This is a shameful place and you deserve to mingle with it."

David reached into his satchel and pulled out a vial of ashes. He poured them into the river and dropped the vial. All he heard was the plop.

CHAPTER 17.

SHIT ROLLS DOWNHILL

Ottawa 1956-62, 1985

David was sitting in Uncle Peter's condo, slumped in an easy chair. Since Poland, he felt like his world was out of joint. He had just come from the hospital where he had been visiting his mother and consulting with Dr. Clift. It was the end of the Labour Day weekend.

"How is she, Davey?"

"Not so good and somehow I feel responsible."

"Don't be foolish, your Dad would say you're being maudlin. It was normal that you'd be out for a run, and unfortunately, all too normal for Meg to be drinking. You couldn't predict she would fall; she'll mend soon enough."

"I'm not so sure. Dr. Clift says that Mom has advanced cirrhosis. She probably fainted on the stairs. I just thought, after reading what she had been through with Sam Carr and Dad's sudden coldness when he got back from Poland, that I'd get her a treat she'd like on my return, quality Polish vodka. Anyway I found the empty Chopin bottle in the bin and Mom at the bottom of the stairs with a broken ankle."

"Hopefully this will be a wake-up call for her."

"I don't know Uncle Peter. She's been sliding for a while. She said she didn't feel like eating when I was away. She was depressed and food made her nauseous anyway. Her mood swings are getting worse. I reminded her that she couldn't be a grandmother unless she stopped drinking and she turned on me. Sometimes I think she's like a serpent sunning on a rock. Warm on the outside and cold-blooded on the inside. She told me to stop blackmailing her, said I spent more time writing and speaking to Lydia than I did to her, and then got vulgar. She said I was like a dog after a bitch in heat. I don't know if it's a personality change or the real her coming out."

"It's the pain and coming to grips with her disease David. No one wants to be mortal. Don't judge her too harshly but at the same time don't let her tie you down."

270

"I know Uncle Peter, I don't suffer the guilt she tries to lay on," he smiled wryly. "But I don't know if she'll stop drinking. Dr. Clift said she's been killing brain cells for a while and her leg swelling and hand shaking will only get worse if she continues."

"Ultimately, that's her choice David; you have your own choices to make."

Peter had poured them each a glass of red wine. "Try this Burgundy. It may not be what your Dad ordered in Kraków but it's good. Napoleon used to like this wine. I think he said, 'nothing makes the future look so rosy as to contemplate it through a glass of Chambertin.' I know you must be feeling a bit bleak but your father used to say that there must be something to celebrate at the end of every day."

"Did he really? So Dad told you all about Kraków and Fred Rose and how he lost his trust and love for Mom. What did you make of it?"

"Yes, we talked long and hard when he returned. He couldn't help it but he believed Meg entrapped him and shamed him; he couldn't forgive that and he wouldn't trust her. He said he had been hoodwinked before in his work but he couldn't tolerate it in his own home. He would not be mocked. I'm afraid he was adamant."

"But he loved Mom and he loved me. How could he just turn that off because an old man in Poland suspected Carr raped her?"

"As he explained, a switch turned off in Kraków. He went from love to indifference; he didn't hate, he said. He would do his duty for his family, he would take care of her and you; he wouldn't hate you, but the love had died."

"I know Dad wasn't religious but it seems like this was Old Testament treatment, the sin of the father, whoever it was, tainting the son. And you couldn't make him see reason?"

"No David, I'm afraid I couldn't. He kept saying over and over and chuckling, 'How ironic, a bastard fathers a bastard.' I didn't understand it and he wouldn't explain. You know how he could be. I said to him, 'People don't disappoint you, Des, unless *you allow* them to disappoint you.' But he wouldn't see it that way.

In fact, I became complicit in a way. Your father said that work was going to take him away more often and for longer periods of time and he asked me to stand in for him when he was away. I said I would be honoured to be there for you, as if you were my own son, and that I would see to it that Meg and you were taken care of in his absence. You became the family I lost."

"So Dad did his duty financially but physically and emotionally he more or less abdicated?"

"Yes, he never communicated anything to Meg as far as I know and I never felt it was my place to tell her. That's why I never judged her too harshly. As I said, I was complicit; she got the wrong messages if she got any messages at all."

Peter sipped his wine and gazed far away for a while. Then he looked back at David.

"Tell me how you felt after Sam Carr's confession."

"Pretty confused actually; I still am. I can see where Dad would be angry but he never gave Mom a chance, nor me. And well, he was at home less and less, wasn't he? But I don't feel like I lost out on a father because you were there; maybe it was even for the best, becoming more independent and all. But really I don't know."

"What else did you find out about Des in the '50s? Maybe I can help you understand some of those times."

"I'd say he thought the world was going to hell in a hand basket and he didn't really care. He just didn't want to go down with it."

"That needs some explaining; here let me refill your glass."

David began. "Let's see, there were a lot changes in his job in the Fifties; it was getting pretty convoluted. Many of the heads of the Special Branch were administrators just passing through on their way to other assignments and promotions. Rivett-Carnac was replaced by Cliff Havrison; both became Commissioners after their stint with Security Service. The Branch changed its name again, to Directorate of Security and Intelligence. Dad wrote, 'What's in a name? that which we call shit by any other name would still stink.'

Anyway, with the Cold War threats and bureaucratic scuffles increasing, Security received more budget money for more resources. Not all of it went to the Mounties though and there was inevitable turf envy. For instance, some new units were created, a Watchers' Service of surveillers, a Movements Analysis and a new Security Panel, none of which the Mounties entirely controlled and that made them jealous. I think Dad missed the independence he had working for Frank Zaneth. It wasn't long after Dad's return from Poland that he started to manipulate the situation to suit his own purposes."

"What do you mean?" inquired Peter.

"Well, for instance, in 1956, the Cold War world seemed particularly topsy-turvy. That fall, Britain and France invaded Egypt after it nationalized the Suez Canal and then the Soviet Union put down a revolution in Hungary. This was only slightly more than a decade after the Second World War. Dad wrote that people kept singing the chorus of a silly song popular back then. Do you remember Doris Day and the song *Que Sera, Sera?*"

Peter nodded. "It was pretty fatalistic really, *'the future's not ours to see, whatever will be, will be'*. Your father may have been getting cynical but he never believed in fatalism."

David agreed and continued, "It might have been his old mantra, 'you may have me, but you don't own me'. Anyway, there was a new initiative from the top that year. The brass wanted a special squad that would investigate homosexuals in the civil service who they believed were particularly vulnerable to Soviet influence. They even had a name for the tests and clinical gobbledy-gook they developed for investigations, called the 'fruit machine'. Anyway, Dad volunteered to be on the squad."

"Why do you think he did that?

David paused to sip. "I think he wanted a new challenge; maybe someone new to lash out at besides Communists. Maybe he wanted to show that he was not a homosexual himself, fight the innuendo that Frank Zaneth first used against him, that and the murder charge, remember? So maybe it was a way to clear his file, to prove he wasn't one of 'those'. I'm not sure Dad even knew why. Do you have any ideas?"

"Not really, I was pretty busy with my practice then too. I only know he was at loose ends after Poland. And he was intent on getting assignments that took him away from home whenever he could, 'selling security'."

Peter put his wine glass down and said, "He used to sing a few lines of a popular song going around back then, a torch song we used to call it."*Show me the warmth of a secret smile to show me you haven't forgot, that always and ever, now and forever, honey, little things mean a lot.*" The woman who sang that plangent tune, Kitty Kallen, actually looked like your Mom on the album cover, wavy light brown hair, roundish soft face, big eyes and winsome smile.

In fact I bought the record for your father for a birthday. It might be as simple as Des being depressed, rueful even. I know he believed your Mom to be dishonest and untrustworthy and he couldn't unbelieve it, so maybe he just wanted to bury himself in a new project."

"Mmm, you might be right. There was one incident from the new assignment that sticks out from the day-to-day bits. In fact he was skipping entries for weeks on end so this one caught my eye. It had to do with Herbert Norman again. Dad was having lunch with some of his colleagues when John Leopold, his old nemesis, joined in, uninvited really. Dad didn't like Leopold very much, thought he was vindictive and a bully, belittling the suspects he interviewed and investigated, a Red-baiter he called him. They got into some banter, the usual stuff I suppose but it turned nasty between Dad and Leopold. Here, let me read it to you."

David flipped through pages and found what he was looking for.

Monday April 15, 1957

Had a dust-up with Leopold today and it put me in a real dark mood. He came barging into our lunch meeting with total disregard for our team, saying things like, "How are the faggot-bashers? I heard you got to another one of those homos last week; a diplomat committed suicide eh? By the way, got a light for my fag? Whaddaya eatin' boys, fruit?" We were getting sick and tired of it...

...He sat across from me, looked at me with squinty pig eyes and said, "You ok, Des? You're looking kinda queer." He started laughing like a hyena and reached for some French fries off my plate. I flicked out my hand with the fork and brought it down, tine-side, hard into his finger. The blood mixed in with the ketchup.

He howled, "Jesus Des, you stabbed me; I was just joking." I threw the plate of fries onto his lap, grabbed his tie and pulled his face to me over the table. "Do we look like we were laughing, asshole?" I pushed him away and the team just gaped at me, shocked.

I left and went outside for a walk to cool down. It's true that we were ferreting out homosexuals and already some civil servants had been dismissed, resigned or retired. Some of the guys in the squad were just as bad as Leopold too, the way they ridiculed the suspects. But I hung around with guys who were professional, not sadists, and definitely not like Leopold.

To be honest, I think I reacted because I was feeling bad about what happened to Herbert Norman last week. More than bad. I'm afraid I might have turned into something evil while I was in Cairo. The whole episode flashed before me and left me tasting bile all over again. The images came back, while I was sitting on the garden bench having a cigarette, my head down, staring at the pathway.

I had flown to Egypt last week to see Herbert Norman. He had been appointed ambassador there in 1956 and did some terrific mediating between President Gamel Abdel Nasser and the West over the Suez crisis last July. But the CIA and the American Senate were reviving the charges against him yet again, that he was a Communist spy and traitor. He called me asking if there was anything I could do.

I reminded him that he lost his chance at a deal, remember? But I added that I would see what I could do anyway. I went to the Director and he sent me to Cairo to meet with a CIA agent and to notify Norman that he was going to be investigated again as a security risk. The Branch believed he may be a homosexual as well and wanted me to question him in that direction. The three of us arranged to meet on the rooftop garden of a nine-story apartment building- Norman's choice.

It was blistering hot up there. We stood close together in the shade of some potted palms. The CIA agent, Chuck, wiped his brush-cut head and brow with a red cowboy bandana but Norman was looking cool in his white linen suit, light blue shirt, dark blue tie and white straw fedora. He still had those round glasses but I felt he looked more like a deer in the headlights than a wise owl.

Chuck was pressing him hard about Commie friends, accusing him of helping Kim Philby to escape via Turkey; and I was badgering him about being seen in the company of the Swedish ambassador, Brynolf Eng, a known homosexual. Eng lived in this building so I played my trump card and accused Herbert of sleeping with him.

Norman's shoulders slumped, like it was the final cut, the last straw. Chuck motioned me to go to the stairwell in case Norman tried a runner but he just seemed defeated. I heard him say, "This will never go away, will it?" I turned suddenly when I heard Chuck say, "Mr. Norman, Herb, stop, where are you going, what are you doing?" I turned just in time to see a white blur athletically vaulting over the low wall.

His straw fedora with a dark band was on the ground. I picked it up and noticed the label on the sweatband, DelMonico Hats, est. 1908, Havana Panama; nothing but quality for Herbert. Chuck and I went to the wall and peered over. I said, "Fuck", and we stepped back in case the gathering crowd looked up. I took the hat, looking carefully and quickly for any other traces of us, and we left the rooftop immediately, took the stairs, and exited via the garage onto the street.

It was not pretty. Herbert had hit the side of a light blue car, putting a hefty dent in it. His body was crumpled, shattered really, a dark red ooze outlining his white linens. Chuck said, "We gotta fix this up in a hurry," so we retraced our steps and picked the lock to Eng's apartment for a quick look around.

Sure enough, Norman had left a note in his own handwriting. "Mr. Eng. I beg forgiveness for using your flat. But it is the only clear jump where I can avoid hitting a passerby. E.H.N." I remember Chuck saying, "That ain't good enough," and he went to the typewriter.

He left the newly-typed message in the machine, "Dear Brynie, I wanted to spend some time with you during these last few days of my life and tell you what has been worrying me. But I fear I can't bring myself to tell you the real reason. I have decided to die near 'our' home. Farewell, Herbert." I put the original note in my pocket and we left, with Chuck saying, "Leave this to me, Dilman."...

Peter and David sat quietly for a moment and then David asked, "What do you make of that?"

"This is one story Des never told me. Not in so many words anyway. He once asked me if I thought a homosexual could be a good lawyer. I said a homosexual was no better or worse and no greater risk than a heterosexual. But it was a theoretical chat and easy to agree. So no, I never thought Des hated homosexuals, if that's what you mean."

"No, not that so much. It's just that he pushed the boundaries, didn't he? He was hunting Communists and got jaded with that so he applied for a new assignment that got him into situations that, if they didn't make him depressed, they moved him towards despair. It's as if he went from being a hunter to being haunted."

"Insightful, David. They were hardly the good old days, were they?"

"Not so bad for me. I remember skiing, ball games; you were fun Uncle Peter. Listen, I should get going. Mom might be coming home tomorrow. Do you want to come over? I do a mean lasagna, if the grocery store has one." They laughed and said good night.

The weather had turned cooler, the first hint of fall, portending frosts to come. Meg was surrounded by pillows in an easy chair, leg propped up and face with a moue. David brought her a glass of wine. "Just one," he said, "so nurse it." She said, "Thanks. At least the weather's cold enough for the oven. That garlic bread and lasagna smell good, dear."

Peter and David were on the sofa. Peter said, "I agree Meg. I bet it feels better to be at home than in the hospital. What have the doctors said?"

She put her glass down on the side table. "Now Peter, don't pretend you don't know. I know you and Davey talk, you always did. I have to go to physiotherapy for my ankle and I have to stop drinking. I have cirrhosis and will die if I don't smarten up. Also I'm hoping Davey can take me to therapy."

"If he can't, I'll arrange to, Meg. What about the drinking?"

"Cheers Peter." She raised her glass again as in a toast. "Oh, I'll wean myself off a bit, I suppose. I hope you're home for good now Davey. Poland changed your father; I hope you got it out of your system."

David looked at Peter and then cleared his throat. "Well, I'm about to start the '60s' box tomorrow so I don't know where it will lead. Yes, Dad had a rough go in Poland, and so did I as a matter of fact. Dad suspected Sam Carr had raped you and Carr admitted it when I met him in Kraków."

Meg put her glass down carefully and looked squarely at the two men on the sofa. Her voice was even, not shrill. "That's nonsense. Sam Carr may have wanted to have sex with me but I would never. It's just the ramblings of old men. Your father was a fool to believe those two Polacks, sorry Peter. You know David, that food smells good but I'm more tired than hungry. Will you help me up to my room and save me some lasagna for later?"

When David came down, he and Peter moved to the dining table.

"Well, that muddies it. Mom just turned that whole event into a 'he said, she said' didn't she?"

"I don't know, David, there's more between the lines maybe. So, you've finished with the '50s then?"

"Yes, pretty much. There were some more newsy current events. Like Lester Pearson winning the Nobel Peace Prize for his role in creating the United Nations peacekeeping force in the Suez. It was announced in October, 1957 about a half year after Herbert Norman committed suicide and Dad wrote that Pearson won the prize on the coat tails of Norman's work. It made Dad wonder if politics always trumped idealism, and ultimately your freedom.

Peter jumped in. "The end of the '50s gave us many changes which I remember your Dad and I discussing at length. We often agreed to disagree. He was usually cynical, especially about Americans, and I was optimistic about things. He used to say I only liked Ike Eisenhower because he played two rounds of golf a week when he was in office and he thought that Diefenbaker caved to the Americans when he cancelled the Avro Arrow jet fighter project."

"Yes, Dad did refer to those things, but he seemed to be rather taken with Fidel Castro and Cuba. He was quite thrilled that the revolution defeated the U.S.-backed Batista regime in 1959. I think he said it was the one bright spot of an old decade ending and a new one beginning."

"Yes the '60s had freshness and hopefulness at the start. I think it began with JFK being elected president. That line from his inaugural speech, 'Ask not what your country can do for you, but ask what you can do for your country' was like a clarion call. But on your home front, I remember Des being away quite a bit for long stretches of time. You were starting high school then too and he used to worry about you."

"Yes, well if he worried, I never knew about it. He did include some entries towards the end of the '50s about me and elementary school in his diary. He was proud that I got top of the class in Grade 5 and was pitcher on the school baseball team, even though we didn't win a game. But he wasn't around much and when he was, it was awkward.

I remember him razzing me for a penalty I took in hockey and saying he didn't know why he bothered to take me to games if I was going to play like that. We had a backyard rink for a few winters and he sometimes played goalie for us boys after church on Sundays. Once he slipped and fell hard though, and that was it. That's what I remember, rare glimpses of feeling that we were out like other guys and their dads, being regular, and then sudden disappointments. I always felt more at ease and comfortable with you, Uncle Peter."

"I'm glad to hear that you liked your time with me, David. It was special for me too. I suppose it doesn't help to say your Dad was doing the best he could, does it? "

"If you mean with his work life, then maybe. But with me and Mom,

I think he blew it really. The best I can say about him so far is that maybe I understand more about him, what made him Des, if you will; and if he couldn't fulfill the husband and father role, at least he provided a wonderful substitute. Now that I'm half way through the cedar boxes, I may empathize more than I did, but I'm still working on forgiving and forgetting."

"That's a fair assessment of your perspective. I'll be curious to see how it holds up through your high school and university years in the '60s. And David, thanks for keeping me involved with your discussions about the project. It helps to keep Des with me in a more tangible way."

They said good-night and David cleaned up before sitting to write Lydia.

He gave her a detailed chronicle of his time in Kraków, his interview with Carr, his feelings on the bridge with the ashes, his mother's accident and prognosis, his enlightening chats with Uncle Peter. His feelings seemed equanimous enough on paper, but Lydia would have some concerns about his reactions to being 'somewhat illegitimate', David's words. And Lydia would also notice that David reported the quest was moving along, as if he were being driven by a following wind rather than being at the tiller. In fact, she would read between the lines and worry that Des might be haunting his son.

The next morning there was a brisk breeze from the north, the feel of a Laurentians' autumn about to start. David got up early to run before his mother awoke and then tended to her recuperative needs before beginning the Sixties' chest. He pulled the cedar box out of the closet and unlocked its contents, perusing while sipping a cup of coffee.

He didn't really relish starting a new decade with his father. He saw the usual collection of journals of course, and newspaper clippings, one on the Bay of Pigs invasion in 1961 and a few of the Kennedy brothers' assassinations almost five years apart, first John in 1963, and then Robert in 1968.

There were also some school report cards of David's. He had accelerated a year, skipping Grade 2 because the nuns said he could handle it, and had started high school in 1961, when he was 13. There was also a blue ribbon for coming in 3rd at an all-Ontario high school ski meet in 1965, his Grade 12 year; and a junior high school commencement program with the announcement that he had won a scholarship for top marks in Grade 10. David shook his head and smiled ruefully at these mementoes, at his father's interest from afar.

Then David picked up something odd. It was one passport made out to Steward 'Paddy' O'Neill, dated 1937, apparently one of the two that Des had kept from Spain. A note stuck inside the document said he was a Company Commissar who died at Belchite. David wondered what happened to the sixth, and last, passport.

David looked outside, the wind had picked up and the leaves were flickering off the branches of the Lombardy poplars that Des had planted thirty-five years ago. Then he considered the irony of his father's possession of an extra passport that Carr might have been able to use. If Dad had known, would he have given it to Carr and saved his Mom's beating? But that was a 'what if', not a reality.

Another cursory look in the box and David saw airplane ticket boarding passes to Vancouver and to Havana. He made himself a peanut butter and banana sandwich and delved into the journals. The first entry he read described some odd reflections about new work, a bleak world, and a failure to communicate with a son.

Wednesday, April 18, 1962

New statistics came down the pipe on our security work: well over 500,000 possible communists investigated and over 100 on the homosexual list. Many have been dismissed from the civil service. Impressive but not for congratulations the way some of the boys received the memo...

...However, I let the powers-that-be know that I was interested in a new case happening on the west coast. Seems my fling at running Lucien a few years back may have given me a leg up. This was the scoop.

They want me to head a team watching an old postal service worker in Vancouver who the RCMP suspect of being a Soviet agent. They want to call this one by the code name Moby Dick. Call me Ahab looking for the old white whale. Also, if possible they want me to try to run this guy as a double agent.

What we know so far is that he belonged to the Canadian Communist Party but was kicked out for some reason; that he served during the Second World War; and that he landed a full time job in 1949 as a letter sorter after part-time stints. Also in his free time, he used to help with tours of Vancouver for the Friends of the Canada-Soviet Union Cultural Exchange Society. After one of those junkets, he made contact with the Soviet liaison at a hotel lobby.

After that meeting, one of our watchers saw him checking out cemeteries and writing down names of deceased and also stopping by bankrupt businesses and writing down particulars. Strange behaviour on a day off but our suspect, George Victor Spencer, is an odd duck. He wears shabby suits and dirty tee shirts under them and goes around without a hat, his white bald pate open to all the weather. Attractive character.

Tonight, David asked to stay up and watch the Maple Leafs play the Black Hawks in the fourth game of the Stanley Cup finals; he was finished his homework so we watched some together. Bobby Hull has a helluva slap shot and Chicago beat Toronto, but neither of us was very interested since Montreal was out. I made sure to blow my cigarette smoke away from him but he still waved his hand at the smoke and wrinkled his nose at the smell. I said not to be so sensitive but he frowned at me and commented on the stink.

I asked him how school was going and he mumbled okay. I asked him what his favourite subject was and he said he liked all of them, but History was good. I told him I was thinking of buying a new car and would he like to help me shop but he just shrugged. I mentioned I was going to be away for a few months, selling security systems. He didn't ask where and just shrugged again, staring at the television screen. I said I might miss his birthday, did he want anything special? He just shrugged again.

I said, "What's with all the shrugging, don't you know anything?" I meant it as a joke but he glared at me and said he knew plenty, and then he went off to bed. He's going to be 14 next month, the same age I was when I was kicked out to work, and he knows nothing of the real world.

I'll have to ask Peter what I can get David, maybe a new baseball glove, or maybe a nuclear bomb fallout shelter. I hope JFK and Khrushchev don't make the latter necessary with all their sabre-rattling and posturing. Things aren't much calmer a year after that whipper-snapper Kennedy okayed the Cuban Bay of Pigs fiasco and Khrushchev got the East Germans to build the Berlin Wall. Shit, Kennedy is spending billions on the American intercontinental missile program and defense system; the Soviets will have to respond somehow.

I just read where Los Altos in California built a municipal fallout shelter. It was 25-by-48-feet, and about 15 feet below the surface, equipped to sleep at least 96 people. How comforting to think that less than a hundred Californians could be all we have to carry on civilization!

Does the brass seriously think that turning some aging postie against his Soviet bosses will make much difference? It's like putting a finger in the leaking dam.

Well I leave on Friday so I better get my things in order here and put extra money in the account for Meg. Lunch with Peter tomorrow...

CHAPTER 18

NOTHING IS EVER BLACK AND WHITE

Ottawa, Vancouver, Havana,
1962-1969, 1985

Des didn't write a great deal of daily entries in his journal although the periodic updates of his time in Vancouver had cynical descriptions, probably written after he did his reports to yet another new Director of Security Services, this time Assistant Commissioner William Kelly.

David pieced together the scenario for Uncle Peter one morning during a round of golf. The day was one of those delightful September ones, temperature in the upper teens, leaves tinged with oranges and yellows, the aroma of freshly cut grass wafting on the zephryean breezes. They were playing at the Ottawa Hunt and Golf Club where Peter was a member, driving off the Blue course's Number One tee, named 'Spyglass' by President Eisenhower after he played there in 1958.

David sliced his drive out of the tree-lined fairway and the whole game went that way, like an Army march, left, right, left, right; striking more shots than a patient Peter did. Along the way David recounted Des's narrative in Vancouver.

"Dad went to Vancouver, or more accurately Burnaby, in April 1962. He joined a team of four with the Vancouver Watcher Service, doing six hour shifts in a shabby two-bedroom upper story apartment across from George Victor Spencer's place. It was off East Hastings and Macdonald Avenue, a district of mixed housing and ma and pa stores, such as variety stores, salons, diner cafés and a good used record shop.

They had a clear view of Spencer's modest grey-stuccoed, raised-ranch bungalow. The house had several windows facing the lookout so they could see Spencer at most times. They had been keeping pretty constant vigilance on Spencer since 1960 and two men trailed him when he left the house."

Peter said after getting on the green in regulation, "It sounds like dreary stuff."

David agreed. "It turned out to be a rather pathetic case to be

284

assigned to. After trackers noticed Spencer meeting with Russian Embassy staff in Ottawa, and after two years of watching his odd behaviour in Vancouver, they wanted Dad to try and turn him, run him as a double, so that they could find out who some of the Russian illegals in this country were. It seemed an exciting challenge at first, but Dad found it very unsatisfactory."

"Mmm, your father wasn't often dissatisfied?" Peter said with raised eyebrows, rather sardonically and smiled. "This putt will break to your left, Davey. That's it, good putt. So tell me how your Dad was less than thrilled?"

"Spencer's bugged house proved very revealing and entertaining enough at first. He apparently spoke non-stop to himself, a virtual conversation of questions and answers, role playing and even mimicking accents. He was also a strange mixture of carelessness and paranoia, giving the team plenty of information that could be used against him. Dad had enough to leverage against Spencer; he could get him for espionage or treason and was impatient to try running him as a double agent."

"Try keeping your left arm straight on your backswing but bring it back, not up."

"That was better Uncle Peter, thanks. So Dad tried to take the case to the next level against Spencer; and it wasn't pleasant work."

On the walk to the next tee, David continued. Des had been pretty detailed about his descriptions at first, as if he anticipated the case would be a memorable assignment. It was, but not for the reasons Des expected.

"One day Dad followed Spencer to the record store and started up a conversation. Dad, who had introduced himself as Dinzy, said he had listened to a singer recently that he really liked and thought George would too, and that he would lend him the album when they next met. That was a big enough carrot for Spencer and they arranged to meet for coffee the next morning.

It had been raining and George showed up, his suit shoulders soaked and his head glistening. He nodded to Dad and they sat at a table in the back corner. George wrapped his hands around the white cup, warming them a bit, his nicotine-stained fingers the same colour as the mug's contents. Dad put the Kitty Kallen album on the table."

"You mean the one I bought him?"

"If not that one, then one like it."

David continued with details and Peter could picture the scene as if he were there.

George turned the album jacket over and commented appreciatively. "She's very pretty, Dinzy, does she sing as well as she looks?" He lit up a cigarette and blew the smoke from the side of his mouth, away from their table...

..."Better," Des answered. "Listen George, I gotta level with you here. This isn't just about music, except that you're going to be facing the music very soon, unless you pay close attention. I'm with the Mounties' Security Service and we've been watching you for some time now, ever since you met those Russian Embassy guys in Ottawa. We know what you've been up to."

Spencer played dumb and his eyes squinted in the smoke. "What are you talking about, Dinzy?"

"Your phone has been tapped for over a year and your house is bugged. We know that you've been giving information to the Russians, things such as the names of Russian immigrants applying to live in Canada or wanting to obtain passports, details of males who died in infancy, bankrupt businesses, all manner of things that might come across your desk at the Post Office. What are you doing that for?"

"It's a free country with freedom of information. They funded some travel for me, more than the Canadian government ever did."

"What? One or two trips to Ottawa? Or that crazy trip you took to Edmonton, taking photos of the Trans Canada pipeline and its pumping stations?"

"I wasn't doing anything illegal, just interested in the development of the country was all."

"Bullshit, you drove a crazy route, backtracking and zigzagging. Plus you ate late meals in diners in the middle of nowhere, stayed in grubby motels. You were following their instructions on how to lose tails or frustrate trackers."

"No I wasn't; I was trying to save money. I don't make much on my salary."

"Don't fuck with me, George. You've been sending receipts to the Russian Embassy for expenses and you met with a nice couple driving with Alberta plates who were Russian illegals."

"Were they? I thought they were tourists and I was just suggesting the sights they should see."

"No they weren't tourists, George, they were Russian illegals and they were judging whether to run you, or to cut your connection to the Embassy. It's what they do."

George lit another cigarette with the stub of his old one and inhaled deeply. "You don't know that, you can't prove that."

"We got tapes and pictures, George. You're blown. Now if you want to help us catch more of those Commie illegals, we can pay you and you can prove to us that you really do love Canada after all."

George leaned over the table closer to Des, his face pale, his eyes red-rimmed and his breath foul. "This country has done nothing for me, nothing. I put my life on the line in '39 and they wouldn't even give me compassionate leave to see my sick mother during the war. They screwed up my application for work and I was forced to do crap jobs. I've had to be a grouter's gofer, and even run a boarding house, just to support me and my mom. And if you know so much, you can see my house is mostly unfurnished. Stalin took care of his citizens far better than this Dominion of Canada does." He pronounced it Dumb Minion and said it with a sneer.

"Well, why didn't you go to Russia then, George?"

"I wanted to; at least all I wanted was a paid trip to visit the Soviet Union, to see Stalin's experiment in action. That wasn't so much to ask of the Russian Embassy. I was just giving them general information. It wasn't hurting anything or anyone."

"I'm not so sure about that George, giving the Russians information so they could provide profiles for their illegals, giving them sites of key resources they could sabotage in a crisis. Here's what we're gonna do. I'll give you 48 hours to think about helping us or we'll arrest you. When you've made up your mind to cooperate, all you have to do is leave your house and walk toward the record store with this album and make sure the pretty lady's face is showing. Her face means you're safe and ready. I'll meet you in this coffee shop a half hour later and give you further instructions."

"And what if I don't want to cooperate?"

"We've got you watched and we listen to you. Don't do anything stupid. This is your only chance to salvage something from your lousy life. I'll pay the bill here, and by the way, George, give a listen to that track, *Little Things Mean A Lot.*"

Spencer got up diffidently, put the album under his arm, face in, and left the café coughing, his collar up against the rain.

Des stayed to sip his coffee and saw no one else leave the café. He did see one of his team trackers go by the shop window though, following Spencer.

Two days later, Des and Spencer were sitting in the same place, Spencer smoking while taking small bites from two butter tarts on his plate. He looked like he hadn't slept, more rumpled than usual, and he also stunk, that unbathed smell.

"You're paying for this, right Dinzy, or at least my taxes are?"

"Ya, of course. Did you like the album?" Des tried to be soft with George.

Spencer responded, food in his mouth and pastry crumbs falling onto the table, "We're not here to talk about music, are we? You know I tried to call the Russian Embassy, don't you?"

"Yes, and we know they wouldn't meet with you. They've dropped you George because you can't offer them anything more and they probably suspect you're being watched too. Do you want to get back in their good graces and help us too? I can give you something they should be interested in and then you can get paid by two of us, the perks of being a double. Whaddya think?"

"I don't know what to think but I feel screwed, no, make that sick and tired. Right now, I feel like both you and they are playing me. I feel pinched; a plague on both your houses." George began to raise his voice and Des calmed him.

"You may be right about both sides being cursed but we're willing to take you under our wing and give you something the Russians should be interested in. The point is, are you interested?"

"I suppose I could be."

"Tell them you have something concrete for them, something more than names of deceased babies; tell them you have a bona fide passport. In exchange, all you want is to be run by one of their agents here so that the Embassy can be clear of handling you."

"I suppose you have such a passport and will pay me."

Des slid a passport across the table, but kept his hand on it. "It's from a Canadian who died in Spain, in 1937, in Belchite, Jim Wolf."

"They'll ask me how I got it."

"You just have to tell them it was in unclaimed mail that you were sorting. And also make sure you call from home so we can monitor it or you won't get paid." George nodded and Des slipped the passport into the album jacket. "Follow the same routine when you want to see me."

Five days later, the trackers spotted George with Kitty Kallen's face looking at them. Des arrived at the café a half-hour later.

"They stood me up, Dinzy. I waited at the movie lobby but no one showed. I guess the passport wasn't enough bait. I called again and they said that maybe I could help by finding farms in Surrey for sale, they wanted to set up a network there, but they didn't get back to me. I did

289

what you said; now I want my money."

Des took the passport and album back and said, "Here's how you're gonna get paid, George." He took out a two dollar bill and ripped it in half.

"Is this some kind of joke?"

"Not at all. Our people just need time to have you meet an evaluator who will pay you. You'll know this person because he will have the other half of this bill. In two days, you'll go to the Vancouver Hotel and at 7 p.m. sharp take the lobby elevator up to the 4th floor. Then just follow instructions. And for chrissakes, George, clean up a bit."...

David and Peter were back at the clubhouse and enjoying a beer.

Peter commented, referring to the conversation during their round, "It all seemed pretty cloak and dagger, didn't it?"

"Yes, I suppose it did," David agreed. "Dad basically handed him over to higher-ups after the Russians balked. The rest he learned from Kelly's post-operative meeting.

Kelly's man was waiting for George on the 4th floor. He was instructed to say to George that a strange thing just happened, that he tried to tip the porter but all he had was a ripped two dollar bill. George blinked at him at first but then the penny dropped. George showed him the match to the bill and they went down together to the hotel restaurant.

Over a meal, Kelly and his man judged whether George could be a valuable double agent or not. They found him wanting and decided to essentially blow him off, watch him a bit longer to be safe, but then press charges. Dad had a few more desultory meetings with Spencer but there was nothing going on, and in the fall of 1963 they closed the operation. It was eighteen months of deadening work for Dad."

Peter shook his head. "I remember getting the odd phone call from your father then, always about ten o'clock at night because of the time zone difference, always short and always from a phone booth. He'd ask about you mainly, wire some money and suggest treats, like a hockey game to take you to or a ski day. But he was away a long time. Your father came home for a while in 1963 but then was gone again. What was he up to?"

"He coordinated some teams, still reported on Spencer and some other cases he was given. But the outcome for George bothered him a lot. Once Dad chatted up the bartender at the Waldorf Hotel on East Hastings about 'Vic', as Spencer was known there, and heard a lot of hard luck stories. Then in March 1965, Spencer had his left lung removed. He had already been fired by the postal service without pension. They said it was because the RCMP claimed he was a spy and he had broken the oath of loyalty he took when hired. He died in April 1966, just before an inquiry into his 'spying' was released. All in all, it was a sad case to be involved in. I think Dad felt sullied by it all."

Peter finished off his beer. "What a miserable experience! That couldn't have been good for Des's mental health."

Both declined a second brew. Peter continued, "I can't say I noticed anything different in your father's behaviour, David. He was good at hiding his feelings if he wanted to; did he write about changes?"

"Sometimes. I do remember something odd with me though. It was early December, 1963, Friday it must have been. I had just finished my first term exams in Grade 11 and I had asked Dad if he could give me a ride to the movies; I was meeting the guys there. Along the way he tried to have a father-to-son talk but it was weird. I almost recall it word for word. Dad said,

'Do you remember what you were doing when Kennedy was shot, David?' Of course I remembered distinctly, it was only two weeks ago.

'I was finishing a Geography exam and they announced it on the P.A., why?'

'It's one of those poignant moments in a life, that's all, and you want to make a note of things that change you.'

'It didn't change me, Dad. It was shocking and I felt badly for Jackie Kennedy and her blood-stained pink outfit, but really, it didn't change

291

me.'

'Oh it probably did, David; you just have to be open to it. Whether it's a big stone or a small pebble that splashes in the pond, they all leave ripples and we should remember the ones that change us. Are you still interested in History?'

'Yeah, why?'

'There's the big show of History but don't forget the little sideshows. Sometimes those sideshows have more influence.'

'Dad, the only show I'm going to watch right now is *The Great Escape.*'

'Escape is good, David, but don't make a habit of it, is all I'm saying,' and he drove off. "

Peter responded, "Sounds like he was just giving some fatherly advice. Did he write something in his diary about it?"

"But that's the point, Uncle Peter, Dad never gave fatherly advice, he just hectored me. Yes, he wrote around it, but it was rambling; if he wasn't depressed again, he was terribly confused. I think Dad may have been in a crisis, maybe even heading for a breakdown."

Later that evening, David picked up where he left off.

Friday, Dec. 6, 1963

I'm back in Ottawa for a while, at least through Christmas. Meg is cordial and David cool but I shouldn't expect more really. The world is looking pretty bleak everywhere. The Sunday after Kennedy was assassinated I went to church with Meg as a courtesy and a memorial. David had gone to an earlier Mass and later, while watching television at home, he saw the suspected assassin, Lee Harvey Oswald, get shot and killed on screen...

...Meg flapped about like a chicken and David was a bit unglued because he had wished someone would kill Oswald and then it actually happened. Now he wonders if that was a mortal sin. I gruffly told him to forget that church crap; that I believed he was without sin, that he was experiencing some of the real world firsthand, even though it was only television.

I find I'm thinking quite a bit about George Spencer. What a victim! He was dealt a bad hand at every turn. Maybe I should've defended him more, I mean, he tried to change his circumstances by spying I know, but hell, am I so different really? Spencer believed in an 'ism' but what do I believe in? Am I really shaping my own Destiny? I've been talking about getting back at the system for years, but really I've just been going about my job with disdain. I don't think it's enough really.

Hurting Lucien or Spencer or even Norman didn't really get back at Zaneth and the Mounties. Who am I kidding? Next chance I get, I'm gonna grab it. I have to stop drifting with the Mounties. I'm not sure how, but I will have to pay attention to opportunities.

At a meeting yesterday, Kelly was talking about some suspected terrorists financed by the Cubans. There is some subterfuge going on between Cuba and sponsoring terrorism in the United States. Is it connected to the presidential assassination? We've just learned that Lee Harvey Oswald may have been secretary for a New Orleans branch of some group called the "Committee for the Fair Treatment of Cuba", financed by the Cuban Embassy at the United Nations.

The FBI is following any possible connections to Oswald, and this committee and its members are suspect. The FBI wants our help in tracking a possible suspected member of that group living in Quebec, a radio journalist who was also sympathetic to some radical bombings. Kelly passed the file to me.

Monday, January 13, 1964

Well, Christmas is over and I started a new file on the Committee for the Fair Treatment of Cuba. Where do they come up with these names? Marianne Lacloche is the young woman I'm investigating. She was working at a Trois Rivières radio station until recently and now is with CFTM television in Montréal. She's young, 26, tall and leggy, given to flirting with men and ideas. She belongs to a radical group supporting Québec independence and was heard to say that a newer, more radical group, the Front de Libération du Québec or FLQ, responsible for a spate of bombings and the murder of a bystander last April, was justified.

How do these young idealists become so flippant and callous?

I see where the Canadiens are playing the Detroit Red Wings next week at home. I think I'll try to see that game on my expenses and catch a glimpse of our Marianne too.

Sunday, January 19, 1964

Damn, the Canadiens lost to the Red Wings, 2-0, last night. Not even the great Jean Beliveau could beat Terry Sawchuk. I consoled myself by going to the *Casa Loma* to listen to some jazz afterwards, on Ste. Catherine and St. Laurent, about a 15 minute cab ride,. That and some business.

I got a tip that Marianne and friends would be at the club too. The crowd was noisy between sets and the room was smoky. I saw her with a mixed group, two lean lawyer-looking fellows with moustaches, heavy into a political tête-á-tête, no doubt. Marianne was smoking and looking languid, but not bored. Her legs seemed to go on forever in her bell-bottoms and her crocheted poncho hinted at long, bare arms and only partly covered her shapely behind. She had long crinkled blonde hair, parted in the middle and a leather thong headband that slightly indented her forehead and coif, very much a hippie look. I didn't mind ogling her from afar.

The conversation got animated and louder and I was able to overhear them talking about the recent bombings and how it was fine as long as no one was hurt or killed. Marianne casually said, as she blew out smoke, that if someone died it would only be 'collateral damage'. How can someone so young get involved in some cockamamie idealism and be so callous about killing people?

Well, now I've seen her and her friends, so I can set some surveillers on them. If they're that careless in public, we shouldn't have any trouble getting information.

Wednesday, April 8, 1964

There is more graffiti going up in Montréal promoting *Québec Libre* and *FLQ*. Our team has gathered plenty on Lacloche, photos of her meetings with suspected FLQ members and even sympathetic comments on air. We're monitoring her work phone; we're picking up conversations with two Americans who are with the Cuba Free Treatment Committee and another radical group in New York, Black Power. Also she's mixed up with some radicals who are calling themselves the Revolutionary Army of Québec and there have been a bunch of bank robberies to fund their plans. Not a bright girl, or at least not careful!

Monday, May 18, 1964

I managed to get home on the weekend, late for David's birthday but better late than never I hope. Meg gave me a bit of cold shoulder for missing his exact day but she baked another cake for the occasion. It was good to see Peter again too. Davey showed me his beginner's driving license and wondered if I could take him for a drive.

I was a bit nervous because the Ford Galaxie 500 was only a year old, but hell it was the kid's birthday. We went on Sunday to the high school parking lot, safe enough I thought. He was starting to get the hang of letting out the clutch slowly, trying not to lurch, but he must have got nervous because he revved it and popped the clutch, running over the curb and gouging some grass. Poor kid, he grabbed the steering wheel tightly and said that mistake never happened with his uncle.

I said there was no damage done but maybe he'd be better with Peter teaching him then. I had given him a cheque in his birthday card but I didn't appreciate his smart ass sarcastic comment, "Gee, that's personal." He was playing some loud music this weekend too, a new group from the U.K called The Beatles and some mumbler called Bob Dylan. It ain't Sinatra. Meg asked me to stop bugging him about it.

Now it's back to work. We tipped off the Québec police that the Revolutionary Army is training recruits a couple of hours east of Montréal and that they are planning to heist some weapons and explosives. We've heard Marianne offering support to them and the American group. She's getting in deeper.

Thursday, July 23, 1964

Damn, it's been hot and muggy, mid-'80s all month. David is working as a camp counselor this summer, a Catholic one. Meg says she asked the Archbishop to get him in and that Davey's really enjoying it, not much money but good experience. I hope he doesn't expect jobs to be handed to him all the time.

Looks like I'll be going to an even hotter place next month. The FBI informed us that Fidel Castro is underwriting 84 students to visit Cuba in August. We also learned from our sources that the two Yanks who Marianne communicates with, Bob Collier and Walter Bowe, will be among the group. Our Marianne updated her passport and bought tickets for a holiday to Cuba at the same time. Time for me to put my cover story into action.

Sunday, August 23, 1964

I've dusted off my writer's accreditation again. I'm here in Havana doing a feature on *Hemingway's Haunts* for *Weekend* magazine. Who knows, I may even write the piece eventually. The *Montreal Star* and *Weekend* supplement owner, J.W. McConnell, is a bigwig and always willing to help the Force apparently. I was on the same flight as Marianne, and staying in the same hotel, the *Ambos Mundos* in Old Havana. It's a five-story salmon-coloured building from the 20s, where Hemingway stayed in 1939. Now I just have to keep tabs on her and hopefully her touring coincides with my cover. Thought I'd try to record a long piece about the weekend for the diary since I have to appear to be a writer anyway.

Hemingway committed suicide in July 1961 but he visited or lived in Cuba off and on from 1939 to 1960. He was also friendly with Fidel Castro and a supporter until Castro planned to nationalize American property, which included Hemingway's fifteen acre farm house outside of Havana, *Finca Vigia*.

There are many Hemingway haunts here which attract tourists. In fact, Marianne joined a tour group from the hotel going to Hemingway's place, about 10 miles east from Havana in the working class town of San Francisco de Paula. I made sure I was part of the trip, for research purposes, of course.

The tour guide was saying Hemingway bought this place for about $12,000 and wrote three books there, *For Whom The Bell Tolls*, *The Old Man and the Sea*, and *A Moveable Feast*. I started chatting up Marianne as we explored the rustic interior. Looking at an old photo, I told Marianne that I had met Hemingway once in Spain. She wouldn't leave my side, duly impressed with my near-celebrity status and stories of him and Martha Gellhorn.

Marianne reminds me of Martha a bit. She's quite attractive, willowy, showing lean tanned legs in shorts and wearing a tie-dyed tee shirt with no bra, her blonde hair in loose double pony tails. I soaked two bandanas in cold water and gave her one to tie around her neck, a heat reliever I said, that comes from experience. She was grateful and linked her sinewy arm through mine as we continued our visit. After a greasy fish lunch at the Marina Hemingway, where supposedly the writer kept his boat, *Pilar*, the bus took us back to the hotel by late afternoon for a siesta or at least freshening up. Marianne and I agreed to meet in the lobby later and go for drinks.

I had told her that I knew two bars that Hemingway frequented depending on whether she fancied daiquiris or mojitos. She was wearing a wonderful fragrance, *Chanel #5* she said, a French perfume. She invited me to sniff her neck. It was amazing and I said "Vive La France." She smiled and said, "No, it's better now to say, '*Vive le Québec*.'"

I didn't want to get into politics so soon but I said that Marianne was the name of the French maid of Liberty in the French Revolution, often depicted with bare breasts. She said that maybe she could replicate that later and smiled beguilingly.

This could become more than flirting. Hell, I'm twenty years older than her. I should be protecting her, not seducing her; or was she seducing me? Anyway, she opted for daiquiris and we walked the ten minutes or so on the smoothly rounded cobblestones of Obispo Street to the sign *la Floridita, la cuna del daquiris* in teal neon, the rose-coloured corner entrance welcoming us.

They already had Papa's barstool cordoned off as a tourist site. We grabbed a table under a ceiling fan and a server approached in a red jacket, similar in colour to the garish interior. I suggested we order the famous rum cocktails, one with sugar and the other without, as Hemingway preferred. She tasted both and preferred the Hemingway, probably because she was sweet enough I intimated, but cringed inside at my obvious attempt at being a Lothario.

She had mentioned earlier that she had some friends here taking a course at the university. I asked if they were students and she coyly said they had engineering degrees already and now were students of life, a better life. I rejoined that we're all students then because we're all looking for a better world; and in fact, I hoped my article would bring more tourists to Cuba and help its revolution along in some small way. She seemed to like that, saying she thought I had worker solidarity.

She had already downed her drink so I raised my hand and said, "*Otra vez, Papa doble, por favor.*" Then I said she could invite her friends here if she'd like, we could collect them in a taxi, on my magazine's expense account. It's a short ride, less than ten minutes, and they could join us for a drink. She thought that would be nice and went to call them.

It was then that I noticed some loud greetings and handshakes at the bar. The object of the attention was a tall, slim, broad-shouldered Englishman with thinning, wispy, light brown hair combed neatly. He was wearing a blue blazer and white linen trousers, a red ascot and matching puff in his pocket. "*Señor Greene, la bienvenida. Si, si, ron Barbancourt.*"

It was Graham Greene, the famous British author. He had just written a successful novel, *Our Man In Havana* in 1958 and did the script for a movie of the same name, starring Alex Guinness in 1960. The daiquiri may have given me false courage because I went up to him by the bar and asked if I could buy him the drink, that I was a huge fan, having just read *Orient Express*.

He seemed stand-offish until he saw I was with Marianne and then he was interested. He asked if I was American since the British title was *Stamboul Train* and the Yanks had changed it for their market. When I said I was a Canadian writer doing a piece for the *Montreal Star Weekend*, he warmed up, saying he was working on a piece himself for the British paper, the *Sunday Telegraph*.

He asked where we were staying and maybe he could repay the drink sometime; that Fidel was treating him like a VIP and it would be good to have a normal night out. I gave my number at the hotel and we made arrangements for tomorrow night. If he calls I would be ecstatic.

Meanwhile, Marianne had returned to the table said her friends would join us and would be happy if I would pay for the taxi when they arrived. In ten minutes, she went outside with a couple of American dollars I gave her and she re-entered with her two black friends, just as Graham Greene touched the brim of his Panama to me and them and nodded on the way out.

Bob Collier and Wally Bowe were in their late 20s, black, sporting Afros, wearing bell bottom jeans, and sandals. One had a tee shirt with Mao and a red star; the other had a rainbow and peace symbol. They looked like twins and markedly different from me in my beige seersucker trousers and green polo shirt. They seemed a bit cocky, slouching in their chairs and an arm slung over the back, establishing that they only had an hour before their curfew and happy enough at the change in routine.

They were guarded when I asked about that routine but accepted the drinks from this bourgeois friend of Marianne's. I said that I only tried to facilitate Marianne getting to spend some time with her own friends, just being thoughtful and spontaneous; and Marianne squeezed my hand. When I said what my assignment was they were dismissive of Hemingway and white American writers in general and said I should be reading Richard Wright's book *Black Boy* if I wanted to know about growing up black in America and how to change it. They said I should write how Hemingway used Cuba and include how Castro's Cuba is a miracle story with advances in health and education.

One of them said (I was beginning to think of them as Tweedle-Dweeb and Tweedle-Dumb), that the revolution was where it's at and Cuba showed how improvements such as the Literacy Campaign could be made much faster than that fat cat Lyndon Johnson and his so-called war on poverty. Besides, they added, LBJ's escalating the military draft so more poor black folks can go fight in Vietnam. It was time, they went on, for the black man to fight back. Like Stokely Carmichael says, their grandfathers had to keep on running but now the black youth were out of breath and wanted to have black power.

"We got plans to hurt whitey Establishment in his pride," they said. They were wrapped up in their own rhetoric for sure, but then suddenly

299

went quiet as if they had said too much. I wasn't disappointed when the hour was up and they left, neither showing any gratitude or bother at being treated by a capitalist. They took Marianne out to the curb while they waited and seemed to be giving her admonishments, probably about hanging out with me and saying too much.

Marianne and I had another round for the road and then wobbled back towards the hotel, having only nibbled on tapas. Outside her room, Marianne wrapped her long arms around my neck, kissed me gently and asked if I wanted to see that French Revolution icon now. I was all a-quiver actually. Partly booze, partly testosterone, but I told myself I'd do this for work, a rationalization for sure.

Anyway, I followed her in. She took a few steps away; her back to me and in a fluid motion took off her tee shirt. Then she slowly turned around. Her small and perky breasts beckoned and I could feel my tumescence. When I told her she was lovely, she came to me, raising her arms to my shoulders and cooed that it was time she showed me what the counterculture's free love was all about.

CHAPTER 19

PRINCIPALS AND PRINCIPLES

Ottawa and Havana, 1964-1969
Ottawa, 1985

It was the following week, the end of August, and Des was back at his desk in Ottawa getting ready to report on his Cuban findings. There had been a furor out of Québec that weekend; on Saturday, August 30th, there was a botched gun robbery by the Revolutionary Army of Québec where two people working at a Montreal firearms company were killed. Five terrorists were captured. Marianne had been in Cuba at the time, so she had an alibi. Des thought back and wondered how much he should reveal about his week with Marianne, or Greene, for that matter.

Graham Greene phoned me at noon at the hotel. We arranged to dine early on the shaded rooftop terrace of the Ambos Mundos before proceeding to the Tropicana for a night of games, so to speak. He said that El Presidente insisted he come by official limo and with a fidelista body guard but would I ask my lady friend along. Marianne was delighted to come...

...The Tropicana was actually another Hemingway haunt. Many celebrities and mobsters had frequented the establishment and she was intrigued. She appeared on my arm in a simple black mini-dress featuring two white horizontal lines at the hem and chiffon sleeves, very attractive; while I tried to look dapper in an open-neck, light blue Oxford cloth shirt and cream linen trousers, with a light-weight blue blazer. Greene, in a white dinner jacket and dark trousers, looked handsome, already seated at the red-clothed table at the Ambos Mundos and sipping a mojito. He introduced his man Raul and kissed Marianne's hand gallantly, saying she was the perfect adornment for the evening.

At first Marianne didn't appreciate Greene's Old World charm and she smoked and drank quietly. The conversation, mainly between me and Greene, wandered down several interesting avenues, such as our writing assignments, pre-revolutionary Cuba, travel, Hemingway and suicide. Greene admitted that, like Hemingway, he too got depressed but could stop drinking when he wrote, whereas he suspected Hemingway's book could have been entitled 'to have and to have another'. Greene also confessed that he had gambled at suicide himself by playing Russian roulette, the only worthy game to come out of Mother Russia, besides spying, he added. I was somewhat taken aback by how candidly he revealed himself, rather openly and seriously.

Perhaps as a way to get us to open up too he confided that at the end of any project, he missed the daily imperative to write five hundred words and his mood darkened. Planning a trip or a different assignment helped. That's why he agreed to the Sunday Telegraph request to feature an article on the revolution 'five years after', with the condition that they send him in August, since he hated Europe in that month.

He was staying at the Hotel Habana Libre which used to be the Hilton and where Castro set up headquarters in 1959. He preferred the Sevilla Biltmore actually and, in *sotto voce*, said he used to love the brothels and cocaine he could get there. Fidel's Havana was decidedly more puritan now. I tried to keep him talking about his writing but after some more mojitos, Greene began regaling Marianne with his anecdotes of revolutionary figures, wickedly flashing blue eyes her way. I asked him about a line from *Stamboul Train*, that if you had a cause, you didn't need scruples.

Marianne perked up at this comment. Greene was smoking a stinky Brazilian cigarette, *Menzala*, and offered some from the yellow and green pack. She agreed that some innocents get hurt in a revolution but it's the cost of the larger goal. He looked at her squinting through smoke and asked her why she was interested in revolution, was she studying or doing a feature for her television station?

Marianne said she had radical friends studying and read their books but she believed violent change was necessary to move the powers that be, even in Canada. Greene raised his eyebrows at that, noting that Canada seemed an odd place for a revolution. At that Marianne excused herself to go to the washroom and said, as her chair scraped, "Just watch Québec, Monsieur Greene. You'll see before the year is out."

Greene admired her curvy backside leaving. He said to me, with a sly grin, "I find her very sexy, Des. And more than a little cocksure, if I might be permitted to observe. She'll find that the world is not as black and white as that dress, more like black and grey, wouldn't you agree? Would you mind terribly if I offered to show her some landmarks of the revolution tomorrow? I'm going with my photographer. And then perhaps we could all dine tomorrow night or have drinks."

I responded that it was Marianne's choice and that I had some interviews to attend to tomorrow for my own piece. With that he asked me about my writing. I told him I wrote the odd freelance article and kept a regular journal but never got down to writing a novel.

"It was my dream to write but I'm afraid my other work interferes," I said.

He waved his smoldering cigarette my way. "Nonsense, it just takes discipline, if you want it badly enough. Don't romanticize the life of the writer Des; it's hard, disciplined labour. The reality is far different than the dream. Oh and before I forget," he said as he reached his hand over to Raul and snapped his fingers, "here's a copy of *Our Man in Havana* for you." I was both grateful and amazed, and he offered to inscribe it.

Marianne came back refreshed and looked stunning. I marveled that it was less than 24 hours ago that she was astraddle me. Her angular hips belied a wonderful smooth rounded bum. Last night, when I'd smiled and confessed I'd never had sex so aggressively, she licked her lips with a pointed tongue and coquettishly replied that it was assertive, not aggressive.

The limo to the Tropicana Casino complex was a twenty minute drive along the seaside road, the *Malecón*. The resort itself was luxuriant with tropical plants over glass arches, the up-lighting effectively throwing dark shadows. There were roulette wheels and card games in side rooms which reminded Greene of side altars in cathedral apses. But the big draw was the open-air cabaret show of lithesome, sequined and feathered girls, the 'flesh goddesses'.

Greene ordered a bottle of champagne and we took in the vibrant colours and throbbing rhythms, our heads moving like searchlights, trying to take it all in. Greene laughed at our awe and said it was more risqué before the revolution. During a break, he asked Marianne to dance and when they returned to the table she announced that she was branching out from bourgeois Hemingway haunts with me to proletarian revolutionary sites with Greene on the morrow.

I took a cab to the hotel alone, Greene and Marianne intent on gambling. The following day I interviewed some officials in the National Institute of Tourism Industry and in the Ministry of Education. Ostensibly I asked questions for my cover, about using Hemingway as a tourism attraction; but casually I also tried to find out about student conferences and exchanges and their role in exporting revolution or training terrorists. They were good at dissembling so it was grinding work. When I got back to the hotel there was a message to meet for dinner at La Gran Sevilla's Rooftop Garden.

When I arrived, Marianne, seeing me, rose quickly, gave me a warm kiss and whispered, "Save me, I'm being held captive and tortured." Greene was effusively grateful when I gave him a package of Montecristo #4 cigars and we chatted amidst the thick blue smoke, the mojitos only making us more light-headed.

Marianne revealed that Greene had been asking her questions about Québec, Catholicism, and her beliefs about sin. She whined, "It has been like spending an afternoon with a father confessor." Greene laughed at that and said it had been a perfect afternoon of talking theology with an angel.

He continued, "I was trying to explain, no, trying to convince Marianne that sin can be turned to good. For example, executing Batista's man, Jesús Blanco, could persuade timid spectators to become active revolutionaries, maybe even true communists. But I'm afraid the concept of sin is lost on her. She doesn't believe in it."

"I believe in action, all action for the cause is good; anything else doesn't matter."

"See what I mean, Des? And what do you believe?"

I felt as if I were being tested. "Oh there are people who do bad things but I don't know if they see it as bad or evil. If they don't feel it's wrong, maybe there's no sin. Even Hitler thought that what he was doing was going to improve Germany. It's complicated, isn't it? I suppose I believe personally in trying to do what's good for the greatest number of people, but I know that I don't always behave that way either. Maybe it's a sin when you knowingly don't do what's good. But what if not doing good brings about something better, like stealing to get life-saving drugs for someone? Like I said, it's complicated."

Marianne said, "See how heavy he makes things with his topics of conversation. Let's drink and dance and be merry."

Greene laughed at that point but later, after our meal, said to me in an aside, "Can I have word in private, old chap, perhaps by the railing?"

We excused ourselves from the table and rested our arms on the balustrade overlooking the rooftops and the moonlit sea beyond. He lit another cigar and asked me, "Des, what other job do you do?"

"What do you mean?"

"Well you can't make a living on a couple of free lance articles, for one. Secondly, I know a thing or two about gathering intelligence. Marianne said you were kind enough to invite her radical friends for a drink and that seemed an odd ploy just to get into her pants, if you'll forgive me.

Let's just say that if you're watching Marianne, you'll have to be very careful about her. She's very determined to aid and abet some very extreme people in Québec and she has no qualms about sinning, shall we say." He looked sideways with his piercing blue eyes and tapped a finger to the side of his nose.

"It's just a word to the wise. I like you Des but Marianne likes celebrities. Right now it's Fidel, Ché and Papa and she's fickle. She's very pro-Cuban, anti-American and very pro-revolution. Indeed she could go to any lengths to be a celebrity herself." We paused and, deep in our own thoughts, watched the wide swath of the moonlight.

Suddenly Greene added, "In the future, if I might be permitted to give you a bit more advice, if you're going to continue to use a writing career as your legend, exaggerate your writing credentials and output some."

I just nodded a grateful acknowledgement and that was the end of it. I shook Graham's hand and we parted company after coffee.

Marianne and I strolled back to our hotel arm in arm. I was lost in my thoughts. Was I not being as good at my job as I believed? Was I behaving a bit blindly because of the attentions of a younger woman? Ah yes, I could go for more lustful sinning with her. Being bad might lead to some good intelligence. A means to an end, the perfect mix of business and pleasure. After all, I was going to have to see her again in Montreal so I mustn't stop contact yet.

"Des?"

"Yes, Marianne."

"Graham said he missed the shoeshine boys and young kids hustling and begging in the streets like before the Revolution. I prefer it this way, don't you, quiet and calm and no economic abuse?"

"Mmm," I absently answered, my mind working on other preferences.

At the hotel I enticed her with a visit to Room 511, Hemingway's room which the manager was intending to make into a shrine/museum. I opened the door and we saw the famous writer's bed in a nook covered with an orange bedspread; his Remington typewriter on an adjustable desk, since Hemingway sometimes typed standing when his leg's war wound bothered him; an antelope's horn, and even a bar tab on the bureau. She wrinkled her nose.

"*Je ne sais pas*, I think I liked his drinks more than his macho hunting."

I spooned behind her and wrapped my arms around her, lightly rubbing her belly and venturing lower.

"I think I like to seize the moment," and nuzzled her. We opened the French doors to the balcony and made love standing at the railing, the creamy moonlight and velvet air caressing us...

Just then there was a loud knock on his office door and it startled him, breaking his day dream. Director Kelly's secretary said he would see him now. Des went to the office of the Assistant Commissioner, who greeted Des with his lyrical Welsh accent and hooded eyes.

Des reported, "Yes sir, I think their revolutionary plans are moving faster than we may have thought. I was able to get visuals on three suspects and overhear enough talk that I think we can safely tell the FBI that these three people bear watching. One of course is Lacloche in Montreal, and two African-American engineers, Robert Collier and Walter Bowe who are members of the Black Power movement in New York City. I suggest we bug Lacloche's phone and apartment; I should be able to set that up. Also the FBI and NYPD should try to get an insider to befriend the New York group somehow. That way we should be able to monitor them. My read is that Lacloche has contacts within the FLQ and the Revolutionary Army of Quebec and might be in the market for weapons or explosives for those radicals in New York."

"Good work, Dilman, I'll pass this on to the Yanks. Carry on and keep me informed."

Not wanting to appear too eager after the Cuban holiday, Des waited a few weeks before contacting Marianne. He said he was in Montreal meeting with the editor about his article and wondered if she would like to have dinner with him.

While Des was waiting at her apartment, Marianne shouted from her bedroom that she'd be about ten minutes, to make himself at home and pour a glass of wine. It was all the time Des needed to install the listening devices in her home.

Meanwhile, the policing counterparts in New York recruited a very good young policeman, Ray Wood, whom Des had briefed earlier on a quick trip to the city. He too was an African-American, a very efficient undercover agent, who managed to gain the confidence of Tweedle-Dweeb and Tweedle-Dumb, as well as the dozen members of the extremist Black Liberation Front group which they had formed after the Cuban sojourn.

Wood even persuaded the radicals that he should be the trusted conduit between Marianne and Collier and Bowe. It was a way, he said, of communicating via a safe liaison and hiding their trail as plans gelled to blow up symbolic American monuments, such as the Statue of Liberty and the Liberty Bell.

Finally Des learned from electronic surveillance that the BLF were planning to execute their so-called Monuments' Plot in February, 1965. Marianne, Collier and Bowe transported thirty sticks of dynamite in Marianne's car from Montreal to New York City. The FBI followed their car but never stopped or searched it. According to Marianne's plan, she stayed in a hotel in a New York suburb and called Ray Wood to come collect the dynamite. He went with Collier to the rendezvous where Marianne and Collier and later Bowe were all arrested...

David read more in the journals.

Sunday, February 21, 1965

The Monument Plotters had their hearing; all pleaded guilty. Marianne received five years in prison for her role. Director Kelly was pretty happy about the result, not only for our part in foiling the plot, but also for a successful collaboration with the FBI. In front of the others, he said, "A real feather in our caps, Des, a real feather, thank you." He doesn't congratulate anyone very often...

...I've been giving some thought to what Graham Greene said about sin being turned to good. Is catching the Plotters an example? Illegal sleuthing and lust being used for the better end, the greater good, saving symbolic monuments and probably lives? Maybe in the big picture, but personally I feel more like I've lost a principle instead. It's the first time I've had sex outside of marriage. Mine may be a marriage in name only but, by my own rules, I was unfaithful. That makes me no better than Meg.

And it's like a domino effect. If I can throw away one principle, why not others? Or can I reclaim the principle of fidelity by asking forgiveness, by pledging I won't do it again? But forgiveness from whom? Certainly not from Meg and her mumbo-jumbo Catholicism. Now it's got me wondering just who I am really? Principled or opportunist, rationalizer or fraud?

Kelly has given me a few days off but hanging around home won't help. Watching Meg bustle about and knowing I'm no better than she is now; I feel like a forged painting hanging in a gallery. And David is absorbed in his own Grade 12 life and notices nothing beyond himself. I feel a little like one of our 'black bag jobs', the new trick of photographing documents instead of stealing them. The victims don't realize anything is missing or different, but we, because of the inside information now, play a whole different game. I need to take a little road trip to think, alone.

Friday, March 5, 1965

I went to visit Greg Clark in Toronto. I read an announcement that he had been short-listed for the Stephen Leacock Award for Humour. It seems his war stories are getting a national chuckle. It was good to see him. I learned that his oldest son, Murray, had died in France and the *Toronto Star* didn't give him leave to go to France from Italy. Greg, who normally didn't bear grudges, felt he had to leave the newspaper and switched to the *Toronto Telegram* in 1947.

After a request to be a reference for Peter, he always wondered what became of me and was happy that I had recovered from my injuries, well mostly anyway. Always intuitive, at least with me, he noticed that something was bothering me. I always felt I could talk to Greg like a father so I told him I had just had an affair, but it was over now and I felt at sea.

He responded with an anecdote, about an Italian woman in the war who had been buried beneath rubble when her village was bombed. Rescuers recovered her, still alive. Greg and other war correspondents heard about it and rushed to the scene, sensing a good story.

"We asked why she hadn't evacuated before the bombing, like everyone else. She held up a flyer that the planes had dropped prior to the mission, telling the locals to leave. Our guide interpreted her answer. 'The words, he said, 'they '*alla inglese and she looka for a someone to a translate*'. Just goes to show that wanting to know all the answers can sometimes be overwhelming, eh?" He chuckled.

Good old Greg, always a funny story to put things in perspective. Maybe there aren't any answers or meanings; it's just what it is. It didn't solve anything for me but I laughed.

When I got back to Ottawa, Director Kelly gave me another assignment. It seems Prime Minister Pearson in 1963 had cancelled surveillance for subversive activities on university campuses, except for those who were actual Communists. Kelly told me he didn't want to put it into a memo but he did want me to surreptitiously keep an eye on campus activities, maybe get some professors to relay information to us about 'subversives'. He wanted me to quietly cultivate that link...

David had been chatting with Peter, filling him in on some of the journal memories of the 1960's material while they had lunch at the Lord Elgin Hotel.

"So your father was showing signs of the classic mid-life crisis, very much at sixes and sevens. I remember him saying he should change his occupation from time to time but he didn't know to what," said Peter. "As I recall, you and I were doing a fair amount of skiing that winter. Wasn't that when you anchored your school team at the all-Ontario Alpines?"

"Yes, he was still at loose ends."

Peter said, "Des was pretty wrapped up in work, I remember, and when we did get together he mainly wanted to know how you and your mother were doing. When we talked there wasn't much information about him, pretty much business. He never confided in me about an affair, not then anyway. Maybe he was too ashamed. And do you think your father sorted himself out on that Toronto trip?"

"The diary doesn't really say specifically. I think Mr. Clark put him at ease, and allowed Dad to be less hard on himself. But did he sort himself out? I don't know. Work helped him I know. He wrote about some sex scandal in Ottawa and that it was a kind of *schadenfreude* for him. Oh, what was the name; I had it in my notes, something 'Mudslinger', I think it was."

"Oh yes, the Gerda Munsinger Affair. I do remember your father getting a kick out of that bit of political comedy. She was an alleged East German prostitute who had slept with Prime Minister Diefenbaker's Minister of Defense, Pierre Sévigny, in the late '50s. She was deported and Sévigny resigned and the whole matter was dropped in the early '60s. But Diefenbaker was always looking for some way to embarrass Pearson and the Liberals. When he had decided to insult Pearson's Justice

Minister, Lucien Cardin in 1966 over the handling of the George Spencer inquiry, the Liberals raised Munsinger from the heap, so to speak, as a counter-embarrassment. Anyway, it backfired on Diefenbaker; she admitted to several affairs with several Conservative politicians. I could see Des liking their misery somehow."

Peter's eyes crinkled and he chuckled at the memory.

"Dad mentions that he visited university campuses and went back to Cuba too in 1967. Apparently the CIA anticipated that twelve of the twenty-three countries to the south of the USA could be overthrown, and were in danger of adopting Castro/Communist models. Since the CIA couldn't operate in Cuba very easily, they asked the RCMP for a liaison of sorts. That CIA guy involved with Herbert Norman, Charles Bumbly I think it was, suggested Dad, and Kelly agreed.

"Des used to bring back good Cuban cigars, Montecristos. I remember us smoking one to celebrate Canada's Centennial and also to celebrate you getting into Western."

"Really? I'm just at the stage in the journals where I'm starting university. Dad was developing two files, university campus surveillance and Cuba information gathering for the CIA report, 1966 to 1969."

Peter ruminated, "It was an interesting time for all of us; the wind blew every which way, didn't it? Québec and the country celebrated Expo '67 and then reeled with separatism; the excitement of Trudeaumania and the tragedy of Vietnam. But of course you remember those things. You were a 'with it' guy," he said with a twinkle, and then continued.

"And you were very involved in your campus politics too. It was a miracle you got your degree. Your father fumed about your goings-on and I listened. It wasn't easy for us older folks with our values being challenged at every turn."

David shook his head and grinned, "I can't believe some of the stuff I got into and the yelling matches Dad and I had. Do you recall the dinner when he criticized my long hair? He used Ronald Reagan's definition, when he was governor of California, that a 'hippie is someone who dresses like Tarzan, has hair like Jane and smells like Cheetah'. I flared back that at least I was standing up to fascists, and their Gestapo police. Now I understand that I was bandying about historical labels loosely. No wonder Dad resented me co-opting them after he himself had fought in Spain and Italy, while I hadn't done much more than hold a placard."

"Don't be too hard on yourself; your father didn't share a lot of his history with you. How were you to know? That's what the journals are doing now."

"Maybe so, but the petty battles of the Canadian Union of Students, the so-called New Left, seem so distant now."

"Don't be dismissive of your own history David."

"No, I don't mean they didn't count; and they weren't always shallow either. Sure we had protests against the war in Vietnam, supported steel workers in their wildcat strike in Hamilton and boycotted grapes as well. We really were trying to get more democratic student involvement in university government. It was all well-intentioned, but now it reminds me of Yasgur's farm after the Woodstock rock festival, all flat, littered, and quiet. I know Dad scoffed."

"Ha, yes, I recall entering your house and you two throwing grapes at each other in the kitchen. You were yelling that we had a duty to support the migrant workers and Des was shouting back that he could buy whatever he pleased. Did you ever think that he wasn't so much scoffing as just being concerned about your safety?"

'What do you mean?"

"Weren't you on the streets of Montreal during the St. Jean Baptiste Day bottle-throwing riot when Pierre Trudeau was on the stage? There were lots of heads cracked that night and I know your dad was worried that yours might be one of them. And then those students were killed at Kent State by the National Guard, terrible. I remember Des being worried that you'd go off and try something stupid, like pushing a flower into the barrel of a rifle."

"I don't remember his concern, just belittling. He had a funny way of trying to dissuade me. Anyway, I'm just reading some of his entries from

1967-1969 now. Maybe I'll get some better insight."

"Didn't you go to a student conference in Bulgaria in 1968? Your father was very worried about you that summer, with those student revolutionary marches in Europe erupting. He used to say that you kept demanding the naked truth; but he felt truth looked better with a little clothing on."

"Yes, that sounds like Dad. And yes, me and some CUS friends went to Montreal that weekend and found ourselves involved, so to speak. That was also the summer I went to Sofia and met Lydia. Right on both counts. Good memory, Uncle Peter. That's got me wondering."

"Oh yes, about what?" Peter asked and signaled for the bill.

"I would like to go to Vancouver and empty a vial. Dad's time there was important to him. But also I'd like to visit Pearson College, to let them know who I am and that I'm very interested in working for them. How is the account doing? Can I go to Vancouver and Victoria? "

"That should work."

"Cuba probably merits a vial too, maybe in November. Then, instead of returning to Canada, I was planning to go to Brazil for Christmas and be with Lydia."

"The trust account is still healthy but, strictly speaking, the money's for travelling to places connected with your father and his journals. The trust could lend you money for the other personal plans though. Let me think about it. When do you want to go to Vancouver?"

"I'll probably leave in a couple of weeks and stay for a week. That way I will be back in late October to have a go at the '70s. I'm seeing an end in sight, probably Christmas or early in the New Year."

"Have you talked to your mother about your plans? I know I'll be here for the holidays so I can ease your absence a little. How's she doing, by the way?"

"No, I haven't broached it with her. She seems to be doing well with her ankle but I think she's still drinking. I'm sure she's getting her Catholic Women's League and card playing crones to smuggle vodka in."

"Let's the three of us get together to talk over your plans then. I may inhibit your mother's anger a bit if I'm there. Perhaps we can keep some clothing on her biting 'naked truth'.

In the meantime, David continued to bear down on his research before going to Vancouver.

Wednesday, August 16, 1967

I've been in Havana for a few weeks. The Cubans had hosted the Organization for Latin American Solidarity Conference from July 19th to August 10th. There were lengthy speeches by Fidel, Che and American civil rights leader, Stokely Carmichael....

...Fidel used the event to commemorate the anniversary of the July 26th Movement, the one he proclaimed in 1955 to overthrow Batista and now to promote further revolution in Central and South America. Che talked about hatred being needed to fuel revolution, to hate the imperialists everywhere. Carmichael, a good-looking and articulate black man, must be one of the few Americans in Cuba.

Yanks are even more *persona non grata* since Castro claimed the CIA was behind the *La Coubre* bombing in the harbour in 1960 and since the trade embargoes after the Bay of Pigs fiasco. Fidel welcomed Carmichael because he can embarrass the U.S. He has moved from a strategy of non-violence to Black Power and now talks of young bloods taking control. He said they would disrupt the United States from the inside while the Cubans disrupted from the outside, amidst huge applause.

I took Greene's advice and beefed up my writer's profile, claiming to have written technical manuals for security systems and for being a ghost writer to make ends meet. I'm here as a *Montreal Standard* reporter, getting a Canadian point of view.

All the accredited journalists are staying at the Habana Libre. The revolutionary motif is unmistakable, the lobby mural of the rebels in arms and the quote on the wall that it is the duty of every revolutionary to make revolution. Many of the writers were in the bar wrapping up their assignments and I got chatting to a Brazilian journalist for the *Jornal do Brasil*, Gregorio D'Silva. We were sitting at the bar sipping strong daiquiris before heading for the airport.

I asked him how Brazilians felt about Carlos Marighella, who had read from his new book, *Minimanual for Urban Guerillas* at the conference. Gregorio was non-committal and shrugged, saying sales were not outstanding. He asked if I had got enough material for an article and what would Canadians think of the conference. I said something facetious about Canadians liking the anti American feelings here.

He nodded and said that his paper would like the leftist rhetoric but that it scared him personally. We got onto the subject of young people and radicals, their anger and impatience for change. He has a daughter in university and is very concerned that she not get involved with the crazies of the left because his country thinks nothing of torturing troublemakers. I shared his anxiety, mentioning David and how it's difficult to advise him. I told him that we can't even laugh at the same thing, that's how far apart we are.

I was telling him something Bob Hope said, that the napalm producer, Dow Chemical, finally got even with anti-war protestors who burned their draft cards by issuing asbestos ones. I chuckled but Gregorio didn't get it. I said not to apologize; my son didn't 'dig' Bob Hope either.

I'm not much of a joke teller but thought I'd try another on Gregorio. I asked if they knew about the CIA in Brazil. Gregorio looked up and down the bar and nodded imperceptibly. It was the joke about asking CIA recruits to take a gun, enter a room and kill their spouses. The men couldn't do it but the woman went into the room and shot six times followed by crashes and yells. It turned out the gun had blanks so she beat him to death. Gregorio visibly blanched and asked if I was CIA. I reassured him that I wasn't but it also made me note how much fear the American organization generated and here I was gathering information for them. I asked him why he reacted that way.

He said that in his country, the CIA backed the right wing forces and the military to oust the president in 1964 and it finished democracy for Brazilians. It's true that Brazil needed aid; it had been suffering from inflation, national debt and higher wage demands. But any United States aid demanded stability in return, he added. The U.S. Embassy actively intervened in Brazil's politics and CIA people engineered the coup. I was incredulous but he said it was true. The CIA backed bogus educational

315

and women's groups as a way to report on leftists, over 400,000 dossiers were collected. There was a parliamentary investigation and it was revealed that the CIA spent more than 20 million dollars trying to rig elections. I was dumbfounded.

He said he was not against stability and certainly not pro-left but anyone who opposed the coup or protested was labeled a communist. He wanted to fly below the radar he said so he was nervous about working for a left-wing newspaper and especially about his daughter's politics. I said I felt for him as a father and ordered another round of drinks, promising no more CIA jokes.

We wished each other well and shook hands. But my antennae are up about blindly helping the CIA.

Thursday, August 31, 1967

I'm just getting ready for the long weekend, the end of summer. Davey is heading back to London and Western, his second year. He said he was going to major in Honours History and English and I wondered aloud what kind of job that would get him. We parted in a snit. I wish I could stop that trend, not a good way to say goodbye, ever.

Met with Director Kelly. I informed him about my university campus surveillance organization and talked over my CIA liaison report with him before sending it on its way to Bumbly today. I told them about Stokely Carmichael's change of beliefs and tactics and that the response to his call for Black Power was pretty powerful. I suggested that Carmichael's speeches could frighten whites in the United States.

I also started privately investigating the Company, the CIA. I don't like them using me as an *ex officio* agent. Kelly does though, especially that we were getting brownie points with our American cousins, but I found their meddling tactics deplorable. The CIA actually advocated torture of detainees involved in radical politics.

I learned that South American police and security services regularly beat prisoners with a wooden paddle called a *palmatoria,* and used electrical shocks on genitalia. The CIA spent money, issued equipment and trained foreign police, including one academy right in Washington. They infiltrated radical groups, financed oppositional parties where they could, and used dis-information to de-stabilize societies, what we'd call lies or propaganda. It's such a double standard because the CIA is the first to decry Communist-fronted organizations. I'm telling you, this assignment eats at my insides and I'm squirming.

I tried to caution David about being overly involved with the Canadian Union of Students when he went back to school. He said that you had to participate to be free. I said that I had been participating all my life and I still didn't feel free. He responded with something glib, something about me being over 30 and not to be trusted. If I had a grape, I would've thrown it at him.

David looked up from the diary and smiled wistfully at the memory of university days evoked from the journal. It seemed a lifetime ago. He skimmed along and then stopped to read one that caught his eye.

Friday, October 20, 1967

I was meeting with some of my watchdog professors about subversives at the University of Western Ontario today. A History professor, not knowing our connection, included David on a list of possible troublemakers to be watched. I hoped to meet up with David and go for lunch or something, but found out that he skipped classes and was in fact on his way to Washington D.C. to march on the Pentagon, a huge protest to end the war in Vietnam. Stupid bugger, he may think he's being a Marxist but he belongs more to the Groucho Marx faction.

David closed his eyes while his flight was droning over the Prairies en route to Vancouver. He was still reeling over the revelations he had read in the last journals. Those entries about him at university floored him. Obviously Des would know about David's public goings-on from his campus files, such as attending the summer conference in Sofia or an occasional protest march. But he knew some private things too, very private, and it shocked David. He shifted in his seat.

The jet's engines didn't interfere with his reflecting on the end of the decade. He had forced himself to carry on reading the '60s box of journals but it was his father's intrusion into his own life that he found particularly upsetting. The most salient revelation, and it made David's stomach flip, was that Des had known he helped a university girlfriend get an abortion and pay for it himself in February, 1968. David wondered how much more his father knew, beyond the journals' entries, and how it affected their relationship. At any rate, his Dad's spying on him stuck in his craw. He was amazed and pissed at how much his dad must have known about his life then.

In addition, the last journals had been a blend of Des's observations on passing events such as Pierre Trudeau being elected, race riots following the assassination of Martin Luther King, as well as the first baseball game for the new Montreal Expos. He also mentioned the new and brash American boxer, Cassius Clay, who upset Sonny Liston for the heavyweight crown, changed his name to Muhammad Ali, and then refused to be conscripted to go and fight in Vietnam. Des fumed about the U.S. stripping Clay of his belt.

Then there was a poignant one involving the CIA, as Des's research continued to delve into the agency he was co-opted to. Apparently the Company was involved in the massacre of several students in Mexico ten days before the '68 Olympics were held there. David remembered those events too and was surprised to find that his father's reaction and analysis of them was not that different from his own. Threaded throughout his writings were also fatherly concerns about David's life.

As the plane hit a patch of turbulence, David was aggravated by the thought that his father had followed his own son's life like a stalker. It left him incredulous, even stupefied. He did agree with his Father on one recurring concern in the journal though. What would become of him in such a fucked-up world? Yes, indeed, Dad, yes indeed!

CHAPTER 20.

CHANGING THE MEMORY OF THE PAST...

Ottawa and Havana, 1970-71
Vancouver and Victoria, 1985

David landed at Vancouver airport in low cloud and rain, the runway lights appearing suddenly out of his window as if by magic. By his own admission he was mentally at sea, confused about his feelings and his purposes that afternoon on Thursday, October 10, 1985. He booked into the Holiday Inn on Howe Street because he figured it would be central to address his several needs, first for his dad and then for himself.

That drizzly night he walked up Howe to fashionable Georgia Street and then Richards Street towards Gastown. West Hastings Street quickly morphed into East Hastings with its flop houses, drug users, alcoholics and bums. Finally David gave in, the rain and the ambience too much for him; and he hailed a cab to take him to the Waldorf Hotel, several blocks further along Hastings. He entered, trying to commune somehow with his dad and Spencer's drinking hole from twenty years ago.

It was certainly rough at the edges, smoky, the smell of cheap beer, couples with heads close together, huddled around small round tables, their hands around their glasses as if expecting to be robbed of their drinks. David could imagine 'Vic' Spencer slouched at the bar on a stool, telling hard luck stories to the bartender, or his dad tucked at the corner inquiring casually what the barflies knew of the sad sack. It was all very depressing.

David ordered a beer, closed his eyes and could feel the stinky smoke and fetid air grasping onto his clothes like osmotic burrs. It felt like his father was grabbing onto him and pulling him down. Suddenly David rebelled against the drowning sensation and quickly opened his eyes. He decided he didn't want a séance with his dad any longer and refused to be lured into one. He had got a sense of his father's working environment but he didn't need to replicate it any longer in an effort to feel his father's life. No, what he needed was fresh air and his own life.

Taking a taxi back downtown, he asked to get dropped off near the water. The cabbie obliged and took him to English Bay, in the West End. David entered the café of the Sylvia Hotel. It was warm and cheery in the ivy-covered heritage hotel across from the beach and the sea. He sipped his coffee and occasionally glanced at the lights of the waiting ships and his own reflection in the window. He could feel the vial of his father's ashes in his raincoat pocket, the fifth that he would scatter.

He asked himself, "So where are you now, David? You've followed your Dad's life through riot, war, and vengeful spying". He thought he had gained some understanding of his father's life and also its impact on himself. He had caught a glimpse of how Des's idealism turned to cynicism and how his father had twisted and turned as a result. Now, even when David thought he was independent, free from him, he realized that his father had bored into his life like a termite.

"Shit, I'm like him in so many ways, even if I'm his bastard son. Talk about imprinting. Ha!. And Des the security man even knew my big secret. What will I do with that one?"

He decided it was time for a walk and some thinking. He paid up, asked if he could get to Howe Street walking along the waterside and got directions. It would be about three kilometres; he was ready for that.

He crossed to the seaside walkway at the corner of Denman and Beach Drive where it was bright with reflected reds and greens and neon signs on the road puddles. He took the lower path along the entrance to False Creek, heading towards the Burrard Street Bridge and Granville Island, his hand gripping the vial inside his pocket and his rain hood up. His sense of smell picked up the redolence of sea air and creosoted wooden moorings and his mind was churning. He was remembering back to his second year at Western, the winter of 1968.

I was going out with a cheerleading substitute, Lindsay was her name, and she and I attended most of the Mustangs' home games that winter. One night after a post-game celebration at the Ceeps, a local watering hole, we rushed home on a cold night and decided to warm ourselves up, under the covers...

...Lindsay was blonde and blue-eyed, a petite, pert girl from Toronto, with an infectious laugh and giving body. She announced a few weeks later that her period was late. We were both a bit frantic. I thought she was on the pill and she thought I would use a condom. It was too late to use the line "not birth-control but self-control" proclaimed on some anti-pill and anti-contraception posters on those Catholic colleges, Brescia and Kings, so I investigated abortion possibilities.

Minister of Justice and soon-to-be Prime Minister Trudeau was talking about liberalizing legislation on abortions but the law hadn't changed yet and we needed action, not talk. Through a couple of friends with the Canadian Union of Students, I heard that there was a progressive, private clinic in Montreal where a Dr. Henry Morgentaler, focusing on women's right to choose, was using a new safe method to end pregnancies. When Lindsay confirmed she was pregnant we both agreed a baby was unwanted. I withdrew $300 from my savings and we took the train to Montreal on our Reading Week. I had a friend's Québec birth certificate and health card and Lindsay and I memorized the data on the trip.

The appointment was friendly and supportive. Afterwards in the recovering room, there were no complications and Dr. Morgentaler wished us well. His female assistant, with no sense of being duped by fake identification, assured us. "Yes, Michelle, you are no longer pregnant."

On the train trip home, Lindsay rested to the rocking clickity clack of the rails. I was still amazed that the clinic charged no fee and our problem was terminated. Although we held hands, we both knew that we weren't in love, and sex had presented complications we weren't ready for. Our relationship faded like the melting snow banks along the campus streets...

David wondered why his father did nothing with the secret. He never confronted David with it. Was it because he wasn't being judgmental or was he afraid of losing his cover as a security salesman? But what would he, David, do with his own secret now? Was he going to be as duplicitous as his father? Was this his crucible, to prove that he was made of different mettle than his dad? A resolution rose in him like rising mercury in a fevered person's thermometer. He made up his mind.

At Burrard Street Bridge amid the susurration of tires above, he took out the vial and poured the ashes into False Creek. "There you go Dad. I know Vancouver and the Spencer case were hard on you, but you continued to play false, with Mom, with me, and possibly with Uncle

Peter. Perhaps with yourself. But I'm declaring here, to myself, to your ghost, and to Lydia, that I choose to tell my secrets and to be true to myself and to her. I will not be like you."

And with that oath, he hurled the vial out into the dark arm of the sea. When he heard the kerplunk, he went under the bridge, like so much water, and turned left on Howe Street towards the hotel, hands in pockets, head forward and with steps purposeful on the slight uphill.

In the morning, the rain had stopped and the sky's ceiling was higher, as if a weight had been lifted. David went for an early run, back down to False Creek and east along its bank, past David Lam Park and under Cambie Street Bridge, where he remarked on the new B.C. Place stadium to his left. Straight ahead, the Science World geodesic dome, slated to be the iconic attraction for the city's Expo '86 next year, looked like a mushroom in the grey dawn.

He slowed his pace and took in the new building and reclamation at the nether end of the creek going on apace for the exposition opening in less than six months. Somehow it buoyed him, that the city was dedicated to renewal. He circled the dome and began to retrace his route, noticing that the B.C. Lions were hosting the Winnipeg Blue Bombers that night. He decided to explore the city, having shed the morose mood he had come to Vancouver with.

David appreciated wandering the city, taking in the West Coast vibes. He visited the art gallery, bought a ticket for that evening's football game, sat for a coffee at the elegant Wedgewood Hotel where the windows with their royal blue and gold trim awnings opened onto Hornby Street and the law courts, and wandered the up-market shops of Robson where he bought Lydia some ski gloves. He was intent on that promise to take her skiing somewhere this winter.

There was a new restaurant on Thurlow honouring the legendary lifeguard, Joe Fortes, who came to Vancouver a hundred years ago. David stopped there and sampled some Fanny Bay oysters. At another coffee stop on Granville Island, he sat on a bench, stretched out his legs in relaxed fashion, and wrote postcards, even though he would arrive back in Ottawa before the cards did. He was having a good day.

In his uplifted mood he felt like communicating. To his mother, on the back of a garden scene from Stanley Park, he was dutiful but thoughtful, saying now that her ankle was better, she would love the walkways and parks here. To Peter, on a picture of a covered B.C. Place, he wrote that he was attending a CFL game there, offering to bet two dollars on the Lions and that they could settle up when he got home. To Lydia, he had carefully chosen a card of the totem poles at the Museum of Anthropology, and wrote that the animals protecting humans reminded him of their own relationship; that he had an epiphany in Vancouver and would explain more fully in a longer letter later, when he saw her in December.

Then he telephoned Pearson College from the hotel and arranged a meeting and tour on Monday, since he was in the vicinity. It would be Thanksgiving Monday but as it happened the Director was on site and would be happy to meet him and show him around.

Now it was a rainy Tuesday and David was on the evening ferry back to Vancouver from Victoria and the college tour. The low clouds and mist hid all but the shoreline of the islands in Active Pass and he felt the ship yawing as it negotiated the narrow passage. Fortunately the hour and forty-five minute crossing he took earlier on Sunday had been in brilliant sunshine and he had enjoyed the cool brisk breeze on deck and the gauntlet of islands heading into Sidney's Swartz Bay terminal. He even imagined sailing here some day. But tonight, he was using the time to sit in the ferry cafeteria and write Lydia.

Tuesday, Oct. 15/85, somewhere between Victoria and Vancouver

Dear Lydia,

I'm just finishing up a week here on the West Coast. You'll be getting a postcard soon of some totem poles I saw. It's one with a carved symbolic eagle and bear, protecting indigenous people in cone-shaped hats. They believed the eagle was intelligent and courageous and the bear was a teacher and strong, both protecting those who took risks. See how they reminded me of us? I feel we have some big decisions and risks to decide soon. I can't wait to be with you and discuss our future.

He wrote about his activities, the colour and noise of the Lions' football game, a long run along Stanley Park's seawall, and more detail on his stay in Victoria too, the inner harbour, the museum and Legislative Building, the coastal walkways.

I couldn't help but be excited driving out to Pearson College. The road winds by the coast and through rock and ancient forests. In fact, there is a trail on the school grounds which runs through the woods that early settlers used to hike to Victoria about thirty kilometres away. I loved the place but the Director could make no promises.

At least they know me in person now. I also chatted with several of the students who had not gone home or billeted with anyone over the long weekend. They were so articulate and committed. I'm trying not to get my hopes up but I'm sure we would love it here; although that is a topic we must discuss when we get together again, face-to-face.

I know you have two months off from mid-December to mid-February; Carnival is February 10th I think, and you return to school after Carnival, right? Could you stand to be with me for most of that time? I'm trying to scheme a way for us to go skiing in Canada during that break too and I've even bought you a Christmas present for just for that possibility, so please say yes.

He mentioned that he was about to begin the 1970s on his Dad's journals and asked her to ask her father if he remembered a conversation with a Canadian journalist in Cuba in 1967, because it seemed that Des and Gregorio D' Silva shared some daiquiris then.

Small world if it was them, eh? I'll try to explain more in a phone call, (damn I miss you and your voice) about this change that came over me in Vancouver. Remember how you were a bit anxious that my Dad might be dragging me into depression or haunting me? Well, I just suddenly decided that I didn't want to let that happen anymore. It was like I was in a stuffy room and had just thrown off an old heavy winter coat. There's more to tell but it'll have to wait, minha preciosa.

I'll try to call you next weekend. I know that this is a long weekend break for you, Teachers' Day right, and that you're going to visit your family in Rio. If I spend Christmas with you in Brazil, would you like to spend two weeks with me skiing in Canada, later in January?

Love, David

Back in Ottawa, David had more bounce in his step. It may have been partially because there was less humidity but whatever the false cause, the effect was pleasant. His mother remarked on his cheeriness but there was no prodding for the reason. She still didn't feel like walking in public so invited Peter to dinner rather than a meal out. David produced a bottle of 1985 Cabernet Sauvignon from California's Napa Valley for the repast.

"I couldn't find anything from B.C. but I thought a New World wine would be appropriate to celebrate Dad's work in North America. I found this in a specialty shop in Vancouver. Stag's Leap Wine Cellars has good vintages and won a French blind tasting competition in France in 1976. It's not from Dad's cellar but worth a try, don't you think?"

Peter was impressed. "David you're getting to know and appreciate good wine, just like your father."

"Oh and this is for you, Uncle Peter." David handed him a new crisp two dollar bill, its distinctive terra cotta colour with two robins on the reverse side of Queen Elizabeth.

"I never thought the Lions would lose two in a row to Winnipeg. But hey, now it's the playoffs, so maybe you'll give me a chance to win that back," and they both smiled.

Meg interrupted to say, "Oh David, this letter came from the Hamilton School Board today." She handed the envelope to her son as he handed her a glass of wine.

"Just one glass, Mom."

"And just one envelope, dear," as she scrunched up her nose at him. "There hasn't been anything recently from that hot Venezuelan girlfriend of yours. Has she gone tepid?"

"She's Brazilian, Mom and no, it was my turn to write. We haven't gone tepid and there's no need to be snide."

"Sorry dear, please forgive me. I'm just grumpy about still not being able to get around."

"But you can get around." The letter caught his attention. "Mmm,
325

seems the Hamilton Board wants to know if I'm still interested in being on their supply teaching list."

"I hope you say yes. Aren't you done gallivanting around with that silly idea of your father's? It's time to get back to our life."

"Mom, you still don't get it. The quest is my life right now. I should be done by Christmas though. I suppose it makes sense for me to stay on their supply list. I'll have to line something up soon, but I really do want to teach at Pearson College."

Peter entered the conversation, in an effort to blunt Meg's mood and to segue onto David's wish. "How did that interview in Victoria go, David?" Meg hobbled off to the kitchen, making audible sighs and groans from time to time.

David recounted his experience on the coast, but heard something being poured in the kitchen. "Just one glass of wine, Mom," he shouted to her.

"Yes dear, it's just one glass at a time, I know."

David gave a questioning frown to Uncle Peter and he just shrugged.

"And what are your next plans, David? Should we raise the subject of Christmas?"

"I'm going to telephone Lydia next Saturday so let's wait until I know things are confirmed."

It felt like the beginning of a work week, and it was for David, in a manner of speaking. He had been for his run, and was rummaging in the 1970s box, sipping a cup of coffee. The fragrance of the cedar was pleasant, reminding him of Vancouver Island. David felt a bit humbled as he scooped the loose artifacts of the box onto the living room floor.

He realized his own life had not progressed much at all since this decade and hoped he was doing the right thing by putting all his eggs in the Pearson College basket. He sighed deeply because he wanted to take his relationship with Lydia further too; his free time and money would run out when Des's project was done. But first things first and to the task at hand. Worrying would not solve anything. He sifted through the items on the rug.

It was an odd collection of memorabilia. David came across a ticket for a ship, the SS *Santiago de Cuba*, dated January 6, 1971, out of St. John, New Brunswick, bound for Havana.

"It doesn't sound like a cruise but I wonder," he thought.

He picked up a December, 1970 newspaper photo and article about five FLQ members exchanging kidnapped British Trade Commissioner James Cross on L' Île Ste. Hélène.

"I remember this, it was the end of the October Crisis and they flew to Cuba as part of a negotiated arrangement. I wonder if Dad had anything to do with these guys."

David reached for an old invalid passport, his own. David flipped through the pages seeing the stamps for Bulgaria, the United States, and Cuba and a sullen face that looked back at him with youthful disdain, his own face over twenty years ago.

"Why would Dad keep this?" he wondered.

David refilled his coffee mug, feeling the need for strong black java this morning. A red and green ticket stub caught his eye. It had the 1976 Montreal Olympics icon on it, like a Boy Scout's three-finger salute and five rings below. The ticket cost two dollars, standing room only for swimming and with the bilingual information, *place debout*, piscine *olympique*, dated July 24, 2 p.m. He remembered his dad asking him to go but David said he wasn't interested. He now felt a bit callow and churlish remembering back.

Next he lifted a newspaper column up, a death notice in the *Montreal Star* for Frank Zaneth, aged eighty, in May, 1971. David's attention was piqued, now realizing the name of the one who hoodwinked Dad into joining the Force back in 1935; and whose name David first heard when Commissioner Simmonds mentioned it at Dad's service. David placed it aside for special consideration later and picked up another faded newspaper article with the headline "Air Canada Jet Hijacked to Cuba".

This story recounted that on Boxing Day, 1971, a guy brandishing a handgun and grenade in front of a flight attendant, demanded that he be taken to the captain. They were only twenty minutes from Toronto where they landed; the passengers deplaned unharmed. Then the six crew and hijacker took off for José Martí Airport in Havana. The hijacker was met by Cuban officials and vanished while the airliner returned to Canada.

"Well, incidence of coincidences, Dad. I bet you spent more time in Cuba in the 1970s and that'll work out perfectly for my plans too. He looked at the cedar box again and noticed a hard cover book among the few journals. It was over five hundred pages and entitled, *Inside The Company: CIA Diary*, written in 1975 by Philip Agee. The name was familiar and David muttered to himself.

"Of course, now I remember. Agee was the CIA whistleblower and a guest at the WFDY conference in Havana in 1978. That's why he looked familiar to me at Dad's memorial."

He recalled that he had skipped Agee's panel discussion at the conference because Lydia and he had just had another spat, but he remembered the posters advertising it. David looked inside the dust cover at Agee's photo. Yes it was Agee, looking younger but with the confident chin, thin lips, long hair and wire-framed glasses. David then looked for an inscription and found one. *The Fascists had it wrong at Auschwitz with their 'Arbeit Macht Frei'. It's not work that will set you free; it's the truth. Hope you're finding your truth, Des. All the best, Phil. Havana, 1978.*

David looked up from the book and realized that his father had met Agee in Cuba the same year he was there working on the World Youth conference. And why was the book in the cedar box rather than on Des's book shelf?

The journals themselves also had newspaper articles and postcards inserted, but he would deal with those later when he read the diaries. David picked up the first one, 1970-71, and went to the kitchen to have a ham and cheese sandwich with a carrot and an apple. Standing and munching at the counter he began to read.

He perused the pages, some sports references stood out, such as the name Bobby Orr scoring his iconic 'in flight' overtime goal to give the Boston Bruins the Stanley Cup in May and Brazil winning the World Cup. There was domestic news too. Dad mentioned Mom getting excited about a new television series in the fall, the *Mary Tyler Moore Show*.

The October Crisis featured often, from Pierre Trudeau's bravado statement, "just watch me" when badgered by a CBC reporter about how far he would go to stop the FLQ (Des thought highly of that), to the FLQ exchange of James Cross for asylum in Cuba and cash (Des thought that was pandering to terrorists). Then David stopped to read about Christmas time more carefully. He remembered he was home for the holiday that year, trying to write some essay for his Masters degree in History.

There was the entry about him and his dad arguing over the election of the Marxist, Salvador Allende in Chile, David saying it was an example of democracy working and Des saying the Americans would never stand for it. "Well, Dad got that one right," he mused.

And then one entry mentioned bickering about Trudeau invoking the War Measures Act. David could picture it as he read and said to himself, "There didn't seem to be much peace on Earth in the Dilman kitchen that Christmas. Every now and again Mom would yell at us from the living room to be quiet because she couldn't hear her television programs. Only when Uncle Peter was around did civility return, it seemed."

David returned to the living room to read, randomly stopping at entries and focusing on the few subsequent pages before browsing again.

Monday, Dec. 28, 1970

The new Commissioner, Bill Higgit, called a special meeting at Headquarters today. Since his background was in intelligence and security, none of us was surprised to learn we have a new name now, the RCMP Security Service. How imaginative! But the meeting wasn't about that...

(David could picture his father looking up from his jottings and reliving the incidents of the day).

..."Gentlemen, we have several crises on our hands that require urgent intelligence, both for us and our colleagues to the South," Higgit orated.

"No shit, Sherlock," someone near me at the back whispered and we had to stifle our laughs.

Higgit didn't hear us, or chose to ignore us, and announced that, as he was speaking, three FLQ members of the cell that kidnapped and murdered Pierre Laporte were being rounded up at a farmhouse south of Montreal. There was a cheer and applause but he quickly hushed us and went on to enumerate other concerns for Canada's security, from France and China, to Vietnam and the United States.

It was a kind of state-of-the-union address starting with France as he held up his thumb. Higgit believed that France was behind the October Crisis, what with de Gaulle's utterance, *'Vive le Québec Libre'* and now his pushing for Québec to be a separate member in La Francophonie. The French would require continued scrutiny on our part.

He held up his forefinger, saying number two. He complained that Prime Minister Pierre Trudeau had recognized the People's Republic of China, cozying up to Mao and ditching Taiwan. "Not only did it tweak the nose of the pro-Nationalist Chinese-Americans but we're going to have to beef up security for upcoming diplomatic missions and visits. And on the topic of the United States," he added holding up his third and middle finger, "the number of American draft-dodgers was increasing by the thousands."

I had my head down marveling that it looked like he had just given the finger to the Americans, a veritable 'fuddle duddle'. His handlers better get on that I thought when I suddenly heard my name. He centred me out by saying that I would have to update the report on the campus groups aiding and abetting the deserters. I corrected him, saying that they weren't deserters, sir, but draft dodgers, and that the groups on our campuses were weakened with the split up of the parent American Student Democratic Society into various quibbling factions last year.

It was more detail than I needed but I'd show that cock-up that I was on top of my file. His face got a bit red, not serge red, but close. I knew I'd be having a separate meeting with the boss after that.

Sure enough, I was called to his office where I met two bumpkins just leaving, Inspector Sid Yelle, the head of Montreal's anti-terrorism unit, and Corporal Dale Boire.

Higgit waved me in imperiously and greeted me with, "Those two know how to do things quietly, Dilman. You, on the other hand, do not. Don't ever show me up in a meeting like that again."

I interrupted, "Well sir, I thought it more appropriate to correct you among friends than have the media catch you in an embarrassing faux pas. If you had called the Americans deserters, sir." He cut me off with a wave of his hand.

"Listen up! I need you to investigate a couple things in particular for me. Go see the Associate Director of Counter-Subversion who will brief you on an assignment we have for you."

I knew Howie Draper by name and Higgit didn't need to be pedantic about his rank. Trying to control my anger, I trodded off to my next office appointment. Something struck me as odd though when I saw that Yelle and Boire were both leaving Draper's office too.

"You guys must think I'm stalking you, or maybe a fly following the smell of shit," I said to them.

Yelle said, "That would be sir to you, Sergeant Dilman." I asked if he meant me to say it was Shit, Sir, or Sir Shit, and ducked into the office.

Draper had two personae. In large groups he was usually a pompous ass with shifty eyes; but face-to-face like now, we got along okay. He was trying to put a handkerchief over a cutaway model of a lock on his desk.

"Pretend you didn't see that or those guys, Dilman."

"See what, sir?" I answered and he snickered his appreciation. "Commissioner Higgit said you would brief me, sir," dissembling any disrespect for rank.

"Yes, yes. By the way, that was a stupid thing you did in the meeting today Dilman. You looking to get cashiered?"

"No sir, just keeping the boss informed," I said with a straight face.

If those guys were threatening me after thirty-five years of loyal service, they would have to outsmart old Dilman. I wasn't worried about limiting my career at all.

"You've been at this a long time Des, you ever think of retiring?"

"I started young, Howie. I just turned fifty-three, lots of meat left on the old bone yet. What are you cooking up with those two guys from counter-terrorism, Howie, the two I didn't see? "

"None of your business, Des, just feathering a nest so to speak, to help out the new Commish. I was just offering those guys a ham sandwich," and he chuckled at some kind of inside joke. I just shrugged.

"What and no lunch for me? Well like I said, I didn't see or hear anything, Howie."

"Good, now down to business. You're lucky you have valuable experience that the Commissioner and brass need right now. Especially in Cuba and with the CIA. You're not indispensible, Des, just hard to replace, but don't let it go to your head. I'm gonna push you on this assignment, Des. Can you juggle? Because it's two jobs in one and you better not drop a ball?"

They want me to go on a junket to Havana, leaving in a few days by boat. I'm supposed to cozy up to a CIA defector who will be on board and send a liaison report to the Americans. Also, while in Cuba they want me to report on the conditions and whereabouts of the five FLQ members now living there. A pretty big New Year's job I'd say.

But when I get back to Ottawa, I want to sniff around and find out what Draper, Yelle and Boire are concocting; like the hags of Macbeth, some toil and trouble no doubt. I can't help myself; I hate it when bumpkins think they're pulling the wool.

Wednesday, January 6, 1971

The *SS Santiago de Cuba* is a real clunker, a World War II Liberty ship on its rusty last legs. It was carrying much needed 'exports' to Cuba to bypass the American trade embargo and about 20 passengers too, among them a self-exiled ex-pat, Philip Agee.

332

He had caused quite a stir among the CIA in 1969 by resigning and claiming that he'd had his eyes opened to Agency misdeeds after a decade or so of assignments in Latin America, and eventually decided he didn't want to be a part of all that anymore. I sat by him at a galley table tonight, the ship lulling in the Atlantic swells. We were having a coffee and chatting, not many others in the room, probably because of the stale kitchen smells, the cigarette smoke and the bucking ship. I liked the guy right away. He introduced himself openly and I said he could call me Dinzy. He looked at me squarely and said, "Why would I do that, it's not your real name."

I laughed heartily at his candidness. We shook hands; he was totally easy to be with. He was a young 36 and said he was on his way to Cuba to do some research for a book he was writing. The conversation was not like 'twenty questions' at all. He spoke freely and, I must say, even encouraged me to reveal aspects of myself; it was like meeting a long-lost friend, or travelling with a hitchhiker, not a spy-deserter.

Later on deck we talked and smoked until midnight. I admired his forthrightness and his ethical courage. He told me why he left the CIA, at first joking that it went against his Catholic upbringing. I understood that was a weak joke, having lived with Meg and her guilt and forgiveness-seeking. What he told me about the CIA I already knew from reports.

His extra details about torture in Uruguay were new though. He also told me about receiving a typewriter from a wealthy American lady who recently befriended him in Paris and how the damn machine kept making weird noises. He took it apart only to find an electronic listening device gone amok and whirring. There I was, elbows on the sticky salty railing on the port side, listening to an earnest young man, throwing over his career because of scruples.

Suddenly those old doubts and questions about myself came roiling back to the surface, like the white wake from the props below. I asked him if he wasn't just having a mid-life crisis a little early. He laughed and said you could call it what you want, but he just knew he had to set things right while he could, and before he got too old. He held my stare as if he were daring me to do something.

Sunday, January 10, 1971

Lots of conversations with Phil, about being a writer, about being haunted by the screams of a man being tortured in Montevideo and wondering if it were someone whose name he had passed along to the police, of being taught that America always backed the good guys and slowly realizing they weren't the guys in white hats at all.

I told him how I became an RCMP security man and he thought it was criminal the way I was used. At least he was recruited fair and square out of university, he said. His beliefs and values had changed, that's all. I even admitted that I never believed in, or at least never bought into, all the assignments I was on, like Spain and gathering information on wet university kids. I was just good at my job and wanted to provide for my family. He was so accepting and non-judgmental, saying that he could sympathize, but it was not the route he was choosing.

Tomorrow we enter Havana harbour. I told him where I'd be staying and that it would be great to have a drink with him before I returned, so we exchanged contacts.

Wednesday, January 20, 1971

On my way back to Ottawa today. Last night I met up with Phil for drinks and a light dinner at the Habana Libre. The Cubans were helping him a great deal with his research. He agreed with me though that the optics were bad; it would look like he had gone over to the enemy.

He made the point that the words 'friend' and 'enemy' might be as interchangeable as 'patriot' and 'terrorist', like holding a child's building block and seeing it differently depending on what face of the block you were looking at. It all depended on one's point of view and values. We tested that simile a little by chatting about my other assignment, the Canadian exiles. Weren't they like him, he asked? They just changed their beliefs about where their government was going.

I disagreed. It was more; the FLQ had kidnapped, robbed, and were in cahoots with political murderers. Did he plan to do violence to anyone in his process of writing about the CIA? He answered that he didn't plan to, but he was going to cause waves and not everyone might have the ability to tread water. It was so 'Phil', probing and exploratory. I enjoyed his company.

We had several Cuba *libres* and it loosened us up considerably. We began to compare our respective country's foreign policies, the U.S. being the global policeman and Canada being the peace keeper, the helpful fixer; us not supporting the U.S. in Vietnam or in Cuba but happy to have the U.S. protect us from the Soviets. We started sniggering uncontrollably when I described Canada as a middle power with middling fuck-ups, and Phil countered that it was a tad better than being a super power with super fuck-ups.

Over coffee, Phil asked what I was going to report to the CIA and my bosses about him. I shrugged and said I would tell them the truth, that he was writing a book and accepting help wherever he could find it, including from wealthy American ladies. He smiled in appreciation. I then said in all seriousness that his former employers were probably going to continue to play hard ball with him and that if he ever needed my help, he only had to ask. I couldn't give him the shirt off my back, but I gave him my Panama hat, the one I picked up after Norman jumped...

David wondered, after reading this last entry, if his father was throwing his hat into the ring with Philip Agee somehow.

CHAPTER 21.

...INTO THE HOPE FOR THE FUTURE...

(Lewis B. Smedes)

Ottawa, Havana, Paris, 1971-74

David was imagining how a conversation went when Des was back in Ottawa at headquarters, reporting to Superintendent Howie Draper on a blustery winter's day at the end of January.

"You got a nice tan there, Des. I suppose those damn FLQ, those flocons, are getting tans too. So what did you find out?"

Des let out one loud burst of laughter.

"Howie, I think they call themselves felquistes, not flakes for chrissakes. Actually, they're like scared kids, not much older than my own son. I tried my journalist's cover and got an interview."

"I suppose they wanted to feed you more of their propaganda?"

"A bit...

... I learned that Jacques Lanctôt was the brains of the Liberation cell and they're in each other's company almost constantly, like a family. Lanctôt was going on about wanting the Cubans to give them better housing, train them in guerrilla warfare, and give them false passports; but I don't think Fidel will accommodate them much. The Cubans are just happy to embarrass us, like they did when they got us to designate the Canadian Pavilion on the Expo site as Cuban territory so the exchange could take place. Talk about rubbing our noses in it. I'm running a local guy to keep an eye on the exiles and report to me monthly."

"Good work. I hate those fucking radicals, Des. They might be scared kids but they've frightened and hurt a lot of people here with their stupid Marxist ideas and separatism shit. "

"More than frighten, Howie. They've been criminals and we can't forget that."

"You got that fuckin' right. More than a 150 bombs since 1963, a dozen deaths, too many injured, and over a hundred thousand dollars stolen in robberies too. I mean they bombed the Montreal Stock Exchange, for chrissakes."

"Yes, but we've been successful at getting them for their crimes, politics be damned. That Chenier cell that killed Laporte, they'll come up for trial."

"They never get enough punishment from the courts, Des; we all know that. Hell, that turd Lanctôt was already charged with trying to kidnap an Israeli diplomat and here he was, out on bail and able to nab James Cross."

"What's the alternative, Howie? We have to follow the law and we can't sink to their level."

"No, but maybe we can bend the rules a little. After all they've killed a cop and set dynamite at an RCMP detachment, Des. They're vermin and maybe we can catch them with some traps of our own, eh."

"Have you been cooking something up with Yelle in counter-terrorism, Howie? I've seen him and Boire in and out of your office a lot."

Des wasn't sure how much to probe.

"Yes, I guess you could call it cooking, like boiling up a 'ham' maybe," and he looked at Des slyly, finger to the side of his nose. "We're just gathering up some guys to beat these *flocons* at their own game. Why? You want in?"

Des declined, "I'm just curious, and I don't think Yelle would be keen on my involvement. Keep me in mind for some jobs though. How many guys?"

"Yelle and Boire are still working on it, more than a dozen, maybe twenty. It will be a good operation but mum's the word, Des, really."

"You can always count on me, Howie. By the way, has anything new come across your desk on counter-subversion? Anything you can feed me to help me look for KGB contacts in high places? I'm hearing about some weird operation looking for Communist connections in External

337

Affairs. Maybe I could help, especially if some mandarin's son at university is flirting with Communism. You know, forewarn your guys maybe."

"You got enough on your plate with those Cuban exiles, that Yank, and keeping tabs on the campuses. But I'll let them know upstairs in Feather Bed that you offered."

Des left him two folders, one reporting on the *felquistes* in Cuba and the other to forward to the CIA on Agee.

When Des left the office later that day, a cold blast of wind blew snow around him and momentarily choked his breath away. When he reached his car, he sat with his gloved hands clutching the steering wheel firmly, and muttered, "Winds of Change, that's what we got swirling here."...

David looked up from his reading at that point. It was the pleasant end of October; the leaves were still emitting their own golden light into the house. His mother was off with the Euchre ladies, one of whom had picked her up. It was quiet in the house. He let his mind drift while he put the kettle on to boil. After picturing what his father was doing, he tried recalling what he himself was doing in that winter of 1971.What changes did he go through?

He must have been working on his Master's thesis, Canadian Foreign Policy in the Caribbean, some esoteric probe into whether Canada would have more influence in that region as a member of the Organization of American States or whether it should chart an independent foreign policy separate from the United States. He didn't go to many activist meetings while working. He had pretty much given up on The Canadian Union of Students; it was becoming a fractious bunch and not fun anymore.

That said David felt that, when his thesis was done, he must renew his radical fervour or do something to rededicate his political activity. He remembered flirting with joining the new Young Communist League (YCL), a fledgling group dedicated to supporting causes as diverse as demonstrating for North Vietnam and for lowering transit rates. Some YCL recruiters were on campus but he found them too intense, especially a University of Toronto fellow, Mike Giordano, who gave a pretty fervent speech supporting Cuba. David was at loose ends and yet didn't feel like joining anything exactly. What was it at that time? Was all that idealism requiring too much work and no play?

Perhaps he was lonely. Back then, he hadn't seen anyone seriously since Lindsay, although he'd had several flings. He was writing Lydia regularly since that summer in Sofia, more than a pen-pal, but where was that going? He had several unanswered questions, university days coming to a hiatus and still no idea of what to do. He considered law, or at least Uncle Peter had suggested law. He considered teaching, but felt it beneath him, a kind of caving to the derisive adage "those who can, do; and those who can't, teach". No, he wouldn't teach, that would feel like a capitulation and sting too much. What then? That's when he considered applying for External, but that went up in smoke also.

His mind moved on, like cumulus clouds crowding in on a clear afternoon. David wondered about his current situation with Lydia. To be honest, he was getting impatient with his 'international affair'. He wanted to have the open-ended, long-distance arrangement with Lydia become more defined and yet there was nothing definite for the future. He had nothing to offer her. Then realizing that he was wallowing a bit in self-pity, he thought, "Let's get my Dad's quest done and then I can focus on my own life; only a couple of months more and then I can be with her."

With a renewed vigour, David kept going through the days of the journals, noting salient ones, giving passing interest to others.

Wednesday, May 5, 1971

I drove up to Wakefield today, to Frank Zaneth's funeral. The trees have that nascent green about them and the Gatineau River is full, running dark with the spring run-off. Frank had a retirement cottage up there in the rolling hills with the higher Laurentians looming further east...

...We heard in the office that Frank had died on Sunday; only three weeks after his wife had died. At first I felt nothing and wasn't going to go, but decided at the last minute to drive the 45 minutes out of town. I arrived late and stayed on the periphery, behind a maple tree. There weren't many in attendance, some older folks and a couple of Mounties in red serge.

It was enough for me to know the bugger was underground rather than undercover somewhere. He'd go to any lengths to get his man including playing a drug dealer in Chicago once. I always bore a grudge against Frank for the way he got me to be one of his boys; but I also have to admit that he trained me well and treated me like he wanted to protect me somehow.

I hadn't seen him in twenty years, not since he retired, but today I felt that I was finally throwing off his grip on my shoulder. I didn't mingle with the mourners, and on the drive back, a bunch of memories drifted in and out. I crossed from Hull back to the city at twilight, and that was that.

Monday, September 20, 1971

I was going to do a campus check this week but something in the office changed my tack. Howie Draper told me to meet him today and we took the elevator to the top floor, 'the penthouse'. Before he opened the door, he whispered to me that I was about to see something on a 'need to know' basis only, called Feather Bed; and he ushered me into a room with a huge seminar table. A few guys I recognized, even a couple who I had recommended myself for counter-subversion investigation. We nodded an acknowledgement and I sat down. There was a thick file on the table.

Howie said, "Des we've been watching carefully some fancy pants diplomats over the last little while. We got wind that there might be some KGB tampering with our Foreign Service officers. We don't want another Herbie Norman incident, do we?" A few laughed and I suppressed some rising anger.

"For instance, George Ignatieff, our former president of the UN Security Council, is one who goes way back to pre-Lenin Russia and the Tsars. He may be a Canadian now but he has deep Russkie roots. He's been highly involved in NATO too and describes himself as a peace monger. He's anti-nuclear too. If he had his way, Canada would be easy pickings for the Soviet Union.

Anyway, his kid, Michael, is at the University of Toronto and we were wondering if you could add to the file here?"

I looked around. These men were good professionals, but their noses were sniffing into this Communism connection shit way too much.

I said, "Last year I noted that Michael was organizing some international conferences on campus but nothing suspicious."

"Just get us the information, Des, and let us decide if it's suspicious."

I decided to fish a bit. "How many diplomats and External stiffs are you investigating?

Someone said about seventy-five but Draper quickly shot him a look and told me to never mind. At any rate, the team would appreciate what I could get on young Michael Ignatieff.

On the way back down to my office, I asked Howie if the Commissioner had sanctioned Feather Bed. Howie put his arm around me and said, "You know Des, sometimes we have to act for the good of the country even if the country doesn't want us to. We don't want to be embarrassed like the British were with Kim Philby types, do we?"

These guys believed they were looking for spies and Communist traitors, but really they're making mountains out of these possible mole hills. I'll play along with them for now, but I won't play for them.

Sunday, Dec. 26, 1971

Prime Minister Pierre Trudeau equaled God yesterday. His wife gave birth to a baby boy on Christmas Day. That was the good news for the country, I suppose. Meanwhile, I received a post card with the Eiffel Tower on it today. Must have been Agee. It wasn't coded, and simply said, 'doing good research, garret near Sorbonne, contact 33 (0)1 40 46 34 08'. He certainly wasn't trying to hide and I was glad to hear from him.

My files are getting more full, if that's possible. First the campus stuff; I learned that David went to a Young Communist League meeting but he hasn't joined. What a 'flocon'!! Fed some information to Feather Bed about high officials' sons, but nothing really substantial. My Cuban contact tells me the Quebec exiles are wearing out their welcome with demands. I have year-end reports to work on.

341

An Air Canada flight en route from Thunder Bay to Toronto was hijacked today and taken to Cuba. I wonder if that might end up on my desk.

Tuesday, January 4, 1972

I'm in Havana to top up my tan again, at the behest of the Americans. Asked me to track this hijacker and get them some particulars. His name is Patrick Critton, a twenty-four year old black man from Harlem with a Fu Manchu and dark framed glasses. The Cubans allowed an interview, so I met him at a decrepit small dorm south of Havana called *Casa des Transitos* or Hijackers House.

The Cuban authorities have given enough skyjackers asylum that they transfer them here and then let them apply for jobs, usually on sugar plantations. Critton said that was good enough for him. He's on the lam because he belonged to a radical group, the militant Republic of New Africa, where he made explosives, and was involved in a botched robbery. I thanked him, calling him Mr. Cretin, and told him he should look up the *felquistes* in Havana when he gets out of the *casa*.

I also confirmed that Philip had left for France after about six months of research in Cuba. It would be great to see him again somehow. Back to Ottawa and winter by the weekend.

Friday, February 18, 1972

While having coffee with a friend over at External, I learned that David had taken the External Affairs exams and had done really well. He said that David had also passed the second interviews and they were about to do security checks before offering him a job. How did I miss that? I poker-faced my way through but I'm going to have to throw a monkey wrench into that somehow. No fucking way am I going to let the so-called public service get another Dilman.

Wednesday, February 23, 1972

Arranged to see Fred again over at External in the East Block. Over coffee, I said, in a low and confidential voice, that I could save the department some aggravation in security. After a lot of soul-searching, I decided I wasn't the only father to be embarrassed by his son. So I wanted to come clean and let them know David was a risk. Fred raised his eyebrows but I indicated that David was not only a likely Communist, but also a closet homosexual. At first Fred was shocked and then he dolefully commiserated. He patted my arm and said thanks; he would let the departmental processors know...

David tossed the diary down in shock; he could not believe what he had just read. His father had actually admitted to torpedoing David's attempt to get into External Affairs. His own father had identified him as a 'homo' and a 'pinko', and ruined his chances at a career in diplomacy, holy Christ!

David said out loud, "Damn his spying and meddling!" He looked outside at the late afternoon; it had turned windy and leaves were being strewn about. He needed a run to clear his head; hopefully it would give him a chance to abate his growing anger. His mother had returned from her cards and he went to tell her that he would be out for a short while, only to find her asleep in front of the television, head back asleep, mouth open and a wet spot on her lap from spilled tea that she must have jerked from her cup. He thought, "What a pair of parents!"

He ran blindly, his head down and thoughts swirling like a squall. He pounded along sidewalks and onto roadsides, against oncoming traffic. At times he fumed at his Dad's tampering with his life, and then he felt rueful, imagining what his life might have amounted to in a diplomat's suit. There was even a glimmer of acceptance that his father hadn't really hurt him because what counted was that he was trying to make a life for himself and Lydia. Maybe not getting a job with External worked out for the best because he loved Lydia and being with her was more important than any diplomatic posting. But that calm was brief, like being in the eye of the storm, and the winds of ire returned quickly. After a half hour of running, he realized he was outside his uncle's office.

David decided to act on the impulse and consult Peter, hoping to see him at the end-of-day appointments. He took the stairs, two at a time, and breathing heavily, asked Nancy if he could see Mr. Nowak.

"He's just stepped out for a coffee, David. He shouldn't be a minute." David paced the waiting room and was about to leave when Peter stepped out of the elevator with two cups of coffee. Nancy said she didn't need one after all and shushed them both into Peter's office, saying she would close up.

"Davey, what a pleasant and unusual surprise! Good workout?"

"I'm as surprised as you, Uncle Peter. I was just running without knowing where I was going and here I am. Have you got a towel or something so I don't get your chair wet with sweat?"

Peter waved his concern off. "So you unconsciously wanted to talk to me? Is it Freud at work? He smiled disarmingly and added, "Shall we commune over coffee then? You like your Americano black, don't you?"

David thanked him for the coffee and then asked, "Did you know that Dad purposely lied to the Department of External Affairs to destroy my chances of being hired by them?"

"What? No, never. Who told you that?"

"I just read it in the journals, in 1972."

"I never knew about that specifically although I do recall him saying that he had done something that he was ashamed of, but couldn't help himself from doing. I asked if it was an affair again and he only snorted and said, 'I wish'."

"So he never said what he did?"

"No, not even in so many words. He may have skirted it with a hypothetical case. We often had those kinds of discussions, those scenarios. I seem to remember one of our conversations focusing on parenting, along the lines of 'if a father put up a hurdle to what a child wanted, knowing that it was not in the child's best interest, would he be a good or a bad father?'"

"But I wasn't a child, was I?"

"No, you certainly weren't." They both paused to sip their coffee and think of what to say next.

David started. "You know Uncle Peter, I feel like throwing all his cedar boxes and journals into a bonfire and wiping my hands of his whole quest."

"I can appreciate that you're angry with your father again, but I wouldn't advise that David. Legally you're bound to finish your Des's dare or pay back to the estate everything that you've spent on it so far. And financially that would add up to a huge amount for you. Also as executor I would have to rescind the loan for your holiday plans with Lydia."

"Jesus, he's got me by the short hairs, as they say. Damn him! Why would he ruin my life?"

"Sip some more coffee and listen for a minute. Stop running on emotion and use your head instead. Your father knew you would get to this part of the journal and that the knowledge was bound to make you see red. He gambled on ruining any posthumous rapprochement for some reason. What do you think he was risking?"

David's face scowled and he shrugged his shoulders.

Peter continued, "I think he knew that you would have to deal with that knowledge somehow. If you quit the quest and it ate you up inside, you'd be the loser he hoped you wouldn't be. If you somehow dealt with it, you'd be the better person. Isn't that what he said in the will?

David begrudgingly said, "I suppose, but;"

Peter cut him off, "Have you ever read the *Rime of the Ancient Mariner*?"

"Yes, in first year English. Are you suggesting that what Dad did, buggering up my life and then telling me about it in the journal was like putting the albatross on my shoulders?"

"Something like that. I'm not condoning what he did and I don't believe he was proud of what he did either. It was another case of him putting himself before others, yet all the while thinking it was for the best."

"Jesus, this is just about all I can bear about his flaws."

"I don't blame you but I urge you to try to see a bigger picture, if you

345

can. I think he was looking for more than forgiveness here. I think your father was too clever to design this odyssey just to get your forgiveness. Do you believe there's a difference between forgiveness and compassion?"

David put his coffee down and looked into Peter's blue eyes before turning away in thought. Then he countered his uncle. "Let me ask you a question. Do you think things happen for a reason?"

"I think that's putting too much faith in Reason, Davey. Reason can be too cruel and cold I've found. No, I believe things happen and you have to use it to the positive or else you'll be less than you can be. What did the Old Mariner say to the wedding guest? Something about praying, if memory serves me; but I always paraphrase it with my own philosophy, 'he lives best who loves best, all things both great and small'."

"That can be a tall order, Uncle Peter," he said as he stood and sighed. Then he noticed a print on the wall for the first time. "Isn't that a new Alex Colville?"

"Yes, it's a serigraph of his recent painting, *Seven Crows*. I've always had a fondness for crows and ravens. Their clever caw usually means to stop and give second thought; at least it does for me. Important for a lawyer, no?"

"Important for anyone." David gave his uncle a hug in parting.

David jogged, weaving his way back home in waning sunlight, a city full of both shadows and golden clarity. Suddenly, an idea emerged like an epiphany. Could it be that his father could no more escape his past and his baggage than those tortured garter snakes that were doomed to never shed their skins? Was he trying to get David to rise above the torture of betrayal? Maybe David felt he could look at things from his father's point of view, but not necessarily be his father.

What if his father acted the way he did because he hated to be left out; being in the know was his element of control. When he wasn't in the know, he felt alone. Being left out was another reminder of that loneliness! Of being worth less! Not knowing about his son's decision to apply for External, whatever the reasons for their estrangement, would have cut his father to the quick. It would be another example of being shunned, of not being trusted, of being unloved, just like when Mom wouldn't share the ignominy of her rape experience. So he went one better; he froze them out.

Was this the compassion Uncle Peter talked about, simply putting himself in his dad's shoes, but not necessarily walking in them? All his dad wanted was to be included, to be on the inside. Was it as simple as that? Perhaps if his dad had felt more part of David's life?

Then David's anger flared briefly like a match. He said to himself, "No, Dad made his choices; he lost his chances." Then just as suddenly, the match went out.

Was it so hard to understand? Could no one in his family rise to the occasion of compassion? His father tried once in Spain at the orphanage; maybe it was David's turn. David found a park bench and sat down, headlights and tail lights racing by like comets. With his elbows on knees and forehead resting on his fists, he felt a deep pathos for his father and a sensation of a weight slipping from his shoulders.

Later at home, he picked up the diary and tried reading with more compassion.

Friday, April 28, 1972

Spent the day in the office working on monthly reports. Knocked on Draper's door to drop off some files and found him in a tête-à-tête with Yelle. They suddenly went quiet and Yelle said I should wait for permission to enter. Howie said, "Nah, Des is alright. Sid. Just put the files there, Des...

...We were just going over some leads we have on the *flocons*. Seems they've stolen some dynamite and are hiding it south of Montreal."

"Good on you guys, how did you find that out?"

"Sid here has been doing some fine work; it's nothing that a little break and enter here and there can't find out."

"Good for you Sid, I mean Sir." The peacock didn't know what to do with all the praise he was suddenly getting.

"Well just good police work, that's all, and a little initiative," Yelle crowed.

Draper countered, "Hundreds of 10-84's are more than a little initiative, Sid. Your bee and ees are breaking the balls of those fuckin' FLQ and their political lackeys in the Parti Quebecois. And planting that TNT onto the FLQ was brilliant."

I excused myself and left immediately. I made a decision. Later I began to document my own secret records of what I was hearing. These cowboys were going too far.

Monday, May 8, 1972

There were lots of guffaws around the coffee dispenser this morning. Seems some guys burnt down Paul Rose's mother's barn in the Eastern Townships on Saturday night. Rumor had it that the FLQ and Black Panthers were going to meet there but a judge still wouldn't permit a wiretap. The counter-subversion team went ahead anyway and ended up burning the barn down by mistake. Embarrassing and illegal, the assholes. I wonder if it's Yelle and Boire and their crew.

Monday, September 24, 1972

Headquarters was buzzing today. The hockey Summit Series was about to re-start in Moscow and there were three games scheduled this week. Boy, the Soviets have been teaching our guys how to play *our* game. They've beaten us in the Forum and in Vancouver. Now it moves to their rinks.

Speaking of moving, I stopped David from joining External Affairs only to find out he took a job with the World Federation of Democratic Youth and will be moving to Europe. Meg is beside herself. He went to Sofia in 1968 and she worried herself sick then. Now he's off to their head offices in Budapest to plan for a festival in East Berlin. I'm pretty sure he didn't join the Young Communist League but he's flying the red flag now, at least that's what the CIA thinks of the WFDY.

Friday, October 13, 1972

Oh boy, Friday turned into an unlucky day, I think. Dale Boire and

Sid Yelle were in the lunch room with some of their cronies, acting loud and slapping backs. I asked, "What are you guys celebrating?"

Yelle said, "We just scored big time, like Henderson's big goal. By the way Dilman, what have you accomplished lately? You just puttin' in time around here? Have you become a pasture boy?"

"What are you getting at, Sid, Sir. If you mean whether I was put out to stud, your wife isn't complaining."

There was a chorus of oohs around the table and Yelle got red-faced. He started to get up from his seat and Boire put a hand on his arm. Yelle shook it off and growled at me, "We just did a Bobby Clarke slash on those *felquistes*. We didn't just fuckin' break their ankle, like Kharlamov, we took 'em out at the fuckin' knees."

I knew I shouldn't, but I couldn't help myself. I was trying to goad Yelle anyway, so that he might give more information away. "Your wife is good on her knees too, Sid."

He lunged across the table at me and I parried just as Draper came into the room. Things settled quickly and both Yelle and I were summoned to his office. Howie asked what that commotion was all about.

I said, "As far as I can tell Howie, Sid here was criticizing me in public and bragging about doing something illegal to the FLQ."

"I was just sayin' we played like Bobby Clarke, Sir."

Draper said, "As a matter of fact, Des, Sid here has done us a service, as big as winning the Summit Series. He's been able to connect some PQ members to Communists and to money laundering."

"Well done, Sid, but it isn't a competition for scoops around here, for chrissakes. No need to belittle my little legal efforts when your illegal ones are scoring big time."

Later I chatted up one of the boys and asked his view of what happened back there at lunch.

He said," Sid made a big deal about having a 'ham' sandwich, some inside joke or operation. He's not too discreet. Anyway, he started bragging that their clandestine operations landed them some information that will cripple the Parti Quebecois and the FLQ for good. He blows more hot air than fuckin' Moby Dick."

With a little more digging, I learned that Yelle and Boire and company had broken into two leftist groups' offices and stole thousands of files and information. These guys are goons and my secret file on Operations Ham and Feather Bed is growing.

Thursday, January 11, 1973

It's a new year, but same old shit. Dale Boire and three others were sitting at a table in the cafeteria. I took a seat near them, but was hidden by a plant. Boire and these guys were deep into conversation about a job they did on Monday and didn't notice me.

Apparently they illegally broke into the office of *Les Messageries Dynamiques* and stole a computer tape containing the Parti Quebec's membership list. They made a copy of it and, while returning the original, they were almost detected. A person was asking Boire what happened to the copy. He said that Yelle or Draper had it locked in his office and they're scared shitless because they didn't know what to do with it. It has over 100,000 names on it and some of them are big movers and shakers in society, like finance and business. I chuckled to myself. These guys are reaching for the brass ring but they don't know what to do with it when they catch the damn thing.

How ironic that this year is the 100th anniversary of the RCMP's founding. If the country only knew what its men in red serge were up to.

Friday, March 30, 1973

Something is afoot in the United States. President Richard Nixon has started his second term by ending the Vietnam War. But there has been a botched burglary at the Watergate Hotel and presidential aides are implicated. Tricky Dicky had the world by the tail but he's losing his grip now. Speaking of which, I think I may be getting close to being able to turn the screws on some of the lads at headquarters, just a little more tweaking of a plan I'm making...

It was intriguing reading but David needed a break. Also he wanted to address his own life. It was a chilly Friday night, the last one in October, and with a scotch in hand, David telephoned Lydia.

"Hello Lydia," David said warmly.

"Yes, it's been going well enough, I guess. I can hardly wait to see you, but this last part of the quest must be like running the last few miles of the marathon. I've read about the physical phenomenon called 'hitting the wall' and I think I've just gone through that with my dad's journals. Now I wonder if I'll ever want to run a real marathon...

Yes apparently you get very fatigued, the brain produces less dopamine, you start feeling you can't go on, and you can even hear voices or hallucinate. No, not good if you're racing.

Well, I've just about half-finished the '70s. My father flew to Paris in 1973 and something very momentous happened there as far as I can figure from the entries. He was working on a couple of files that seemed to be his main official assignments but I've got wind of an unofficial project that was becoming pretty consuming.

No, I'm not getting consumed by it myself, but it is fairly captivating. He was amassing material that could be pretty damaging to colleagues at the RCMP.

Not to him if he played his cards right, and I suspect he did.

Hmm, I think I'm going to have to fly to Paris for a week and then Havana; I've got a hunch from the journals that those places will warrant leaving some ashes. I know he was in Havana in 1978. Yes, exactly, when we were there. No I don't think he was spying on me then, but I wouldn't put it past him.

Yes, he has entries where he admits that he was spying on me, mostly in university. In fact, I learned that he told lies about me and totally ruined any chance I had of getting into External Affairs.

It did bother me for a while but I had a good chat with my uncle. Yes, he's very good at getting me to see perspective; a lot like you.

Nope, nothing from Pearson but I did agree to have my name go back on the supply teaching list in Hamilton in the New Year. Does your school need a gardener maybe?

Yes, I watched the U.S. Open finals on television, the women's singles was very exciting, and Martina Navratilova just missed out, didn't she? Yes, I'll have to take up tennis. It's a deal, tennis lessons from you, skiing lessons from me.

I love you too."

It was getting late. David took the journal to bed and opened it to the bookmark.

He started at **Sunday, July 8, 1973** and Des was flying to Paris for a few days. Commissioner Higgit wanted an update on the five exiled FLQ people who reportedly left Havana for France. And the CIA had requested his cooperation on Philip Agee too. Once again, it was a 'two birds and one stone' assignment. Des held a tumbler of scotch and water with ice at 35,000 feet, his head back and eyes closed, trying to gauge where he stood with his own oath of loyalty.

CHAPTER 22.

THE WORLD IS A DANGEROUS PLACE BECAUSE OF THOSE WHO LOOK ON AND DO NOTHING (Albert Einstein)

Paris and Ottawa, July 1973

David couldn't get to sleep and continued reading Des's journal into the wee hours.

Des was on an Air Canada flight returning from Paris after spending two weeks on his assignments there. He was reflecting on what he had accomplished and what he planned to do next. The image he kept seeing was him peering into a cesspool. It were as if he were walking along the edge of a it, following a catwalk with railings and looking at the dirty stinky water bubbling in the vat below. Lately his job was like that, he decided. Draper and Yelle and their lackeys had no compulsions about adding to the filth even if they believed they were cleaning up society. And eventually their mess would leach out and besmirch the others trying to keep the Force on the up and up.

He reviewed the last fortnight. He had reported to the Canadian Embassy, a place he hadn't been to since meeting the plenipotentiary there in 1937 on his way to Spain. Now he was greeted by the ambassador, Leo Cadieux, who had joked with Des about FLQ threats to castrate him if Trudeau didn't release political prisoners. The ambassador made Des laugh when he said off-handedly, "They threatened the least active part of my body." The ambassador then directed Des to liaise with his first secretary who would facilitate contacting the FLQ exiles.

Des wasted no time. He arranged to meet Louise Cossette-Trudel in the *Jardin du Luxembourg*, with its randomly placed benches, geometric hedges, and nannies with prams. Louise was the sister of the hothead FLQ cell leader, Jacques Lanctôt. Des was hoping that by meeting with her, he might be able to conduct more candid and less party-line negotiations.

The July day proved to be overcast and humid, portending a storm. To Des, Louise looked quite attractive still, after being away from Québec for three years. She had alabaster skin and a slender neck framed by black hair in a bob style. However, she did have dark bags under her eyes, most likely from her ordeal in Havana. They shook hands and Des decided to come to the point, that the exiles had broken a condition of their exile agreement by leaving Cuba.

Louise hadn't had an easy time in Cuba, she told Des; cramped apartments, heat and humidity, and boredom, even though they were better off than most Cubans. They were working for the Cuban press agency, *Prensa Latina,* but she'd had enough of Fidel's multi-hour speeches and the radical rantings of her brother.

She had given birth to a son, Alexis, who was 18 months now and asleep in the stroller as they spoke. And she was pregnant again, just beginning to experience the recognizable queasiness. Yes, France suited them much better, but she and her husband really missed Canada. Des thought she was wallowing a bit in self-pity but didn't let her whining make him judgmental.

He came straight out and hinted that his report might influence their ability to return to Canada and perhaps persuade the government to pardon them. Louise sighed and smiled at the glimmer of hope. She suggested that what they had done was no worse than what the Mounties had been doing with their own arson and break and enters. She pleaded; didn't they deserve a pardon, didn't the Mounties' crimes really amount to the same thing as the non-violent kidnapping she was charged with?

She knew of the dirty tricks and Des acknowledged that her lines of communication with home were good. He also fumed inwardly that Operation Ham could be used as leverage against proper justice. The toddler began to stir and Louise looked enviously at the nannies, wishing she could afford one. They parted with Louise promising to arrange another meeting with the exiles and Des.

As he was leaving, his shoes scrunching the cinder pathway, he noticed the pockmarks on the walls of the Luxembourg Palace. The Nazis had strafed the building when leaving in 1945 and the French kept the bullet holes as a reminder. Why is 'lest we forget' rarely about forgiveness?

Des gave the exiles a couple of days to mull things over and, in the meantime, collaborated with the embassy's first secretary, getting their information packages coordinated. Des was able to inform him that he and the RCMP had set up a bogus FLQ group in Algeria with some funding, hoping to snare some roaming members. Next he called the Sorbonne, asking to leave a message for Philip Agee.

When Des returned to the Trianon Hotel in the *Rive Gauche*, there was a return message from Philip, arranging to meet him tomorrow at the *Bibliotèque de la Sorbonne*, not far from the hotel. Philip met him in the foyer at 1 p.m., jaunty in a blue beret, jeans, white tee shirt and red back pack slung over a shoulder. He hugged Des heartily before suggesting a latté at a nearby café.

"How's the research and the book coming along?" Des asked.

"Really well. I got a bunch done in Havana and my sifting is pretty much finished. I've decided to write it as a diary and I'm about half done."

"Do you think you'll be able to get it published?"

Agee grinned boyishly and said, "There's a young guy, a like-minded fellow, who's interested. Jeff Steinberg. He was with the book division of *Rolling Stone* magazine but has started his own publishing house. Looks promising."

A server set down two huge mugs, more bowl-like, of steaming milky froth. "Merci, Philip, and congratulations," Des said with heartfelt feelings, raising his cup to Agee.

He added, "Have you had any more harassment from your former employers?"

"Nothing major or obvious, but you never know what might be going on behind the scenes. So what brings you to Paris?"

"You mean besides seeing you?" They laughed good-naturedly and Des added, "I need some information for the liaison file with the CIA. What do you want me to put in it?"

"That's some sleuthing, Des," and they laughed again. "Tell them the truth, or most of it anyway. Say I'm writing the book as a tell-all diary and I have a European publisher; that should get under their skin some."

"Actually, I'm looking for some advice too," Des said.

Philip leaned in closer while stirring the sugar in his cup. "Anything I can do to help, you got it."

"You know how I admire what you're doing, spilling the beans on the CIA. I'm in a bit of a dilemma myself; I can't write a book about what I'm observing in the RCMP, but I still want to put a stop to some illegal business. How do I expose the dirty tricks, which some of my colleagues are committing, without giving myself away?"

"Wow, this is pretty heavy, Des," and Agee looked around at the other coffee-drinkers surreptitiously. "Let's meet for dinner in a loud bistro, a jazz club I know, just to be on the safe side. Tell me about your son in the meantime. Or what you can tell me about your assignment here."

Philip laughed heartily when he heard about the exiles' complaints about living in Cuba. "The ravages of radicalism strike again." About David working in Budapest and East Berlin, he was empathetic. He asked Des, "Do you want me to see if I can keep tabs on him?"

Des was a bit surprised, "How can you do that, unless all those rumours about you being helped by the KGB are true?"

"No, I don't work for any foreign intelligence gathering service, but I do take help wherever I can get it. I have some contacts that might be able to get me information. You think about that, and I'll think about a good strategy for you to be a whistle-blower, your way." He smiled genuinely.

Agee went off to do some more writing and Des worked on his FLQ file in the hotel until meeting Philip at *Aux Trois Mailletz*, a legendary jazz club and cabaret not far from the Sorbonne. The old stone walls and individual tables with white table cloths could not absorb the noisy ambience entirely. But, if it was difficult for Des and Philip to discuss things, it was doubly hard for anyone to overhear them.

Des started, "I've become aware of two operations, both covert, which the RCMP is conducting, semi-officially. One is surveillance of upper level diplomats in External Affairs and their university-educated offspring. The surveillance team is trying to find any connections to Communists in case the diplomats can be compromised or be double agents. The other is full of dirty tricks like arson, illegal break-ins, theft, and even acting as fraudulent *agents provocateurs* in an attempt to root out the FLQ. The first one shows an obsession with the Soviets, a paranoia about possible moles in foreign affairs, and generally just throwing a net too wide and possibly ruining careers. The second one is illegal and is going to backfire someday. I'm convinced that the whole service is going to get tarred with the same brush, the good and professional ones too "

Agee listened patiently, sipping his wine, sometimes closing his eyes and bobbing his head with the music. After a lull, he asked, "So what do you want to do and why? The 'how' we can tackle later."

Des took in a deep breath. "I want to stop the bastards from doing their dirty work before it goes any further and people get hurt. As for why? It's a good question.

Part of it is certainly pay back for the rule-benders and lawbreakers. And I guess I care about the good members of the Force. I hate to see some of them influenced by the bad apples. I don't need to screw all the Security Service, just the rotten ones."

Philip was lightly tapping a finger on the base of his wine glass. "Are you telling me that you want to be a source of good against evil? Sounds pretty Catholic to me, Des." And they both smiled.

"Phil, you know I'm not you; I don't want to take on the whole RCMP. Maybe I don't have your courage either. Maybe I want to have my cake and eat it too. I mean, I still want my pension and benefits after all the years I've put in. And I still want to provide for my family. But at the same time, I hate those guys who think they can get away with murder; I hate their impunity, their self-righteousness, their paternalism. I'm not lily-white myself; I've done some things I shouldn't have. But this eats away at me. How can I take on some of my superiors and their underlings and dismantle whole operations?"

"I don't know if you can do this without having to suffer some or sacrifice even, Des," and then he put on his impish grin, "but Christ, it would be fun if you could."

The music had stopped, the set finished, but the noise of silverware and clanking plates still reverberated. Phil downed his wine and re-filled both glasses from a carafe of house red. Looking at the menu, Phil said, "They do a good *boeuf bourguignon* here that would make Julia Child proud."

"OK, let me buy a good, rich, robust Rhône wine to go with that, a Chateauneuf-du-Pape. And maybe it will make you more serious about my problem."

Phil protested, "I am serious; I just need you to be clear about your motives and consequences."

"How would you proceed if you were me then?"

"For starters, I'd keep a file. But I'd have three copies, and well hidden."

"Why three?"

"Well, I don't think you should go it alone. You need to find someone who has the ear of someone in power, someone outside of the Force that can lower the boom on these guys and their tricks. You'll need to set up a clandestine meeting with that person who will be the conduit to the power. You'll have to keep a file yourself, give one to the conduit, and give the third one to someone else in case anything goes wrong. Do you have someone you can trust to keep the files and can you find people who have influence like that?"

Des nodded, "I think I can. So you're saying this will have to be an external power, like the government or news media, or something, rather than internal?"

"Absolutely. If it's internal, trust me, they'll get you rather than the perpetrators."

Des leaned back in his chair, his goblet in his hand, sniffing the twirling red before sipping. Just as the waiter brought their order, he said, "Well, that's some food for thought."

After enjoying their stew and the songs of a meandering chanteuse, Des thanked Philip for his candid advice.

"No problem, man," said Agee. They clinked glasses and drained the last dregs. "Welcome to the coterie of whistle-blowers. And what about David?"

Des shook his head, declining any help with information about David. "He has to go it alone sooner or later, unless you happen to hear something ominous by chance."

On July 14th, Bastille Day, three members of the Liberation Cell, the Cossette-Trudels and Lanctôt, agreed to meet with Des in the *Jardin du Luxembourg*. They gathered four chairs together behind the balustrade that overlooked the pond and the palace.

"*Bonjour.* Where's the little boy today?" Des asked Louise. She answered hesitantly that he was with a sitter.

Jacques Lanctôt sat with his arms crossed and kept scuffling in the cindered ground. "What do you want with us anyway; why don't you leave us alone?"

"Like I told Louise the other day, you've broken your conditions of exile. There's a new government in France and President Pompidou doesn't want any embarassing business between himself and Monsieur Trudeau. You read the news. Canada may be asking for your extradition. Like I told Louise, my report on you might influence consequences."

"Pfft! If you really wanted to help us, you'd be getting us some of the money that Algeria is giving to that so-called external delegation of the FLQ there. The 2,000 francs each month would come in handy."

"*Ferme-la*, Jacques, pipe down," Louise said. "So if we give you some information, you'll put in a good word, is that what you're saying?"

Des cautioned, "I can only do so much, but if I tell the authorities that you cooperated freely, then it might help. I'm given to understand that if you admit to the kidnapping, you won't have to go on trial and the government may be more lenient too. Let me be more specific though about what I want.

There's a strong suspicion that there was a sixth member of your cell, a Brit who was at McGill. We might be willing to offer clemency then, if not a pardon, if you give us the name. All we want to do is watch him and see who he meets with. You must know we've been gathering up FLQ members one by one anyway; it's only a matter of time. Why not get some benefit from something that is going to happen anyway?"

"Oh, *je sais pas,* I don't know," Louise said. Lanctôt, shifted again and spat. "It's just like you and the fucking system again, grinding away at us like my chair on this dirt."

Des countered, "First of all no one thinks you're dirt, Lanctôt. You're careless with your comparisons. Besides, it's the system that's offering you a deal here." And looking at the Cossette-Trudels, he added, "Two names in exchange for a better life for you and your two children."

"Leave the kids out of this," Lanctôt raised his voice.

Louise said shrilly to her brother, *"Tais-toi! Tu es leur oncle, maudit,* shut up, remember you're their uncle, dammit." Then to Des," It's very difficult what you ask. He's like family to us."

"Yes, but now he's living in Canada, holding down a job most likely, and maybe raising his own family, while you're suffering over here. Is he treating you like family?"

"You said two names," as Louise rubbed her pregnant bump.

"Yes, we understand that there's a person in Algeria who had trained in Jordan." Looking at Lanctôt, Des added, "Learning advanced terrorist methods. He's wanted for violent crimes in Canada, bombings, threatening assassinations. Your cell always said it was non-violent. This would be a way to prove to the world, or at least to Canada, that you don't believe in violence."

Lanctôt erupted again. "What do you want to do, smack him on the head and kill him like *les flics* did two years ago to my good friend, Mario Bachand?"

"I wasn't involved in that. Look, I've lain it out on the table what I need. Go away and talk about it, like a family, do what's good for the family. I'm going to go watch the celebrations, maybe take in the parade and the fireworks, *le feu d'artifice.*"

Des's pronunciation was not particularly good and he looked at Lanctôt when he said what sounded more like *fou d'artifice,* 'you tricky fool'.

"You know how to get in touch with me, but I'm only here for a couple days longer."

Two days later, Louise and her husband, Jacques, were strolling with Alexis in the park when Des sidled up beside them, as arranged. They exchanged envelopes, two names for 8,000 francs, about $2,000.

Des returned to work in Ottawa. Back at headquarters, he concentrated on his two reports, and he gave some thought to implementing his own strategy to uncover the covert. He entered Draper's office and put his files on the desk.

Howie looked up and said, "Well how was it in gay Paree? Hard to come back to the farm, eh?"

Draper pulled the Liberation Cell file towards him and opened it. Des thought how ironic to call the Security Service 'the farm', the same term used for a CIA training facility.

"It was good, Howie. I managed to get an update on the exiled members and also got two additional names that should help catch more FLQ."

"Mmm, it says here you spent some unauthorized money. Is that coming out of your own budget?"

"Howie, my budget, your budget, it's all the same. Look at the results. You got the sixth member of the exiles' cell, Nigel Hamer, an electronics professor at McGill; and an FLQ terrorist in Algeria, Normand Roy. That gives you, and Operation Ham for that matter, a leg up. You're welcome."

"Oh right, thanks. Between Ham and PROFUNC we've been adding

FLQ suspects like crazy; students, communist bookstore owners, you name it. We've been busy."

"Are they real FLQ, Howie? My names are real ones."

"Flocons, Commies, felquistes, same diff, right? Listen Des, you're coming up to 40 years with the Service, aren't you." He tapped the folders on his desk. "This was good work you did here and may get you a promotion before you retire; help the pension eh?"

"Sure Howie, whatever."

Des left Draper's office without any qualms about what he planned to set in motion. First, he had lunch with Peter and asked him to keep two files in his office safe. Of course, Peter agreed. Des explained it was meant only as a fail-safe. It was a simple procedure; the green folder would be given to a person who would use a code, which Des would give Peter in due course; the red folder was to be given to the journalist whose name was stapled inside the file, in case anything happened to Des.

"It sounds very secretive, Des, like James Bond; what are you up to, or can't you say?"

"Something I should have done a while ago probably. Let's just say something happened at work that was like the straw on the camel's back. I'm hoping to produce a show, Peter, but I want to keep us out of the limelight. I'll fill you in on details later, once the curtain opens."

Next Des contacted Jacques Hébert. He was a Quebec intellectual and friend of Pierre Trudeau, now working with the Canadian World Youth, a non-profit organization he had founded in 1971. The CWY was Hébert's brainchild, an idealistic venture just getting off the ground. He was trying to organize teams of Canadian youth to exchange with a similar number from developing countries on projects. By all accounts, Hébert was an indefatigable worker and completely committed to his new scheme to promote peace and understanding. A secretary put Des through.

Des said, "You don't know me at all, but you may want to soon. I have information that could damage Pierre Trudeau. I understand you're his good friend and would do anything to protect him. I need you to convey this security information to the prime minister or it could be worse than Watergate is for Nixon."

There was a quiet lull on the phone. Des filled the dead space with a direction.

"Meet me at the Maclaren cemetery in Wakefield this Sunday, August 5th, at 2 p.m. I will be waiting by Lester Pearson's headstone."

It was sticky, muggy weather that Sunday afternoon. Des was wilting as he waited under a shady sugar maple near Zaneth's grave. At 2:15 he moved out into the glaring sun and walked uphill to Pearson's gravesite. He turned and saw a car pull up by the gravel drive and park. A balding man got out, looking roundish, his white shirt with fully buttoned sleeves, no sports jacket, beige pants showing the wrinkles in the humidity, and dark sunglasses under a Panama hat.

Des kept the headstone between him and Hébert.

Des said a trifle peevishly, "You're a bit late, Monsieur, but I'm relieved that you came, for everyone's sake."

"I could have said the same," Hébert replied. "I was watching from the car park by the river; I saw no one until just now." He pulled a white handkerchief from his back pocket and fully wiped his whole head and face, from his grey, fluffy sideburns and eyebrows to his freckled pate. He had a round soft face with laugh lines at his eyes, but to think of him as soft would be to underestimate him.

Des realized this; if it was going to be difficult he preferred moving into the shade and shadows again. He looked around wondering if the handkerchief had been a signal. But there was no other movement.

"It's hot, but so is what I have to tell you," Des began. Both men lit a cigarette, needing to calm nerves and nascent excitement and walked into shade nearby.

"*Bien sûr.* I hope what you have is paramount," said Hébert, betraying a certain resentment at being out in the humidity. "I'm very busy and hope this is worth it."

"I think so, but you be the judge. I'll try to be brief and then you can ask questions. I've learned recently that some RCMP Security Service agents have gone excessively beyond the law in trying to find FLQ members and possible Communists in External Affairs. They've acted as *agents provocateurs*; they've burned a barn, planted dynamite, set off explosives claiming it was FLQ, conducted several illegal break and entries, opened mail without authority, stolen membership lists for a certain Quebec party, and spied on the young sons and daughters of leading diplomats. I can give you the names of the offending agents and some of the names of those they've victimized."

"That's terrible. *Mon Dieu*! But what does this have to do with the prime minister?"

"Well, in the first place, it's Trudeau's watch. The RCMP need to be shaken up and these dirty tricks stopped. I'm hoping Trudeau may be able to do something. He won't listen to me, but he will to you."

"Perhaps, but you said he could be damaged; you intimated that he may be in danger and needed protecting."

"You remember that he was banned from the United States in the '50s for having suspected Communist links?"

"Yes, but he appealed and his ban was lifted. How did you know that anyway?"

"It doesn't matter how I know. The FBI and CIA still keep a file on him. You know that Nixon has tape recordings of all his presidential meetings? Well, I happen to know that the president referred to Mr. Trudeau as an asshole."

"Pierre would say he's been called worse by better people. That's not damaging."

"No, but Nixon's involved in a cover-up, and that will hurt his presidency irreparably. If it ever got out that Trudeau knew of his own federal Security Service's wrong-doings and also tried to cover up, or worse did nothing, then it would certainly look bad on him, especially since he only has a minority government."

"How would it get out that he knew?"

"You were a journalist once; you know what a scoop can mean. If you don't agree to receive a file with all this information and pass it on to the prime minister, then I will make sure an investigative journalist will get it."

"Now don't be hasty, who said I wouldn't take a file?"

"I'll give you a week. If you don't call this number by next Monday and send a trusted third person to pick up the file, then I'll be sending it to John Sawatsky, the Ottawa correspondent for the *Vancouver Sun*. Just a week, Monsieur Hébert, or it goes public. You might want to ask your good friend, Mr. Trudeau, what he would like you to do." Des gave Hébert a card with Peter Nowak's law office number on it and a coded message written on it. Hébert frowned as he read, "Just say, 'Frère Jacques sent me'".

Des continued, pointing at the card. "If you use this, you'll receive a green file folder. I'll check with you in a month, for an update."

Hébert then crushed out his cigarette, blew a lungful of smoke into the air, and started walking out of the cemetery.

Des made his way towards the Black Sheep Inn in the village. He needed a beer and another cigarette. What were the odds that Hébert would start the ball rolling? Would Trudeau order an inquiry; how would Des know it had started? Would he be forced to contact John Sawatsky? He was anxious because it might be harder to stay anonymous if Sawatsky made it public. Well, he had a week to wait. On the drive home, he noticed big black billowing clouds rising over the Capital City and hoped it would clear the air.

The following Saturday, Peter said at lunch that someone had come to sing Frère Jacques to Nancy on Friday. "Most odd. Is that the best that clandestine operations can do?"

Des laughed, relieved. The green file was a go.

Finally David put the diary down and fell asleep. The next day, while having lunch with Peter at the Lord Elgin restaurant, David couldn't stop yawning. He could hear the autumn leaves scrabbling outside the restaurant window and see them swirling over in Confederation Square. The trees were mostly bare now. The Remembrance Day parade was over; the Grey Cup was set for Montreal next Sunday, November 24th.

Peter said, "You look like you haven't slept and your mind is a million miles away."

"Sorry Uncle Peter. I was up late reading the diary. Hey, I just realized. You've got to let me bet on the BC Lions again, Uncle Pete. Let's make it five dollars this time."

Peter agreed good-naturedly and added, "So that leaves me cheering for the underdogs, the Hamilton Tiger Cats. Okay, only if you spot me a touchdown. Will you be still be in town for that game, Davey?"

"That depends on the business part of our luncheon, Uncle Peter."

"Well you've been holed up with the journals the last few weeks, so your Mom tells me. I'm really glad you didn't decide to abort the project. Why don't you bring me up to date?"

David inwardly winced at Uncle Peter's choice of words but reported matter-of-factly.

"I've finished the '70s and have started the '80s. You played a professional role, if I understood correctly."

"Merely peripheral, I'm afraid. Your Dad asked me to hold two files for safekeeping and pass one on to some secretive fellow, if contacted properly."

"That would be the green file; what happened to the red one?"

"Oh, from time to time your father asked me if it was still safe. Sometimes he wondered about sending it to a reporter he knew. Des got very impatient with the slow process of a political and judicial inquiry."

"That was the McDonald Commission, right?"

"Yes, it lasted a long time too. Your father found out that Trudeau started looking into the circumstances by interviewing certain RCMP officials and getting the Solicitor General involved. It seems he wanted to get things right so that he could change the law. So, it was almost four years after your Dad gave one file away before the judicial investigation began in July 1977. And another four years before the final report was released in 1981."

"And that's when Dad retired, May 1981."

"Yes, he felt he had worked long enough to see the changes to the Security Services and lived long enough to see at least one blackguard convicted for his wrongdoings."

"That would be Sid Yelle in 1983."

Peter nodded and David continued."It seems Dad was pretty much put out to pasture for the last five years of his career. He was promoted to Staff Sergeant in 1976 with two files left to work on, and he conducted the odd course or seminar for the Security Intelligence Transition Group in Ottawa."

"Yes, that promotion helped with his pension too; it gave him his best five earning years. He always wanted to keep a low profile during the inquiry so he could keep his job and leave the family with a good future. That was always his concern."

"I guess I should thank him then for his perseverance. He certainly threw a spanner into Security Services though, and its operations went into a kind of limbo. Dad continued to monitor the FLQ exiles who returned to Canada. The Cossette-Trudels arrived in December 1978 and Jacques Lanctôt the following month. He also was the Canadian go-to guy when the CIA asked for assistance monitoring Philip Agee."

"He never told me precisely what his assignments were. I remember him being available for lunches more often in the '80s." Peter looked around and added, "In fact we used to sit at this very table."

"Did Dad keep you up-to-date with his work?"

"Not really, Davey. I knew he went to Paris again and I recall a holiday to Cuba, both in 1978 I think, but no details and I didn't press.

Your father and I were very close, brothers really, but he still put me in a 'need-to-know' category about work, I expect."

"That last trip to Paris was to escort the Cossette-Trudels back to Montreal. They asked for him personally because they trusted him. And the Cuba trip was just before that, a junket to see Agee. I don't think there was any more travel in the '70s."

"So that leaves you the '80s and your quest is finished, I believe. What are your plans now?"

"I guess this is the business part. How are we doing with the trust fund and the ashes? I would like to leave a vial in Paris. It seems appropriate given his connections there; his first and last overseas assignments. Then I would like to go to Havana with a vial. Cuba's a pretty obvious place to leave some of Dad. That will take me to mid-December. Instead of returning to Ottawa, I would like to take an extended holiday to Brazil over Christmas. I know that's personal but I'm prepared to borrow from the trust, if I can."

Peter nodded, put down his utensils and sipped some white wine. "How many vials have we deposited so far? Mine at Monte Cassino, and how many by you?"

"Five, so far. Paris and Havana will make seven."

"I looked into both the money and Des's remains a couple of weeks ago. There are plenty of both for your plans. Yes, the trust can manage it easily. Have you spoken to Lydia yet?"

"Yes, we're both excited by the prospect of spending some quality time together."

"And your mother?"

"That's a totally different story, as you might well guess. She was pretty mad with both Dad and me about the continued interference, as she calls it, of the quest. Her other term is 'gallivanting'. When I told her about me not being here for Christmas because of spending the holiday with Lydia, she said I was like a mutt sniffing where it shouldn't be. She sure has a vulgar and mean side that erupts when she's drinking. I'm afraid she's sneaking vodka with everything now, even her cereal."

"I'm sorry you're on the receiving end of that behaviour, David. It's difficult to remember the better times when you're caught up in that. I'll look in on her often while you're away. I must say I'm impressed with how you kept on with the quest. You were very angry with your father a few weeks ago. How did you re-apply yourself?"

David grinned. "Part of it was the financial reality check from you. But the biggest was Lydia. When I told her on the phone what my father had done to interfere with my life, she was pretty philosophical."

"Can you share that?"

"Sure, I know she wouldn't mind. Apart from pointing out that things may happen for a reason, that we might not have re-met had I gone with External; she also mentioned something she's learned from yoga. She said that I should remember that the sun is always shining; the amount of light that gets through depends on the number of trees surrounding our house. I guess what she was saying was that, as far as my Dad was concerned, perhaps I should cut down some trees."

"Sounds like she's very level-headed, wise even."

"Oh she is, Uncle Peter, she really is."

Back at the house, David had to be firm with his mother when she saw him packing his bags again. She shouted and used histrionics to make him feel guilty but David remained impervious. He even tried to explain that he understood that Dad had behaved unfairly toward them but that his father also tried very hard to make up for his deficiencies in other ways, like the economic arrangements, for instance.

"Money wasn't enough to save Judas, was it?" she yelled. When he asked her if she could find it in her religious beliefs to forgive Des, she shrieked back, "Tell you what, sonny boy, I'll overlook that whole dreadful marriage, if you'll overlook my drinking."

When David tried to reason that the two processes were not the same thing, his mother glared at him and hissed, "Both experiences have played their role in my miserable life, David; only one I've enjoyed. And now if you'll excuse me while you go off gallivanting, I have to get ready for my Euchre Club."

In a calmer voice, she added, "You know, Davey, in life, you just have to play the cards you've been dealt. That's all I can do; that's the best I can do."

So David prepared to leave for Paris, with arrangements in place for a two-month sojourn to Cuba, Brazil, and maybe Whistler, before returning to Ottawa. There had only been two journals in the '80s box and he took those along without rummaging much the box for paraphernalia; he would do that afterwards. He packed his uncle's travel gift, a copy of Victor Hugo's *The Hunchback of Notre Dame*, to give him a feel for French literature, he had said. While trying to sleep before his flight next day, David realized he was too restless to start reading anything new. So he closed his eyes and recalled the trips Des described in his last journal entries of the '70s.

The Cossette-Trudels had had a quiet plane trip with Des back from Paris, just before Christmas. They were homesick and excited about returning to Québec but Des had reminded them that things had changed a great deal in Montreal. He cited the Thomas Wolfe line, that they could never go back home again, not really. They were immediately arrested when they landed and charged with conspiracy to kidnap, kidnapping, attempted extortion and forcible detention, before being released on bail. In May, 1979 they pleaded guilty to their charges and in August received a two-year sentence, with no trial.

His father's trip to Cuba was of a different ilk. In September, Des had gone on a week's holiday, not an assignment. Philip Agee's exposé had come out in 1975. In it, he named over 250 Foreign Service officers, front companies for the CIA, and foreign agents in their employ. The American government fumed at the perceived perfidy. Some in the US government even blamed Agee's revelations for the assassination of a CIA agent in Greece.

Des had been in contact with Agee surreptitiously over the years and had learned that he had moved from France to Britain where the book was published. Des's journal entries also mentioned Agee being spied on and him having to move to the Netherlands, West Germany, and Italy. Finally he returned to Cuba in 1978, learning that the United States planned to revoke his passport.

That was when Des booked his holiday and met Agee. Philip and Des met in old Havana, at the Café Paris, a fitting haunt for locals and foreigners interested in Cuban music and a cheap beer and sandwich. During their meal, Philip passed Des a copy of his book, *Inside The Company, A CIA Diary*, and Des passed it back to be inscribed, having inserted a passport inside the front cover. It was the last document Des had from the Spanish Civil War, the passport of a Canadian, Jim Wolf, who had died at Belchite. He hoped Agee could use it to his advantage somehow. They shook hands and that was the last time Des and Agee would see each other.

Des wrote later in the diary.   *Sept 18 6:24pm*

Monday October 2, 1978

I feel so far away from my boy these days. I was able to get his expired passport and thumbed through his travels since 1973. A lot of European countries' stamps. My goodness he looks sullen, such an angry young man...

...I feel as if he has moved so far from me that all I can do is hold onto is his old travel document, like a comet's tail. I actually hugged it to my chest and cried a few tears of self-pity. I must be getting maudlin in my dotage.

I finished reading Philip's book last night. I've decided to put it in the cedar box rather than on my bookshelf, at least until the damn inquiry into the RCMP wrongdoings unfolds. What a slow process!! But I don't want anything that links me to whistle blowing to be out in the open. Maybe later, and then his book would hold a place of honour...

And so a life goes. No matter how one tries to be the master of their own fate, one can't predict how the best-laid plans can get altered. It was that way for Des and Philip; and it would be that way for David.

He was no exception. His plans and his life would change dramatically in the next two months. Indeed, he would need his best navigational skills to chart his course.

CHAPTER 23.

A WIND CAN BLOW OUT A CANDLE OR KINDLE A FIRE

Paris and Ottawa, 1985

It was Monday, November 25th. On the Air France flight, David was fidgety. He and Peter had watched the Grey Cup on television yesterday and David won his five dollar bet with the Lions winning, 37-24. But that escapism was over and he faced his quest again. He found he couldn't concentrate; even reading was providing no solace. His mind wandered. For the last few weeks he had almost willed himself to avoid recalling memories of his own life; he had concentrated on his Dad only, and the journal entries of the '70s were behind him. Now he had hours to think of nothing but his own context.

David looked at the cover of the book on his tray but was loathe to begin reading. His uncle had given him a used Penguin classic by Victor Hugo, *The Hunchback of Notre Dame*, intended to put him into a Parisian frame of mind. Instead, he remembered his Dad taking him and some young friends to a movie matinee of the same name one time. He was about eight years old and it was part of a birthday party. The film starred a voluptuous Gina Lollabrigida as Esmeralda and the content was too adult for him and his friends; but he did remember Quasimodo drooling and grunting around the bells of the cathedral and of beautiful Esmeralda being killed by an arrow.

It was a confusing plot but still he could see the image of the bones of the two misfits, Quasimodo and Esmeralda becoming dust and blowing away during the credits. One of the more precocious boys kept saying, "What a waste to kill Esmeralda; did you see those boobs?" David smiled now remembering those early coursings of sexual fantasy.

With his eyes still closed, random images and thoughts tumbled through his active brain. From Esmeralda's body to Lydia's, then how to tell Lydia about his former girlfriend's abortion, and wondering how she would react. Where would his life have gone if he had successfully been hired by External? He shook his head, as frustrated by the idle daydreaming as a pre-pubescent boy's fantasy of lolling on Gina.

Then his thoughts were off again. Had he forgiven his dad? Forgiveness alone seemed somewhat dismissive and insufficient, like brushing oneself off after a fall and just carrying on again, as if nothing required changing. Compassion, however, was made of sterner stuff. It asked one to feel like the other person, to put oneself in his shoes. If David truly put himself in his father's shoes, actually feared for a son's choice and loved him enough to forestall it, would he have behaved any differently? Wouldn't David actually have to change himself to avoid the pitfalls of being his father? There was the rub.

But surely compassion did not mean to necessarily become the other person; shoes maybe, but not all the clothes. He was not the father; he was the son. And he had proclaimed often enough that he didn't want to be like his dad. Suddenly, he thought he heard his father's voice ask, "So, what have you learned, Davey?"

He opened his eyes quickly, almost in a panic. The plane hummed along. David stopped a flight attendant and asked for a demi-bottle of wine, a Merlot. Indeed, what had he learned?

One thing for sure, he told himself, was that even if he wasn't entirely successful at not judging as his dad did, at least he could judge less. And maybe he could think more of others, even before thinking about himself. That would be a concept, he laughed to himself.

The wine tasted cold and the tannins coated his teeth like mittens. Was it enough to feel for his dad, but not feel like him? Would that make him better than his father, not that it was a competition. He wanted to be an improvement on his father. Was he, David, learning to be a gentler self? He took another sip of wine, warming it in his mouth before he swallowed; the wine and the last idea felt better.

And what about his mother? It was increasingly difficult to feel sympathy for her, especially with her self-destruction. Was he being compassionate toward her, or even patient with her needs, for that matter? His mind was completely clouded over now. He needed some clarity. So he pushed away the thoughts of his own future, Lydia, his mother, and focused on one thing. He wondered where his father would like his ashes to be dispersed in Paris.

David had never spent time in the City of Light and only planned to be there for a few days now. It was Tuesday and he intended to combine exploring places that mattered to his father and some historical ones that he, David, had an interest in. He felt somewhat confident that he would know the spot for the ashes when he saw it.

He booked into the same hotel his father had stayed in, the Trianon in the *Rive Gauche*, a few blocks away from the Sorbonne and the Luxembourg Gardens. The first day he spent meandering the winding streets near the university and sat on the benches in the gardens, just like his dad had done. He smiled, realizing he was dealing with jet lag and desiring expedience when he was tempted to drop the ashes in the huge ornamental pond. The next day he traipsed some more, including a pass by the Canadian Embassy, but he wasn't getting any sense of appropriateness. Instead he crossed the Seine and walked east along the river, absorbing the city's richness.

Still trying to intuit the right place for the ashes, he considered pouring the remains into a street dedicated to the likes of the social critic and *philosophe*, Voltaire, or the revolutionary, Danton. But he dismissed that as being convenient more than appropriate, being a bit like a guttersnipe perhaps. Besides his father was not a political activist like those two. David returned to the hotel, footsore and despondent. When he collected his key, the desk clerk said there was a message asking him to call Peter Nowak.

It was 5 p.m. in Paris and David caught Peter at his office at 11 a.m. It was a terse conversation.

"David, I'm afraid your mother collapsed at home and is now in hospital. She's in a coma actually. Everything that can be done is being done."

"I see," answered David. "I'll change plans as soon as I can and fly back to Ottawa. Havana can wait for a bit. I may not get out tomorrow but certainly the day after. I'll call your office and leave details with Nancy. No, I can take a cab from the airport. Should I get some of my mother's things from home or go directly to the hospital? Okay, and thanks for being there, Uncle Peter."

David had known that if his mother kept up her drinking, her condition could worsen at any time. He had done some research and talked to their doctor who laid it succinctly on the table. Women are more prone to cirrhosis, especially if alcohol is involved. Hepatic encephalopathy, which he suspected his mother had, most often occurred when cirrhosis has been present for a long time. Toxins get into the bloodstream and can cause confusion, changes in behaviour, and even coma. His mother's course was a predictable one.

David was able to re-route his ticket; he would fly home on Friday at 10:45 a.m. and be in Ottawa at 5:00 p.m. He had one more full day in Paris.

Whether it was the thoughts of his mother and her Catholicism or his perusal of the novel, David decided he would visit Notre Dame. The next day was clear and the urban air redolent of street garbage and diesel fumes. He walked ten blocks up Boulevard Saint-Michel past Boulevard Saint-Germain, occasionally tempted to tarry awhile in the Latin Quarters' alluring cafés and or peruse booksellers' wares. But he resisted and crossed via the Petit Pont over the Seine with its murky brown waters and onto the Île de la Cité. The medieval cathedral with its Gothic twin towers loomed on the right.

The cathedral was cavernous and ornate, giant rosette windows at the ends of the transept, diffusing soft purple hues onto the nave and apse floors. For centuries this building was the focus of Christian faith; David entered a pew and sat down to contemplate.

His mother had wrapped herself in the trappings of the Catholic Church, using its forgiveness to help her get by her failings, but not really able to practice the love it preached. Or was that her disease that made her seem like a harpy? Both he and his father had kept his mother company from time to time at church but with no conviction. So what caused David to keep an arm's length from his mother and his father, as well as Catholicism? No matter the ultimate cause, the effect was the same. He stopped being close to them. To David, they had subverted the golden rule of 'do unto others as you would have them do unto you'; his dad with sarcastic abuse and his mother with hypocrisy and double standards.

He realized his family was very fortunate to have Uncle Peter as a friend, and maybe he was the only one that brought out their occasional glimmers of goodness. There was a loud cough and the bang of a kneeler hitting the floor. It echoed in the recesses of the transept and brought David out of his meditation.

He left, fingering the vial in his pocket. He had to find a place to spread the ashes. He walked east, outside along the length of the cathedral. As he weaved among the tourists, he crossed the *quai* and entered a park by a wrought-iron gate. David's feet scrunched along a cinder walkway. He noticed a triangular rose garden to his left and continued straight ahead to a concrete and tile memorial dedicated, he now read, to those deported to concentration camps from Vichy during the Second World War. David suddenly felt this place was speaking to him.

The eastern tip of the island was meant to replicate a ship's prow but it reminded David of a bunker along the WW II Atlantic Wall. He walked down a few stairs that brought him to an open geometrical floor with an iron portcullis at the very end, a veritable prison's window out onto the Seine. At one side of the courtyard he noticed a narrow opening guarded by two upright plinths. He entered and inched along a long, narrow, claustrophobic hallway with little lights dedicated to all the deportees who would never return. Also, he was struck by the raw and powerful aura of the urns set at the end of the tunnel. They contained ashes of deportees gathered from the Nazi camps. There was an excerpt from a poem by one of those victims, a Resistance fighter, Robert Denos.

David read, "All that remains to me is to be the shadow among shadows...to be the shadow that will come and come again into your sunny life." David was awed by the sad existential message and could sense his dad shouting at him, "This is the place."

David returned along the tunnel and approached the portcullis, taking several deep breaths of fresh, reviving air. Withdrawing the vial from his satchel, he unstopped it and let his father's ashes be borne away by the west wind, out and away onto the Seine. He clutched the empty vial in his hand a moment and then tossed it over the barrier into the river. Finally David felt that he and Des had made their peace with Paris.

Now his thoughts turned to his mother.

It was hard to believe he had been in Paris only yesterday and now was being chauffeured by taxi to the Ottawa Hospital during a Friday night rush hour. The sleety rain of early winter splattered the windshield and the metronomic window wipers were hypnotizing. By 7:00 p.m. he and Peter were sipping a watery coffee from Styrofoam cups at the hospital cafeteria. David, fighting tiredness, was being brought up to speed regarding his mother who was on life support in the intensive care unit.

Peter was reporting what he knew. "They're monitoring her breathing and her blood pressure, David, but I must be honest, it's a very deep coma. The doctor was describing something called a Glasgow Coma Scale and your mother was somewhere around three out of fifteen. Eight or less is very severe. She can't open her eyes, she doesn't respond with any alertness when addressed, and she can't move to commands. If she were younger, there would be more optimism, but."

"There's no need to be apologetic, Uncle Peter. Mom was a train wreck waiting to happen and she consumed more alcohol in the last year than any of us realized. Hell, I can't believe it's coming up to only a year ago that Dad died and here's Mom on her deathbed."

"Those Catholic Women's League Euchre Club ladies have been up to visit and they started theorizing that she was dying from a broken heart, what with Meg's husband dying and her son always travelling." Uncharacteristically he added, "How do they come up with such bunk, Davey?"

David and Peter looked up, caught each other's eyes, and began to laugh with a certain relief, like air escaping from a balloon. David said he would visit his mother before going home to call Lydia and then get some sleep. They agreed to meet again on the weekend.

When David saw his mom in the ICU, he was taken aback by the tubes and oscillating machines emanating from her shriveled body. He took her hand and marveled how her skin felt wrinkly soft and thin, like phyllo pastry. He smiled down on her, thinking of the Laurel and Hardy line, "Well, this is another fine mess you got us into." He kissed her forehead and whispered that he would be back tomorrow morning, and asked her to wait for him please.

He had a quick call with Lydia, explaining how his time in Paris was short but fulfilling and that plans had changed somewhat because of what happened to his mother. There was no need for her to fly up to be with him; just being on the other end of the phone to chat was a wonderful support. He promised to call her often and especially if there were changes. Then he showered, lay on his bed and went into a deep sleep almost immediately.

It was the last day of November, one of those cold damp days that works a chill right into the bones. David made himself a coffee and retrieved the '80s box from the closet, putting it on the kitchen table, along with the two journals he had taken to Paris and almost completed. He didn't open the diaries or the box however. Instead he gazed into the back yard and the bony arms of the trees and thought of his mother.

He remembered seeing those thin arms at the kitchen sink, yellow rubber gloves on and up to elbows in dish soap. She and his father had made a sudden 'day trip' to visit him in London at his university digs...

...She insisted on cleaning up the kitchen mess and when David remonstrated, she turned on him angrily, "Can't you let me do anything for you anymore? I want to clean up, there's little left you need me for." Another time, he recalled coming home from high school and walking into the den where Meg was watching her new favourite soap opera. She greeted him in an exaggerated salutation, saying how she could relax now. "It's happy hour with my cuppa tea, my *General Hospital*, and my boy." He wondered if she was adding vodka to her tea with lemon even then.

Not long after that, it was Grade 10 he thought, he arrived home to find his mother sobbing. She said she was so lonely during the day and so happy when he got home. But she shunned him when he tried to put his arm around her. His dad was away so he called Uncle Peter. Within an hour Dr. Clift arrived, sedated his mother and prescribed some anti-depressants.

David felt a bit guilty when he remembered how once he used her need to be needed. He wanted to skip a test at school so he asked if he could stay home until lunch and talk about something important. Meg agreed readily and later boasted to Des in an argument that David loved her more and confided in her. His father took him aside afterwards and told him never to try that stunt again, face the music at school and be prepared. David wondered how his dad found out so fast...

He wanted to remember more times with his Mom but the phone jangled; he was summoned to the hospital. He went to the nurses' station to get a report before entering the ICU. His mother's blood pressure was way down and her breathing was congested, suggesting that the coma was even deeper and the death process progressing. She may last hours or days but soon they would need to know about intrusive life-support. David understood. If his mother was letting go then it was time for him to do the same. He sat on a chair at her bedside. Her cheeks were warm to the touch but her hand, when he held it, was cold and lifeless. Her breathing was irregular and raspy.

David tried talking to her, asking if she remembered the movies they had seen and he began recounting plots. There was no response at all so he opened his book and began reading *The Hunchback of Notre Dame* to her. "This might seem like a soap opera to you, Mom." He quietly recounted the intricate love and lust triangles, the supposed murder victim showing up alive, the monk who was evil, the beautiful woman who was kind and generous but taken advantage of, the hunchback swinging on a rope to the rescue; all the while reading in a soft voice and abridging scenes as he went along.

Suddenly the door swished open. A priest in a black soutane entered with the accoutrements for the Last Rites, some holy water, some oil and a consecrated host as food for the journey, the Catholic viaticum. He invited David to stay but David declined and left the room. At the nurse's station, he said he was going to the cafeteria and, if it was convenient, could someone let him know, nodding his head in the direction of the room and the sacrament being administered, when it was over.

He thought of calling Lydia or his uncle but since nothing appreciable had changed, but instead he opted for a coffee and donut and kept reading the book mindlessly. Without realizing it, more than an hour had passed by. Just then an orderly appeared at David's table and asked if he was Mr. Dilman. He was sorry, he said, but Mrs. Dilman had just died and they were notifying him as requested. It seemed the nursing station thought he meant to be told when his mother died, not when the priest left.

Damn, that Dilman cross-communication, he thought, a trait that he had obviously modeled well. He'd have to work on that, he chided himself. First he called Lydia and surprised himself with a sob that burst out when he told her the news.

"I'm sorry, I don't know where that came from," his voice croaked. "I must be really tired. No, it wasn't a shock really but I guess one is never prepared when it happens. No, I wasn't with her at the time; a priest had given her the last sacraments though. No, I'm going to call him now. I'll call you again later tonight, and Lydia? I'm so happy to hear your voice, alive. I love you too."

Next he notified Peter, asking him to call the church. Then he went up to the ICU. Last duties instead of last rites were his to attend to now.

Most of his mother's arrangements were handled by the church. Blessed Sacrament Church, about five blocks from home, seemed to be his mother's locus of spiritual and social needs. The Spiritual Director and members of the Pastoral Care Team were very helpful and seemed to know his mother's wishes better than he or Peter did, for that matter. That evening, Peter and David had a quiet meal at Glebe Avenue. David had made a quick pasta and ready-made salad and they sipped glasses of wine from a bottle of Chianti Classico.

"So, Uncle Peter, this is a sombre Saturday night. You're my remaining family now. I'm officially an orphan. Just so you know, I'm prepared to let the church handle my mother's affairs for burial; those would be her wishes anyway and I'm not going to impose mine on the proceedings. They and 'she' are going to have a vigil visitation at the funeral home on Tuesday, no cremation; I insisted on one visitation only in the evening, and the funeral will be a requiem Mass on Wednesday at Blessed Sacrament, followed by the interment. I would understand if you didn't want to attend."

"Don't be silly, David, of course I'll attend. We may not believe the creed but we can still be gentlemen. By the way, you need to know that I'm the executor for your mother's will, not the church. Everything stays in the estate and goes to you. Meg didn't change anything even if she may have implied differently to the church. You won't be independently wealthy in your new-found state," he smiled with a raising of his glass, "but your life will have a good financial underpinning."

"Thanks for being on top of all that, Uncle Peter. My inclination would be just to walk away and get on with my life. Apart from you, I don't have much connection to this house or city for that matter." He paused and scanned the living and dining room quickly. "I don't really want any furniture, and I thought I'd suggest that St. Vincent de Paul take what they can and the Catholic Women's League could go through my mother's clothes. I may go through her jewelry but; Uncle Peter, is there anything you want?"

"No, I don't want or need anything. Maybe you'd like Lydia to have something though? We can talk about the house and your plans later."

David looked at the '80s box now on the coffee table. "You know, I'm just about finished with the journals as well. Should we be having a signing-off, something to verify I've completed the dare?"

"Yes, I thought you might be getting close to the end. Let's talk about that after the burial on Wednesday."

David bade goodnight and called Lydia. She was concerned for David and wanted to fly up but he dissuaded her. He was fine and Peter and he would tidy up loose ends as quickly as possible so that he could finish the quest and be with her. It would be enough to talk to her each night on the phone, he reassured her.

His mother's room had always been a private sanctum. David felt her presence like a fleeting shadow and a trace of her perfume still hung in the air. He decided to keep for Lydia a set of pearl earrings and necklace which he always admired on his mother; but for the rest, he felt no sentiment. He realized that for years he had felt a duty to his mother, but no deep affection. He didn't feel any resentment either when allowing the Catholic Women's League Euchre Club ladies to go through her things after Sunday Mass. It seemed appropriate somehow although he remarked to himself as he returned to the living room that the women reminded him in a way of the Roman soldiers playing dice for Christ's garments.

It was late afternoon when they left. David poured a glass of scotch and put on Gabriel Fauré's *Requiem* on the stereo, its dirge fitting. He opened the '80s box; the cedar exuded a pungent sweet scent. When he dumped out the memorabilia something heavy fell out, a medal. He picked it up, seeing it was a silver medal from the RCMP. Attached to it was a three star clasp and royal blue ribbon with two vertical yellow stripes, and an inscription, 'For long service and good conduct'.

"Well both you and Mom deserved that award, I daresay, at least the service part," he thought.

David shuffled around the odds and ends. Then he picked up a movie ticket stub for *On Golden Pond*. It was an Oscar-nominated film and Mom must have talked Dad into taking her, thinking it would be a good one on retirement. A hockey article caught his eye, about the 'Miracle On Ice' game where the U.S.A. beat the Russians at Lake Placid and then went on to capture Olympic gold. And there was an envelope too.

He glanced at it noticing Des had written "Finally it's done". Instead of opening it though, he decided to complete the journals. He was intent on finishing the project before he left for Havana, if he could. He took another sip of scotch, and began to leap frog over selections.

Saturday, April 12, 1980

The Cossette-Trudels were released from prison last week; they served less than one-third of their sentence. I was at the hearing and Louise nodded and smiled to me. I'm not sure if it's justice but something in me felt it was the best route for her and her children...

...And a young man, Terry Fox, is planning on running a marathon per day to raise funds for cancer research. He started today in Newfoundland by sticking his artificial leg into the Atlantic. Unbelievable. Maybe it won't be so bad handing the world over to younger people...

Sunday, May 11, 1980

Meg called Davey today for his birthday, he's 32 tomorrow. He said he was going to stay in Hamilton to teach summer school and maybe get a sailboat and that he wanted to take some lessons at the sailing school there. I told him he was crazy to sail there; the pollution in Burlington Bay was so bad that the government says it is an environmental area of concern. Concern! Hell, don't fall in the water, the fish sink to the bottom because they're filled with heavy metals, I said.

He just asked me to put Meg back on the line; the boy has no sense of humour.

Wednesday, November 5, 1980

I arranged to see a hockey game at the Montreal Forum last night with Jacques Hébert, old Frère Jacques. The game was refreshing. *Les Canadiens* had not had a good start to the season but are inching back to .500. They beat the Nordiques last night 5-4 in the battle for Quebec.

Jacques' update on the McDonald Commission was a relief. He knew I was impatient about the inquiry. It had been sitting since July 1977, for chrissakes. However, he was able to tell me that the report should be tabled sometime in the next year, that they've heard hundreds of allegations and needed legal counsel, as well as highly qualified investigators, independent of the RCMP. Apparently the commission has relied on the Ontario Provincial Police, the National Defense, and even the National Harbours Board Police as the overseers.

They've had hearings across the country and filled volumes with transcripts already. This is big. They've had over 300 hearings, interviewed about 150 witnesses, and examined over 800 exhibits. No wonder it's been taking so long. I thanked him for the information and went home a happy man. It's a lot easier to be patient when you can see the possibilities close at hand.

Thursday, December 25, 1980

Some Christmas! David didn't make it home; some skiing trip he had planned with buddies. Meg was really disappointed. I didn't know when or how she did it, but she was completely plastered by late-afternoon. I had to put the old girl up to bed. It wasn't easy. She punched me and slurred something about at least Mary had her son and Joseph and the ox and lambs at Christmas and all she had was a pig and a piglet, me and David.

Oh well, maybe I'll take her to a dinner and show on Boxing Day. I managed to salvage the turkey and fixings and Peter and I finished a good portion of Pinot Noir with the meal. We reminisced on Christmases past, pretty maudlin really.

Saturday, December 27, 1980

Took Meg to a nice Italian restaurant and then went to see the new movie, *Ordinary People*. It cut pretty close to the bone with the couple's bickering. A perfect family on the outside but being ripped apart inside. I could feel Meg tensing beside me, not a relaxing night. One line hit me between the eyes, "Everything is in its place, except the past."

And so it went. David decided to switch to coffee and while waiting for the brew, he couldn't help feeling that reading his father's entries was like a peeping Tom looking into the window of a dysfunctional family of which he was both an observer and a distant participant. He read quickly over the spotty entries of sports events, lunch chats with Uncle Peter, quiet evenings around the house with occasional 'dates' with his wife, and less and less reference to work.

The entries didn't contain a lot of minutiae and its recordings were fairly mundane. The journals seemed perfunctory, even forced, as if he were writing only out of a life-long habit. Often he would write summary entries covering chunks of time, a couple of weeks, even a month. It was as if his father was putting in time.

Then David's attention was caught when he came across a series of longer entries towards the end of the summer of 1981.

Wednesday, August 26, 1981

Finally, the McDonald Commission was officially tabled yesterday, two volumes and a total of over 1,200 pages of the *Inquiry Into Certain Activities of the Royal Canadian Mounted Police*. I was able to stay under the radar for the whole procedure, thanks to Frére Jacques' discretion.

Almost a hundred members of the RCMP were called as witnesses. I know of some guys because I overheard them in the lunch room, people like Sid Yelle, Dale Boire, and Howie Draper were rarely discreet. Even Commissioner Higgitt and Deputy Commissioner Kelly were called to testify. One of the witnesses, a Constable Robert Samson, was actually arrested, and gave my whistle-blowing a perfect cover, although I didn't know it at the time.

Hébert had said the commission had taken so long because Samson gave Mr. Trudeau more motivation to make major changes and get it right. Apparently Samson had been setting an illegal bomb, free lancing for the Mafia, and blew off some fingers. While being interviewed for that crime he revealed that he also did illegal stuff for the RCMP, worse than planting bombs, and started naming names. What an incidence of coincidence for me.

The report went on to say that there were so many dirty tricks and wrong doings that it had become institutional in the RCMP Security Service. Anyway it's done. Heads will roll and huge changes will be on the way. Over 280 resolutions! We'll see!

Thursday, August 27, 1981

I handed in my notice to retire today. Howie was despondent and said his own retirement was imminent too. There is more immediate fallout starting to happen from the inquiry also. Hell, four Quebec RCMP members, part of the Ham Operation team, were charged with kidnapping among other things today. Those guys!

Apparently when they broke into the *Agence de Presse Libre du Quebec* office, they changed the lock so if anyone legitimate came by, the real key wouldn't work and the person would leave, giving the Ham team a chance to get out. But they took a crowbar with them as well, and left it behind. Would they have used it in case they were ever caught? They had been told to avoid detection, whatever the means. What a mess!

Howie started going on about being hung out to dry. But he realized the folly of that bluster and just shook his head. He stopped and asked me why I was retiring now and what was I going to do. I told him that there were going to be a shitload of changes after the inquiry, hopefully the good members wouldn't be tainted too much by the bad apples, and I was too old to deal with all that bullshit. So maybe I'd go fishing, maybe write a bit, who knows?

Besides, I had been in it long enough, 46 years; I was sixty-three and it was time to hand it over to younger ones. He saw my point. This commission was a game-changer. He congratulated me and said I always kept my nose clean, made sure my files were up-to-date, and was an asset to the Force. Faint praise from a guy who didn't seem to recognize assets from asses.

Saturday, September 26, 1981

There was a retirement dinner scheduled for tonight but I had already declined, saying my family didn't really know what I did for a living so it was too complicated to come out now. Instead, Peter took me and Meg out to dinner tonight, a quiet affair...

David continued his reading past midnight. Generally his father's life seemed lonely, going for walks, attending sporadic sporting events alone, occasional lunches with Peter, rare outings with his estranged wife, and reading. Sometimes he would comment on the pains stemming from lung cancer. Then there were several blank pages, as if the narrative were finished. At least David thought that was the case until he turned a page onto one more entry. It was written the day before his father died.

It began **'*Friday, December 14, 1984'*.** Appropriately, David heard the strains of Fauré's choir singing *Requiem Aeternam* in the background.

Hello David, if you accepted my challenge from the grave to read my journals and got this far, then you deserve my congratulations. It has been quite a journey, if I say so myself. Peter and I often discussed if it were ever too late to become what one might have been. The journals were my belated attempt to be a writer and a father.

I have a bonus for you. I know you got into sailing and probably sold your boat to take on my deathly dare. Even though I never said it, I was both proud and envious of you getting into sailing. But I never said it; now there was something I was guilty of often. Anyway, you will find an envelope behind the Potato Eaters, the print in my room. Use the money to get back into sailing, why don't you? Or anything you want. After all, it's your life now.

Love, Dad

David went up stairs to his father's room. He hadn't been in it for a year. He lifted the dark wooden-framed print of Van Gogh's Belgian mining family, carving slices of potatoes for their meal, with their chiseled and gaunt faces, gnarled hands, all dark greens and black hues under one light above the table.

David always thought it was an odd picture to keep, especially in the bedroom. Depressing, except now he noticed the look of cautious love, mutual caring, and sharing among them. David gently placed it on the bed, the back facing up, and there was an envelope stuck into the edge of the frame with some discoloured tape. He opened it and let out a low whistle. In his hand he was holding a cheque for ten thousand dollars.

Part Three: A Life Lived For Others

CHAPTER 24.

ASTRIDE TWO WORLDS

Ottawa, Havana, and
Ihla Grande, Brazil, 1985

It was now Tuesday evening, time for the funeral visitation. Uncle Peter picked David up and David told him about the discovered largesse. Peter said it was certainly generous, but knowing the accounts as he did, not an issue. He reminded David that he was the only heir to the estate. The financial prognosis was all a pleasant surprise for David.

Both he and Uncle Peter had agreed to cede arrangements to the Catholics for both the visitation and the funeral, although David had asked Peter to say something at the church mass, not trusting his own emotions in public. Both men were astonished to hear stories recounted about a Meg they didn't entirely recognize. The euchre ladies told of Meg being the life of the party with jokes and organizing knitting nights to raise money for the poor with their baby outfits and mittens. The pastor told of Margaret Mary, Meg's formal name, being at the church regularly to change the flowers, taking cuttings from her own garden. There were lots of people who shook David's hand and said what a good woman his mother was, with kind words and works. It was a public side of his mother that neither he nor Uncle Peter was aware of and it left David wondering how well can we really know anyone.

The next day was gray with occasional dustings of snow flurries. Although the church was not packed by any standard, the CWL members, in colourful sashes, formed an honour guard in the aisle as the casket was wheeled to the front of the church and a picture of his mother placed on top. Peter was dignified and correct with a few words, saying how long he had known Meg and the family; how they had included him so warmly as a member of their circle; that one of his fondest memories was being able to take her to England to fulfill her life-long wish to travel; and that it was a blessing that she didn't suffer long with her illnesses and the loss of her husband in this last year.

They were driving to Beechwood Cemetery, appropriate because it was the resting place for Armed Forces' veterans and RCMP members and family, about ten kilometres across town. Suddenly Uncle Peter put a hand on David's forearm and said in an aside.

"You know Davey, we both heard stories over the last couple of days of a side of Meg that we didn't glimpse really. I guess she and your father had 30 years or so to cultivate their separate lives. That's a side of the story those church people would not have realized, or, if they did, it would be as Meg would have told it. We all have a private and public persona, I believe. The more you know both personae, then the more intimate you are.

Your father and I were about as intimate as we could be, but not so much your mother. It's important that you realize something. You were dutiful to your mother without submerging yourself to her whims. That tells me you have a balance of love and independence. Ultimately that's what every parent should want for their child. Remember that David.

And now, I have my own request to make of you. I know you plan on spreading a vial of your father's ashes in with your mother's casket; but to honour both their memories, would you mind not unstopping the vial? Could you just throw the container into the grave, whole? It would be hypocritical to intermingle them more than they were in life, don't you think?"

David agreed.

After the interment, Peter and David had a glass of scotch at the house on Glebe to toast both Meg and Des. The topic of 'those church people' was broached again and they asked each other how and when they lost their own Catholic beliefs. Peter explained how he lost his at the end of the wartime trek around the Caspian Sea when he was left alone.

"How could a loving God do that, David? And you?"

"It was much more mundane and carnal, I'm afraid. I went to confession to admit that I was having sex out of marriage but with a woman I loved. The priest asked if I intended to continue and I answered, of course. So he said he couldn't forgive me since I wasn't truly contrite. I thought how could a loving God be represented by so

390

many men who make up so many rules that get in the way of loving? I decided that the Catholic religion was like a house of cards; take one elemental card away and the house falls. My card was sex, I'm afraid, and the beliefs all came tumbling down."

"Interesting," said Peter. "And this wasn't Lydia, I suspect."

"No, but I do love her, and I'll talk to her tonight and tell her so."

Peter smiled at him warmly. "Well, why don't we spend tomorrow afternoon together to read the will. Later we can arrange to sign you off your father's behest, and let me help you make plans to see Lydia, without any concerns here in Ottawa. However, I have to leave you with a question.

As part of the end of Des's dare, he left instructions to ask something, not that the signing off depended on it. He wrote something that he paraphrased, citing the RCAF pilot and poet who wrote *High Flight*. Your father was often respectful of sources. Anyway he wanted me to ask if, by completing your task, you 'have you broken the surly bonds that held you'? "

"Hmm, that's an interesting question to leave me with, something every orphan could ask themselves. I'll give it some thought." They clinked glasses, saying good night until tomorrow.

David and Lydia had a brief phone call. It was a work night for Lydia, marking papers. He told her about the two sides of a person that he and Uncle Peter had chatted about and he asked her the same question about faith. She said that philosophically she couldn't abide hypocrisy and the concept of 'leap of faith' was too much for her Reason. Then Lydia got practical and warned David that it would be difficult to be themselves in Brazil, too many students on the island and her parents in the city. He would have to adapt to her public side. He was going to question her on the double standard of that strategy, or the honesty, but discretion intervened.

David missed Lydia and wanted to be with her as soon as possible. However she was still teaching until the Christmas break. His new plan was to go to Havana and dispense with his dad's ashes as a finale to the quest, fly to Rio de Janeiro by December 18th, then carry on to Lydia's

Costa Verde island digs and school. This would be a couple of days before her term ended and he hoped to surprise her.

It was the second full week in December; Ottawa was in the grips of a cold snap of -20 Celsius and the city was festooned with Christmas decorations, although there was no appreciable snowfall to help the illumination. David was running the canal path along the parkway with his newest device. He had told Lydia that he bought a Sony Walkman, a sporty yellow one that he attached to his belt when he ran. He usually liked to disassociate from the act of running, letting his mind work on solutions; but on a whim he decided that some music might be a pleasant alternative.

He told Lydia that he purchased the hit album, *Brothers In Arms* by Dire Straits, which was topping the charts. One tune in particular, *So Far Away,* he couldn't get out of his head, and it was perfect for his running pace and frame of mind.

He hummed and mumbled the words to his gait, "And I get so tired when I have to explain, when you're so far away from me. See you've been in the sun and I've been in the rain; and you're so far away from me." As the tune ended he said excitedly to himself, "But not for much longer."

David's last wintry days in Ottawa flew by. Uncle Peter and his secretary, Nancy, had been very diligent about flight and travel arrangements for him which cleared him to leave this Friday, December 13th. Triskaidekaphobia aside, he felt an odd admixture of emotion, some residual grief over his mother's death and the anniversary of his dad's, and a rising euphoria at soon being with Lydia. Fate he couldn't control, only his own choices, he reasoned.

It was Thursday evening. David had completed his paperwork with Uncle Peter and they were having a glass of wine in Uncle Peter's condo after being out for a Christmas celebration and *bon voyage* dinner at the historic Courtyard Restaurant nearby. Peter had said that once David took his leave, he, Uncle Peter, would begin to expedite the estate settlement and would also put the family house up for sale. As for personal effects, David and his uncle had the mementoes they wanted and the church was grateful for the rest as donations. There was one item that David wanted to revisit though. David asked Uncle Peter if he still had the signet ring of his father's.

"Actually I do; would you like to see it?" Peter brought out the simple gold ring and placed it in David's palm.

David said, "You know, at one time, I thought the D stood for Desmond, but now I see how it could be Dad, David, or even Dare." He chuckled, "It's funny that a year ago I could only see one meaning and now I can see several. It just depends on your point of view."

"And perspective, Davey. You know you can have it if you want."

"Mmm, that's a kind offer. I might take you up on it. You know, Dad had written on an envelope in the '80s box, 'finally it's done'. Did you know about that? I feel a little bit like that now. The letter was a hand-written one from Pierre Trudeau to Dad. Jacques Hébert had passed it along."

"Yes, I remember your father mentioning it, a kind of throw-away comment at lunch one day, but I could tell he was proud of it and so I pushed him on it. He explained it had to do with the whistle-blowing on the RCMP's dirty tricks."

"I must say I was glad that he got some recognition for that even if it was quiet, secret, and informal. Not unlike Dad, now that I think about it. It was good of the Prime Minister to thank him."

"Agreed. And what about you, now that the quest is essentially over? Have you broken the surly bonds of your father and the past?"

"Yes, I feel I have, as much as one can really leave the past behind. It hasn't been smooth sailing though. Lydia's certainly noticed my angry flare-ups about my father from time to time and we've spoken about it."

"It sounds like you two do a lot of talking. I'm glad to hear that," said Uncle Peter.

"Oh we do! She allows that there may have been just anger occasionally on my part, but a person really should rise above it. She explained it once, that anger is actually a delusion of the mind, that it's really about ego. I've thought about that a lot on my runs, let me tell you."

"Well this past year has certainly been eventful for all of us; it's given us all a great deal to ponder."

"Learning about dad has truly been a gift. Not just the travel and the money, but how a life lived is not a solitary endeavour; it ripples like a stone thrown in a pond; and it has effects far beyond the initial splash. I guess the biggest thing I've learned is that now I have to live my life and share it with Lydia in such a way that our waves break gently onto the people around us."

"Hmmm, may your sailing skills help you out there. Do you think you'll get back to sailing, David?"

"I'd like to some day. Certainly Dad's gift makes the dream a possibility. But I want to get a teaching position first."

"I'll keep my fingers crossed for you."

"You know, Uncle Peter, this quest has made me appreciate you more too. Thanks for all your help and support. And by the way, if you're willing to part with it, I will accept that ring of my dad's please."

"I always hoped I was merely keeping it safe for you."

They hugged, not goodbye, but 'so long', wishing each other a Merry Christmas.

David promised to stay in touch with his godfather. "You'll always be in my loop, Uncle Peter."

On the way home, David said to himself, "I'm coming, Lydia" and he started singing, "I'm tired of being in love and being all alone, when you're so far away from me."

His plane touched down in Havana and he took a taxi to the old town, to Obispo Street a few blocks from the port. It had been several years since he had been in Cuba's capital, not since the World Festival of Youth and Students in 1978, and it felt like re-acquainting with a long-neglected friend. Absent-mindedly, he twirled the gold signet ring on his right hand pinky, like breaking in a new pair of shoes, and acknowledged it was becoming more familiar.

He got out at the Hotel *Ambos Mundos*, the cheery inn with the salmon-coloured façade where Des had stayed in 1964 with Marianne Lacloche. David took a standard room, trying to be economical, opting for air conditioning but not a balcony. The hotel name meant 'both worlds' and the multiple meanings weren't lost on David. Many facets of his life were brought together at this point of time and place; the past and present, father and son, as well as moving forward and looking backward, all in this propitiously-named inn.

He didn't want to stay long though. Like Paris, he wandered the cobblestoned streets, waiting for something, anything to suggest a suitable place to leave his father's ashes. It was a bright and muggy mid-morning when he started checking out the city. He hired a driver to help speed up his search. They moved slowly, honking occasionally through the winding streets of Old Havana, appreciating once more the exotic lime, yellow and blue fronts of the hotels and shops. They toured by the new Havana too; the mammoth Revolutionary Square with the statue to José Marti and murals of Ché, which seemed less impressive than the first time he saw them. He also climbed the worn steps of the unused parliament building and wandered the largely empty airy halls, noticing that the old wooden senate seats smelled of mildew, like democracy decaying. Finally, toured out, he went to the Habana Libre Hotel where he sat at the dark, air-conditioned bar and ordered a *Papa doble,* the Hemingway drink. The mixture of rum, lime, grapefruit juice, and maraschino liqueur cocktail had little effect on him.

So David went back to his hotel to write postcards for Lydia and Uncle Peter, had an early meal, and went to bed. He was reading *For Whom The Bell Tolls*, a book Hemingway had written in this very hotel while in Cuba in 1939; but he fell asleep after a few chapters. Next morning, after a strong coffee and pastry, David was ready to attack his task, hoping that if there were such a thing as spiritual pheromones out there, then his father had better stir the internal filaments of his mind somehow, and quickly.

He wandered in the direction of the old port where he saw the sign by the plaza indicating the *Castillo de la Real Fuerza*. Suddenly it happened!

David could feel the hairs on his neck tingle and he smiled at the irony of it all. Of course! The Fortress of the Royal Force, like the Royal Canadian Mounted Police *force*, that was it!

He entered the star-shaped defense built slightly inland to repel pirates; a monolithic, cannon-bristling edifice with a four-leaf clover shaped moat around it; an imposing and impressive heritage site that in reality never entirely fulfilled its purpose. How appropriate! David entered the museum and then went outside onto the inlaid brick parade ground. He could see the green water of the moat just beyond a thick, waist-high wall. Yes, this was the place! He smiled. Taking the vial from his trouser pocket, he let the ashes fall into the moat and threw the empty container into the briny watercourse that was designed for protection and security.

"There you go Dad; you honed your skill here in Havana for the RCMP and found a better side of yourself with Philip Agee. Today I am commemorating you as being an integral part of the Royal Police Force and letting part of you rest in this namesake fortress and all that it entailed. Adios."

He turned back towards his hotel. He was done here. It was time for him to go to Brazil and Lydia. He finished reading his Hemingway book on the plane to Rio de Janeiro and then re-read a marked place near the end of the novel.

"Today is only one day in all the days that will ever be. But what will happen in all the other days that ever come can depend on what you do today." Simple yet prophetic, he thought to himself.

The plane landed in Rio on Monday mid-morning, December 16th, and David hurried to make the rendezvous happen, to surprise Lydia on Ihla Grande.

He took a cab to the bus station, the *Rodovieria,* and caught the earliest one he could to *Angra dos Reis*, Refuge of the Kings, on the Costa Verde. It departed at 2 p.m. and took three hours over beautiful winding coastal roads, with glimpses of white crescent beaches and bays, lush lumps of emerald islands, and beautiful azure sea. The darkening mountains on his right used to be the source of Portuguese gold and coffee, shipped down to the coastal coves. The scenery was gorgeous but until he was with Lydia it meant little. He was so close but still separated and he couldn't get to Ihla Grande until tomorrow, there being but one ferry a day and he had missed it. It was a mere an hour and a half ferry ride away, although it could have been an ocean and several time zones as far as David was concerned.

The next afternoon, David stood at the bow of the ferry removed from the other travelers who lounged under a canopied shelter. To pass the time until then, he had tried to read his travel guide and study some Portuguese vocabulary while drinking several mugs of strong Brazilian coffee. Now he felt a bit buzzy and caffeinated hoping to be refreshed by the breeze, leaving behind the Angra pier, the white beach, the even whiter Naval College, and rising hills of shanties behind the town with its potential mudslides. Ahead were blue seas, a bit of wave chop in a gentle wind, and emerald isles to the east. The approach to Ihla Grande and its only town, Abraão, was magical, like entering an Eden.

There was a tall mountain, partly shrouded, the *Pico do Papagaio*, or Parrot's Peak, just visible; and the green jungle came down to the shore like arms ready to embrace visitors. He disembarked with about thirty other passengers, the fishing boats and white buildings awash in a setting sun. Lugging one large suitcase and a backpack along a wooden pier and rough road, David decided he needed some sustenance before he got his bearings and searched for Lydia. He saw some umbrellas along the beach and headed in that direction.

David ordered a Brahma beer and fried calamari, fumbling with his phrase book. Then he stretched his legs out, taking in the scene. The guide book had said that the paradise island had come to eco-tourism only recently; and Abraão had been residence to pirates, lepers and criminals in the past, all outcasts. Now the jungle was overtaking those residential ruins just outside of town. He looked up as he sipped his beer and suddenly saw Lydia in the street plaza.

She had been playing tennis apparently; and before he shouted to her, he took in her presence as a spy might. She was wearing a yellow Polo with the Brazilian emblem of a blue globe and the motto, *ordem e progresso*. Long-legged in white tennis shorts, a blue tie used as a head band to keep her hair off her face, she looked both athletic and alluring. Then David saw her lean forward toward her tennis partner. She had her hand on his shoulder and kissed him twice on the cheeks and then he drew her back for another cheek peck. They laughed, said *"tchau"* and waved goodbye casually, turning in opposite directions.

David could feel his face becoming thrawn, an irrational jealousy rising up like bile to contort him. He tried to suppress it but was unsuccessful; and then Lydia spotted him. She squealed his name and dropped her tennis racket as she ran to hug him. She kissed him longingly on the lips, but he was cool in his response.

"What a surprise, Dahveed! This is like an early Christmas present, no?"

Realizing he was being silly, he drew her close, breathing in her scent of shampoo and coconut oil, feeling the damp back of her shirt, nestling his nose in her hair.

"Did you have a good match? Who was that?"

"Oh, that guy, Alex. Nobody really. A colleague at school and we play tennis sometimes." Then Lydia took a step back and looked closer at his face.

"Dahveed, what is it? You look ill. No wait, you look like you did when I used to talk and laugh with Mike Giordano in Havana. Are you jealous, *querido*? Sweetheart, you are jealous!" And she looked askance at him in mock-shock.

David smiled sheepishly. "I must be more tired than I thought. When I saw you with him, a rush of old doubts came over me, like being abandoned, and I wondered if I had made a mistake coming here."

"Your only mistake is not trusting how much I love you." She took his hand and guided him to the shadows at the side of the bistro, the twinkling white fairy lights of the town beginning to glimmer behind her. She demonstrated to David, "This is the Brazilian custom, especially for an unmarried woman, to wish her luck. Kiss me three times on the cheek." He did obediently and then Lydia came in closer.

"Now this is an unmarried Brazilian woman with the man she loves."

Lydia put her arms around David's neck, pushing her breasts and hips into him, and probing his teeth and mouth with a firm, darting tongue. She arched back from her pelvis and through a beautifully wicked white smile she added, "And Alex did not go away with a *tesão*, a chubbie, as you would say, *querido*."

David laughed heartily at that.

They went off to book David a room. Lydia explained it would be impossible to stay together. She suggested the aptly named Paradise Inn on a quiet street back from the beach. Decorum and lack of space precluded him staying in Lydia's small apartment and only decorum from taking her to his room, since too many of her students lived in town. He checked in and then they went for dinner al fresco. With their hands entwined, two glasses of wine and a candle between them, David began.

"Lydia, there's so much to tell you, I'm not sure where to start. This international relationship and living apart has to end; I mean I can't go on much longer living without you in my life."

She smiled, "Well in both our cultures, I think it is up to you to change that predicament, no?"

He laughed, "Touché. Where shall I start?"

"You told me on the phone late in October that you had something to discuss face-to-face. But a great deal has happened since then and we haven't always been the best at weekly letters, have we? Why don't you start with that news that couldn't be spoken until now?"

He took a deep breath, released her hands and took a sip of wine. "Here goes then." He put his glass down. Lydia reached for his hand again and said, "We are connected, my love, no matter what you tell me."

"You remember that I told you I found out that my Dad had been spying on me in university?"

"Yes, how he ruined your chances for diplomacy but Fate brought us together," and lightly squeezed his hand.

"That part, yes, but there's more. Lydia, I don't want secrets between us. I don't want to be like my Dad, always keeping another life hidden. But I'm also worried that by opening all of my life to you, I might push you away. I'm nervous really."

Lydia felt a cold hollowness briefly, thinking the worst but with an attempt at humour, she gave him permission to go on. "If you are telling me you are a murderer, perhaps we could arrange to have you spend it in a cell of the ruined prison here, so we can be nearer, no?"

David smiled ruefully.

"Just tell me, *querido*. Remember you are just cutting down some trees to let more sun in."

"Okay. When I was in university, before we met, I helped a girlfriend to get an abortion. We thought we were in love, but we weren't, and we didn't want to be parents. So we terminated the pregnancy and our relationship ended shortly after too." He let out a long sigh but kept his eyes on the table and their hands.

"My Dad knew about it from spying on me. It was one of his files on student radicals and I was just caught in the web. He never used it against me or even revealed that he knew. Maybe he just figured it was mine to deal with, one of those rare times he treated me like an adult. Anyway when I read that in his journals, I was shocked and angry and then frightened of your reaction; because I vowed that I would tell you."

Lydia looked pained. "O *meu amor*. Is this your way of telling me you don't want to have children?"

David looked up, noticing her aggrieved voice. "No, it's not about that at all. I just didn't know how you'd feel about that decision, being raised Catholic and all, and me keeping it from you. I would love to be a father, as long as you were the mother."

"I don't know how I feel about abortion but I do admire that you risked so much in telling me. In actual fact though, you risked very little. I'm not angry or disappointed; well not very much. It's your past after all, and it's more important to discuss our future together, despite our separate pasts."

He picked up her hand and raised it to his lips, "I do love you so much; I must say I'm very relieved."

"But Dahveed, the pressure on you is just beginning. Remember you will be meeting my family for Christmas." And she gave a throaty laugh, confessing that she was very relieved as well.

They met at his *pousada* for coffee in the morning and he walked her to school. They strolled hand-in-hand slowly along the beach road, past a fisherman doing a samba with his net. Further along, they met some school children in shorts and blue tee-shirts who smiled and looked big-eyed at Lydia, lilting loudly, "*Bom dia, Senhorita D'Silva*", before they skipped off giggling. Soon the path took them to another secluded bay where the school was situated. David and Lydia kissed, not on the cheeks; and they parted to conduct their separate days.

During the last two days of Lydia's term, David hiked the Parrot's Peak in the morning and read in the afternoon, then he and Lydia played some tennis and swam after school before they leisurely dined, generally melding into each other's life again after an absence that had made them fonder, if not actually intimate. Lydia wanted to show David some of the island before they made the transition to Rio on Monday. So on Saturday they planned a picnic and hiked to the other side of the island.

They started right after an early breakfast; David carried the full backpack of towels, lotions, a beach game, books, and packed lunches from the *pousada* (crackers, cheese, salami, palmitos, bananas, and bottles of water). It was a two hour hike over jungle paths, across a ridge with stunning views back to the sweep the beach at Abraào, and occasionally scrabbling over rocks. Finally they reached their destination, sticky with sweat, and jumped down onto the most idyllic beach imaginable.

The sand was so fine, compact and white that it squeaked like Styrofoam, and stretched in an uninhabited crescent for a mile at least. Bound by rock outcrops at either end and jungle mangrove and palms to the rear for shade, they had the clearest gin-coloured water in front, and only each other for company.

"This is called *Praia Lopes Mendes*, one of the highlights of the island; do you like it?" Lydia asked.

David was amazed. "Absolutely! You know this sand sounds just like snow crunching while walking during a clear and frozen night at home; it's such a contradiction of sensations for me."

"Come; let's go for a quick swim to cool off. Then we must talk."

"What do you mean? asked David.

"We need a united front before we face my parents so we must discuss our future."

"You say that like the holiday is over," he laughed and pulled her into the warm surf of gentlest waves.

Afterwards, Lydia caressingly lathered David in suntan lotion, and they walked hand-in-hand toward the far off rocks.

David began, "So our future, eh? Shall I start? I've been thinking about how I might be able to support you."

"Why you support me? Maybe I can support you."

"Let's do some real assessment, Lydia. My situation has changed. I realize you don't make a lot of money and realistically, what can I do down here. Being a gardener was merely a jest. I'm not wealthy but Uncle Peter assures me, my future, our future, is looking bright. We can be together for a good bit of time now, even without definite jobs."

"Não, *necessitamos profissões*, we need our occupations! I love teaching, you do too; we must not go into *aposentadoria*, how do you say, retirement, no! Look how my language goes when...aagghh!" And she threw her hands in the air.

"Lydia, *basta! obrigado*, enough already!" He caught up to her and turned her to him with his hands on her shoulders. "I'm not suggesting we never work; I'm just saying I don't have to wait until I land a good teaching job before we decide to be together."

"But if I go with you to Canada, I must quit my job here at the *escola primária*, which I love."

"That's true, but Pearson College will be a place where we can both teach perhaps and be involved. Besides, your English is much better than my Portuguese. It would be both practical and romantic in Canada." He smiled and raised his eyebrows, suggesting fun.

"Has Pearson offered you a job yet?"

"No, but something will come up." He continued, "You said you wouldn't have me back until I knew myself better. I think I do now. And practically speaking, I can earn more in Canada for us than you can down here."

"*Ay caramba*, you are asking me to move to Canada and quit my job and you haven't asked me as what...your mistress? *Não serei uma concubina*! I will not be that."

"Wow, you're getting as hot as the temperature, let's go for another dip."

Refreshed again and silent but holding hands, they proceeded with their beach stroll. Lydia said, more calmly, "We have some practical problems if we are going to stay together, my love. I have been thinking about them too but it was always in the future, not now. Suddenly it seems, well, sudden. It's important for you to understand my needs too, Dahveed."

"You're right, and I thought I was. Let's give it some more time to sink in. But I do think I know myself well enough that, as much as I'm loving being here with you, I would start to feel like a fish out of water here in Brazil."

"And I might feel like a fish in an ice cube in Canada," she smiled and looked at him sidelong. Impulsively she jumped into the shallows and kicked warm water at him.

As they approached the end of the beach, David saw a white chapel hidden partly inland among some palm trees. He took Lydia up to stand in the shade of the chapel wall.

"You know we could establish some immediate plans that could satisfy everyone. Christmas with your folks, maybe a little side trip to show me more of Brazil, and then go to Canada to ski in January. And here's a token of my commitment until we can decide on our definite intentions." He slid the pinkie ring with the **D** off and slipped it on her right ring finger.

She looked up at him with a huge and satisfied smile. "I meant to ask you about this ring. It's new, no?"

"It's my Dad's. The **D** could stand for many things but right now, let's say it stands for *dois,* the two of us."

After lunch, they played some paddle ball, read a little, and just as David's breathing indicated he was close to a nap, Lydia asked him, "Dahveed?"

"Mmmm?"

"Do you think your parents, or your Uncle Peter even, had their needs met in their relationships?"

The query woke David fully and he rolled over onto his front beside Lydia.

"That's very deep, my love." He stroked with the back of his finger the fullness and firmness of her breast beneath her bathing suit top. "I know that I need you at the moment, and want you too."

"Me also, but I'm serious. Talk to me." She mildly slapped his hand and pecked him on the cheek.

"Well, Peter certainly had what he needed in his family, the love of his wife and child, respect and love of his in-laws, but they also had great adversity with the war. They had to get on with it and make the best of a bad situation. I suspect he wanted more but I don't think he needed more. He had, or should I say 'has', a great capacity for love. Sometimes I wondered if we were poor vessels to pour it into, my family and me. We weren't always worthy, I'm afraid."

"*Sim,* but he chose to love you. He had his reasons and you had your qualities, no?"

"I suppose. My Mom needed attention and coddling, what she thought was love, but she could never get enough; she was like a bucket with a hole in it. My Dad needed to be accepted and recognized but could never really accept himself, in many ways like the vials, emotionally dried like ashes with stoppers on, never letting himself out or anyone in really, except for Peter as best he could."

"And you, *querido,* do you know what you need?"

"This is hardly the lightness of being of a holiday; why all the third degree?"

"Don't put me off, Dahveed. I'm serious. Do you know what you need?"

"I need you Lydia, to come home to, to talk to, to be physical with, and intellectual with, and emotional with, and even spiritual with. You are my best friend. You complete me. I hope you need the same things. I need to share with you, make you happy; and if you're happy and content, then I am." He was getting frustrated with the line of questioning and raised himself up off the towel.

His bathing suit revealed some remaining tumescence and he said a bit brusquely, "I'm going for a swim."

"Good, you need one, and by the way, your answers were sweet, but I think we need to talk more," she called after him.

As David was wading out to deeper water, Lydia surprised him by splashing up behind and taking his hand.

"Come out with me, I think we deserve this," she smiled at him, melting any coolness of the previous conversation.

They waded up to their chests, a bit higher on Lydia. She glanced back at the beach and scanned the jungle and noticed no one. Putting her finger to her lips to indicate no protest, she said to David, "Just go with the flow, *querido.*"

Suddenly she dunked down and pulled David's bathing suit down, releasing one leg and letting the other ankle anchor the trunks. She came up a bit breathless and gasped for air. "Now you do the same to me," she instructed.

David smiled, but he accused, "Olá, you've done this before."

"No, but I have lain on my bed and thought how it could be done."

David took a deep breath and dunked, gently pulling down Lydia's bikini bottoms as she had instructed. Up he popped, rubbing his eyes. The salt water stung. "I had to open my eyes; a beautiful sight, but what a price!"

She moved into him, the warm ocean swells caressing them from chest to neck. She put her arms around his neck and let the buoyant water raise her onto him.

She closed her eyes and muttered, "Mmmm, I've missed this and wanted you."

"Me too," replied David with contentment, "but I was beginning to wonder if you did." He gently squeezed her buttocks and guided her up and down with the swells. She had her arms propped against his shoulders, arched back from the waist and they appeared to be apart to anyone who might be watching, two people gently bobbing with the waves. David's eyes were closed and he was lost in time, only this moment with Lydia mattering. They came almost synchronously and embraced again, nuzzling each other's necks, smelling and tasting the fresh sea.

"*O meu amor,*" they mumbled into each other's neck and laughed with release.

"Now would you be a gentlemen and help me get dressed?"

David dunked and nuzzled his nose on her vagina while helping her get her leg back into her bottoms. Then Lydia reciprocated. They dove and swam a bit apart from each other and then started to wade back in.

"We still have to talk, you know."

He put his arm over her shoulder, and the warm water splashed from their legs as they moved in the shallows. "Oh I know. I know."

Although David hinted at a shower together after the sweaty trek, he knew it was a vain attempt. They both returned to a restrained and respectable relationship.

The night was like soft velvet. David arrived for dinner first, looking tanned and nattily casual, dressed in a blue Oxford cloth shirt and white trousers with his rope-soled navy blue espadrilles, called *alpagartas* in Brazil. He had the sleeves rolled up on his forearms and top shirt buttons undone, an urban look. He ordered a Brazilian specialty drink on ice, a *caipirinha*, the national cocktail of lime and sugar with *cachaça*, the local rural sugar cane alcohol. It was smooth and refreshing, what the bartender had jokingly called 'medicine', and David sipped at it that way. Lydia arrived later, and plaza eyes followed her. She wore an emerald green cotton mini-dress, the neck loose so it fell off one shoulder and gold ankle-wrap sandals, looking tanned, fit and supple.

"*Boa tarde*", he said, rising partly from his seat.

"Good evening, sir. I had to wear gold to match my new ring, *ouro por ouro*" she said and smiled. "This means a lot to me, *querido*."

David had ordered two more drinks and the *caipirinhas* arrived as Lydia was seated. David raised his glass to her.

"You look like a veritable girl from Ipanema."

She laughed and bowed her head at the compliment. "But wait until you see those real girls in Rio; you might change your opinion."

"Can we come back to the topic on the beach about needs?" David asked. "I think I got a bit angry there; it might be that I'm not used to being so open. But I want to be open and honest with you. I'll try to be less frustrated but I might have to work on it, with your help."

"*Certamente*. And on that topic, would you like to know my needs?"

"*Sim. Por favor.* How was that pronunciation?"

"Mmmm, *optimo,*" she said taking another sip before gazing at him. "To begin, I need you. But what does that mean? Sometimes, I think that to be with you means giving up my life, here in Brazil, my students, my family. That's asking a great deal. So, I need to think and feel my way to the next step, no? What you suggested of letting things sink in was very helpful. But I get a bit *apprensivo*, you know, anxious. Sometimes I feel like the dog that chases the car; and when it catches the car, the dog doesn't know what to do with it. I kind of chased you and now that I've caught you, what will I do?"

He flashed his most coming smile. "Trust me, you're not a dog." But Lydia was not to be deterred so easily.

"When you got jealous a few days ago, your face, *oh meu Deus*. At first I was flattered but then I worried that you haven't changed, not really."

David leaned back in his chair as if jabbed, but nodded as if to parry and came forward again to the table.

"Lydia, I may not have changed completely, but I am changing. I'm not the guy in Havana from ten years ago, surely you realize that?"

"*Sim*. Deep down I know, but..."

"But what? Like we're butting heads here?"

"Don't joke, *meu amor*, I have to know what we're getting into. Both of us have seen many people who give up so much of themselves for love. When I saw your jealousy and your anger again, I worried that you still are full of some old ways."

David looked at her trying to comprehend. She saw his questioning frown and explained.

"When you got jealous, you said you were tired and that might have been part of it. And then you stopped talking abruptly today. Did you ever consider that it might be your ego speaking? Jealousy and anger are such wasted emotions, Dahveed."

"Sweetheart, aren't you over-analyzing?"

"No, I don't think so. You must trust me and treat me like a partner. You can't assume to plan for me just like you can't control who I will be with. That's my choice. You have to trust that my choice is you; and, if I choose someone else, it's also my choice."

"Is there someone else?"

"No, don't be silly." She took his hand again across the table. "You are my choice, but that's for me to control, not you. I need to know what my choice entails."

"I thought I was making plans for the two of us. As for changes, I'm afraid I can't offer any guarantees about my faults. Just that I'm working on them, I mean it."

"It? So you always find room for a joke; you have some faults, *meu amor*, but neither of us is perfect," she laughed."I don't need guarantees and, don't be defensive when I say this. I need to know that you want what is best for me also, and not just for you."

"Ah. So do you think you might be surrendering too much to spend your life with me?"

"Surrender, no. You make it sound like a conflict. No, I prefer it be an alliance, no?"

"So what do you need from this pact then?"

She sent him an air-kiss. "So now you ask what I need. Finally. I need to have meaning in my life; work is important, teaching is important, contributing is important. I need to know that Brazil is not closed to me, that both of us will spend time in Brazil as well as Canada."

"That sounds fair. But is there something more?"

Lydia cast her eyes away, trying to see the stars above the plaza, maybe the Southern Cross. After a pause, she answered.

"Two things. You haven't actually asked me to spend my life with you. And I want to have a family. Soon. Neither of us is getting younger, *querido*.

David pushed his chair back, got up and went to Lydia. He squatted in front of her, cupped her face in his hands, kissed her gently and said, "Just when I thought I couldn't love you more."

CHAPTER 25.

THE BEST GIFTS ARE
WELL-THOUGHT OUT SURPRISES

Rio and Buzios, Brazil, 1985-86

So David and Lydia left Ihla Grande in time for Christmas at the D'Silvas. Lydia's family was very welcoming; after all they had their only child home with them and were anxious to meet David. Although Christmas was a special *dia de festers* for Brazilians, the D'Silvas were low-key about it, displaying a small crèche only and no colourful lights. The four of them sat chatting over coffee in the modest living room after dinner on Christmas Eve. Lydia's parents asked questions about her future plans. Although they meant long-range, Lydia told them only the immediate ones: show David the sights of Rio, go to Buzios for New Year's, and fly to Canada to ski for a couple of weeks before coming back for Carnival.

Senhora D'Silva got up to gather the dishes and put them in the sink until later.

"We must go to bed early or *Papai Noel* won't bring presents, " she said over her shoulder.

Lydia got up to help and answered her mother, "It doesn't matter what time the poor ones go to bed, they still won't be getting gifts in the *favelas*, Mama. Anyway, it's more about renewing our love for one another because the Christ Child was born, no?" And she kissed her mother on the cheek.

David and Lydia washed up and then sat to talk a bit before going to their separate spaces, she to her bedroom and he on the sofa. David was lounging, fully satiated after their wonderful meal. He said to Lydia, "Do you remember that epistle from St. Paul to the Corinthians about love?"

Lydia stifled a yawn, "Not really, *o meu amor, por que?*"

Giving her shoulder a squeeze, he continued, "Love is patient; love is kind; it never fails; and that's all I can remember."

"Dahveed, are you getting soft at Christmas time, what's the expression, mushy?"

"Maybe a bit. So here is something that hopefully will keep you warm in a Canadian winter." He reached into his backpack and showed her a small box. "Would you wear this on your finger? Will you marry me?"

"*O meu amor*, this is more commitment, no? Yes I will but, if you're going to be like that, I won't be needing this. Here is your father's ring back."

Early on Christmas morning, David was awakened by movement and noise in the kitchen. Lydia's mother clapped her hands and squealed, "*Quão maravilhoso, minha querida filha.*"

He threw off his sheet and stumbled to the kitchen in shorts and t-shirt, ready to protect against whatever might be the cause of the alarm. Lydia was hushing her mother quiet, wishing not to wake the men. Then she and her mother clutched each other warmly in a bear hug. David was not used to such familial intimacy but enjoyed seeing it.

When Senhora D'Silva saw David, patting down his hair from pillow effects, she waved him over to join in the hug, calling him "*meu genro*", my son-in-law.

"You must call me Maria now."

Lydia laughed and said, "*Bom dia, meu noivo*. My mother saw the diamond ring and couldn't contain herself, I'm afraid. Sorry if we awakened you. Merry Christmas, Dahveed." Lydia showed off the diamond on her right ring finger, the Brazilian custom, until married.

By then Senhor D'Silva entered the room in a ruffled way, learned of the cause for the commotion, and soon there was shaking hands and kissing and hugging all around again.

David said that this was too much excitement so early in the day without coffee.

"*Sim, sim*, some steamy strong coffee *é necessário*," Lydia's father agreed.

Suddenly David remembered and went for his back pack. "I almost forgot. Here sweetie, this is for you." He handed Lydia a battered package which she tore open quickly revealing some black leather ski gloves.

"*Obrigado, querido.* Will it be this cold in Canada really?" The sun was up and already it was in the mid-twenties Celsius, making the gloves seem oxymoronic. They all laughed at the prospect.

Inevitably Lydia's mother started with questions. She asked, when will the wedding be, where will it be, and what work will David do in Brazil? Lydia answered in two languages that they hadn't decided anything definite yet, that they were going to enjoy the day's event and, since it was the feast of the Christ child, would they like to go for a picnic to the Corcovado?

While Lydia and her mother prepared a picnic lunch, David and Senhor D'Silva took their coffee and the favourite Brazilian breakfast treat, a cheese bun, *pao de queijo*, to the patio garden.

"Mmm, this is a tasty, sir, Mr. D' Silva."

"Call me Gregorio, please. I'm glad you like it; it's a traditional Christmas treat for our family. I'm sorry to hear that you lost your father and your mother last year, Dahveed. It mustn't have been easy for you."

David was touched and grateful for the condolence. "Thank you, sir, I mean Gregorio. No, not easy but my Uncle Peter has been extremely helpful. You know, I think you met my father once, in Havana, the summer of 1967, I believe."

"You think I met your father?"

"I'm pretty sure. He mentioned a Gregorio D'Silva in his journal. It was at a conference in 1967. He was writing for a Canadian magazine and you were working for the *Jornal do Brasil.*"

"Yes, it could be me, although I switched to another paper shortly after. I seem to recall him. He was asking many questions about Brazilian politics and it frightened me somewhat. At first I thought he was CIA and I was worried for Lydia and her politics."

"Ha, that would be him. He wasn't CIA, but he did work for the Canadian security service. He could be a bit nosey in his way. Did you like being a journalist?"

"Yes for the most part. I liked it better when I switched to *O Globo*. It suited me better and I was sent on some interesting assignments. They sent me to Canada once, to Montreal to cover the Olympics in 1976."

"Did you like Canada, or at least Montreal? It's only one small part of the country," David asked.

"*Claro! Sim.* There was a da Silva in those Olympics, different spelling and no relation, who came in 5th in the 200 metres. Lydia is the only athletic one in our family." He patted his belly and pointed at the *pao de queijo*. He continued, "Lydia says you like to run and sail too. Brazil got a bronze in sailing that summer I remember."

"Yes I like to run but I sold my sailboat a year ago. Maybe again someday."

"Lydia tells us you are a teacher too. Will you be able to find similar work here in Brazil?"

"Oh, I don't think I'll be able to teach in Brazil. I have a couple of job offers in Canada though."

"I see," and Gregorio nodded slowly and looked away. He added, "It will hurt both Lydia and her mother a great deal if she did not stay in her own country." And with that revelation, the conversation waned, until Gregorio asked, "Are you liking Brazil; it's your first time here, no?"

"Yes, I think it's very beautiful, what I've seen so far. The people seem quite warm, or is that just the temperature?" David's attempt at humour earned a smile.

Lydia drove the family car up the winding road to Mount Corcovado where the air was slightly cooler and the panoramic view spectacular. They could see the iconic Sugar Loaf; the sweep of the famous beaches, Ipanema and Copacabana; and the super-stadium, Maracana. They climbed the steps at the base of the Christ Redeemer statue and decided to have their lunch there overlooking the city.

Maria, said, "I haven't been up here since Pope John Paul's visit in 1980. He was blessing thousands and we couldn't get this close to the statue. We were lined up down the road. The vista is quite good, no?" She paused then asked, "Dahveed? Lydia says your mother was a devout Catholic. Are you also?"

"I suppose she was in her way," David answered. "Me, no I'm lapsed I'm afraid." Maria looked to Lydia to translate.

"*Caducou*, Mama. It means he doesn't practice anymore, like me."

Maria and Gregorio exchanged glances.

Maria added, her voice a bit strained, "*Mas das crianças*, what about the children?"

Before an argument ensued between Lydia and her mother, Gregorio said, "*Chega, obrigado*! Enough, thank you. They are not even married yet, Maria; and remember today is the day of peace, no?"

Although David and Lydia spent most of their days together out and about, when they returned to the D'Silva's, Lydia's parents often returned to questions about Lydia's future. It was clear they wanted to influence the couple's plans. David was conscious that they were anxious and understood their prying questions, such as what he planned to do to 'take care of' their daughter. However, the effects of the line of queries were wearing on him. Eventually he asked Lydia if they could leave earlier for their road trip to Buzios. She was agreeable.

David insisted on renting a car, a yellow Brazilian-made Ford Corcel fastback, rather than accepting the offer to use the family's car. Their destination was a bucolic peninsula just a three-hour drive east from Rio and they would be away for a few days. As they crossed the Niteroi Bridge, the aqueduct-looking link leaving the city, David let out a deep sigh.

Lydia was driving and looked over at him. "Are you okay?" She laughed, "Are you that pleased to be getting away from my parents?"

David smiled back a bit sheepishly. "Did it show that much?"

"To me it did; but to no one else, I'm sure."

"I thought your father was a bit insulted that I refused his car."

"He may have been somewhat. He probably took it that you thought his car was too old and just felt a little rebuffed that we wanted to be so independent."

"Maybe I shouldn't have chosen something so flashy. Anyway. It's not just that I wanted to be alone with you, but I was also feeling a bit prodded by your folks."

David decided to plunge ahead. "You know, Lydia, your parents are going to push hard to influence the way you want a wedding, even the way they see our future together. Some people give advice and leave you to decide; others give advice but expect you to follow. I think your folks might be like the latter," David said this while looking out the window.

Lydia glanced over quickly. "My mother maybe; my father less so, no?"

"I suppose. Who would have thought that getting engaged would mean having to map out a future life in such detail?"

"*Querido*, it is a big decision after all."

"Yes, but your parents want so many details worked out in advance. Your dad even asked how I expected to care for you as my wife, and in between the lines he intimated that it be in a style that he and your mother approved."

Lydia laughed her throaty amusement. "I guess it comes with being an only child and a girl."

"Perhaps. While we're on the topic, I'd be curious to hear your ideas about a wedding," David pursued.

"Ah, *meu amor*, are you getting cold feet already?"

"No," he chuckled. "If I can have any input though, I think I'd prefer a small civil affair."

"Ah, you're just like a man," she scoffed in good humour. "Actually I agree. I think we're too old to have the 'kitchen shower' with all my school girlfriends. And the cost of a big reception afterwards would cripple us, or my parents, financially. My parents may protest; they'll want us married before God in a church, but I don't need that."

"Oh upright judge, oh learned judge," David crowed.

"But I do think I would like to get married in Brazil; my parents can at least invite friends and relatives to the house."

"I see you've been doing some thinking about it."

"*Claro!* Probably we should go to the civil registry in the New Year. The paperwork might take a couple of months because of you being a foreigner. You see I have looked after some details about my future, no?"

David teased, "And why am I not surprised? I think I would like to invite one person, Uncle Peter, once we nail down a date."

Lydia sighed and David noticed. She added, "This event takes on a life of its own, doesn't it, Dahveed? It was only a few days ago we were saying we would let things sink in. I don't want to lose control of our lives."

"I agree. It seems that becoming *noivos* has changed the rules of engagement, so to speak.

"Do you dislike my parents, Dahveed?"

"No, it's not that at all. They're welcoming and generous, but they seemed so controlling about you and a bit judgmental about me. It was getting a bit oppressive for me, if you must know."

Lydia laughed. "You are the interloper, my darling; but seriously, you're marrying me, not my family."

"You have no idea how good it is to hear that. I really appreciate being alone with you and recovering my energy to face them. Let's hope that soon we can be more definite about our future. So, step one, we'll declare our intent for a *casamento* in the New Year. When should we get married?"

"One step at a time," she teased. "I must let things sink in, remember?"

There was a huge lurch and thump in the car. "Can you try missing a few potholes though, love?"

They had left the main highway, and the road into the peninsula of Buzios was a blend of bumpy cobblestones, uneven pavement, and dirt so that it seemed to have undergone a mortar attack, forcing them to skirt around obstacles slowly. Buzios was still a quiet, dusty fishing town with over twenty beaches, but an inexorable sense of future development. Big villas were growing like buboes on the hillsides above the beaches, *pousadas* popping up in town and beachside streets, and quaint restaurants catering to growing tourism were aplenty, a veritable getaway respite from the city.

It was the busy season but Lydia had managed to get a room with a view of the ocean at a comfortable *pousada, Casas Brancas*, close to the promenade along the bay, the *Rua das Pedras*. The accommodation was simple and fresh, but most importantly, allowed them some privacy for intimacy. Their hunger was mutual; their ardour barely cooled by the overhead fan and the ocean breeze.

David said as they lay sweating side by side, barely touching, "When I make love to you, when I'm with you, I feel like I'm home, like I'm in a nest."

Lydia chortled, "Are you calling my vagina a nest?"

They laughed and David said, "No, well maybe," and he stroked the coarse hairs of her *mons Venus*. "I meant it more figuratively than literally."

With their few days alone, they fell into a pattern that soothed their long separation like an aloe balm, lovemaking, napping, and strolling the streets in search of trinkets and tee-shirt deals. Their days in Buzios took on a lazy, hazy routine. It started with breakfast on the patio watching the street and the bay; choosing a different beach to sunbathe and swim; buying food for a picnic; and after showers and naps in the afternoon, treating themselves before dinner to the famed *caipirinha*. After dinner they promenaded along the sea with the suffusing sunsets. All in all it was an idyllic celebration of their engagement, their *noivado*.

One afternoon David bought Lydia a buzios shell necklace. The shiny, brown-spotted shell with the labia-looking underside was said to be a gift from the goddess of the ocean, and when given as a present it signified wealth, improvement, and good luck in weddings.

"See, marrying me is going to be great according to the goddess," David deadpanned as they left the shop hand-in-hand.

Of the beaches, they liked the relative privacy of Forno and the majestic sweep of Geriba where they took a photo of their footprints in the wet sand for posterity. But their favourite of all was Ferradura. Plato would have considered horseshoe-shaped Ferradura the ideal beach if he hadn't already had a Greek one in mind.

The dark blue Atlantic was tamed as it entered the bay, fended off by two forearms of rocky headlands, covered with green shrubbery and cacti and a few new villas. The waves became calm vestiges fringed with white as they lapped the perfect curvature of golden sand in the cove. There was a *barraca*, called *Claudio's*, at the main parking entrance. They bought a fruit drink and strolled the firm, gently sloping sand.

There was little activity that day. One fishing boat was throwing its netted catch onto the shore; some children and nannies were drawn to the spectacle of one small beheaded hammerhead shark; and a lone sailboarder was kicking up a rooster tail parallel to the beach.

Lydia, wearing stylish sunglasses, looked up to the sky and said, "Mmm this is lovely, but it can't be our real life, you know."

"You mean romantic isn't real? You're joking, right?" David teased in response.

She tugged his arm pulling him off balance and into the warm shallows. They embraced and David said, "I realize that sweetie, this is a romantic respite. But damn, it's beautiful. How many beaches like this does Brazil have?"

"A lot, but not enough to make you want to live here, I suspect."

"You're probably right, but enough to make me promise that I would want us to spend time here every year."

"So an annual pilgrimage to Brazil?"

He looked at her squarely. "Realistically, I think Canada is where our future lies. Remember what the búzios seller told us."

Lydia decided to lie on the beach for a while and David took the opportunity to go for a run to the far end of the cove. There was something dark blue, almost like a beached whale in the distance. Indeed, it was the whale watching season, but as he got closer, he noticed it was a derelict sailboat lying on its side, blue hulled with a white water line.

David slowed his run and then stopped to wade around the boat. Already buried partly in sand like a treasure chest, David saw it had been stripped clean, no mast or boom, and the remaining teak trimming was bleached gray making the topside look rather ashen in its death throes. The bottom had a scar where the lead keel was missing and a few waves were lightly smacking the transom as if spanking it for being naughty.

"Hard to keep on course without a keel, for sure," David thought and he began to consider whether he should try to repair the boat as a project, feeling a bit angry that someone had just left a sailboat to rot. But the rules of salvage, ownership and maritime law were complicated, so he let the idea go. He continued running to the far end where there was another lean-to *barraca*.

He stopped to order a coconut water and tried to ferret out information about the boat. It had been washed ashore about a month ago, abandoned with no apparent owners; the fishermen had taken anything of value long ago; and now it was garbage, *lixo*.

When he got back to Lydia, he reported on his find. "It's such a shame; to discard a sailboat like that. Fucking *nouveau riche* and their throwaway mentality. Now it's flotsam, useless, and a danger to the beach. The owners ought to be shot."

Lydia sat up and rested on her elbows. "*Querido*, what are you going on about?"

"It's just that this is a perfect place, a perfect beach, a *linda praia*, correct? And some idiot blighted it. Too lazy to clean up his mess!"

"Dahveed! Calm down. It's something in you, not the beach, that's making you angry. Maybe you need to meditate or do some yoga, *querido*."

David sat beside her and exhaled deeply. "Maybe you're right. Maybe I'm angry because I want our world to be perfect."

"*Perfeito?* No you're not that much of an idealist. Something else must be bugging you."

"Perhaps." He smiled. "You do know me well, don't you? Another thought crossed my mind too. Seeing that wreck seemed to rekindle a desire for a sailboat again. I realized I missed sailing."

"Oh really, what do you miss?"

"Paring life down to simplicity; a bit of gear, just what you need; being with nature, the wind, the water, taking what it gives you; self-sufficiency; and being far from the crowds. It was like I wanted to recover that part of my life. You'd love it Lydia."

"Maybe, but it seems to me that you are complicating your life, not simplifying. You have so many desires, Dahveed, maybe too many. Let's go for a swim."

Back on their towels, Lydia returned to the conversation. "You have many projects in mind, Dahveed. Marriage, moving me to Canada, and now a sailboat. Maybe you have too many possibilities. Be careful. "

"Hmm?"

"*Querido,* we need to have these projects together, but too many make me nervous. I've agreed to be married but it has big risks for me. It's like what I teach in science, with magnets. The opposite poles attract and the similar poles repel."

David interrupted, "And then we spend a lifetime dealing with it."

"Don't try to make jokes, I'm serious. There is more to the lesson. Yes we attract now, but like electro-magnetism, when the electric current is gone, the magnetism is gone. In marriage we have to keep the current, no?"

"What are you saying exactly?"

"Maybe I am also a strong magnet and we will repel at some time. I don't know. There are risks and I'm nervous. Maybe that's why we, or I, can't decide for sure."

"Lydia, I can only give reassurances that things will work out; I can't give guarantees."

"I know *meu amor*. There is so much change coming for us and I should be happy but sometimes I worry that the smallest change can make a total difference. I remember a phrase; a difference in degree becomes a difference in kind."

"Are you getting cold feet now? David asked. Lydia smiled.

He said, "Look there isn't a cloud in the sky and all you can see are clouds. It's not like you to see the glass half empty. What's up?"

Lydia said nothing, so David chattered. "We used to play a brain game in university about small changes making big differences. It started as a joke really. A monk was concerned about copying manuscripts from the original. When he checked it out, he realized the original said 'celebrate', not 'celibate'. You change a letter or a sound in a word and it becomes something else. Like the word 'peruse' can become 'pursue'; so looking something over can become chasing something madly. Or 'cavalry' can become 'Calvary'. Horses to the rescue can become a place to die on a cross, for example."

"I'm not playing a game, Dahveed. I don't want you to change me in little ways so that I become something else. You should appreciate me and my needs. Respect me also. Love is kind, no?"

David said, "I don't know what to say."

"Don't say anything right now, just think. Besides we have been in the sun so long maybe your brain is coddled, no?

David was going to say the expression was 'addled' but then realized that coddled in the sun was equally appropriate.

He felt chastened, "You're right. Let's go back and nap."

"Yes and only nap. We have a big night tonight. It's New Year's Eve in Brazil."

It was a special night. They strolled the promenade; David in a white tee-shirt and pants with a yellow sweater over his shoulders, Lydia in a white batik sun dress. The sunset cast a pastel peach hue, and the fishing skiffs' silhouetted on the beach looked like the cowrie shells of Buzios. The air was satiny soft. They were a handsome couple, their tans attractive, the gold ring and the diamond on their hands reflective in the shop lights. David brushed Lydia's fingertips diffidently.

"I owe you an apology, my love." He had avoided the topic directly during their *caipirinha* cocktails but it had to be faced. There was loud music, samba and bossa nova, beginning to emanate from several sources, but David guided Lydia out onto the pier, needing isolation to continue.

"I've thought about what you said earlier and if I've been egotistical in my planning, I'm truly sorry. It's a small leap from arrogant to ignorant, isn't it? I learned that both my father and I share that trait. I don't want to be that way with you. But, sometimes the genes come out."

Lydia had been gazing into the water but looked at him and smiled, her white teeth like a beacon. She remonstrated with a joke, "You weren't wearing jeans, my love. And I accept your apology. We can finish off the year on a new footing, no? I forgive you; you respect me."

He nodded and his smile beamed back. David put his arm around Lydia and she rested her head on his shoulder. He nuzzled her hair releasing wafts of subtle musky fragrance.

He said, "I do love and respect you, you know. So are you ready for dinner? And then you can show me the special Brazilian celebration for *Ano Nove*."

Lydia looked at David coquettishly, "Usually we have dinner after midnight but I have other plans. I reserved a restaurant to dine at ten.

They do a great *moqueca* and *farofa*, and it's not far from the beach."

David loved Lydia's choice. He found the dishes exotic. Firm white fish in a stew of coconut milk, with onions, garlic, bell peppers, tomatoes, and cilantro, with the *farofa* of manioc, bacon and onions on the side. After a couple of glasses of Pinot Gris they were feeling expansive and a bit giddy.

"Oh that was delicious, what's next?"

She was fingering the buzios amulet on its leather cord around her neck and asked. "Do you want to know why we wear white?"

"Because we want to leave the old year shorn of our sins and greet the new one with purity? And show off our tans?"

"Good guess, smart guy. It's for good luck." A flower lady was moving about the tables with white gladiolas and chrysanthemums. "And we take flowers to the beach to make wishes and remember people we are fond of."

David raised his hand to beckon the lady. "*Uma dúzia, por favor.*"

"What? So many?"

"It'll be fun to see how we use them up, don't you think? Six each shouldn't be too difficult."

They joined a stream of people walking down to the beach at midnight. Some were jumping in the waves and counting to seven, for good luck explained Lydia. The white clad people and flowers being tossed into the water seemed phosphorescent in the moonlight. Suddenly fireworks began booming from each of the headlands, a show for the masses put on by two corporate big-wigs who owned estates up there.

David took Lydia by the hand and they moved away from the crowd to a more dark and quiet part of the beach. They stood in the shallows and Lydia curtsied to him, inviting him to go first. He took a flower and tossed it into the bay.

He announced in mock solemnity, "I wish that we always have room in our lives for some romance."

Lydia laughed and threw a flower. "I wish that we have good health and live long together."

David responded. "So practical." He threw another. "I wish for our happiness."

Lydia threw one out further. "I wish you to get a teaching job."

"That was a good throw, a long shot even. I throw one to remember Uncle Peter and all he has done in the last year."

Lydia thought a moment, threw another flower and said, "I wish a minimum of suffering for my parents in our future decisions."

David replied, "This could go on all night at this rate." He took two flowers, smelled them and then lobbed them high into the velvet night. "To my mother and father, may they find more peace now than they did while alive."

Lydia said, "That was sweet, *meu amor*. I don't know what to do with the flowers I have left."

"*Minha beleza*, my beauty queen, maybe you could wish for world peace," David teased and she kicked water. David grabbed her around the waist and said, "On the count of three, let's throw our last flowers together."

"Okay, but what should we wish?"

"That our decisions will be the right ones for us."

She liked that, and before the petals hit the water, David and Lydia were embracing and wishing each other a Happy New Year.

It was Tuesday, January 7, 1986 and David and Lydia were arousing themselves after a long flight and shuttle to Whistler. They were both trying to shake off the jet lag and the fact that they had come from a hot 30 degrees Celsius in Rio to a cold -5 in the ski village. Yesterday morning before getting on the plane, David had telephoned Uncle Peter from the Rio airport. Now he recalled the conversation while he waited for some coffee to brew in their room in the new Blackcomb Lodge Hotel.

He played it over again in his head. "Happy New Year or more accurately Happy Epiphany," he had begun. "I know it's early. Oooh 6 a.m. eh? Sorry. Listen Uncle Peter, I don't have much time; we're getting ready to board a plane for Vancouver. Yes everything is going well. Yes, a ski holiday at Whistler. I just wanted to tell you that Lydia and I got engaged and we want you to attend the ceremony, when it happens. Thank you. No, it will be in Rio but we don't have a date yet. Could you say that again, please?"

Peter had relayed that he had received two important telephone messages for David, one from the Hamilton School Board and one from Pearson College. David reassured him that he would call once they were settled in Whistler.

While Lydia showered, David made his two phone calls. Both were excellent news, as if brought by the Magi themselves. Hamilton School Board was offering David a term of work, teaching History and English from the end of March Break to June. But the headmaster at Pearson was offering much more. Their History teacher had just informed him that she was pregnant and due during the summer. She would be resigning her position then, not going on maternity leave. Would David be interested in filling the vacant post starting in September? David had asked for twenty-four hours to consider both proposals and when he put down the phone he whooped, making Lydia jump.

"Sweetheart, we're going downstairs for breakfast. We have some big decisions to make and some shopping to do for ski clothes."

CHAPTER 26.

LOVE'S LABOUR

Whistler, Victoria and Rio de Janeiro, 1986

David and Lydia were talking about his job offers before beginning Lydia's ski lessons.

"Until we set a date to get married, I think I have to take both jobs, Lydia," David said while reaching for his coffee. "While I'm in Hamilton, I'll earn some money for the wedding and honeymoon, or a boat. You'll be working anyway. That way you and your parents can plan the wedding. Shall we get married in July and then come to Victoria to start teaching at Pearson in September? What do you say?"

Lydia was not as excited. "It seems like you've already decided."

"No, I haven't. But what do you think? I said I would call them back by tomorrow."

"I think it's a good plan and I'm thinking it's great that you're offered not one, but two teaching jobs. This is the career you've wanted, but what about my career? The problem is how I feel, *caro*."

She gave a wry smile to David's questioning look, and added, "I feel cold."

"We can fix your body temperature with good winter gear. If it's something else then we have to talk about it. Once I call them with the decisions, I'm pretty well locked-in."

"Mmm, being away from you again until July and then being away from my parents and students for a long time."

"Is it such a hard choice, really," he asked, a bit hurt.

"Let the idea settle a bit. Come, teach me to ski first. I need to realize that you keep your promises, no?"

David bought them both some good down ski outfits and they got fitted for ski rentals. They clopped the short distance through the village to the gondola in their ski boots. David assured Lydia that there were easy green runs up at mid-mountain and a children's lesson area that would be perfect to start, but she was understandably nervous.

David was a patient teacher and Lydia an apt student who listened willingly to his instructions. He had her walking figure-eights on the flat to get used to the long skis and her balance was excellent. Then he helped her on the t-bar as they got some elevation, and worked on some beginner turns and putting weight on the downhill ski. With David skiing backwards to guide and Lydia maneuvering some turns and a stop, her confidence and her excitement to try more escalated. She was agreeable to David suggesting they take Olympic Chair to the next level.

Lydia marveled at what she was doing. It was a bluebird day, and although the snow-covered mountains surrounded her, she no longer felt cold. David wasn't surprised. "You look hot in that powder blue outfit." She smiled at the compliment and then was amazed by the views.

"Look where I am! If my parents could see me now," she laughed and their ski goggles clunked as she tried to kiss him. He grabbed her to steady her when she lost her balance.

"Now this is a longer run, Lydia. It's a bit steeper too but it's groomed; otherwise it's the same as below. Just remember this; it is only one turn at a time. I'll stay with you but you have to focus on what you learned down there. When you make your turn, tap your hand on your lower knee, when you want to turn again, stand tall, turn your toe gradually to turn your ski, and then tap your lower knee. If you have too much speed, hold your knee longer and turn up the hill. Here watch me."

He demonstrated what he said and waited for Lydia to reach him. Her first turn was fine and when she stood tall to make her next turn, she gasped with the sudden rush of speed and her eyes widened. With a squeal, she passed him. Out of control she leaned into the hill and fell, not too hard but down-hearted.

"What happened, *querido?*"

He laughed, but not at her. "It's normal, love. If you get scared, most people lean into the hill. That puts their weight on the wrong ski and down they go. It's called banking. I know it sounds counter-intuitive, but you have to reach down. It's like embracing what frightens you, but that's the way it's done."

He helped her back to her feet, brushed some snow from her toque and said. "Okay? How about you follow me exactly now and listen to what I say. Get right in behind me and follow my tracks."

They went through six or seven turns and on the last one he got her to finish a C-turn up the hill to slow down and stop.

"Fantastic!"

Lydia beamed but acknowledged that she could not have done it without him. He said, "So what! Look what you've just skied." They both looked up the hill and Lydia felt proud.

David asked. "We're half way down the run, do you want to follow me or do it yourself?"

"I will follow you, *meu amor*, for the rest, but can we do it again and I will try myself?"

"*Cert-a-ment-ay*," David responded in over-enounced Portuguese. "Let's go."

David was aware that Lydia had skied several firsts today and not wanting to get her too tired, he suggested skiing down the green Lower Olympic run. They took their time, stopping to listen to birds and the occasional marmot whistling.

"Lydia, I hope you realize how much you accomplished today. First time skiing, first time on a gondola, a t-bar and a chairlift. Let's get a picture together at the bottom so we can show your parents."

They could see the village below. "Dahveed, you have been the perfect teacher. I love this and can't wait until tomorrow. Go down and watch me finish. You have fulfilled your promise, *querido*, I'll show you."

Back in their room, unrobed from their winter layers, Lydia put her arms around David and said, "While I'm showering, why don't you call the headmaster, and tell him you'll take the job at Pearson. At least it's one turn at a time, no?"

He kissed her warmly and he phoned to make arrangements to go to Victoria with Lydia next week and sign his contract.

"We'll have to decide about Hamilton too. I can only call tomorrow morning because of the time zones."

"Let's talk over dinner, *meu amor.*"

The hotel recommended a relatively new place, Araxi, for a fine experience, which suited David and Lydia who felt like a celebration. They both had some oysters with a glass of Sancerre.

David said, "You know what oysters do to sex drive, don't you? Casanova was reputed to eat fifty of these for breakfast."

"Well, we're sharing a dozen as an appetizer; figure out the ratio," Lydia responded, looking over the rim of her glass. "I've been giving your ideas some thought. As much as I'd miss you, maybe taking the supply teaching job would be the best in the end."

They clinked glasses; it was a start to more definition in their lives.

The next ski day was overcast. Lydia had a slightly queasy stomach and they thought it might be the oysters or maybe a little case of grippe. The sick feeling passed after some breakfast toast and they took the gondola for another day on the slopes. Lydia was confident and enthused, and promised to remember her new skills. But the flat light frustrated her a bit, so David coached her.

"Imagine you're getting ready to receive a serve in tennis. Don't be on your heels. Your weight is even over your feet so you can react to anything. Now bend your knees a bit more. That way you can absorb any bumps you don't see. You have to feel them."

"Feel bumps? What bumps? Isn't this run groomed like yesterday?"

"Yes, but bumps happen when it gets skied on; you have to feel them and react if you can't see them."

Their few runs at mid-station were good but then Lydia asked around lunchtime, "Dahveed, would there be clouds all the way to the top?"

"Sometimes they get sun above the cloud. They have a new restaurant up there too called the Roundhouse and green runs down. Want to try it?"

Lydia exclaimed that it was like being on the top of the world; she loved the view of mountain peaks, treeless terrain, and what appeared to be a sea of cloud below. After lunch they took a long slow run down gentle trails called Pony and Papoose. It flattened out near mid-station and was hard slogging, poling until they got back to the lifts. Lydia observed that the flat part was not so much fun so David suggested a blue run with more pitch; and she was game. She did well with the incline and occasional small mogul, following David, but her thighs were beginning to burn.

"You can take a rest, but you still have a way to go to get all the way to the bottom. You're into it now; you can't quit. All I can promise is a refreshing beer and a hot tub for those aching muscles when you're done. You've been amazing today, sweets."

"*Muito* o*brigado*, but take me down slowly, *por favor* and lots of stops."

That evening at dinner, relaxing with a glass of wine, Lydia leaned against David and said, "I've been thinking about my skiing."

He interrupted, "You've been excellent."

"Shh, but thank you. I've loved it; the feeling is fantastic. But also, I think there were lessons for me, for us. Maybe I must be more willing to think of one turn at a time instead of the enormous long mountain run."

"I was just helping you to ski, not trying to give you heavy life lessons," he replied, hoping he hadn't attempted too much.

"No really. I think we should decide on a date to get married before we arrive back for Carnival; and I would like to see this Pearson College of yours too, if you'd like me to."

"Really! Great! Well, our choice of dates for a wedding is getting limited; it will have to be February since I start teaching in March, or it will have to be July when our terms are over. Why not as close to February 14th as we can, Valentine's Day?"

She kissed him and said, "You are a *romântica incurável*, a hopeless romantic."

They left Whistler after a week, happy and settled. Lydia was thrilled that she had even skied a blue run or two and proclaimed again that she loved skiing. David felt gratified and satisfied that it had worked out well. They agreed it would be a part of their lives in the future.

Lydia loved Victoria, the green of it especially and only a couple of hours from the winter she had been ensconced in. The purple heather, winter pansies and odd rhododendron were in bloom, and the couple loved staying by the waterfront, walking the Inner Harbour and the long paths of Dallas Road. They were enjoying the city that felt like a town. Mid-week, David rented a car for the short drive out to Pearson College.

"How quickly we get into wilderness here, Dahveed. It's so quaint."

"I hope you like it, sweetheart; it might be home."

They parked and walked through the campus up to the administration office. David shook hands with Hamish Simpson, the Director of the school and introduced Lydia as his fiancé. Simpson was a tall, slightly stooping, 'proper' gentleman in tweed, and they chatted over coffee in his office. What he said resonated with both David and Lydia and their values as educators.

"We have students drawn from all over the world here. We even have two from South America. They are given a two-year immersion in education, not just in the International Baccalaureate curriculum but also in an environment designed to stretch both mind and muscle. We are also mindful of being a peace college so we attempt to draw students closer to their neighbours in a shrinking world on the premise that, although you may not love people you know well, it's very difficult to hate them." He looked at both of them with a sly smile then and added. "Well, now that I've delivered the official spiel, you must have some questions yourselves. By the way, when are you getting married, if you don't mind me asking?"

"We don't have an exact date set yet."

"Well, don't let me rush you, but we are willing to offer you a married residence here. It means you'll have to do some supervisory duties but it's a wonderful and inexpensive accommodation that can be helpful to newlyweds."

David and Lydia glanced at each other. Mr. Simpson asked, "Lydia, I'm sorry; I should have asked before; what do you do? I have David's résumé here, which is commendable, but can you bring anything to the table?"

Lydia looked at David; she was caught a bit off guard. "I teach in Brazil right now, science mainly to girls aged 10-14."

"I'm afraid I have no position open for that right now, but would you be willing to offer any coaching to the students maybe?"

"She's a fantastic tennis player," David offered.

"That could work; have you ever thought of being a mentor, coaching a few girls with essays, tutoring, that sort of thing?"

"*Sim*, I mean yes, that could be a possibility. I also could teach yoga classes."

He smiled warmly, "Well, I think we may have an extra-curricular pair developing here. Why don't you take a look around the campus? I'll arrange to have you see one of our married residences too. We can meet you for lunch at the cafeteria; I can try to answer any other questions before signing the paperwork. Ah, here's someone to be your guide, one of our senior students, Linda." He gave her some quiet instructions and added," I'll leave you in her capable hands then."

Linda was a sweet, seventeen- year old from Penticton. She showed them around the dun-coloured buildings and described their functions, house residences and meeting rooms, classrooms, and gym, plus a huge hall part way up a hill. There was even a round cabin, the spiritual centre, which was on the rocks overlooking the inlet above a little cove at the end of a wooded path. It had an open room for meditations, or multi-faith gatherings, or just a place to hang out, with big windows that allowed in any light available. As they continued to walk the campus, they smelled the trampled earth and grass co-mingled with kelp and seaweed on the ocean breeze. The high stands of cedar dripped with mist, the air was moist, and no doubt both were contributing to the green moss on the roofs. One might almost think it brooding if not for the youthful exuberance that the scarf-muffled students exhibited while walking to and fro with purpose.

David and Lydia were struck by the friendliness bordering on easy intimacy, and the pride of community they all seemed to demonstrate. After all, there were only 20 staff and 160 students, a small and effective relationship so that everyone felt close. The young emissary, Linda, was very upbeat, forthright and optimistic, a confident teen with serious ideas for improving the world. They chatted randomly of her scholarship, missing her parents and friends back home, and the friends she was making here, all the while perambulating the surroundings before she took her leave to catch a class. She pointed out the married residence that David and Lydia could investigate alone, but not before they reassured her that they could find their way back to the cafeteria for lunch.

David and Lydia walked up the path to a breezeway which provided access to the 'house', a student dorm on one side and the vacant suite on the other. They pushed open the ajar door and poked their heads in. There was a small foyer that presented some stairs to two upstairs bedrooms, and beyond to the right, there was an open area for the living and dining room plus a small kitchen. There was also a small office on the main floor.

The residence seemed much bigger in spite of the shade from towering cedars because there were large windows that opened onto a patio and fenced yard. David and Lydia wandered about separately, nodding and assessing possibilities, before heading back to the cafeteria. They sat at a table with the headmaster and Linda, along with two international students, Alonso whose father was a Venezuelan fisherman, and Cyvia from Peru whose parents were teachers. The conversations were easy and David and Lydia commented on how welcome they were made to feel. Afterwards, David signed his contract with Lydia watching and hands were shaken. Their visit over, David and Lydia, walking hand-in-hand, meandered through the campus before returning downhill to the parking lot.

While David was driving down the long access road back to the highway, Lydia put her hand on his knee and said. "Congratulations, *querido*. I know you've wanted this position for a long time. I loved the kids there, so sociable, so idealistic; they were so positive but not naive. And the campus is perfect for contemplation."

David looked at her and smiled, "Did you notice the tennis courts and the pool? And they have a dock for mooring a boat in the inlet. But what did you think of the digs? I thought it was dark but plenty of room. Could you see yourself living there; I mean us?"

She squeezed his knee again affectionately. "*Sim*, I am beginning to see myself there. It's more concrete; more real now, isn't it? Not just a plan."

David excitedly asked, "Does this mean you'll do it?"

She was not as effusive as he was but said, with a huge smile and twinkle. "Yes, I believe I will." Then she added a little hesitantly, "But can we announce it in such a way that my parents can accept it more easily perhaps?"

"Sure, but what do you mean exactly?"

"Let's announce that we will get married at the beginning of July. And let's say we're going to try Pearson College for three years, as an experiment. And then as a carrot, let's commit to either helping them to visit us here; or we go visit them each year in Brazil."

"You mean it? Yes, it's a deal. Yahoo!"

Suddenly Lydia moaned. "Eeeah, Dahveed, can you pull over, por favor?"

He looked over with raised eyebrows. "Can't you wait until the hotel, you hussy?"

She laughed and then grimaced, "Not that, *caro*. I have to pee in the worst way."

"Are you okay? You've been doing that a lot lately."

"No, I haven't."

"Yes. You went right after lunch and now again. And remember last week, having to find a place quickly when we were skiing."

"Dahveed, I was cold; it was winter after all. And today I've been drinking lots of water."

David clenched his lips, deciding to drop the topic, but resolving to observe her and insist on a possible medical check-up, if need be.

They dropped the car off at the rental behind the Empress Hotel and returned to their hotel on the Inner Harbour, the Laurel Point Inn. David went for a run along the coastal pathways and sidewalks past Fisherman's Wharf and out to the end of the Ogden Point Breakwater, hoping to catch the sunset. He was just enjoying life, basking in the sunlight and the memory of the day's events.

Lydia, on the other hand, showered but cast a thought towards David's earlier concern. Was she urinating more? And then, while lathering, she noticed her breasts were sensitive. She too made a mental note to monitor her health and perhaps get a doctor's appointment back in Rio if there was a concern.

David returned, saying he had talked to the concierge downstairs who recommended a fun dining experience within easy walking distance, called Pagliacci's. But he wanted to call Uncle Peter before it got too late back in Ontario. The call exuded bonhomie, as David conveyed the good news of Pearson College, the decision to supply teach in Hamilton, Lydia's success with skiing, and remembering Peter's attempts to teach David to ski before giving up and investing in a professional instructor.

David, on an impulse, surprised himself and Peter by asking him to be best man, whenever the Brazilian wedding took place in July, but that yes, he and Lydia would be living on the West Coast come September. Then dressed in jeans, sweaters and ski jackets in the cool evening, the contented couple ambled by the Legislature outlined in fairy lights, past the Captain Vancouver statue gazing on the Empress, down Government Street, and then followed directions to Broad Street. It was a touristy thing to do; the restaurant having hosted several celebrities whose pictures adorned the walls. And tonight there was live music as well. David ordered the Hemingway Short Story pasta dish and Lydia was bemused by the Girl From Ipanoodle, deciding it was indeed fun, if somewhat twee.

"Is there anything else in particular you want to do in Victoria, sweetheart? We have to head back to Vancouver tomorrow evening and our flight leaves on Friday. So tomorrow until noon will be your last chance until the summer."

"I think I'll shop for some souvenirs. And you?"

David said, "You know me and books. I'm going to browse in Munro's. It's just moved into a great building on Government Street and we can rendezvous for a coffee. How's that for a plan?"

"*Perfeito*. Can we go now; I'm feeling very tired. It must be what happens when you are planning a life," and she put her arm around David's waist and rested her head lightly on his shoulder on the stroll back.

While tilting his head to read titles on book spines, David thought he recognized someone along the aisle of Munro's the next day. He inched toward the person, trying to make sure of the identity. Finally he said, "Excuse me, but you remind me of someone I knew in university. Did you work for the WFDY? I'm sorry the World Federation for Democratic Youth."

The fellow turned to face David. "As a matter of fact I did, a lifetime ago."

"Are you Mike Giordano? I'm David Dilman. What a small world."

They were looking at each other after almost an eight-year hiatus. David's hair was thinner and Mike was in a suit and tie. His former wispy moustache was now a full handlebar but he was still a thin guy who conveyed openness and honesty. After the surprised shock of seeing each other in a West Coast book store, they shook hands and commenced to chat cordially.

"The last time I saw you," David said self-deprecatingly, "I was trying to talk you into some nefarious fund raising from homosexual groups."

Mike blushed a bit. "Yes, we were mere neophytes then."

They each did a quick résumé of their lives since then. Mike told how he started working with non-profit organizations to help homeless people, starting in Winnipeg and then Vancouver before coming to Victoria. He recently started working with a group that had been helping to improve the lot of the least able since 1968, the Victoria Cool Aid Society. David said he had just agreed to a teaching contract and would be in the area in the fall. They decided to go next door for a tea and pastry and continue their reconnection.

"Tell me about this thing you did for your Dad," Mike asked. He still had the knack of being genuinely interested in others and listening to their plight, making each person feel special. David found that he didn't mind sharing his thoughts and narrative and wondered if that was a measure of how he himself had changed or of Mike's interest. Last time he was with Mike, David was a wiseacre, hiding behind one-liners, and giving no one else much of a consideration. It was a sobering revelation for David.

Mike was passionate about a new project he was working on, increasing affordable housing, soliciting a volunteer dental and doctors' clinic, and being a financial manager for Cool Aid.

"You know I really feel I'm making life a little better for others every day. I work inside the system for those who are outside, or at least on the periphery. How about you? Why do you want to teach?"

"To come to the point, it's because I like working with young people, love creating lessons that light a spark and make them want to learn. That, and giving them a sense of counter-control, I guess. If it's not going to be revolution," and they both laughed, "then I find it important to equip kids with skills to learn the game and be oppositional from within."

"I guess we've both toned down a tad and here we are over 30. Will they trust you?"

"How long have you waited to throw that Yippie line back in my face? Jeez, it's good seeing you, Mike." He looked at his watch. "But I've got to run; I have a rendezvous with Lydia."

"She's here too?"

"Yes, we're getting married in Brazil actually and then moving out to Pearson College."

"So, you and Lydia. You two were like an erupting volcano each time you got together."

"Well, the volatility is a bit more dormant, if not extinct," and they both laughed.

"Good for you. You'll have to look us up in the fall, my wife and me." Mike gave David his business card and they parted.

Could it be that the past could come into his present so easily? He shouldn't be so surprised really. Wasn't it Cicero who said that to be ignorant of one's history meant one would remain a child? Wasn't he proof of that maturing, after having just spent a year letting his father's past catch up to the present? And now Lydia was part of the same process, his past, his present and his future. He walked out into the sunshine, feeling philosophical and existential while float planes loudly droned a descent over Bastion Square.

"You'll never guess who I met in the bookstore?" David took a shopping bag from Lydia as they went to a nearby coffee shop. David told her.

"And you didn't get jealous, *caro*?"

"Ha, I deserved that. No, in fact it could be fun to re-acquaint in the fall. So, what have you bought?"

Lydia showed him the requisite smoked salmon in a cedar box, some maple syrup and even several souvenir tee-shirts for some students. "They were on sale," she parried.

"Aren't you finishing your coffee?"

"No, I don't like the metallic taste. It might be the water or maybe I just miss the Brazilian blend."

"Well tomorrow you'll be able to indulge your taste buds, darling."

The panoply of Carnival, the seemingly continuous samba sashay, and the drumming hubbub were over now. It was a heady experience, but David wanted to turn his attention to lesson plans while Lydia was getting ready to return to Ihla Grande. The D'Silva household was resigned to their daughter leaving, first to go back to her job, then for Canada; but they put a good face on it and were actually excited about an early July wedding reception. The only fly in the ointment of leave-taking was Lydia.

She still seemed tired, and the other symptoms of nausea, semi-incontinence and skewed tastes persisted. She kept shooing concern away, saying it was just stress. But when nausea started occurring more regularly in the mornings, red flags went up.

Lydia admitted to David and then to her mother that she had missed her period in January and it was late now. She had put it down to external issues like the anxiety of skiing and making life decisions; but it couldn't be ignored any longer. She and Maria went to the doctor in late February and it was confirmed. Lydia was pregnant.

"I'm so sorry, Dahveed," she wept into his shoulder. He laughed softly and whispered back to her, kissing the top of her head.

"Don't be sorry, this is wonderful. We'll make it all work out."

"But you don't want children, you said so."

"Nonsense! I said as long as you were the mother, it was fine."

"I don't know how it happened, *querido*."

He held her back by the shoulders, "You mean you don't know about birds and bees?"

She sniffled and laughed. "Of course, but I'm on the pill, no?"

"Well, the pill isn't foolproof. I understand that if you miss a day or even take it at a different time each day, there's a chance of conception. Who knows, my being here probably put you in a fluster," he smiled coyly.

Lydia blew her nose and smiled back. "What will we do now; I've ruined everything."

David reassured her. "I believe 'we' did this. You know, this is the first time I think I'm hearing new hormones talk."

They both laughed and then David began exploring a plan.

"You can quit your job now or go back to your classroom an honest woman."

"What do you mean?"

"I'm suggesting we get married now, as soon as possible. Tomorrow if you want. It has to be now because I can't delay going back to Canada. Maybe your Dad can use his influence for a speedier civil ceremony."

"No, I mean yes. I understand that you have to go to Hamilton. I'll miss you, even more now. But I feel I want to go back to school for the last term. And yes, being married will be good as I begin to show. Do you hate me?"

"Hate? Don't be silly. This isn't even an adverse wind. A minor resetting of the sails is all that's required."

Gregorio and Maria were sitting at the kitchen table when David and Lydia entered and sat down too.

David said, "I'd love a cup of coffee and a *pão de queijo* right now, if you have. It seems we have some family plans to make and would love to have your input." To which Lydia said, "*Sim, por favor*, except for the coffee."

The D'Silvas were not judgmental at all, to their credit. They were excited for the couple and the future as grandparents, saying "*avós*" several times, and shaking their heads with a smile. Fortunately, David and Lydia had registered their intent to marry at the Civil Registry Office already and Gregorio called in some favours to expedite the process. The civil service was a total family affair and a dinner out afterwards.

David put down the phone after calling Peter. He told Lydia that his uncle had joked about them being busy beavers but he was thrilled. Peter understood about the hurried wedding and not being able to act as best man, as it were; but he and David would fly down together for the wedding reception at the end of June. And that night, David and Lydia retired to Lydia's bedroom, canoodling and talking of the future, as husband and wife.

CHAPTER 27.

WHO HAS SEEN THE WIND? NEITHER YOU NOR I... (Christina Rossetti)

Rio de Janeiro, July 1986
Victoria, September, 1986

David and Peter were on the long flight from Toronto's Pearson airport to Rio-Galeao International. The journey would take fifteen hours with one stopover but both men were content to have the time with each other. They had a great deal to catch up on, teaching, wedding reception plans, estate details, and Lydia to name a few, and not necessarily in that order. Plus Peter's caseload and golf.

David was telling his uncle, "The teaching term went well. It gave me a sense of how to manage a classroom again. Plus I had the evenings to go over the International Baccalaureate curriculum, when I wasn't writing Lydia."

"Is there a big difference between the IB and the traditional one?" Peter asked.

"Demands on the teachers and students are bigger for sure and it's much less Euro-centric. It will be exciting to study South Africa, China, and Cuba; and the themes about democracy are thought provoking."

"I guess it stands to reason, if students are coming from around the world."

David agreed. They moved on to other topics quite randomly.

"You know, I had dinner a few times with my aunts when I was in Hamilton; do you remember meeting them at Dad's memorial? Aunt Barb and Aunt Elsa."

"Yes, of course I remember. They were fond of Des as I recall."

"Yes, they were. They made no apologies about not attending Mom's funeral, not that I was expecting any. They are lovely ladies with nice families."

"Did they add anything to what you know about your Mom and Dad?"

"A bit. Dad used to send them money from time to time; Aunt Elsa's husband was out of work once or twice. It reminded me of a diary entry of Dad's not too long after I was born where Dad said he and Mom had harsh words about his being generous to his 'degenerate' relatives and Mom made him promise to stop. He wrote a letter to them that was pretty difficult; he said something about the price of love can be costly. I didn't really understand it then."

"He told me about that too, much later on, one of those hypothetical cases he liked to raise at a meal. He asked, 'Are there limits to the lengths one can go for love?'"

"They told me his early life was pretty rough; Dad's father beat him often apparently, especially when Dad would try to stop him yelling at my aunts when they were girls. They loved Dad for that. Come to think of it, I don't recall Dad ever smacking me. He'd get angry and you know we could yell, but I don't remember him ever beating me. It just dawned on me; he was a big improvement over his own father, I guess."

"Perspective, Davey; it's everything. And Lydia's pregnancy, has it been a good one?"

"Yes, excellent. She had a rough patch at the very beginning, but that was all. I've tried to have some input to the wedding reception but she and her mother have it all under control."

"And are you two going to be alright at Pearson College?"

"Perfect. All the pieces are falling into place. Thanks again for the way you helped with the sale of Glebe Avenue."

"I could have sold the house for more money perhaps if we had waited longer; but you never know how that will work out. An unconditional offer and fair price seemed best. I'm glad you agreed."

David patted his uncle's forearm. "More than happy. Didn't Dad buy that house for about $10,000 when I was born? And you sold it for $110,000 almost forty years later. That's over a thousand per cent profit.

I think any bourgeoisie, or capitalist for that matter, would be satisfied."

"So tell me about this sailboat you bought. All I know was that I wired you money for it. Will I ever get a chance to sail on it with you?"

"Maybe, you're always more than welcome. And you always look fit and agile enough for any activity. How old are you now?

"Seventy-two and before my memory goes completely, here's the last vial of ashes, as you requested. And I have a bit left in his urn for my safe-keeping. Is this the ninth one for you? Very auspicious number, you know. It stands for wisdom."

"Yes, it's the ninth and last one for me. And I believe I have grown some in wisdom. Where were we?" David glanced at Peter with a smile, teasing him about forgetting.

"The sailboat, smart guy."

"Oh yeah. I found this Truant 33' advertised as a private sale. It's used but not too old, five years only. The owner had an accident while sailing in Mexico and it rendered him too disabled to continue boating; so he had to sell, at least that's the story."

"Truant? How appropriate for an educator."

David laughed appreciating the connection. "It was built and registered in Victoria. And you'll like this; the Director of Pearson is thrilled to let me moor it at the school and use it to teach sailing. The college will take care of insurance, getting me qualified as a sailing instructor, and will help to defray costs."

"Fantastic arrangement. Do you have pictures?"

"Yes, of course, here. I have them to show Lydia and her family too."

David produced several photos and Peter genuinely admired the white sloop with its aggressively-angled bow, designed to cut through the water easily; maroon sail covers, and teak gunwale. David pointed out several features, especially those that would make it a good cruiser for the cool Pacific coast, for example, the pilot house open to the stern and the Antarctic oil stove.

He said, "Lydia and I talked long and hard about it and with Dad's money as a down payment, it went smoothly. Thanks again for arranging the financing, at least until the estate is settled. We're both excited. We're going to use it to cruise as a honeymoon before mooring it in the inlet by the school."

"And I see the name is *Margarethe*. You Dilmans are forever tied to that name."

"You're right, Uncle Peter," replied David, as the penny dropped. "Dad's first love in Spain, Mom, and now this lovely sailboat."

"Your Dad would be happy that you got back into sailing, you know. I am too. Say, will you and I be able to get in a golf game while we're in Rio. I know it's their winter but what's in a word. I looked in the newspapers and it will be sunny and in the mid-20s Celsius this week. Maybe Lydia's Dad would like to join us."

"I'm sure Gregorio would love to. If he doesn't play, then at least he'd like the walk and he would be good company."

The week of the wedding reception went swimmingly. It was a small and intimate gathering preceded by visits from individual neighbours and various relatives, all accompanied with typically Brazilian fare. For the reception itself, they had a *churrasco*, a buffet barbecue of assorted meats like *linguiça*, the cured pork sausage with garlic and paprika; lots of *fraldinha and picanha*, both typical Brazilian cuts of juicy sirloin beef; side dishes of potato and carrot salad; plus David's new favourite, heart of palm and tomato salad.

There were several toasts with the requisite *caipirinhas* and Peter had arranged with a Rio wine merchant to provide several cases of red Montepulciano d'Abruzzo to commemorate when David and Lydia recommenced their relationship. Of course, guests wanted to hear the story several times, about their tenuous letters back and forth, romantic Rome, and athletic Abruzzo. And Lydia exaggerated how cold it was at Whistler, to delighted laughs.

Lydia was radiant. She was dressed in a new, strapless, yellow maternity evening dress, full length and flowing elegantly, gathered and sash-crossed at the breasts. She glowed and both prospective parents and grandparents were proud of her seven-month bulge. Her pearls from David's mother were beautiful; her dress and the jewelry handsomely fulfilling the new and old criteria of weddings. When asked about the borrowed and blue, she pointed out that she was borrowing Peter as *'meu tio'*, her uncle, and that David had blue eyes.

There were no bridegrooms or bridesmaids as such but some friends from Lydia's school, including Alex, her tennis partner, were in attendance, as well as some of Gregorio's workmates and a few aunts and uncles and cousins.

Peter was tanned and looking distinguished for a septuagenarian, or any age really, dressed in a smart white linen suit. David was also nattily attired in a new beige linen suit, sky-blue shirt and no tie, only a dark blue puff hanky. As was the custom, no one wore black because it was considered bad luck. And speaking of luck, Lydia showed off two gifts that she kept in a small clutch purse. One was the buzios amulet from David and the other was a *figa*, the Brazilian symbol of the clenched fist, thumb held between the index and third fingers which signified good luck and fecundity. It was given to her as a going-away present from her school, a carved blue lapis amulet with a silver cap. Lydia put it and the buzios together hanging on the leather thong.

"This will be my everyday necklace," she said.

"And this will be my special good one," putting her hand on the pearl necklace. And of course both she and David had been wearing their exchanged gold bands on their left hands since February.

After everyone seemed to be sated with food and wine, there was a short lull before the desserts came out. Then there appeared the *bem casadas*, those slices of wrapped souvenir wedding cake, and *casadinhos*, the traditional wedding cookies. The specialty of two sugar icing wafers representing the happy couple, with *doce de leite* caramel filling, were gobbled up quickly. But Lydia and Maria, aware that David's favourite was carrot cake, had one made and decorated with both the Brazilian and the Canadian flags. They pinned flag lapel pins on each other and the guests too, kissed and thanked everyone. By then the tables were cleared away and a live 'backyard' samba band with dancers entered, with drum and acoustic guitars, again courtesy of Peter.

"Since I can't samba, I thought I would hire someone who could," Peter explained somewhat abashedly, with Lydia translating to much appreciative laughter. There was a new popular variation of samba making the rounds, the *pagode*. Everyone sang along and swayed to the music late into the night, including neighbours who swelled the patio garden celebration.

"Wasn't that memorable, *caro*?" Lydia said to David as the party wound down and they retired to her room, making sure once again, as they did after the civil ceremony in February, to place her right foot over the threshold first, good luck in the Brazil. Lydia lay down on the bed exhausted. David reclined on his side and put his hand on her belly. Suddenly they felt the baby kick, looked at each other and laughed.

"Is that a samba move I felt?" David asked.

"Or maybe the baby wants to go for a run with its daddy," Lydia answered.

It was Saturday, September 13th and the first week of classes was over. The day was calm and partly cloudy, with the temperature reaching a pleasant 17 Celsius and only a slight breeze from the southwest. David waved to Lydia standing on the dock and cast off, *Margarethe*'s engine putting quietly as he went out into the inlet of Pedder Bay heading toward the Juan de Fuca Strait.

He held the image of Lydia's profile for a long time, long legs in jeans and hands caressing her blooming belly under her green maternity top. She had his old cardigan draped over her shoulders too. The baby was due at the end of the month and she had insisted that David take on this afternoon's sailing task alone, while she promised to nap.

They had spent a relaxing morning in their 'home', with coffee and newspaper. In mid-August, they had moved into their residence in McLaughlin House, one of the five on the Pearson College campus. They enjoyed outings to Victoria, going to a few garage sales and browsing in Antique Row on Fort Street, and had added a few pieces to their place. They were contented with the fruits of their labour, and unlike Hercules, awaited their next labour at the end of September with anticipated pleasure, ignoring any prospects of pain.

They were comfortable and David was recounting his endeavours of the past week. He had successfully introduced an idea for a lesson plan that he had devised while still teaching in Hamilton.

"Do you think the students enjoyed your concept of personal history, *querido?*"

"Yes, I do actually. At least I noticed them sharing their findings with each other in the cafeteria at lunch."

She was leaning back in the comfy armchair, legs slightly splayed to better carry her bump, more like a mogul now. "Tell me all the details, please."

He looked over at her, the framed Potato Eaters behind her. They had had words already about that painting of the wizened peasant family looking over the dining room table. He had argued that it gave some perspective to their good fortune but knew that he would move it to his office this weekend, because he loved her and it was one of those battles to lose.

"I thought there were several aims in the International Baccalaureate that I could cover, like promoting the study of history as a discipline and using the past in a systematic way to understand their present, besides being a good way to get to know each other."

She sighed from the discomfort of being pregnant for nine months and asked how he accomplished all that in a couple of lessons. He asked if she was alright.

Lydia smiled and said somewhat sardonically, "*Sim,* Buddha says that good can come from suffering, no?"

He smiled and began, "Well, I explained that it all starts with our own personal history. I asked how old they were when they had their own first memory, or if their parents told them of earlier memories. Then we got into brainstorming to establish any evidence for the memory."

"Mmm, I think I was maybe four or five."

"Me too, but I can't be sure if it was my own or if it was something I remembered overlaid by my Dad's diary. Anyway, then I asked them to start making a list of big memories in their life but going backwards from 'coming to Pearson College'. My only hint was that it could be a person, place, thing, or event that was memorable in their life."

"Oooh, that could be a big enough task for us 'older' folks, but would a sixteen year old have so many?"

"Yes, they didn't find it difficult. So I said there had to be at least ten, one a year. I gave some examples from my own life to break the ice. I used our marriage, buying our boat, travelling to Italy, and my father's death."

"I would have some of the same ones, but it's an interesting exercise, no? Meeting you in Sofia would be one also."

"Whoops, yes, I better revise my list for the next time. Then I asked them to put a date or year beside each significant item so they could track the memorable chronology and to see if there were any years that had more occurrences than others. So their homework was to make sure they had at least one memory for each year, on the premise that each year had to have something worthwhile whether it was good or bad; and have a maximum of twenty items recorded."

"That could be a fun party game, Dahveed."

He laughed and teased her, "Well, maybe one of your parties. So that was evidence gathering and some sorting in the first lesson. The next skill was to organize it and begin to analyze what they had. I had them number their items chronologically. Then label each with a P for person, PL for place, E for event, and Th for thing. That way they could see what seemed to play more of a role in their life."

"Was that it?"

"No, the next step was to see their life or personal histories unfold visually on a line or bar graph. On one side they put the numbers one to ten, one being pretty devastating as a memory and ten being pretty fantastic. On the bottom horizontal, they marked the age of their first memory to the age they were now, evenly spaced to allow room for the items they had decided were memorable depictions of their life. I was also doing mine on the chart to illustrate. I placed my Dad's death as an 8, which surprised most of them."

"Me too, *caro*. How did you explain that?"

"I said his death opened up my world. He set me on a quest, I got to travel and learn about my father and myself which I couldn't do while he was alive, and most importantly, it allowed us to get together again."

"Come give me a kiss." He did and asked if she wanted more coffee. She thanked him and asked, "Did the students have interesting graphs, like life lines I suppose."

"Yes they found them really revealing, as individuals, and to others. I asked them to share with at least three classmates, unless they could make a case to me that their evidence was too private. We talked about balanced lives, whether the class would have enough diversity, whether we tended to be a positive and optimistic group or not. It was a really good discussion. Enough shop talk now. I want to discuss another project for today."

David said he felt that the time was right to dispense with the last vial of ashes, the ninth. He intended to sail out this afternoon for a few hours and asked if she wanted to join him.

"No, I think it best that you do this yourself, *caro*. It's between you and your father, no? I'll go for a little walk along the campus road only, no hiking I promise. Then I'll have a nap or putter with baby things."

Lydia watched him get smaller as he motored to the middle of the inlet. Soon the *Margarethe* would disappear around a bend. There were zephyrs on the water, she noticed, and she shielded her eyes from the glare as the sun momentarily moved from behind a cloud. She saw what appeared to be a glint of gold on his left hand and it made her smile. "*Boa viagem!*" she called out and caressed her belly after feeling some kicking.

Pedder Bay was one of the few good harbours that the Hudson's Bay Company's Vancouver Island factor and first colonial Governor of British Columbia, James Douglas, considered for settlement, along with Sooke and Victoria itself. Although it was a good long sheltered inlet, he dismissed it as a desirable harbour with nothing else to recommend it. For years the rocky and treed shores seemed to live up to his evaluation.

It was home territory to the Songhees and the T'sou-ke peoples and twenty years ago an archaeologist discovered evidence of a trenched village dating back 1,700 years ago. Now a marina and recreational vehicle park occupied the end of the bay; the inevitability of change. Between here and William Head at the south-eastern end of the bay, there were but three features of note, a large burial ground composed of stone cairns with no associated village, Pearson College, and a minimum security prison. All this David had learned from local history research.

Now he was experiencing this mostly natural environment from the water and considering a fitting place to release Des's last ashes, and in a way to finally release himself. He felt he was just beginning his own real life now, with Lydia and their newborn on the way, and his teaching work at Pearson. However, he was also mindful of all the antecedents that went into his being in this time and place; the Songhees and T'sou-ke for instance. They traded, celebrated potlatches, and defended themselves against marauding Haida. As David peered into the impenetrable forest, native peoples must have looked out from the same foliage and marveled at Captain George Vancouver's 53' ship *Chatham*, a 'big canoe with giant blankets' and 'thunder sticks', when it first entered here to navigate the coast.

As he entered the estuary, he looked to port and saw the glint off the razor wire topping the prison not far away, and Victoria itself, about ten nautical miles in the distance to the north-northeast. He didn't want to think of how the natives, the students and the inmates might all consider themselves imprisoned in a way; that was too cynical. And he definitely didn't want to run in that northerly direction with the vial even though it was with the following, easy southwest breeze.

"Since when was your life easy, eh Dad?" So he pointed *Margarethe* into the wind and raised her mainsail and jib, trimming them on the port side so that he headed south towards Race Rocks, loving the purling sound along the boat's hull. It was a gentle sail, in five knots wind, but the currents and ebbing tide could make for confusing waters. David had to keep his wits about him, especially as he got closer to Race Rocks.

As David got closer to the rocks, he could smell the wild and pungent odour of the California sea lions and elephant seals. So he let out his sails to a beam reach and went beyond the rocks on his starboard, taking a more easterly course. And then it occurred to him."Why not the estuary?"

The more he thought about it the more it seemed right, even perfect. It signified everything that his Dad and the quest were all about. The co-mingling of fresh and salt water was like the intermingling of two generations of Dilmans; the once disregarded inlet now offering hope to students, rehabilitation for wrong-doers, and survival for natives. Wasn't it the Spaniard, Juan de Fuca, who was the first white to see this area and wasn't it Spain where Dad had his baptism of fire? Didn't the tidal waters carry the ebb and flow of macro-history from cultural conflict of peoples such as the Coastal Salish and Captain James Cook, to the global forces such as the fur trade of otter pelts and endangering infectious diseases? And what of the many micro-histories which had passed by Pedder Bay, including that of James Douglas who was the son of a Creole mother from British Guyana, and his own wife Amelia who was the daughter of a Cree woman; and now his own students with the significant event of coming to Pearson lodged in their personal histories. And yes, weren't Des and David's live effected by their experiences on this very coast?

"Who knows, maybe these ashes south of Victoria will mingle with the ones dropped into False Creek," he mused, remembering that the Japanese current keeps sending flotsam and jetsam to the Pacific northwest shores, reminding him that the world is small. He had his main sail out to port, sailing northeasterly on a following wind. So he did a controlled gybe and gradually headed westward again on a starboard reach.

Trimming the sails to head in towards Pedder Bay again, David navigated not far off his intended point of sail, having calculated the apparent wind. Off of William Head he started the engine and turned into the breeze to let his sails down. Bobbing on the rolling waves, he took out the vial and uncorked a bottle of wine for the occasion, a Mouton-Cadet Bordeaux.

He took a swig from the bottle and said to himself and 'Des', "I know you shared many great bottles of wine with me and Uncle Peter, but I'm on a teacher's salary now so this will have to do."

He opened the vial, leaned leeward over the cockpit and let the ashes blow. When he was done, he put the empty vial back in his pocket to keep as a memento and poured the wine as a libation over the spreading ashes.

"So there we have it, Dad. You shared a great deal with me, even if posthumously, and it helped me learn about us and about me. Now I am returning you to the elements. Thank you for the quest; a son couldn't ask for anything more memorable. So long."

He looked around to get a fix on his position, so he could point the approximate location to Lydia or Uncle Peter, or even Des's grandchild. Then he put the engine in gear, motoring back to the mooring at Pearson.

When he entered their residence at McLaughlin House, the aroma of a spicy repast reached him. Lydia was at the stove preparing a favourite pasta meal, *spaghetti alla puttanesca*, redolent with garlic, onions, capers and anchovies. David hugged her from behind and nuzzled her neck.

"Did it go well, *caro?*" she asked.

"*Perfeito!* I bought two bottles of the same wine. One I poured with my Dad's ashes and the other will be for us. I know you won't have a drink, but I might have your glass too." David smiled at Lydia. He felt tired but fulfilled somehow.

"Look Dahveed. I thought I'd try a nautical touch with the *puttanesca*. Red and green peppers for port and starboard. See, I'm beginning to think in 'sailing'." She was chuffed with her creativity.

She continued, "Next year I thought we might try growing a little garden of our own, some tomatoes and peppers and herbs, no?"

"You bet, love. I've always wanted a little plot of vegetables and flowers. You know what Voltaire said at the end of *Candide?* After every tribulation the world threw at him, and after he realized he might not be living in the best of all possible worlds, he concluded that the best anyone could do in this life was to cultivate their own garden."

He sipped from his glass, raised it to Lydia and said with a pensive smile, "I wonder if our little one will be taking its first steps by harvest time."

∞

GLOSSARY OF CHARACTERS AND METAPHORS, REAL AND FICTIONALIZED:

There are historical characters in this narrative but any connections to the main character, Des Dilman, are fictitious even though feasible. Any dialogue between Des and the historical figures is completely fictional.

Agee, Philip: He was a CIA case officer from 1957-1969, serving mainly in Latin America (Ecuador, Uruguay, Mexico). He soured on his job with the Agency and resigned, going on to write a whistle-blowing book on CIA tactics, titled *Inside the Company: A CIA Diary* (1975). Harassed by the CIA for resigning and while writing his book, he found refuge in Cuba, England, France, Germany and even Grenada. He also wrote a memoir on his ordeal of leaving the CIA, called *On The Run* (1987). It is feasible that Des would know him in his role as liaison between the RCMP and CIA. Even David would have seen him because he was an invited guest to the Havana conference on World Festival of Youth in 1978. Growing up in a wealthy Catholic Florida family, educated at the University of Notre Dame, and later married to a German ballet dancer, Agee also wrote a newsletter criticizing the CIA called *Covert Action Information Bulletin*. He died in a Cuban hospital in 2008 at the age of seventy-two.

Alinsky, Saul: A community organizer and writer, popular in the '60s and '70s. His ideas, written in his book, *Rules for Radicals* (1971) were adapted by some U.S. college students and other young counterculture-era organizers, who used them as part of their strategies for organizing on campus and beyond. He died in 1972.

Bachand, Mario: He was a friend of Jacques Lanctôt, leader of the Liberation Cell that kidnapped James Cross during the October Crisis. An FLQ organizer and activist, he spent time in jail for his role in bombings.

More a socialist than a nationalist, he fled Canada to Havana and then to Paris in 1970 where he was shot and killed under curious circumstances in March, 1971.

Blanco, Jesús Sosa: He was a colonel who served the Cuban dictator Fulgencio Batista until 1959. He was caught by Castro, accused of over 100 murders, put on trial in 1959 and executed before 17,000 spectators.

Bland, Salem: A Methodist social activist in Winnipeg and Toronto. He supported the Republicans in the Spanish Civil War but was anti-war. He argued for fund-raising to assist those displaced by the war, including an orphanage for 100 orphans in Barcelona, named the Salem Bland House.

Buchanan, Judd: Liberal Member of Parliament for London West,1968-1980. He was a Parliamentary Secretary in Indian and Northern Affairs and then Finance in 1972.

Buss, Ernie & Stan Stanyer: Two gunners who actually drove a water truck the wrong way on May 20, 1944 near Pontecorvo and the Hitler Line. Buss was 25 years old, wounded in the leg. Stan was shot in the shoulder. Both survived. I found this story in *The D-Day Dodgers* by Daniel Dancocks, (Toronto: McClelland and Stewart, 1991), p. 245.

Canzoneri, Tony: Multi-division boxing champion from New York in the 1930s, he held titles in lightweight, light welterweight, and featherweight.

Capa, Robert: He was a world-renowned photographer. In 1938, he was twenty-five and photographing the Spanish Civil War. He would go on to cover wars in China, WW II, and Vietnam. He is accredited with the photo, *The Falling Soldier*, although it is shrouded in controversy and he wouldn't talk about it.

Carr, Sam: Born in Ukraine in 1906, he and Fred Rose were Communists, organizers for the Young Communist League in the '30s, and Carr was also an On To Ottawa Trekker. Carr was national organizer of the CCP front party, the Labour-Progressive Party, in 1943. He was named by Igor Gouzenko as a spy recruiter too but went underground to the States in February 1946, just as the round up of suspected Soviet spies began. In the novel, he contacted Meg in August 1947 to get a false passport. Since he was convicted of conspiracy to get a false passport it works for the story. He was caught in 1949 and jailed. After seven years, He wrote a magazine there under the pen name George Lewis and died in 1989.

Central Intelligence Agency (CIA): It is the United States' principal intelligence gathering agency. It succeeded the WW II group, Office of Strategic Services (OSS) in 1947 and its job was to collect and analyze information that might have a bearing on American national security. However, the CIA began to use extraordinary measures to achieve American political ends and added covert operations as one of its jobs to influence foreign governments. The CIA conducted nonconsensual drug experiments on Americans and Canadians, assassinated and attempted to assassinate foreign leaders, and spent millions of dollars on foreign police training without oversight. For instance, the CIA was heavily involved in anti-Cuba activities like the Bay of Pigs invasion, an attempt on Castro's life; and it was claimed to have bombed the French munitions ship, *La Coubre* in Havana harbour, March 1960. Philip Agee blew the whistle on many CIA operatives in his book, *Inside the Company* (1975).

Clark, Greg: Born in 1892, he was fifty-two when covering WW II in Italy for the *Toronto Star*. He had the reputation of being Dean of the Canadian War Correspondents, sometimes called 'warcos'. In WW I he won the Military Cross for conspicuous gallantry at Vimy Ridge. Clark loved fishing, knew and befriended Hemingway in 1920 at the *Toronto Star* newspaper. He was an accomplished short story writer himself and won a Leacock Humour Award for War Stories in 1955. He lost his son, James in the war on Sept. 17, 1944. When the *Star* wouldn't give him leave to go to his son's funeral in France, he left the *Star* after the war to work for the Toronto *Telegram*. Clark wrote, "May your first love be your last." He was diminutive, only 5'2", and was affectionately called Tom Thumb in WW I.

Clarke, Bobby: In 1972, the Soviet Union and Canada played each other for hockey supremacy and bragging rights, the Summit Series. In Game 6, Bobby Clarke slashed Valeri Kharmalov, the Soviet's best player who had a sore ankle. Whether the slash was a 'tap' as Clarke maintained, or a 'chop', Kharmalov was out of the game and the Canadian professionals squeaked out a win in the game and ultimately the series.

Critton, Patrick: An American citizen, he hijacked an Air Canada flight from Thunder Bay to Toronto in December, 1971. Brandishing a gun and grenade he demanded to be taken to Cuba. In 1971 there was no extradition treaty for hijacking and he had been released to Cuban authorities. He returned to the States in 1994, where he had resumed his teaching job, using his own name and social security number. As forensic techniques improved, he was arrested in 2001 in New York for the hijacking using fingerprints on an Air Canada soda can.

Draper, Howard: While Assistant Director of Security Services, he, along with Inspector Sid Yelle and Corporal Dale Boire of Covert Operations, ran some activities that were illegal. One was a file called *Operation Feather Bed* which investigated 68 Canadian diplomats and politicians suspected of having Communist connections, including George and Michael Ignatieff and Herbert Norman. New RCMP members assigned to the file were fresh from university and good counter-espionage agents whom Des could have trained and recommended. Another file was *Operation Ham,* which embroiled the Mounties in dirty tricks in Quebec, including illegal break-ins, stealing Parti Québecois membership lists, burning a barn, and illegal wire tapping. Their activities were the catalyst for the McDonald Inquiry. Yelle was charged in 1983 and he took the fall, so to speak, although he later was promoted to Superintendent.

Garner, Hugh: A Canadian author, he wrote *Cabbagetown* in 1950 (Collins/White Circle) about growing up poor in Depression-era Toronto. He also won a Governor General's award for Best Short Stories in 1963. He was hard drinking and hard living; he spent time in the Spanish Civil War too. Certainly he would have experienced riding the rails during the Depression and it was feasible to see Des in Banff and for Des to visit him in Toronto and/or for the award ceremony. Also it was feasible for Des to receive an inscribed copy of *Cabbagetown* *(To Des, it's hard to escape our history, it's just one damn thing after another, all the best, Hugh,* which was the title of his memoir in 1973).

Giordano, Michael: Based on a real person who was a Vancouver and then Victoria social worker. He was known to be handy, spiritual, give when you are well, and expect friends to reciprocate when you're not. Described as "warm, very compassionate, and very passionate," he felt very strongly about peace, poverty and social justice. He died suddenly in 1999. He had been a leader/recruiter for the Young Communist League in the 1970s, a resurgent group of student activists organizing as the Canadian Union of Students was dissolving. I had Giordano show up in Victoria in 1985, ten years before the real person actually did. From 1995 he was there as a key member of the Cool Aid Society, dedicated to affordable housing and betterment for the homeless in Victoria.

Gouzenko, Igor: He was the young Soviet cipher clerk who defected in 1945 with documents that incriminated Fred Rose and others with developing a spy ring in Canada. He was given a changed identity, George Brown; and he and his wife and eight children lived clandestinely in Clarkson, Ontario (near Toronto) until he died in 1982. Some of the people he named as spy suspects were Israel Halperin, a Queen's University math professor, Richard Boyer, an atomic scientist at McGill and Bruno Pontecorvo, the scientist who helped with nuclear fission experiments in Canada and defected to the Soviet Union in 1950.

Greene, Graham: He was a prolific British author who spent time in Cuba both for his novel, *Our Man In Havana*, published in 1958, and for the film, based on the novel, in 1959-60. He also wrote some articles for the British newspaper, the *Sunday Telegraph* in 1963 - 1966. Des could have met him then on those junkets, although I set their liaison in 1964. It fits with Des's wish to be a writer and had Graham Greene inscribe Des's copy of *Our Man In Havana* (*To Des, a romantic is always afraid reality won't match expectations, GG*). Much of my research on Greene came from Norm Sherry's biographical trilogy, *The Life of Graham Greene* (Jonathan Cape, 2004), including Greene working for MI6 as an intelligence agent and information on the execution of the Batista army colonel, Jésus Soso Blanco in 1959.

Griffin, Fred: He worked at the *Toronto Daily Star* for over three decades, wrote a book on observations of the Soviet Union in 1932, saw the siege of Madrid in December, 1936, and was also a war correspondent through Italy. It would be possible for Des to meet him in Spain. He died of a heart attack at age fifty-six in 1946, shoveling snow in Toronto.

Gross, Margareta: This character was based on Margarethe Michaelis-Sachs, a Polish woman, born in 1902. She would be thirty-five in 1937 when Des would be twenty. She could be the photographer that Des met in Barcelona. She was married but separated from husband Rudi Michaelis; I connected her to the idea for the Robert Capa photo of the

Fallen Soldier. She later moved to Sydney, Australia in 1939, got remarried to A. Sachs in 1960, and died in 1985.

Hébert, Jacques: He and Pierre Trudeau were good friends. They travelled to Red China together in 1960, meeting Mao Zedong and Zhou Enlai there. Hébert was a journalist and wrote for *Le Devoir*, as well as a publisher. In 1971 he founded the organization *Canadian World Youth* and in 1977, *Katimavik*, aimed at involving Canadian youth in world cultures and promoting peace. In 1978 he became an Officer of the Order of Canada for his outstanding service to Canada and was appointed to the Senate in 1983 where he served until 1998. Always close to the Trudeau family (he accompanied Alexandre to China in 2005), it was feasible that Hébert would be a reasonable conduit for Des's files on Operations Ham and Feather Bed, giving them to Prime Minister Pierre Trudeau and opening the door for the two inquiries, Keable and McDonald.

Hemingway, Ernest: A revered American author, Papa was in Spain in 1936, along with Martha Gellhorn who would become his 3ʳᵈ wife. His book *To Have And Have Not* was published in September 1937. *Farewell To Arms* was published in 1929. His boxing prowess and proclivity to take his shirt off at a party to box was told in *The Paris Wife* (Paula McLain, 2011). I had him inscribe *Farewell To Arms* (*To Des, may you learn to fight and write in España, all the best, Papa*). Hemingway spent time and lived in Cuba off and on from 1939-1960, even buying a villa there. Hemingway also supported and was friends with Fidel Castro. Papa committed suicide in the U.S. in 1961, aged sixty.

Hernández, Jesus: Aged thirty-one at the outbreak of the Spanish Civil War, Hernández was a member of the Spanish Communist Party and a communist newspaper editor. As Minister of Education, 1936-38 he played an important role in promoting the government's literacy campaign. In April 1938 Hernández became head of the War Commissars in the Central Zone. In 1939 Hernández fled to the Soviet Union and became an executive member of *Comintern*, a Soviet organization to promote international communism. He soon became disillusioned with the rule of Joseph Stalin and went to live in Mexico, working in the Yugoslav embassy.

Hindmarsh, Harry: He was the long time editor of the *Toronto Star*. He joined in 1911 as a cub reporter, became managing editor in 1928, and president in 1948. He died at his desk at sixty-nine, in 1956. He was noted for spending huge amounts to get stories, sometimes sending thirty writers and photographers to key spots. Hemingway disliked him because Hindmarsh sent him to the hinterland of Ontario for stories, an event told in *The Paris Wife*, when Hemingway's wife, Hadley Richardson was expecting.

Kelly, William: He was the Deputy Commissioner at retirement in 1970 but Director of Security and Intelligence, 1964-1967 and a liaison officer to Ottawa in 1967. He very well could have been Des's direct boss during his Cuba file. Kelly spied on Tommy Douglas, the former premier of Saskatchewan and a Federal Member of Parliament.

Lacloche, Marianne: Her character was based on a real person, a twenty-six year old, part-time Québec radio and television personality who was involved in the 'Monuments Plot' of February, 1965. She belonged to a fringe separatist group and aided and abetted the black American co-conspirators, Robert Collier and Walter Bowe, members of the Fair Treatment For Cuba and Black Power Movement groups. They would be familiar with black pride concepts as well as Stokley Carmichael and Richard Wright. They were apprehended because of a NYPD, FBI and RCMP coordinated investigation and the clever work of a young undercover detective, Ray Wood, acting as an insider. She received a suspended sentence and was appointed in 2002 to be Premier Bernard Landry's Parti Québecois government's representative to Algeria.

Leopold, John: A sergeant and inspector with the RCMP, he was reputed to be a rabid anti-Communist and instrumental in convicting Tim Buck, the Canadian Communist Party leader, who was on trial in 1931. I used references from Reg Whitaker & Gary Marcuse, *Cold War Canada, The Making of a National Insecurity State, 1945-1957* (Toronto: U of T Press, 1994).

Liberation Cell, FLQ: This was the cell that kidnapped James Cross, Britain's Trade Commissioner. Another cell, the Chenier, murdered Pierre Laporte. The Liberation Cell of the Front de Liberation du Québec was like a family of five: Jacques Lanctôt, Jacques Cossette-Trudel, married to Lanctôt's sister, Louise, Yves Langlois, and Marc Carbonneau. A sixth member, Nigel Hamer wasn't identified until later in 1978 and convicted. The cell negotiated exile to Cuba in 1970 in exchange for Cross. After three years they moved to France. Algeria sponsored several external wings of 'progressive independent' groups like the Black Panthers and FLQ. The RCMP set up a bogus FLQ group in Algeria, hoping to track more members abroad.

Mackenzie-Papineau Battalion: It was an international brigade thusly named in June, 1937. About sixty per cent of the 1, 500 Canadian volunteers who went to Spain were members of the Communist Party or sympathetic to it, although only about 400 former On To Ottawa Trekkers themselves went.

Mallon, Thomas: He was with the other two (Red Walsh and Sam Witczak, retreating with Des (and David) in the Spanish Civil War. Mallon was a machine-gunner during the Republican retreat in 1938. He was in Red Walsh's group and shot by a sniper. Walsh gave to Des Mallon's and Sam Witczak's passports plus Tony Babich, Bill Keenan, Paddy O'Neill and Jim Wolf.

Marighella, Carlos: A Marxist and activist in the Brazilian Communist Party who promoted revolution and urged urban guerillas to oppose the military government of Brazil in 1964. He ran afoul of the security police, being shot and arrested in 1964, then killed in 1969. He wrote *Minimanual for Urban Guerillas* and in 1967 also attended the 1st Conference of Latin American Solidarity in Havana where he wrote *Some Questions About the Guerrillas in Brazil*, dedicated to the memory of Che Guevara. It was made public to the left-leaning *Jornal do Brasil* on September 5, 1968.

McDonald Commission: Judge David McDonald set up a federal inquiry into the RCMP Security Services' wrongdoings. It sat from July 1977 and tabled its three-volume report in 1981. It recommended that police must follow the law, get judicial approval before opening mail, and that national security should be undertaken by a civilian group, CSIS. There was also a provincial inquiry in Quebec at the same time, the Keable Commission, looking into Quebec police misdeeds while fighting terrorism in the aftermath of the October Crisis.

Morgentaler, Henry: A Canadian doctor who dedicated his practice to providing safe and therapeutic abortions for women as their right and choice. He spent time in jail for his belief in 1975 but his persistence won several court cases and earned an amendment to the law in 1988. Morgentaler himself was a survivor of Nazi concentration camps. He died in 2013.

Morrison, James: In 1983, Morrison admitted that he had sold the identity of a Soviet double-agent to the KGB for $3,000 in 1955 to cover his debts. Morrison had been on the counter-espionage surveillance team watching the Soviet Embassy after the Gouzenko affair and by chance learned the identity of 'Gideon'. Morrison's code name was "Long Knife" and the Mounties kept the case quiet for twenty-five years after Morrison left the organization. Why? Perhaps to hide their own lack of security in the face of CIA doubts about Canada and the U.K. at the time, but that is conjecture on my part. I used research from John Sawatsky, *For Services Rendered* (Toronto: Doubleday, 1982).

Nine: There were nine Muses from Greek mythology who were the inspiration for the Arts. They were also known as the goddesses of knowledge. Hence the number nine is symbolic of wisdom. I thought that number of vials had a certain symmetry and significance. Ten vials of Des's ashes were dispersed in all, nine by David, who grew in wisdom, and one by Peter: Regina, Belchite, Monte Cassino (Peter), Ortona, Krakow, Vancouver, Paris, Havana, Ottawa, Victoria.

NKVD: It was the acronym for the Soviet security police, *Narodnyy Komissariat Vnutrennikh Del*, abbreviated to NKVD. The security police were involved in the Spanish Civil War, controlling Republican troops, as well as WW II mass executions such as the Polish Katyn Forest massacres in 1940. They also infiltrated British MI5 intelligence and MI6 counterintelligence in the 1950s. The NKVD were behind the spy rings in Canada that Gouzenko revealed. New acronyms have since followed. The NKVD became the KGB, the security service acronym from 1954 after Stalin died.

Norman, Herbert: He was a talented Canadian diplomat who committed suicide in Egypt on April 4, 1957 after being investigated several times for being a Communist spy. He had some Communist friends from Cambridge days but there was no real proof of his being a Communist or of being a homosexual, which was also alleged. It is conceivable that agents hounded Norman because the RCMP investigated Norman twice at American CIA urgings and were about to begin a third time at the request of the U.S. Senate. There is sufficient mystery about his suicide. CIA leaks to the *New York Daily News* in April, 1957 were forged. Starting in November, 1956, the RCMP were also focusing on investigating homosexuals as being vulnerable risks. Lester Pearson was a colleague and defender of Norman while serving as Secretary of State for External Affairs, 1948-1957; and some in the U.S. and Canada suspected him also of having Communist leanings.

Nowak, Anna: Anna's fate was based in part on the biography of Genowefa Kasprzyk, who was transferred from Eastern Poland when she was fourteen and sent to Siberia, then later to Tehran in 1942, before going to an orphanage in South Africa. I also heard the Caspian Sea migration and cholera story from a friend whose father experienced these very events. Other historians estimated over a million people were released from Soviet gulags and over 120,000 fled to the Caspian Sea, Iran and Iraq.

Palmer, Aileen: She was the daughter of Vance and Nettie Palmer, Australian writers and anti-fascists. The family was travelling in Europe in 1935 and Aileen stayed behind in Barcelona. She volunteered for the British Medical Unit in Spain but the war took its toll. She suffered a nervous breakdown in 1948 and became an alcoholic.

Pearson, Lester B.: 'Mike' was Canada's prime minister from 1963-1968 when he was succeeded by Pierre Trudeau. He also won the Nobel Peace Prize in 1957. He was buried with little pomp in 1972 in the Maclaren Cemetery at Wakefield, Quebec, with a simple headstone and near two diplomat friends. The United World College in Victoria, where David got a job teaching history, is named after him.

PROFUNC: It stood for prominent functionaries of the Communist Party. In the 1950s, Royal Canadian Mounted Police (RCMP) Commissioner Stuart Taylor Wood, had a PROFUNC list of approximately 16,000 suspected communists and 50,000 communist sympathizers to be observed and potentially interned, in event of a national security state of emergency, such as a Third World War crisis with the Union of Soviet Socialist Republics (USSR) and Red China. A separate arrest document, known formally as a C-215 form, was written up for each potential internee and updated regularly with personal information, including but not limited to age, physical descriptions, photographs, and vehicle information, until the 1980s.

RCMP Security: Security was part of Criminal Investigations. It went through many name changes over the years. With Zaneth it was known as Secret Service, Security, and Liaison and Intelligence Section, among others names. Later during the Second World War it became known as Security Services and in 1950 it was called Special Branch. It morphed into the Directorate of Security and Intelligence in 1956, Security Services again in 1970, and finally CSIS or Canadian Security Intelligence Service which took over the role in 1984. The RCMP often took liberties with investigations under the Official Secrets Act, 1939 which involved illegal opening of mail, investigating on campuses even though the government forbade it, and electronic surveillance. These issues were the subject of an investigation by the McDonald Commission, 1977-1981.

Reed, Robert: He was used as a basis for Taffy Stockdale's character, that is Reed's history and also on a friend, Michael Stockman. Reed was a Texan who fought with the Mac-Paps and died in 2005. He sailed on the *SS Volendam* and was also torpedoed on the freighter *City of Barcelona* en route to Spain. He was a poor farmer's son but went to high school and also the Commonwealth College in Arkansas, joined the Communist Party, trained at Albacete with Canadians and fought in Aragon with them. Stockman believed in giving to friends when able and the same will come back in return.

Rivett-Carnac, Charles: Commissioner for one year, 1959-60 but he was directly in charge of the PROFUNC portfolio during the '50s. Under Chief Intelligence Officer Superintendent Charles Rivett-Carnac, the Security Branch became its own jurisdiction. Another Commissioner in Security was Clifford Harvison who was a friend of James Morrison and used him as a chauffeur even though Morrison was suspected as a thief and security risk.

Rosasharn: The bush commonly known as the rose of Sharon is also called Rosasharn. It was also the name of a character in John Steinbeck's *Grapes of Wrath*. Significantly the rose of Sharon is the name of a Canadian charity dedicated to young, pregnant women. I felt it was appropriate to have this bush outside of Meg's office.

Rose, Fred: Born in Poland in 1907, he came to Montreal at age nine in 1916. He was a member of the Canadian Communist Party and also was a two-term Member of Parliament for Cartier under the Labour Progressive Party, the CP in another guise. He knew Norman Bethune and supported volunteers going to Spain, including a Lucien LaTulippe, where I got the idea for Unlucky Luke. Igor Gouzenko identified Rose in 1945 as being involved in a Soviet spy ring and as arranging false passports as early as 1936. Much of my research was gleaned from David Levy's book, *Stalin's Man in Canada*, (Enigma: 2013). Rose was imprisoned from 1945 to 1951.

S.S. Volendam: A Dutch vessel, part of the Holland America line, built in 1922. In 1930 she carried First, Tourist and Third Class passengers. Robert Reed sailed on her April 24, 1937 and I put Des on the same voyage. She made her last voyage between Rotterdam and New York in 1951 and was scrapped in 1952. The name has been reincarnated but the earlier ship is not to be confused with the 1999 version of the R-class ship currently with Holland America.

Savage, Robert (Doc): He was born in 1911 and died in 2006. He was one of the eight Trekkers to meet Prime Minister Bennett in 1935 and then Brian Mulroney in 1985. Savage was a real outdoorsman and retired to Quesnel, British Columbia.

Sawatsky, John: He was the Ottawa journalist for the *Vancouver Sun* and he won awards for a series of articles and books depicting the workings of the RCMP during the 1970s and '80s. In 1976 he won the prestigious journalism award, the *Michener*, for his articles on the RCMP and I used his books, *Men in the Shadows* and *For Services Rendered*, in research. It is believable that Sawatsky could be a go-to journalist for whistle-blowing and no doubt he would have some clout.

Shapiro, Henry: I found this episode In Mark Zuehlke's *The Gallant Cause* (Vancouver: Whitecap, 1996) where I got much of my information about the Mackenzie-Papineau Battalion. Shapiro and the other ringleader, American Robert Eisenberg, both had less than three months duty in Spain and had lost their nerve during battles. So they stole an ambulance to escape. They were executed, it seems.

Sharp, Mitchell: Canada's Secretary of State for External Affairs, 1968-

1974. He was a Trudeau stalwart and would have been in charge when David was applying for External Affairs and when Des was beginning to be concerned with the RCMP 'dirty tricks'.

Simmonds, Robert; He was the RCMP Commissioner for ten years, 1977-87. The McDonald Commission took the Security Service out of the RCMP purview in 1984 and CSIS replaced it, under Simmonds' watch. Earlier in 1966 he was stationed in Burnaby as Sub-Inspector and would have been aware of Des and the Spencer Case. Simmonds emphasized ethics and professionalism. He joined the Force in 1947 and would have known Zaneth in Regina at the Depot.

Simpson, Hamish: He was born in Victoria in 1936 to Scottish parents, attended private schools, and was Oxford-educated. He was director at Pearson College from 1982-1986 before moving on to be headmaster at Upper Canada College. His spiel about the college in the novel was attributed to an earlier headmaster at Pearson, Jack Matthews, who delivered it in 1975.

Spencer, George: A Vancouver mail sorter for the Post Office since 1949, he had been a member of the Canadian Communist Party and admirer of the Soviet system. He contacted the Russians starting in 1956 after a Soviet goodwill tour in Vancouver and started doing tasks for them, approximately from 1959-62. He was the focus of an RCMP investigation, code-named *Moby Dick*, and charged with treason. He died of lung cancer in April 1966 before an official inquiry was completed in May. My biggest source of information was John Sawatsky, *For Services Rendered* (Toronto: Doubleday, 1982).

Tellier, Lucien: Unlucky Luke was born in 1918, only nineteen at the time he was sent to the Battle of Brunete. I developed his character based on research in *The Gallant Cause*. Like so many, he experienced shelling, bombing, and machine gun fire, and became depressed, feeling the waste of life and lack of purpose. Over three-quarters of his battalion were casualties. After the Aragon Front, Tellier was only fit for non-combatant duty, the post office. Des would try to run him as a double agent on Fred Rose, Sam Carr, and the Labour Progressive Party in 1943-1945; and again as a source to identify Communists in Quebec in 1954. Rose actually had a fellow named Lucien LaTulippe work for him in Spain.

Trudeau, Pierre: Canada's 15th prime minister from April 1968 to June 1979 and again from 1980-84. His name crops up several times in the novel. He supported the workers in the Asbestos Strike in 1949 and became a lawyer in labour and civil rights issues in the '60s. He was likely monitored as a leftist and possibly even for Communist leanings. Trudeau travelled to the Soviet Union in 1952 to an economic conference, to China in 1960 on a sponsored trip (with Jacques Hébert), and to Cuba in 1964. He was not necessarily antagonistic to Communism and criticized American foreign policy from time to time. It was also Trudeau who called the McDonald Inquiry into RCMP illegal activities in 1977. Trudeau's first two sons, Justin and Alexandre (Sacha), were born on Dec. 25, hence the quip about being better than God. John English's book, *Just Watch Me*, (2010) is an excellent resource.

Waffle Group, NDP: In 1969, this was the name of a splinter group within the New Democratic Party who wanted to push the NDP further left. It published a manifesto, *For An Independent Socialist Canada*, wanting stronger unions, Canadian national ownership and it was decidedly anti-American. The Waffle Caucus was purged from the NDP in 1972. It would be plausible for David to be interested in their politics and for Peter to ask him why he didn't consider joining them.

Walsh, James 'Red': He was a Relief Camp Workers' Union organizer, Communist Party member, and one of the eight, along with Doc Savage, to have a meeting with Prime Minister Bennett. He also volunteered to go to Spain and became a Mac -Pap commissar. Walsh was badly wounded crossing the Ebro; and survived to return to Canada.

Watergate: In June 1972, five men were arrested for breaking into the National Democratic Party offices in the Watergate complex. They had money on them from the Nixon's *Committee to Re-Elect The President*. The White House kept trying to cover it up but, by July 1973, it was revealed that President Nixon had damaging tape recordings of conversations and, if made available, would incriminate the White House in criminal wrong-doings. The novel implied that it would be unwise for Trudeau to ignore damaging information that Des was providing; it would be seen to be like Watergate. Because of the Watergate scandal, Nixon resigned the presidency in September, 1974.

Waugh, Robert: First Lieutenant with the U.S. 85th Infantry Regiment, part of the American 5th Army. He fought at Monte Cassino on May 11, 1944, capturing several German bunkers, but died a week later, May 19.

Witczak, Sam: I learned his real name was Ignacy from Michael Petrou's, *Renegades, Canadians in the Spanish Civil War,* (UBC Press, 2008). The Soviets had his passport and had thought he died. The passport expired in 1945 and the Soviets got Carr to use it to get false identification. Gouzenko linked Carr to a Russian spy ring in 1945. Another author, Mike Gruntman, *Enemy Among Trojans* (2010) said Witczak was a code name.

Yelle, Sid: Inspector Alcide Yelle of G section was the only Mountie officer convicted for the RCMP dirty tricks after the October Crisis. He stole the Parti Quebecois membership list of more than 100,000 names in 1973 as part of Operation Ham. He was charged in 1983.

Zaneth, Frank: Franco Zanetti, aka Harry Blask, Operative No.1, was a medium-height, Italian immigrant who joined the Mounties in 1917, aged twenty-eight. The following year he was appointed to the nascent Secret Service as an undercover agent. He was known as a tenacious detective. He did help to prosecute Communists such as Tim Buck. He was a Detective Staff Sergeant in 1934, becoming a Superintendent in 1945 and an Assistant Commissioner in 1950. Remembered as a dynamic teacher, many recruits admired him. He retired in 1951 and died May 2, 1971 in New Glasgow, Quebec, north of Montreal. I moved his burial to Maclaren Cemetery, Wakefield, Quebec to be closer to the locale of the narrative. Actually Lester Pearson who died Dec. 27, 1972 and his diplomat friends, Norman Robertson and Hume Wrong, who died in 1968 and 1954, were also buried in Maclaren Cemetery. Robertson and Hume were also investigated under Operation Feather Bed, but that was after Zaneth's retirement.

ABOUT THE AUTHOR

James Ellsworth lives in Victoria, BC. He has honed his writing for several years including a stint at the Banff Centre.

James Ellsworth has contributed several feature articles to the magazine *Inspired Senior Living*, as well as being a co-author on the best selling text, *Exploring World Religions, Aboriginal Spirituality* (OUP, 2001), and writing for other magazines, web sites, and the Globe and Mail. *Apparent Wind* is his debut novel. More information about James can be found on his web site, www.wordsworthwriting.org.

He is an avid traveler having visited most of the locales in the novel. Apart from spending time with his family, he tries to stay fit by running, skiing, golfing, and cycling. He especially loves research and history and is planning a second novel in the Dilman Diaries.

Will David and Lydia have a happy marriage? Will their child grow up, protected in the Dilman 'cultivated garden'? What world and Canadian historical events may buffet their family unit?

Continuing in the story-telling style of a Ken Follett or Hilary Mantel, look for the second novel, *Wing on Wing*.

Made in the USA
Charleston, SC
08 February 2017